Love Me,
Love Me Not

3

IO SAKISAKA

Contents

Piece 9............3

Piece 10.........49

Piece 11...........91

Piece 12..........133

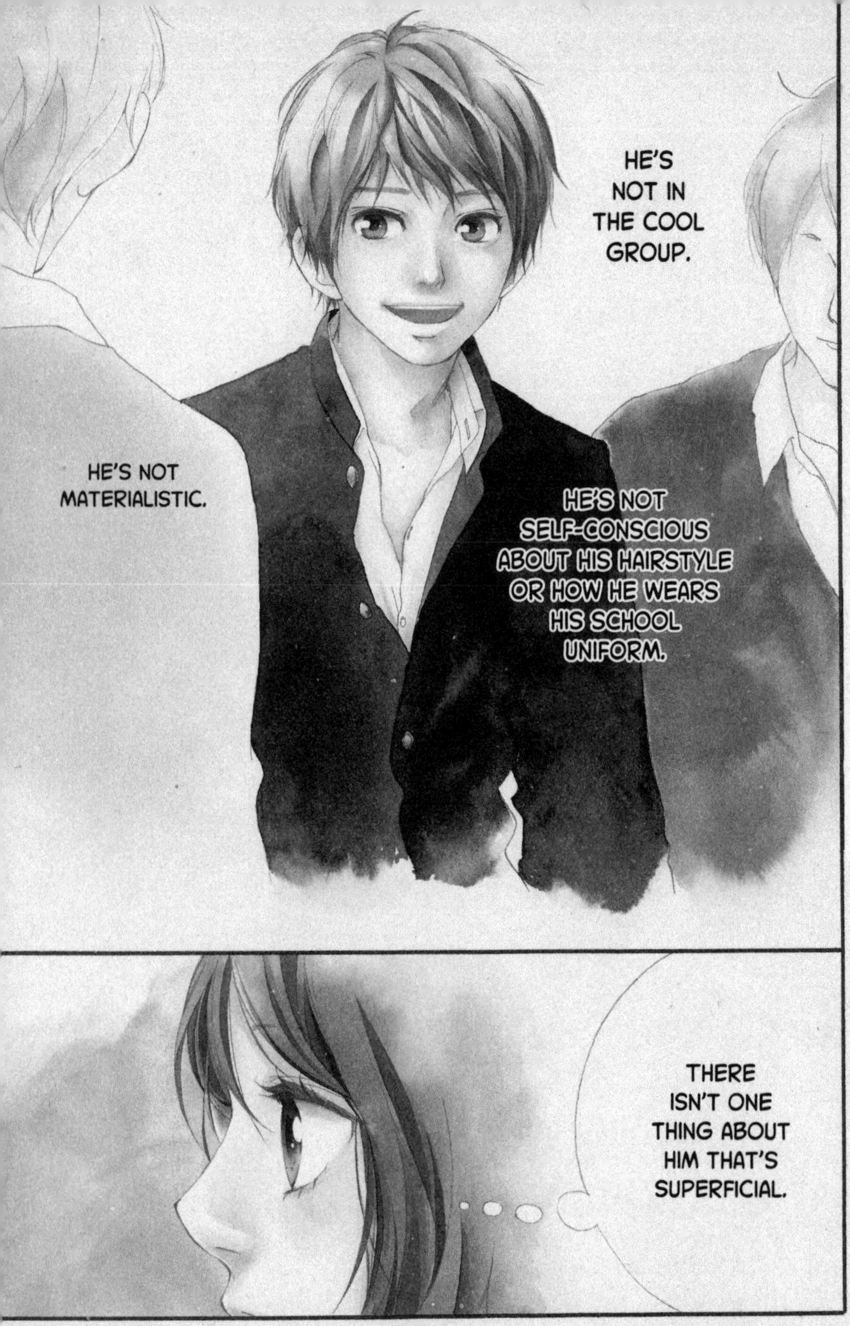
HE'S NOT IN THE COOL GROUP.
HE'S NOT SELF-CONSCIOUS ABOUT HIS HAIRSTYLE OR HOW HE WEARS HIS SCHOOL UNIFORM.
HE'S NOT MATERIALISTIC.
THERE ISN'T ONE THING ABOUT HIM THAT'S SUPERFICIAL.

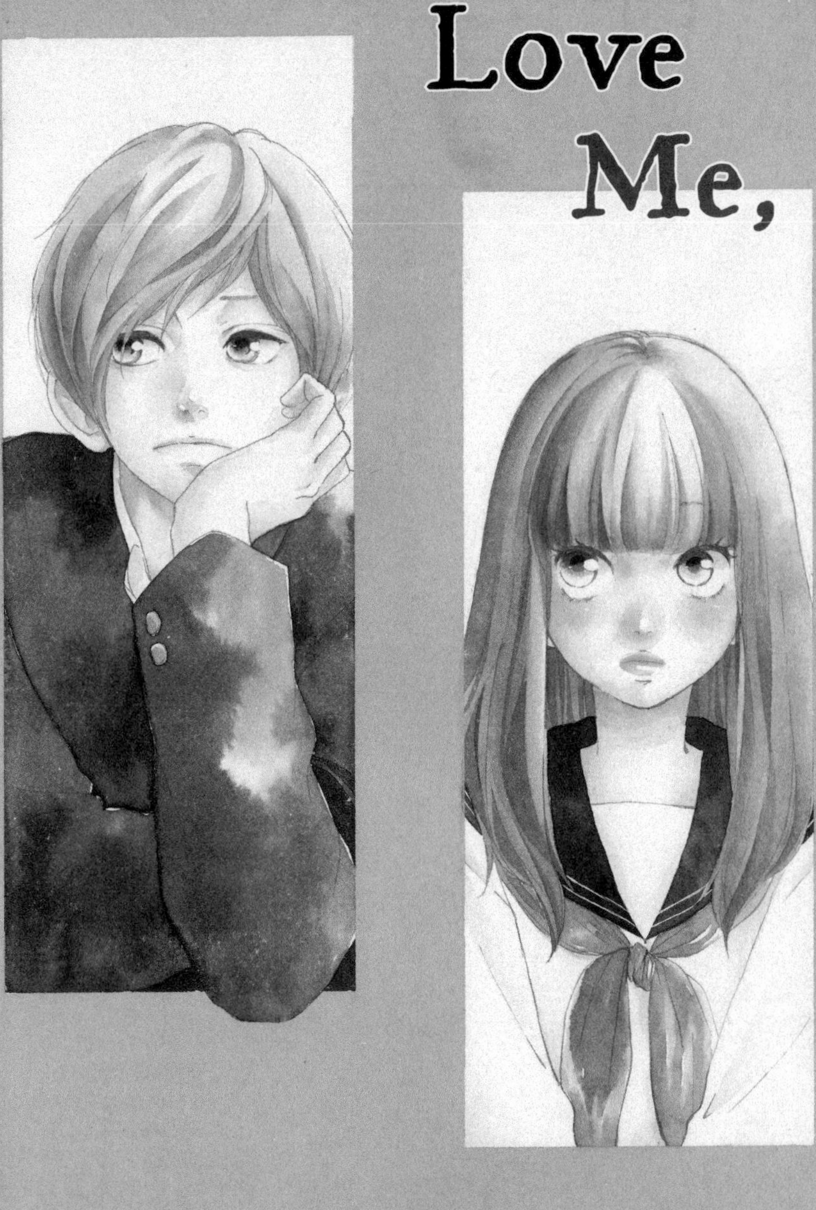
Love Me,

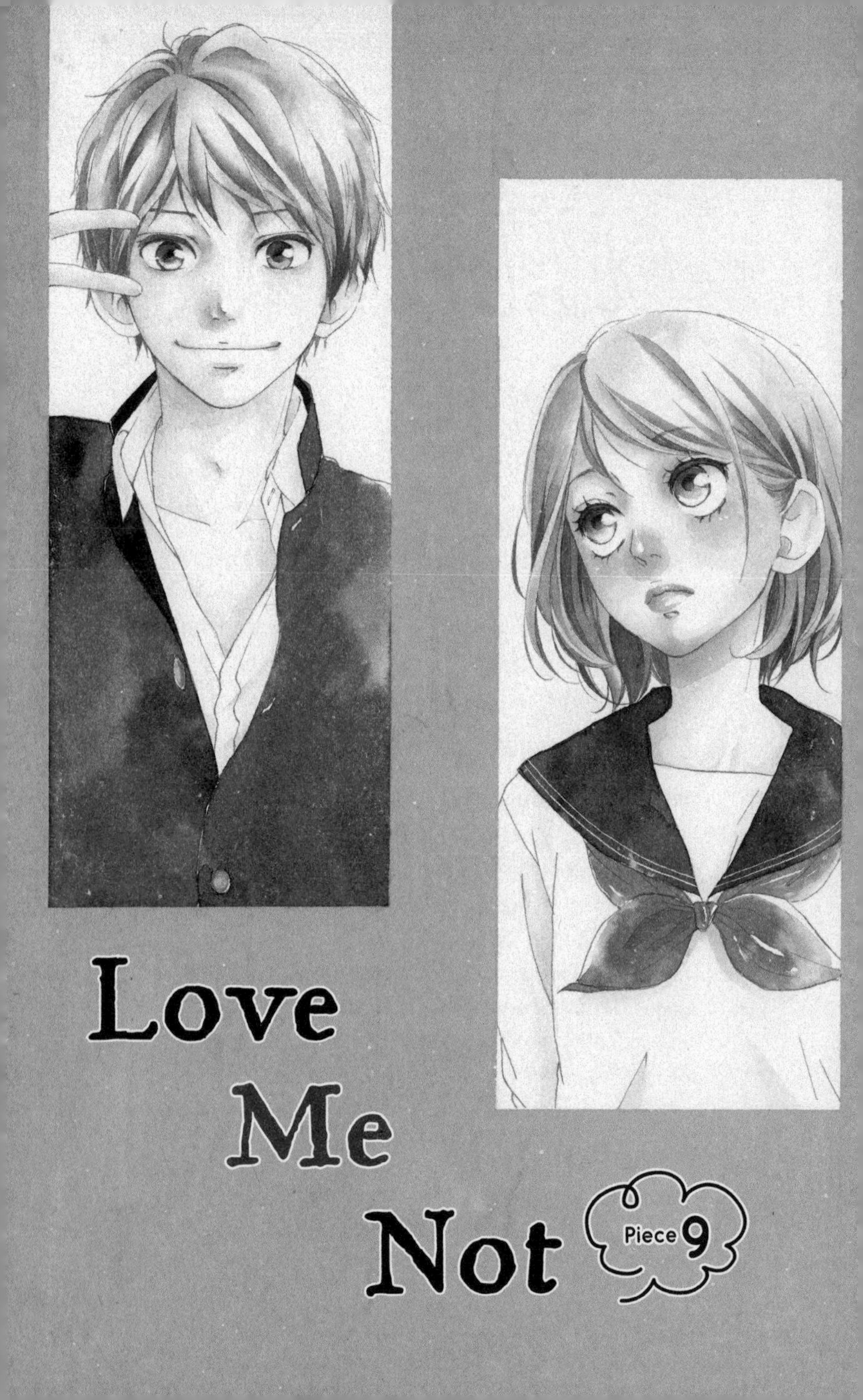
Love Me Not
Piece 9

★ GREETINGS ★

Hello. I'm Io Sakisaka.
Thank you very much for picking up volume 3 of
Love Me, Love Me Not.

The pen I've always used for drawing shiny black shades
has recently been discontinued. It's the one I liked best
after trying many different ones. I suppose that's the way it
goes sometimes. There are other good pens out there, but
this one had consistent high quality from pen to pen, and
everyone found it easy to use. (Thank you for your long
service! Farewell!)

This is the kind of thing that probably makes people switch
to digital. And as a result of people going digital, many of
the tools we use will begin to disappear. I briefly mentioned
this in the last volume, but with the help of various people,
I finally set up my tablet. I haven't touched it since. The
empty box it came in is collecting dust. I knew this would
happen, but this was too predictable for comfort. Now a
mini quiz! Will this situation have changed by the next
volume? Yes or no?

Now please enjoy this volume until the end.

Io Sakisaka

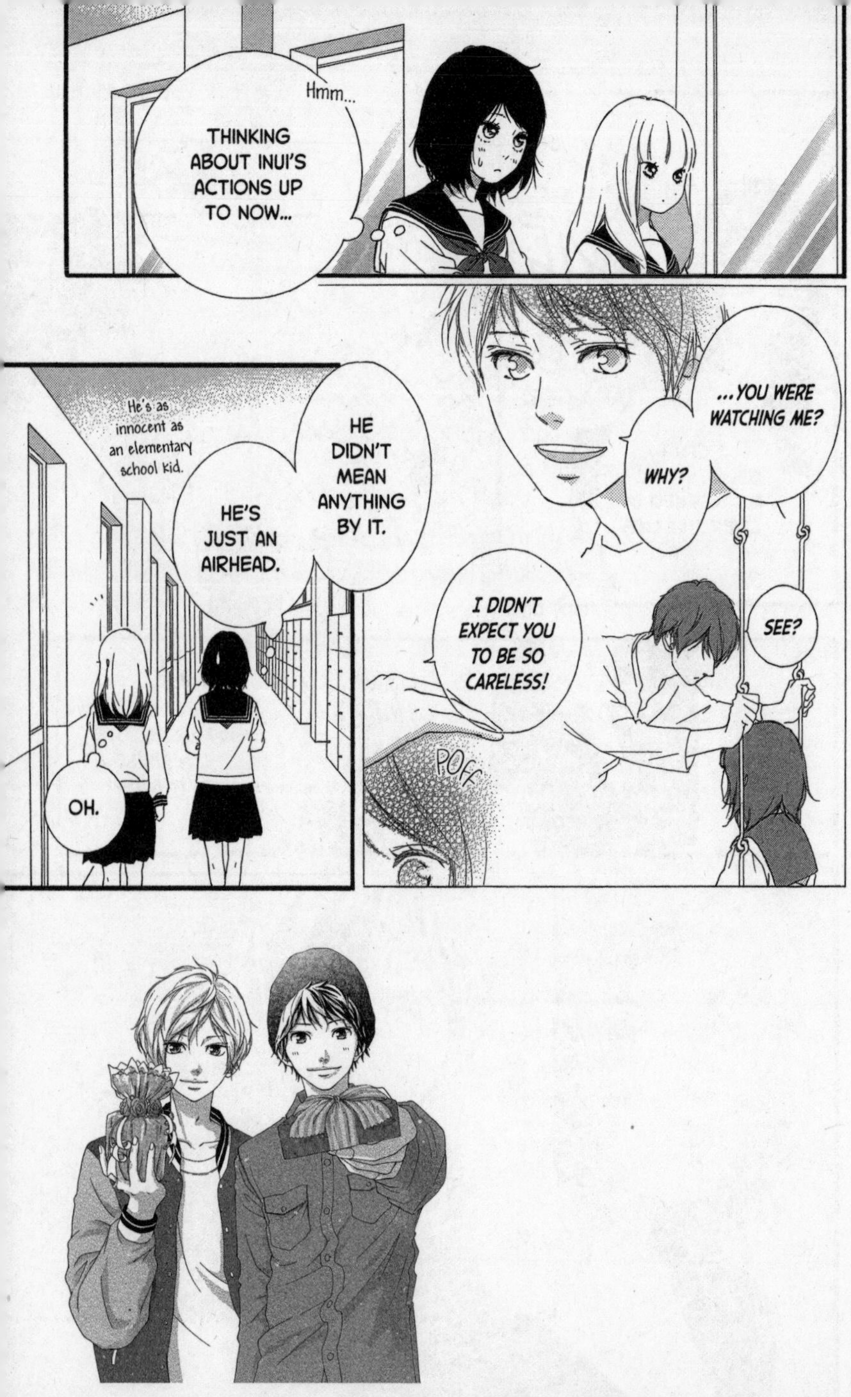
Hmm...
THINKING ABOUT INUI'S ACTIONS UP TO NOW...
...YOU WERE WATCHING ME?
WHY?
SEE?
I DIDN'T EXPECT YOU TO BE SO CARELESS!
POFF
HE DIDN'T MEAN ANYTHING BY IT.
HE'S JUST AN AIRHEAD.
He's as innocent as an elementary school kid.
OH.

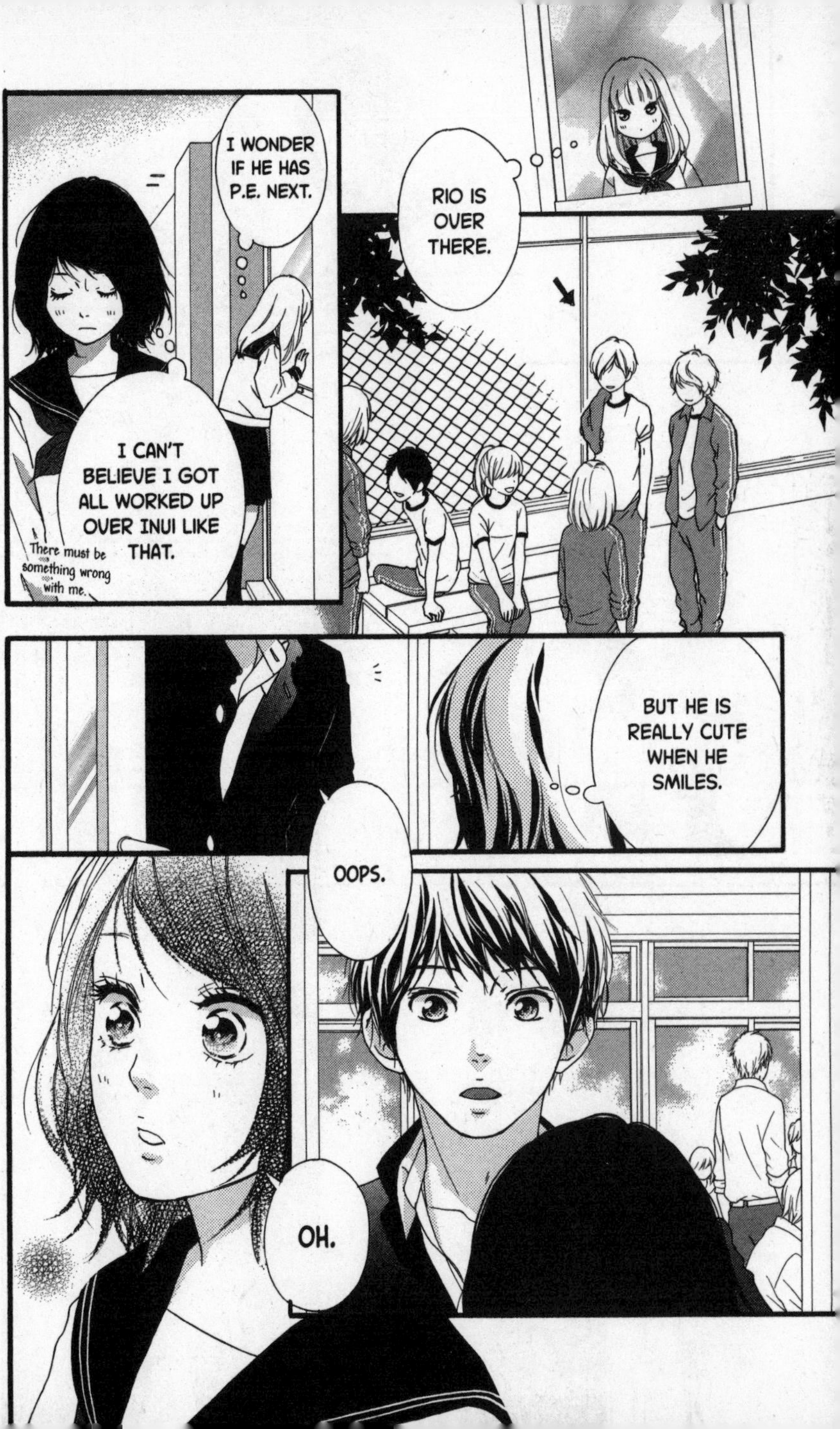
RIO IS OVER THERE.
I WONDER IF HE HAS P.E. NEXT.
I CAN'T BELIEVE I GOT ALL WORKED UP OVER INUI LIKE THAT.
There must be something wrong with me.
BUT HE IS REALLY CUTE WHEN HE SMILES.
OOPS.
OH.

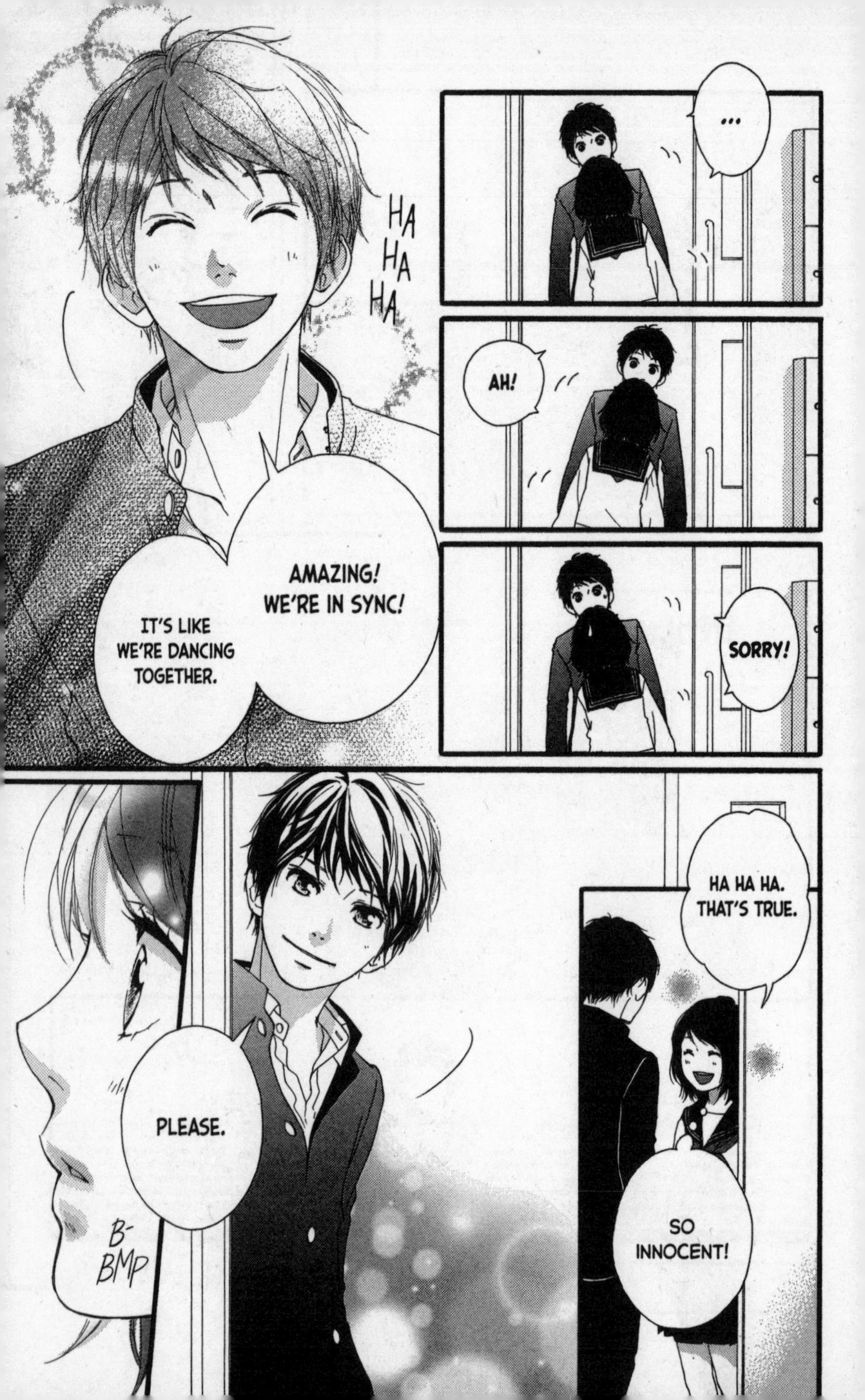
...
AH!
SORRY!
HA HA HA
AMAZING! WE'RE IN SYNC!
IT'S LIKE WE'RE DANCING TOGETHER.
HA HA HA. THAT'S TRUE.
SO INNOCENT!
PLEASE.
B-BMP

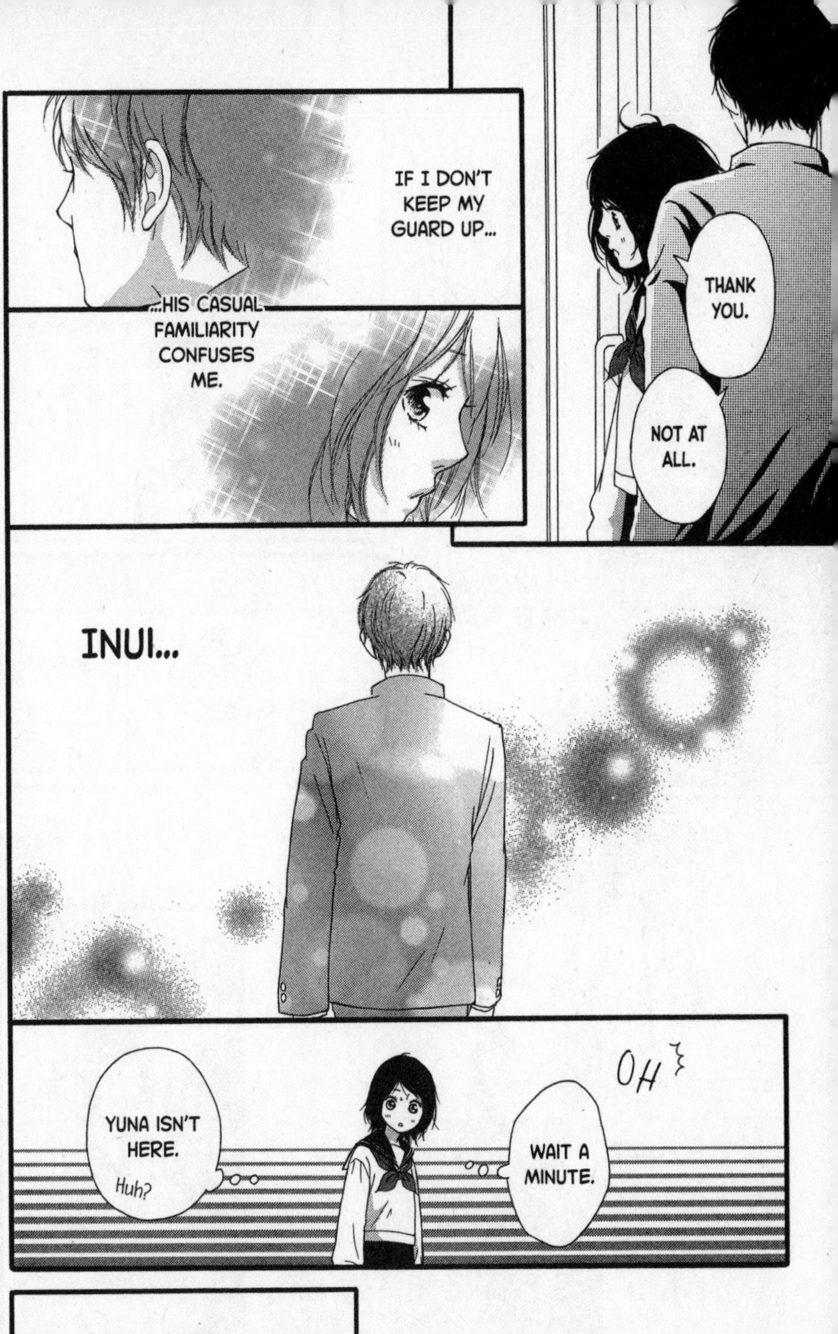
THANK YOU.
NOT AT ALL.
IF I DON'T KEEP MY GUARD UP...
...HIS CASUAL FAMILIARITY CONFUSES ME.
INUI...
OH
WAIT A MINUTE.
YUNA ISN'T HERE.
Huh?

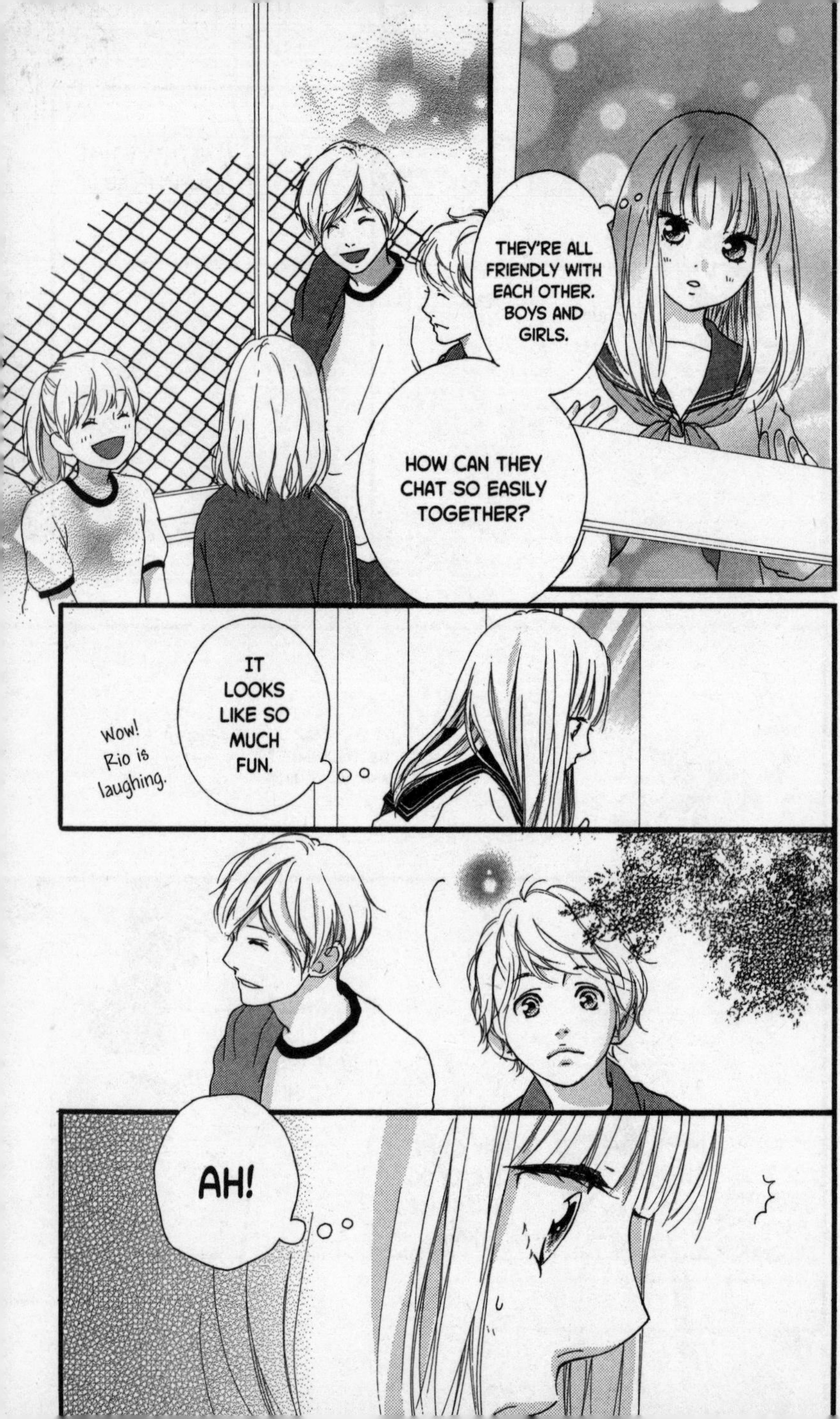
THEY'RE ALL FRIENDLY WITH EACH OTHER. BOYS AND GIRLS.
HOW CAN THEY CHAT SO EASILY TOGETHER?
IT LOOKS LIKE SO MUCH FUN.
Wow! Rio is laughing.
AH!

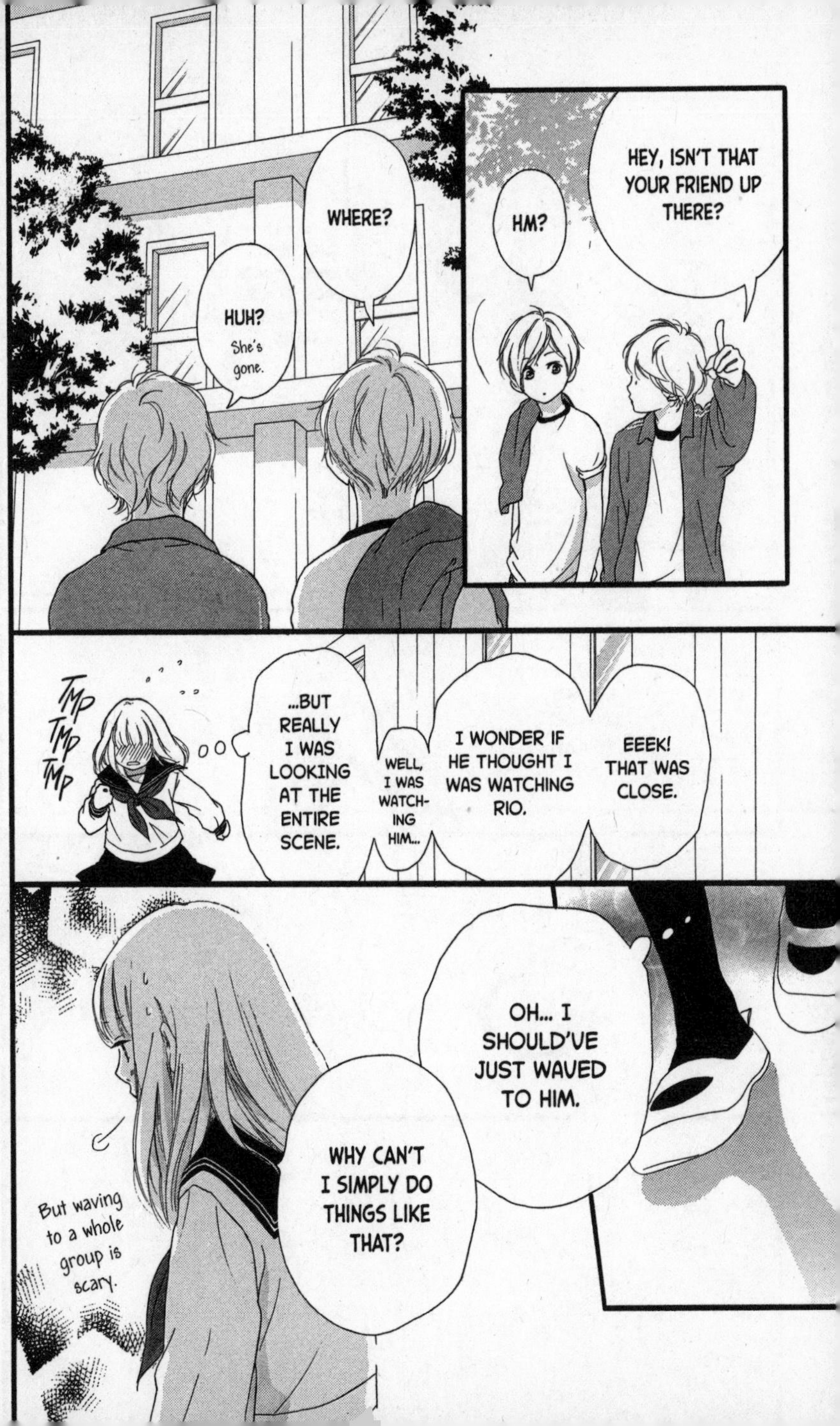
HEY, ISN'T THAT YOUR FRIEND UP THERE?
HM?
WHERE?
HUH? She's gone.
EEEK! THAT WAS CLOSE.
I WONDER IF HE THOUGHT I WAS WATCHING RIO.
WELL, I WAS WATCHING HIM...
...BUT REALLY I WAS LOOKING AT THE ENTIRE SCENE.
TMP TMP TMP
OH... I SHOULD'VE JUST WAVED TO HIM.
WHY CAN'T I SIMPLY DO THINGS LIKE THAT?
But waving to a whole group is scary.

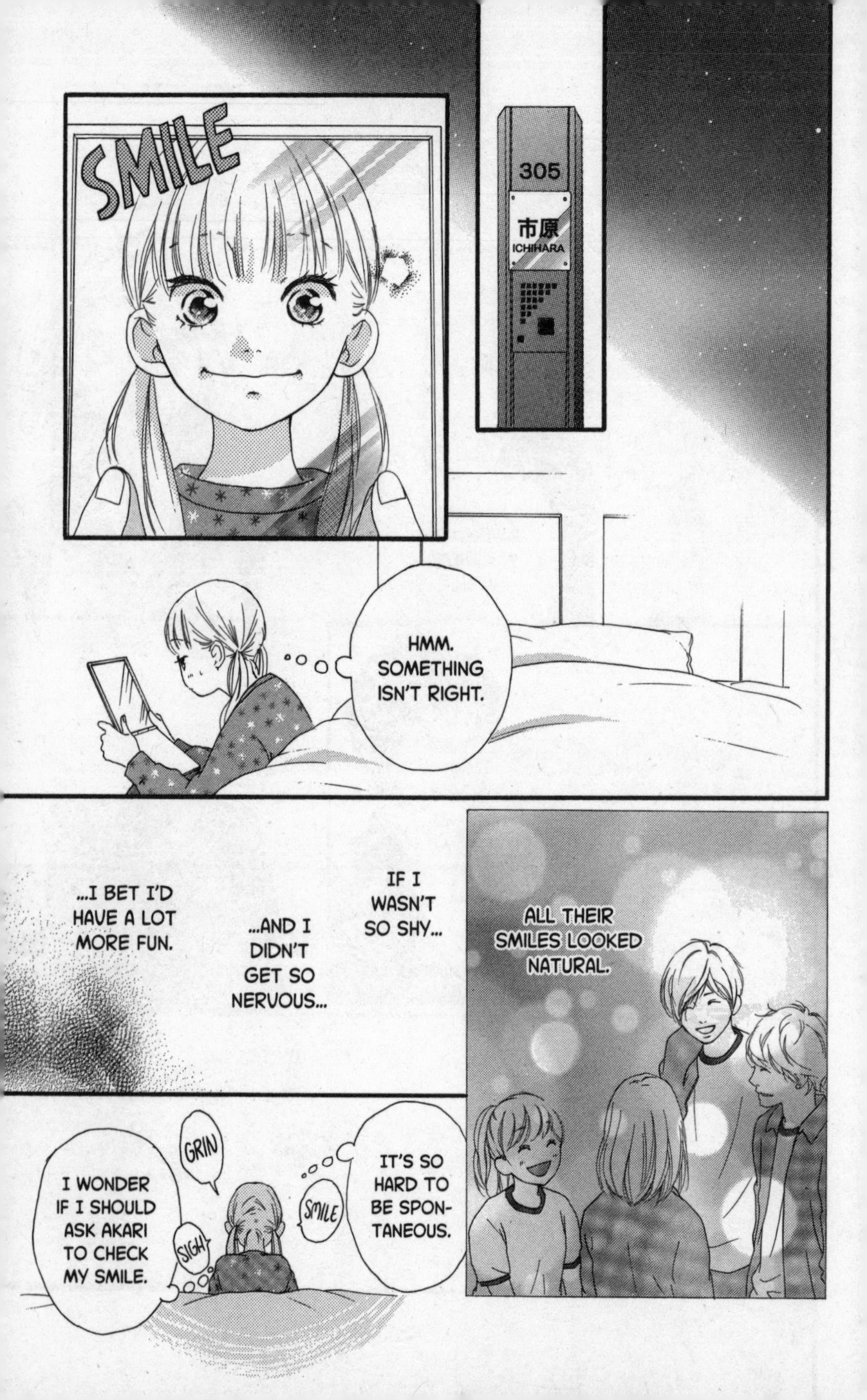
305
市原
ICHIHARA
SMILE
HMM. SOMETHING ISN'T RIGHT.
ALL THEIR SMILES LOOKED NATURAL.
IF I WASN'T SO SHY...
...AND I DIDN'T GET SO NERVOUS...
...I BET I'D HAVE A LOT MORE FUN.
IT'S SO HARD TO BE SPON-TANEOUS.
SMILE
GRIN
SIGH
I WONDER IF I SHOULD ASK AKARI TO CHECK MY SMILE.

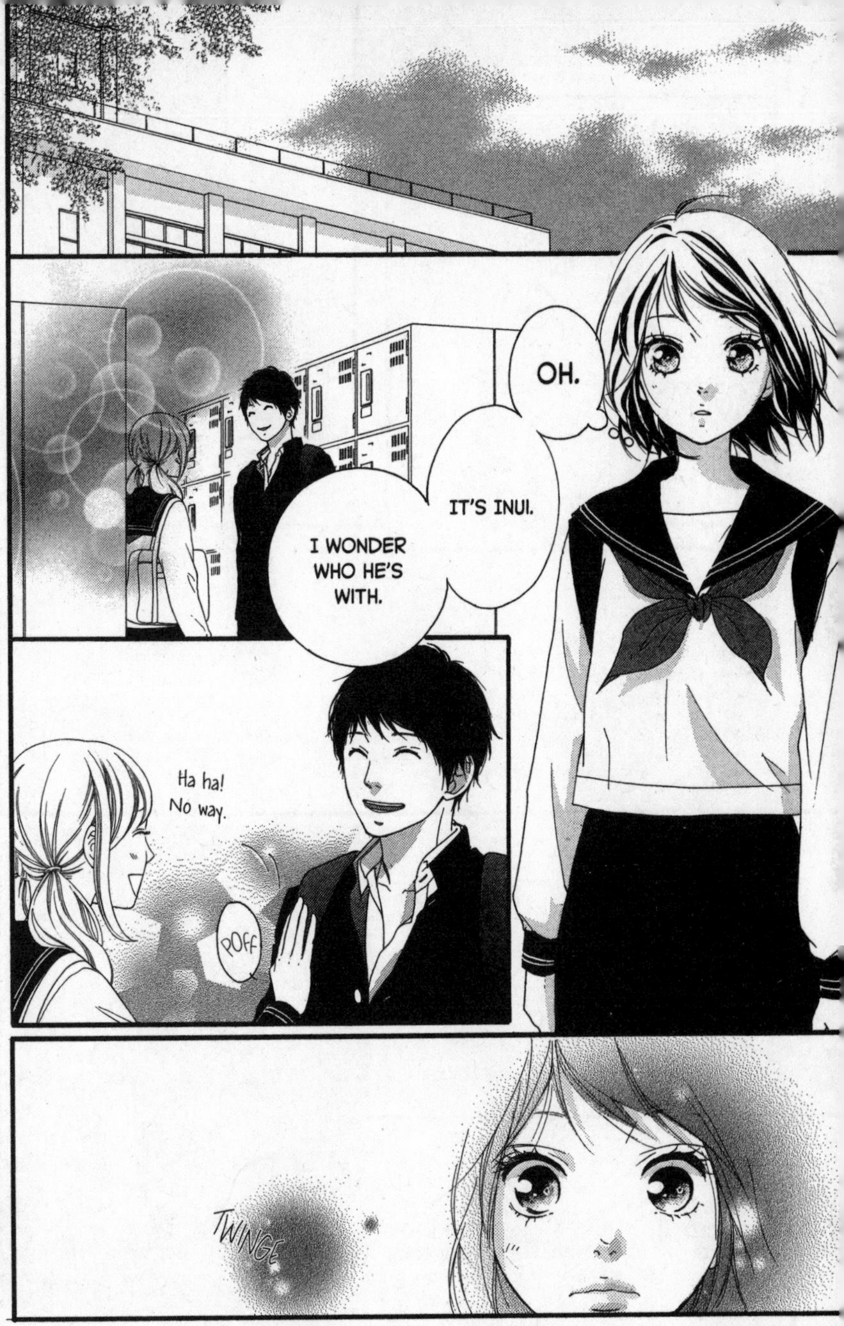
OH.
IT'S INUI.
I WONDER WHO HE'S WITH.
Ha ha! No way.
POFF
TWINGE

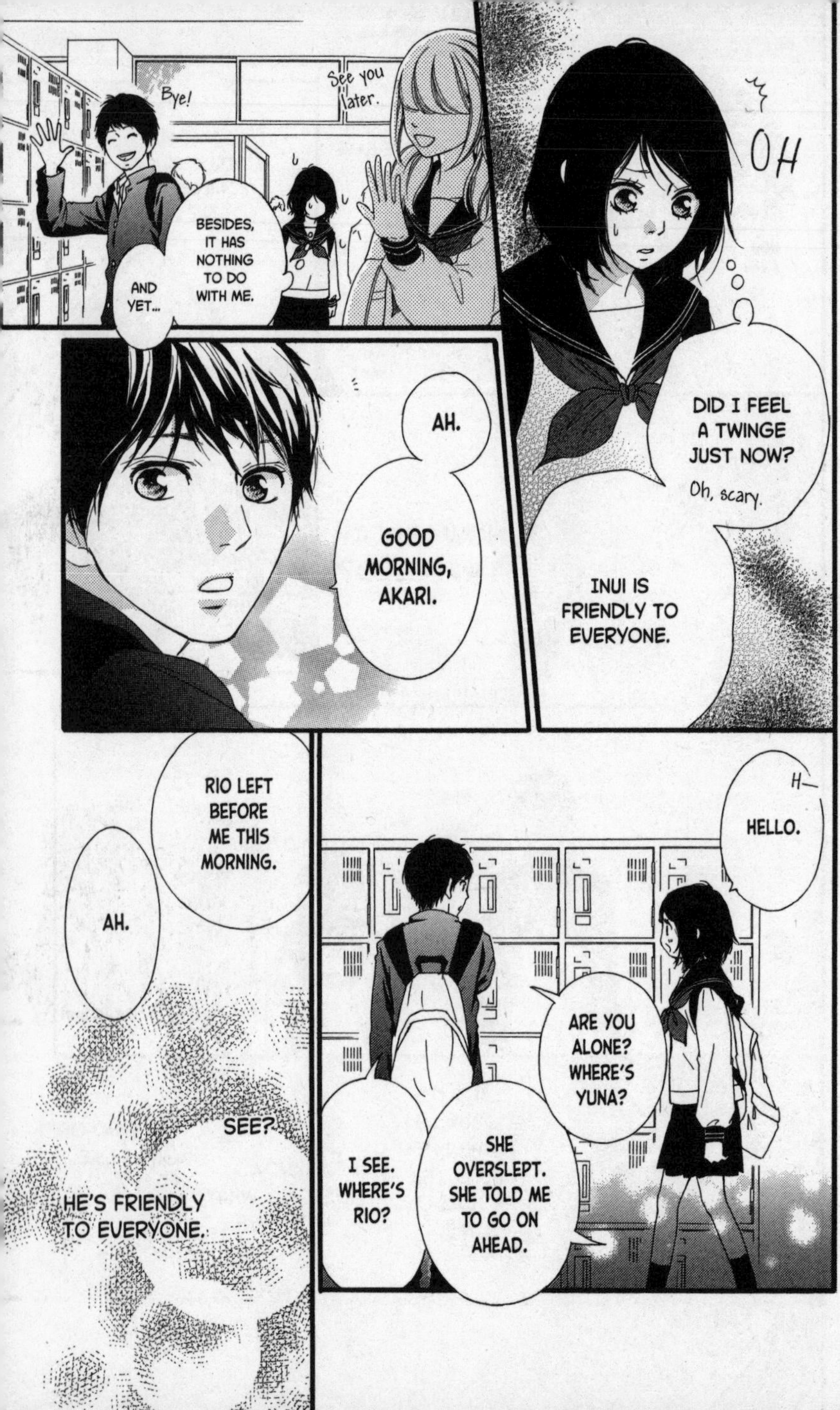
OH
DID I FEEL A TWINGE JUST NOW?
Oh, scary.
INUI IS FRIENDLY TO EVERYONE.
See you later.
Bye!
BESIDES, IT HAS NOTHING TO DO WITH ME.
AND YET...
AH.
GOOD MORNING, AKARI.
H—
HELLO.
ARE YOU ALONE? WHERE'S YUNA?
SHE OVERSLEPT. SHE TOLD ME TO GO ON AHEAD.
I SEE. WHERE'S RIO?
RIO LEFT BEFORE ME THIS MORNING.
AH.
SEE?
HE'S FRIENDLY TO EVERYONE.

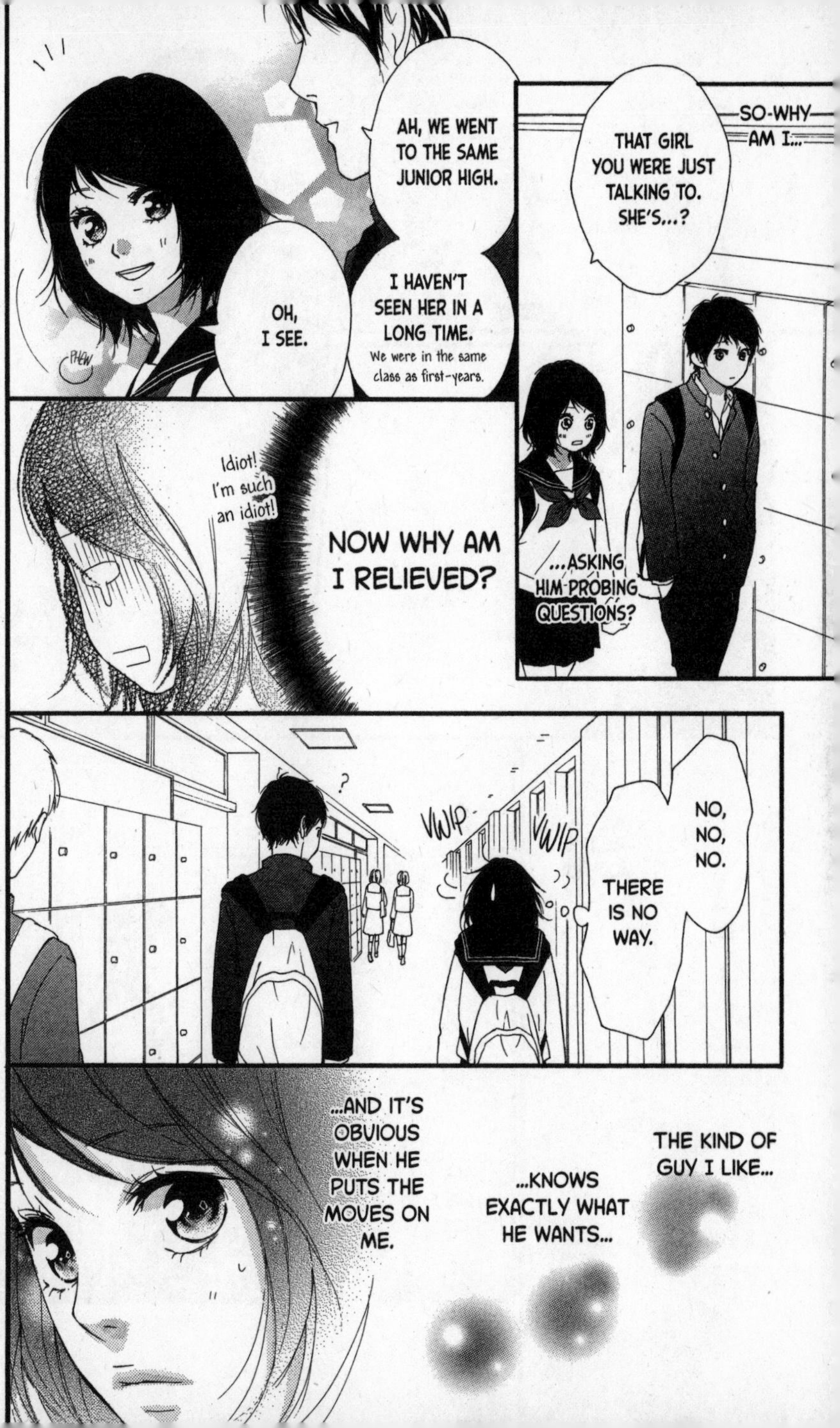
THAT GIRL YOU WERE JUST TALKING TO. SHE'S...?
SO-WHY AM I...
...ASKING HIM PROBING QUESTIONS?
AH, WE WENT TO THE SAME JUNIOR HIGH.
I HAVEN'T SEEN HER IN A LONG TIME.
We were in the same class as first-years.
OH, I SEE.
PHEW
NOW WHY AM I RELIEVED?
Idiot! I'm such an idiot!
NO, NO, NO.
THERE IS NO WAY.
VWIP
VWIP
?
THE KIND OF GUY I LIKE...
...KNOWS EXACTLY WHAT HE WANTS...
...AND IT'S OBVIOUS WHEN HE PUTS THE MOVES ON ME.

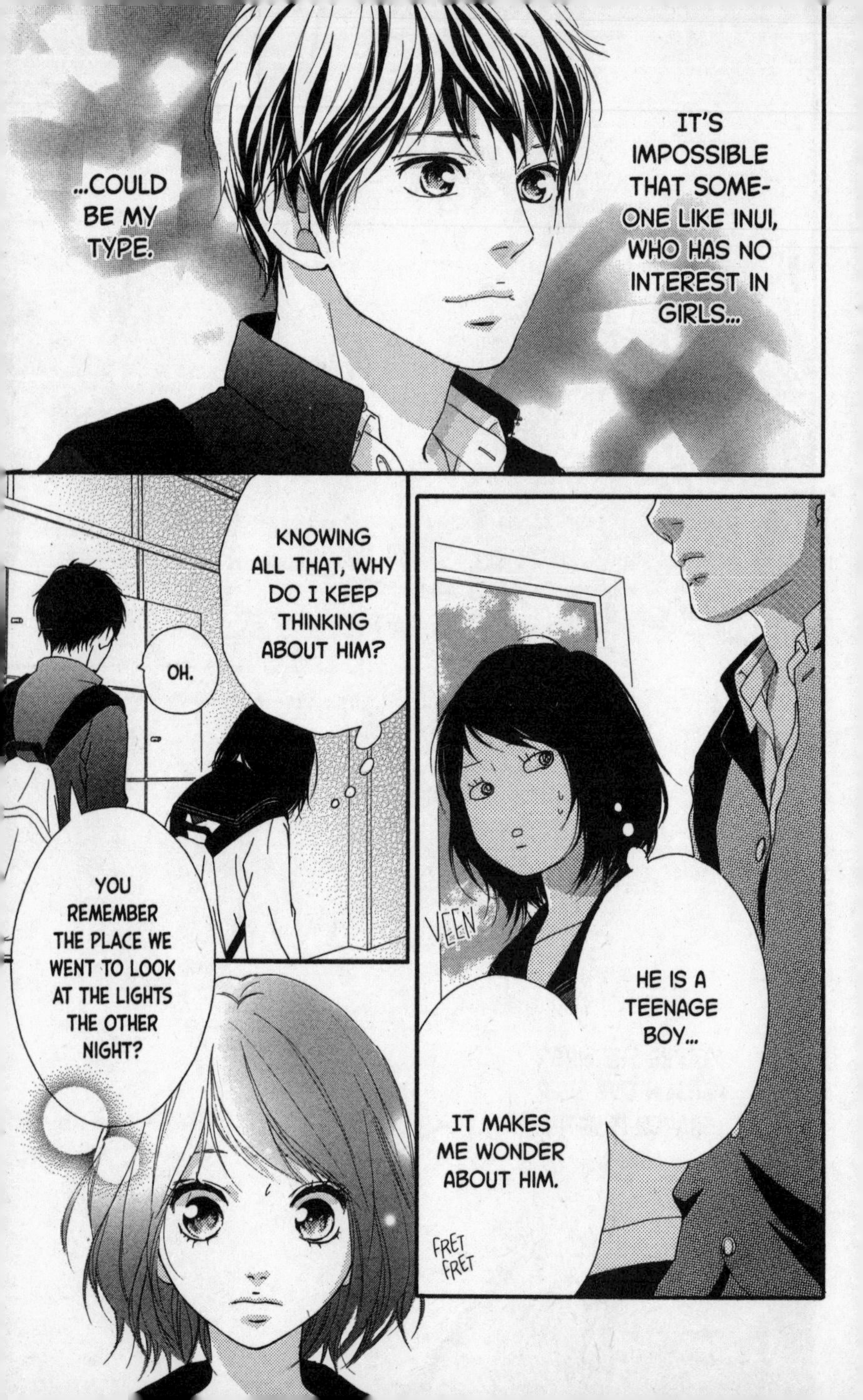
IT'S IMPOSSIBLE THAT SOME-ONE LIKE INUI, WHO HAS NO INTEREST IN GIRLS...
...COULD BE MY TYPE.
HE IS A TEENAGE BOY...
IT MAKES ME WONDER ABOUT HIM.
VEEN
FRET FRET
KNOWING ALL THAT, WHY DO I KEEP THINKING ABOUT HIM?
OH.
YOU REMEMBER THE PLACE WE WENT TO LOOK AT THE LIGHTS THE OTHER NIGHT?

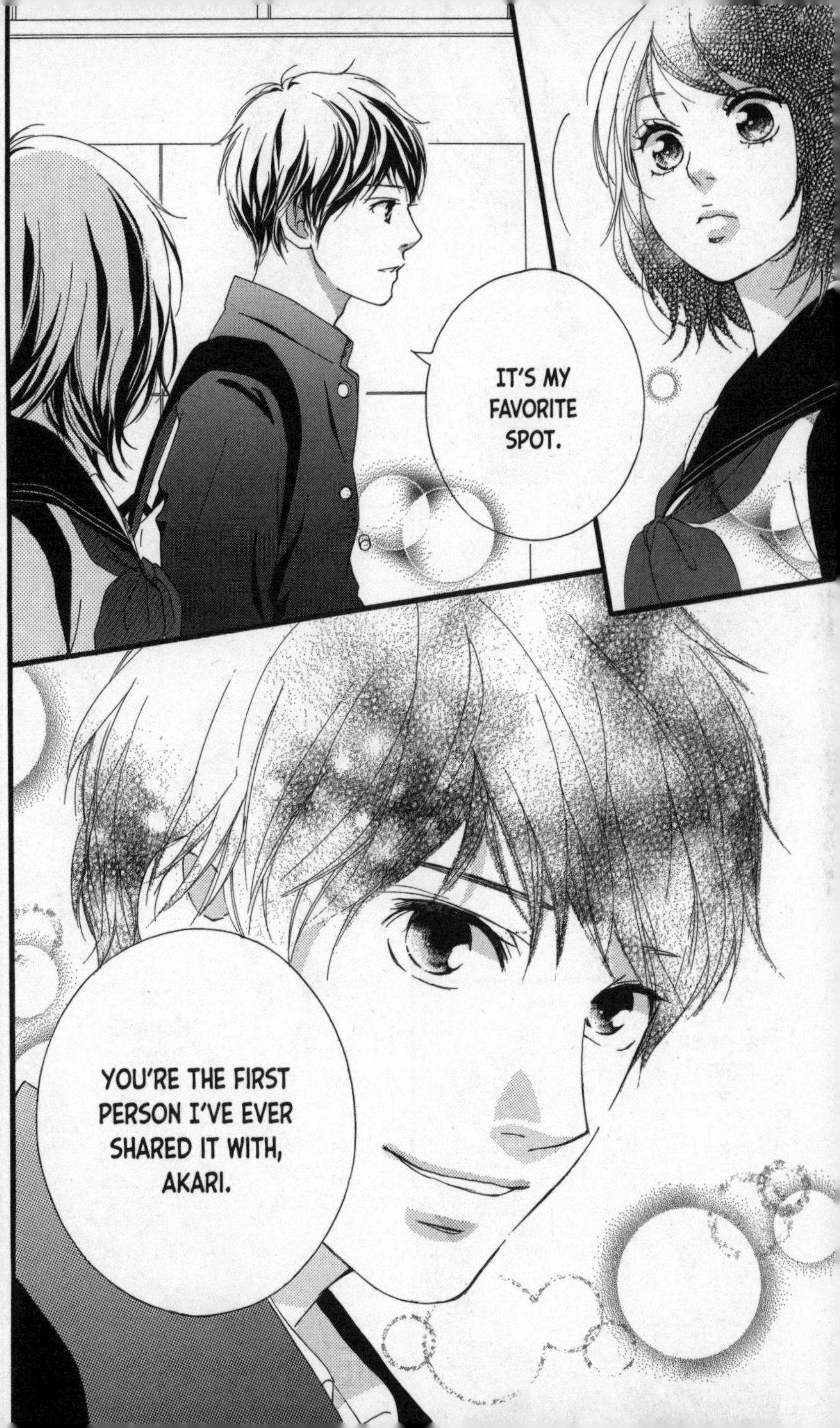
IT'S MY FAVORITE SPOT.
YOU'RE THE FIRST PERSON I'VE EVER SHARED IT WITH, AKARI.

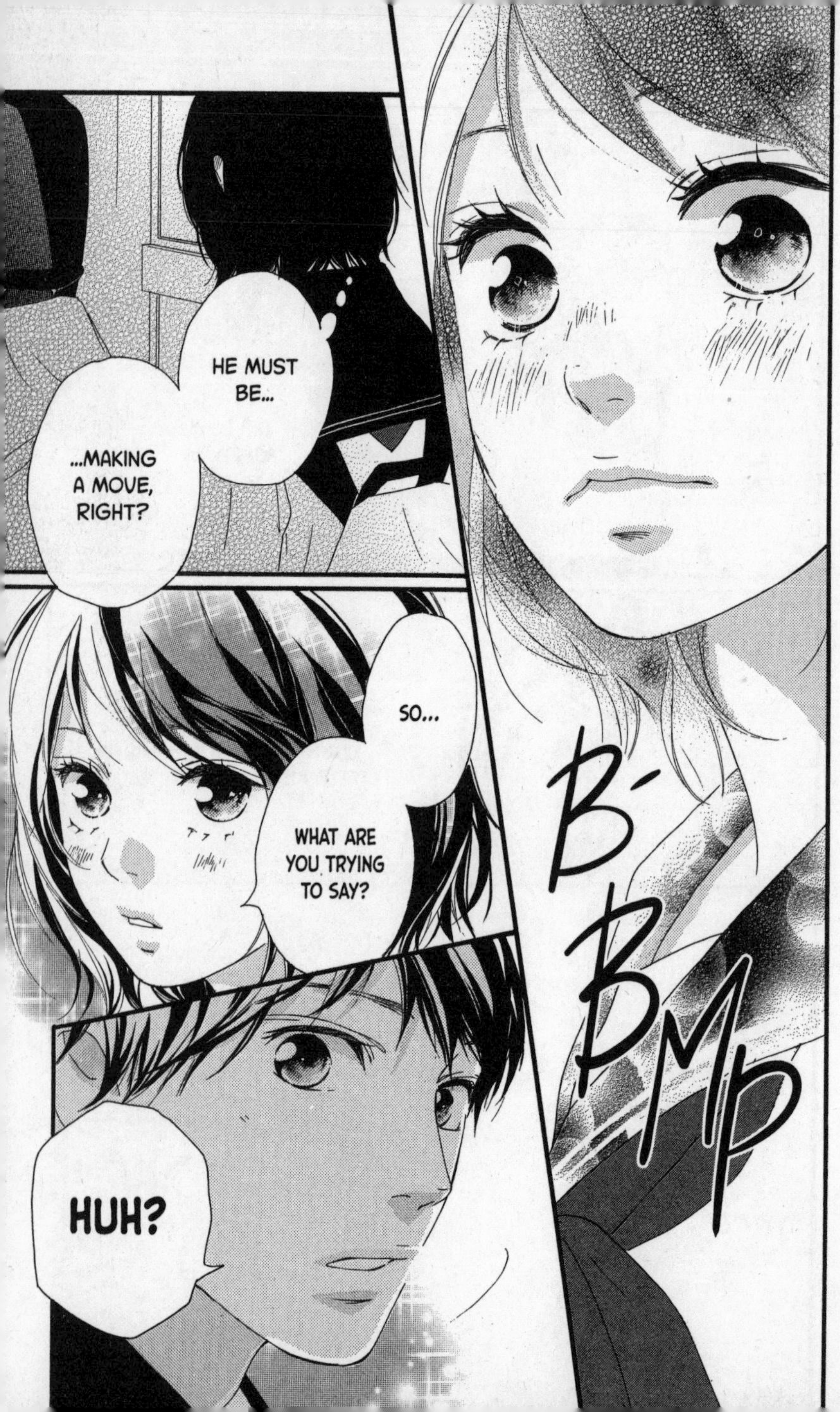
B-BMP
HE MUST BE...
...MAKING A MOVE, RIGHT?
SO...
WHAT ARE YOU TRYING TO SAY?
HUH?

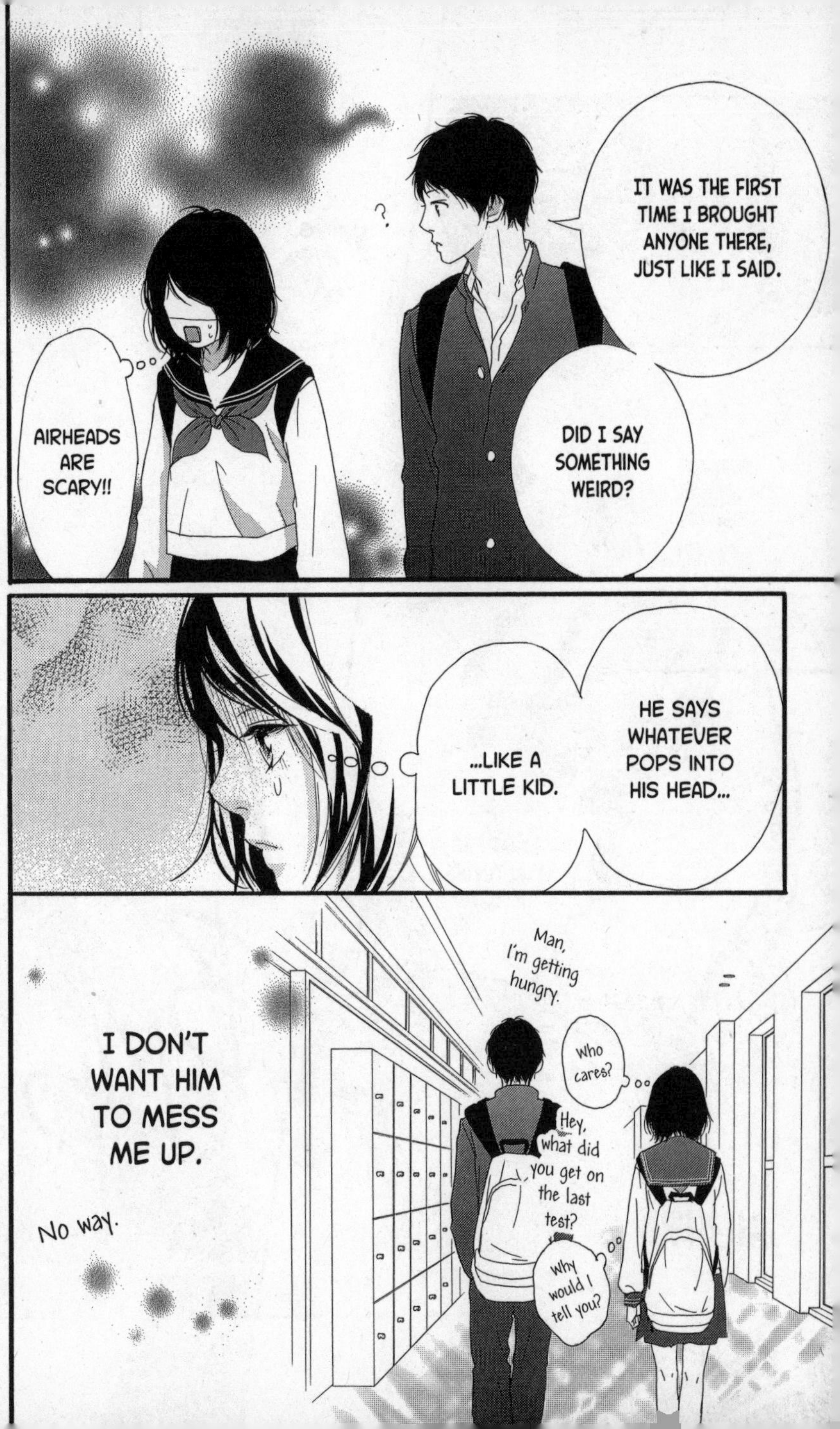
IT WAS THE FIRST TIME I BROUGHT ANYONE THERE, JUST LIKE I SAID.
DID I SAY SOMETHING WEIRD?
AIRHEADS ARE SCARY!!
HE SAYS WHATEVER POPS INTO HIS HEAD...
...LIKE A LITTLE KID.
Man, I'm getting hungry.
Who cares?
Hey, what did you get on the last test?
Why would I tell you?
I DON'T WANT HIM TO MESS ME UP.
No way.

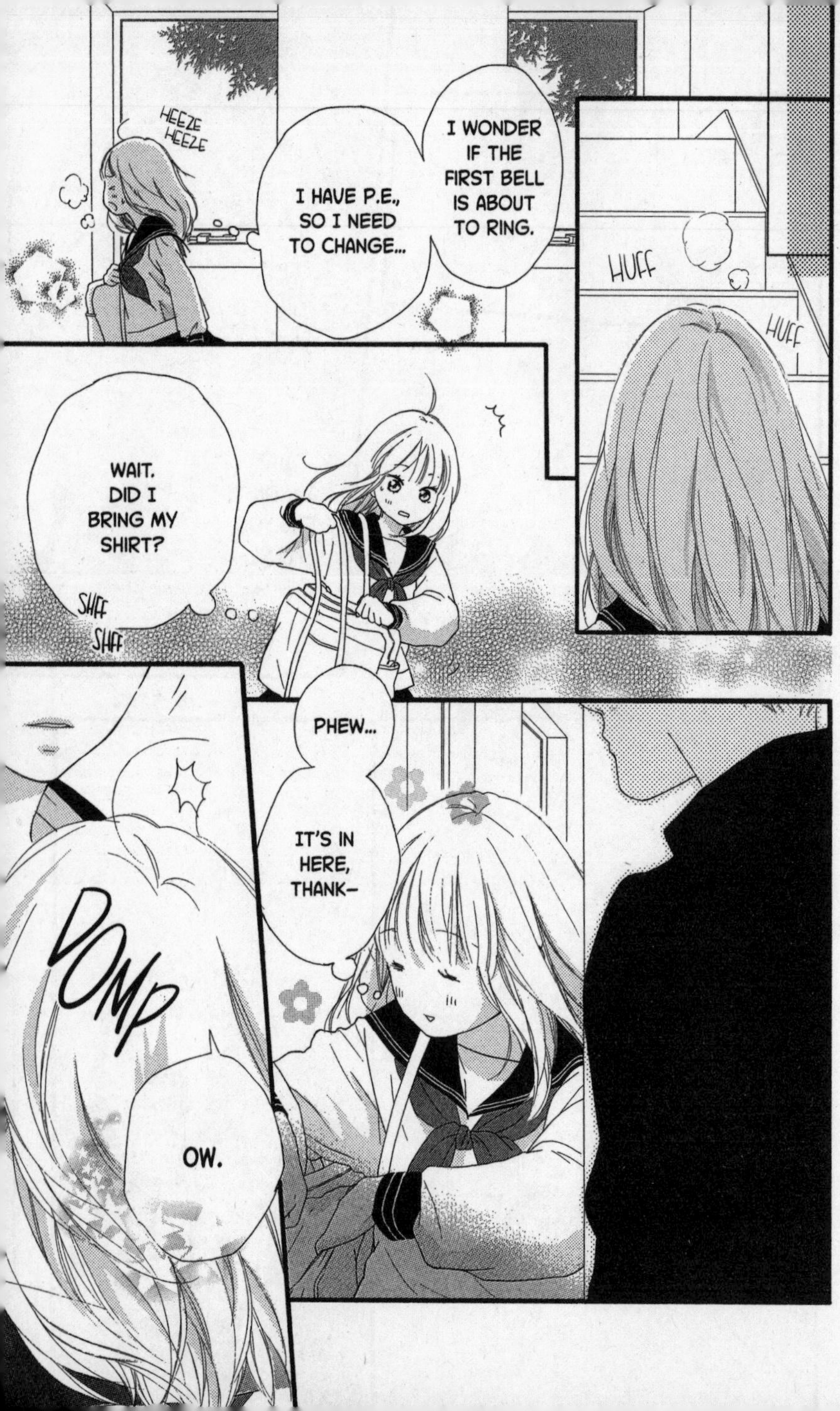
I WONDER IF THE FIRST BELL IS ABOUT TO RING.
I HAVE P.E., SO I NEED TO CHANGE...
HEEZE HEEZE
HUFF
HUFF
WAIT. DID I BRING MY SHIRT?
SHFF SHFF
PHEW...
IT'S IN HERE, THANK-
DOMP
OW.

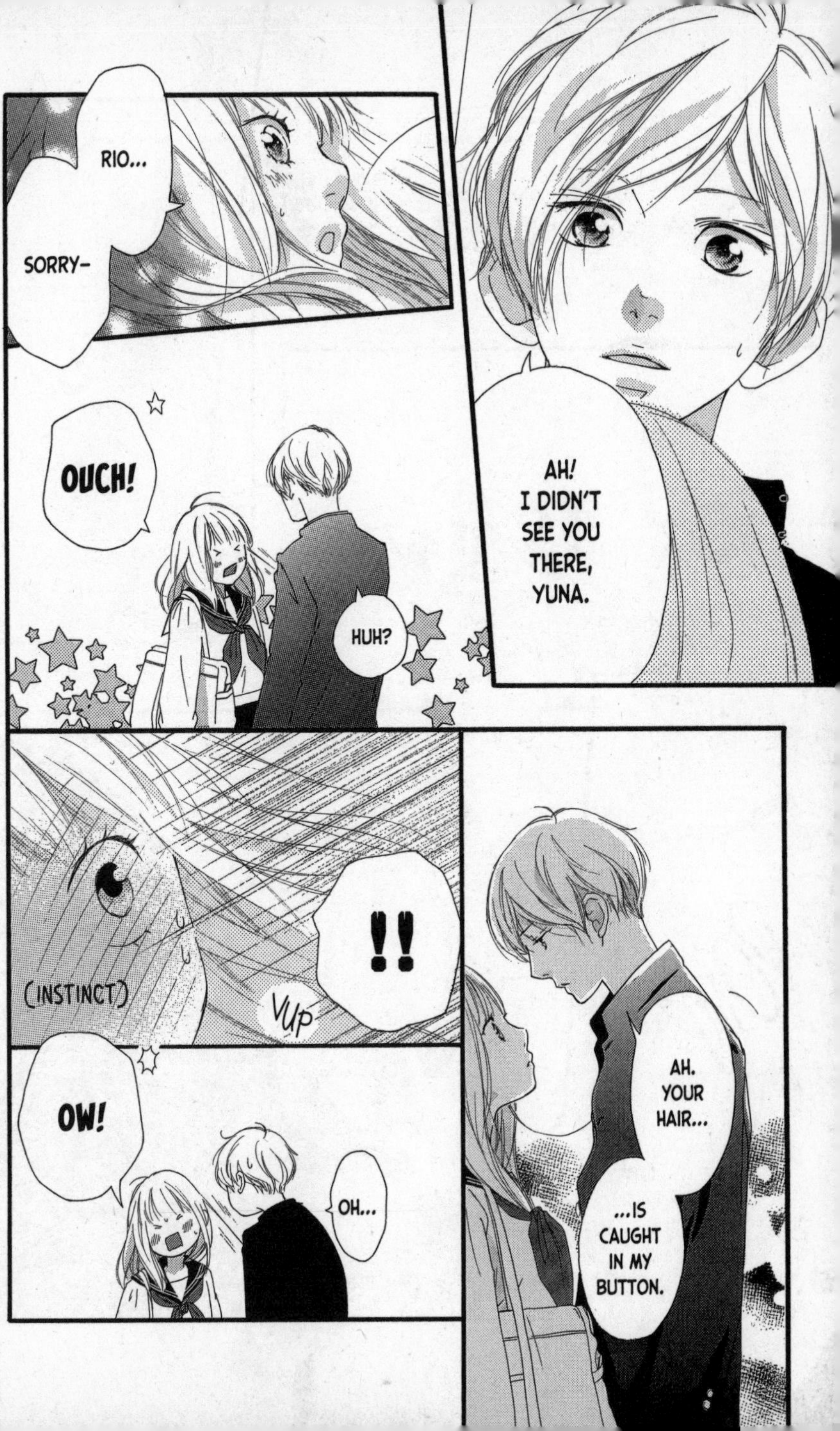
AH! I DIDN'T SEE YOU THERE, YUNA.
RIO...
SORRY-
OUCH!
HUH?
AH. YOUR HAIR...
...IS CAUGHT IN MY BUTTON.
!!
VUP
(INSTINCT)
OW!
OH...

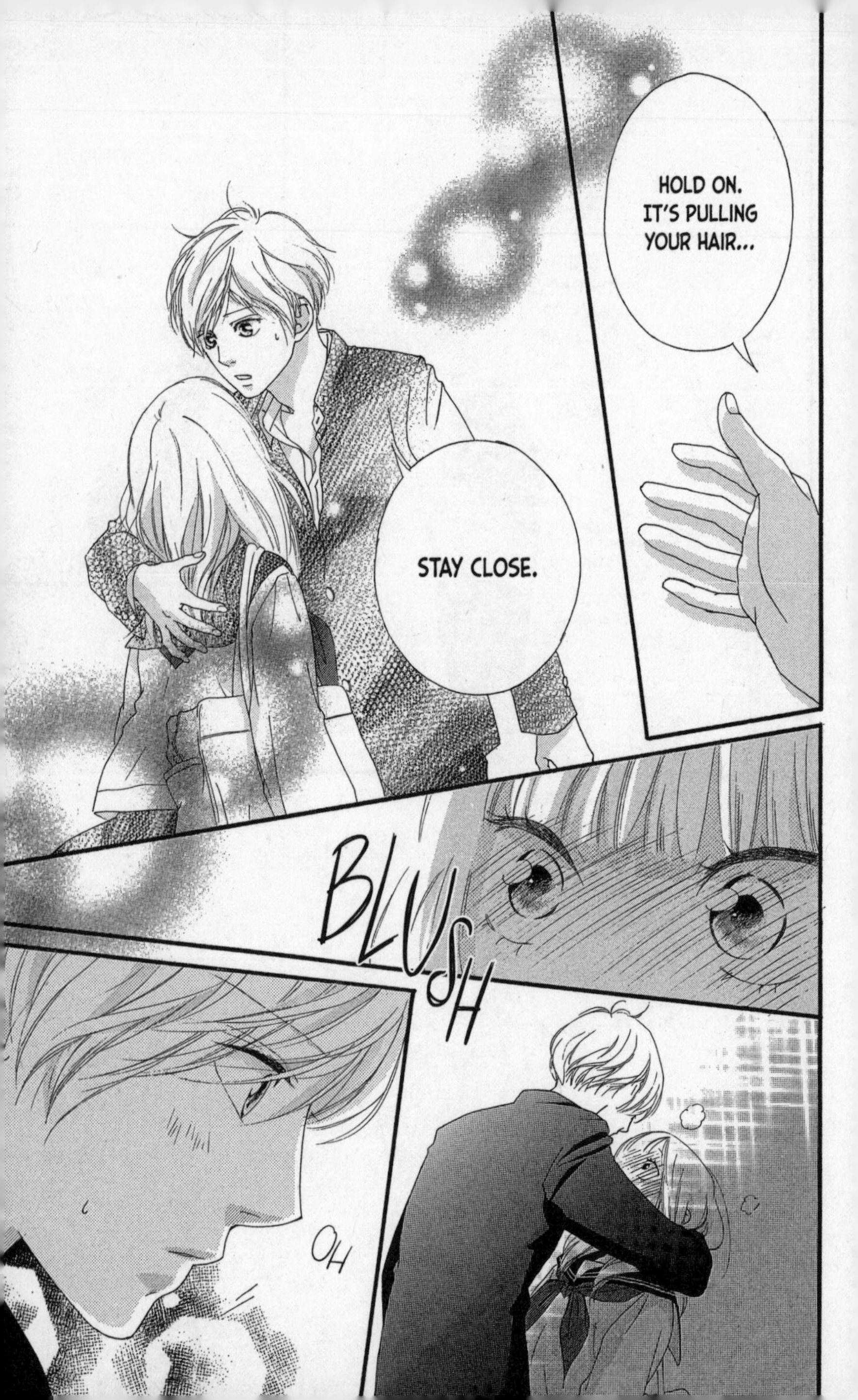
HOLD ON. IT'S PULLING YOUR HAIR...
STAY CLOSE.
BLUSH
OH

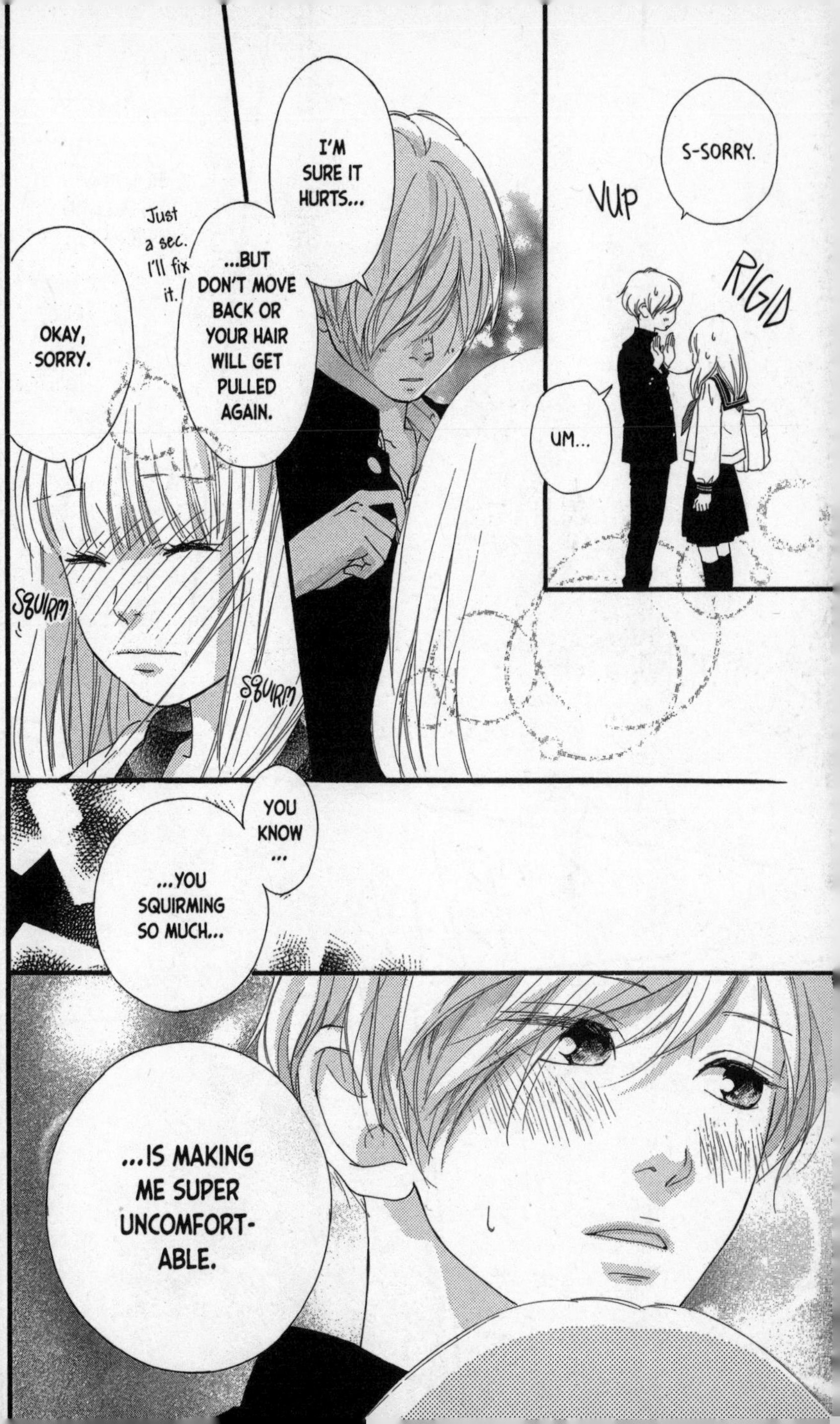
S-SORRY.
VUP
RIGID
UM...
I'M SURE IT HURTS...
...BUT DON'T MOVE BACK OR YOUR HAIR WILL GET PULLED AGAIN.
Just a sec. I'll fix it.
OKAY, SORRY.
SQUIRM
SQUIRM
YOU KNOW...
...YOU SQUIRMING SO MUCH...
...IS MAKING ME SUPER UNCOMFORT-ABLE.

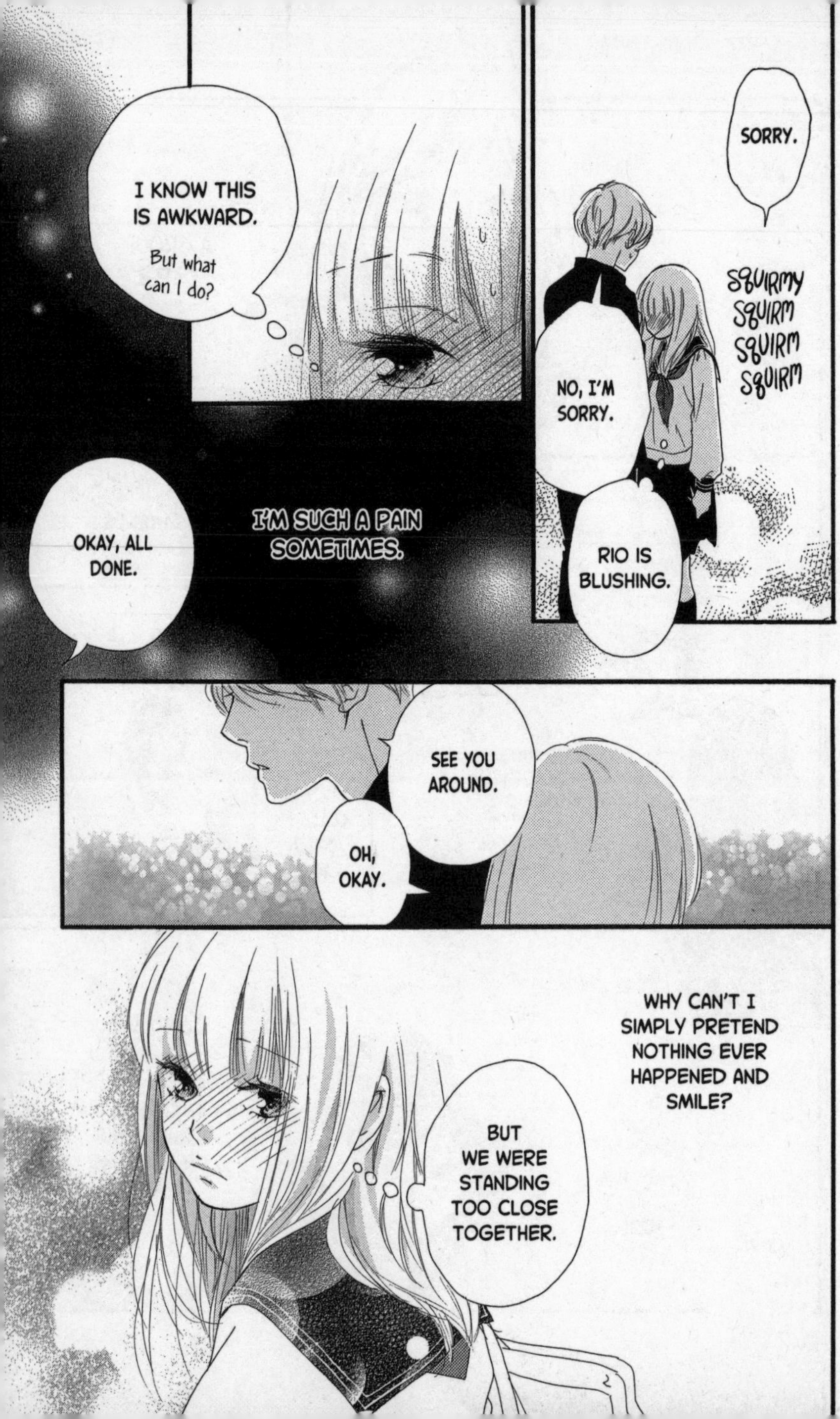
SORRY.
SQUIRMY SQUIRM SQUIRM SQUIRM
NO, I'M SORRY.
RIO IS BLUSHING.
I KNOW THIS IS AWKWARD.
But what can I do?
I'M SUCH A PAIN SOMETIMES.
OKAY, ALL DONE.
SEE YOU AROUND.
OH, OKAY.
WHY CAN'T I SIMPLY PRETEND NOTHING EVER HAPPENED AND SMILE?
BUT WE WERE STANDING TOO CLOSE TOGETHER.

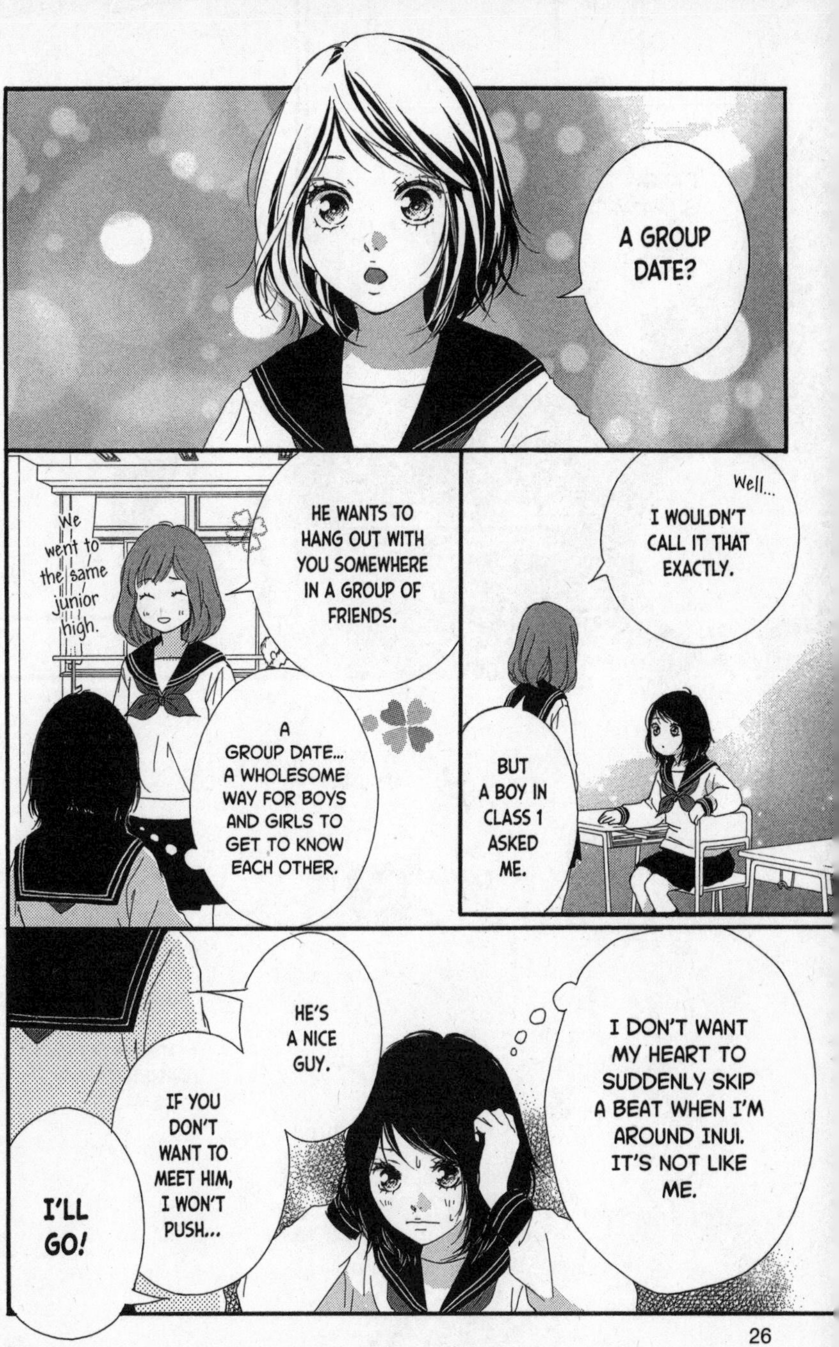
A GROUP DATE?
Well...
I WOULDN'T CALL IT THAT EXACTLY.
BUT A BOY IN CLASS 1 ASKED ME.
HE WANTS TO HANG OUT WITH YOU SOMEWHERE IN A GROUP OF FRIENDS.
We went to the same junior high.
A GROUP DATE... A WHOLESOME WAY FOR BOYS AND GIRLS TO GET TO KNOW EACH OTHER.
I DON'T WANT MY HEART TO SUDDENLY SKIP A BEAT WHEN I'M AROUND INUI. IT'S NOT LIKE ME.
HE'S A NICE GUY.
IF YOU DON'T WANT TO MEET HIM, I WON'T PUSH...
I'LL GO!

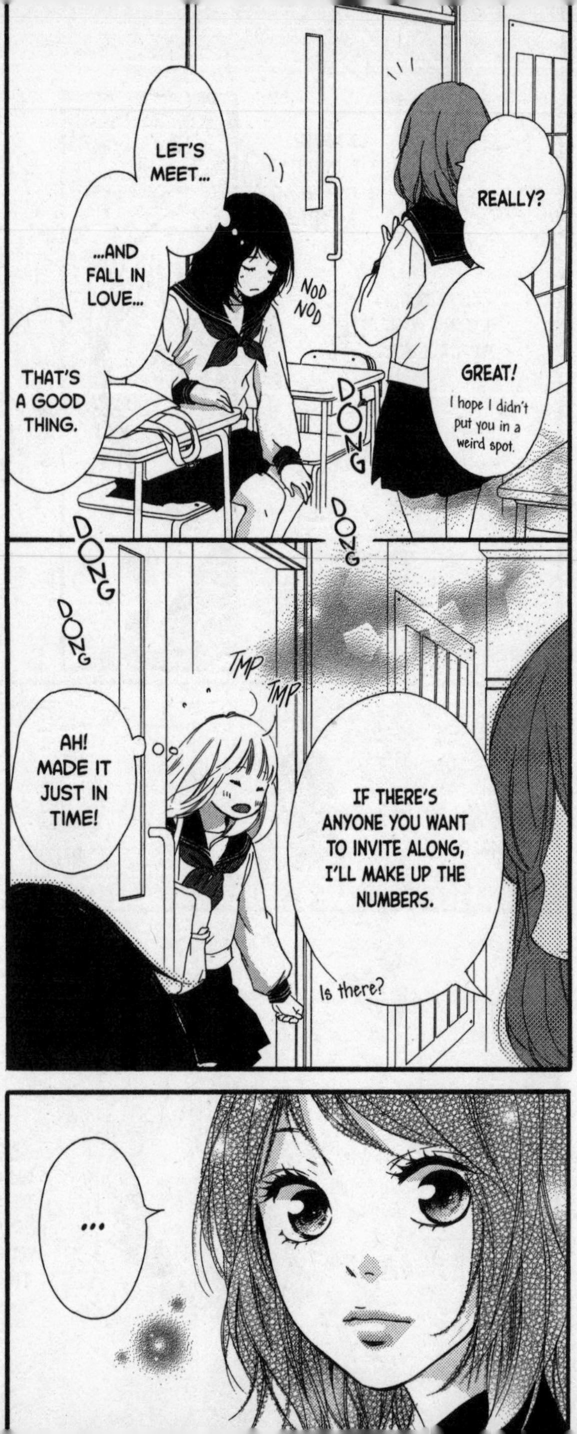
REALLY?
LET'S MEET...
...AND FALL IN LOVE...
NOD NOD
GREAT!
I hope I didn't put you in a weird spot.
THAT'S A GOOD THING.
DONG DONG
IF THERE'S ANYONE YOU WANT TO INVITE ALONG, I'LL MAKE UP THE NUMBERS.
Is there?
DONG DONG
TMP TMP
AH! MADE IT JUST IN TIME!
...

The other day I finished moving all my manuscripts out of my old house. It was such a huge task that I understood why I had put it off for so long. The quantity!! The weight!! I know I was wrong not to have them organized. They were randomly strewn all over the house, and finding them used up a lot of my energy. But in the midst of all that, I found my first work. I knew at the time I shouldn't throw it out, but I couldn't remember where I'd put it away. Finding it was a "wow" moment! Somehow the timing didn't work out back then, so my debut piece is not included in any compilation. It will probably never be seen by anyone. I wasn't brave enough to read it again either, so unseen by me, it has become part of another layer in the new strata I have formed.

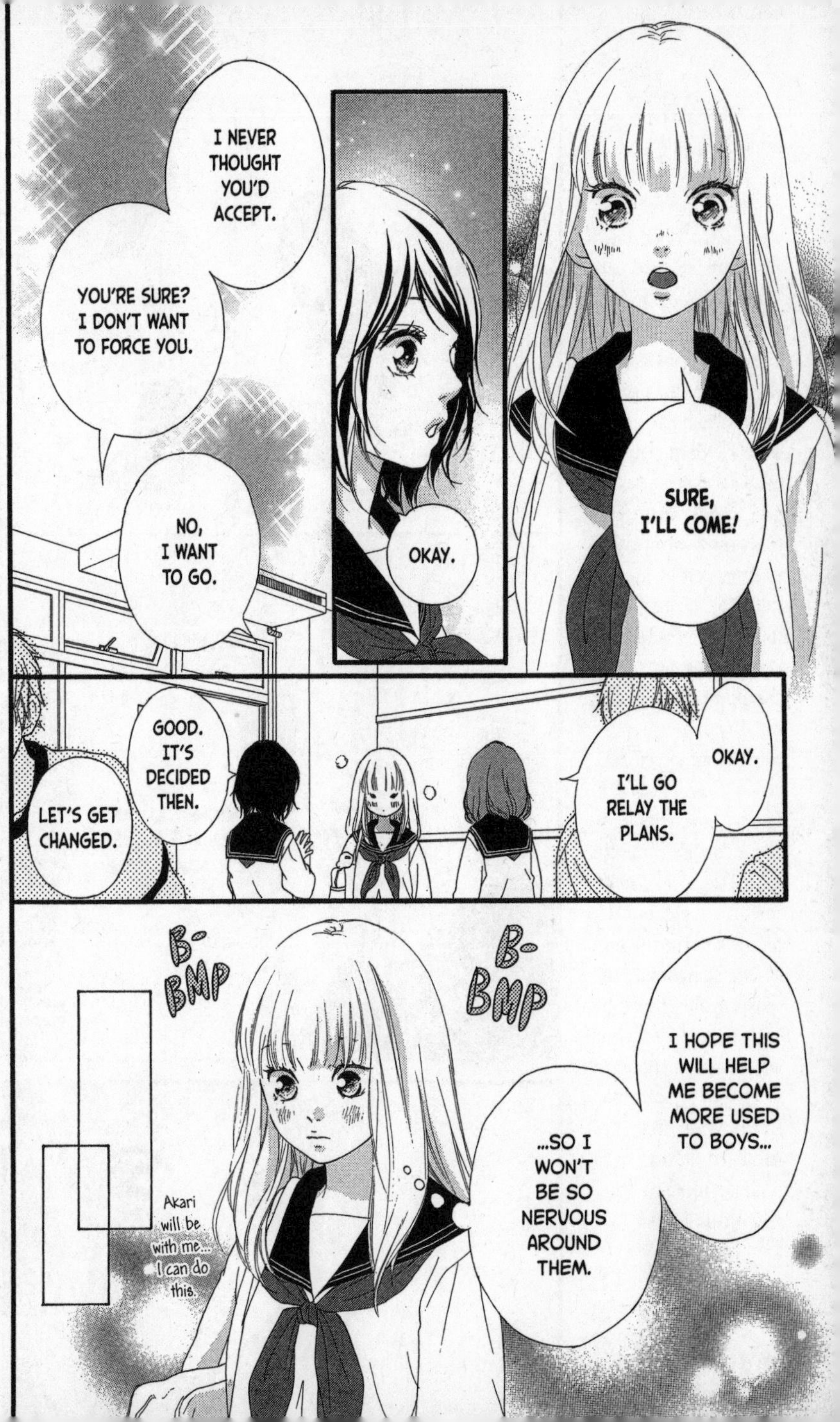
SURE, I'LL COME!
OKAY.
I NEVER THOUGHT YOU'D ACCEPT.
YOU'RE SURE? I DON'T WANT TO FORCE YOU.
NO, I WANT TO GO.
OKAY.
I'LL GO RELAY THE PLANS.
GOOD. IT'S DECIDED THEN.
LET'S GET CHANGED.
B-BMP
B-BMP
I HOPE THIS WILL HELP ME BECOME MORE USED TO BOYS...
...SO I WON'T BE SO NERVOUS AROUND THEM.
Akari will be with me... I can do this.

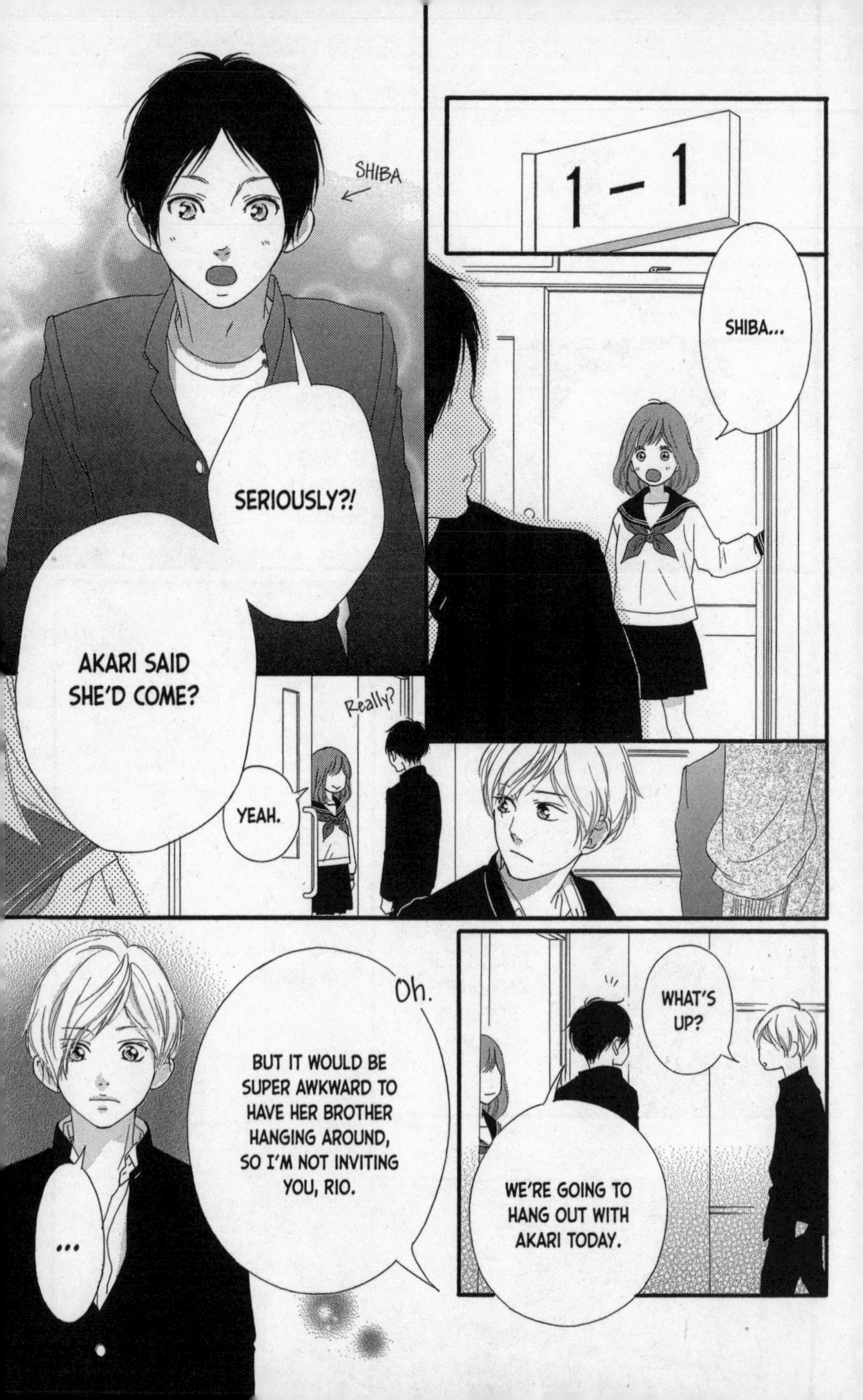
1-1
SHIBA...
SHIBA
SERIOUSLY?!
AKARI SAID SHE'D COME?
Really?
YEAH.
WHAT'S UP?
WE'RE GOING TO HANG OUT WITH AKARI TODAY.
Oh.
BUT IT WOULD BE SUPER AWKWARD TO HAVE HER BROTHER HANGING AROUND, SO I'M NOT INVITING YOU, RIO.
...

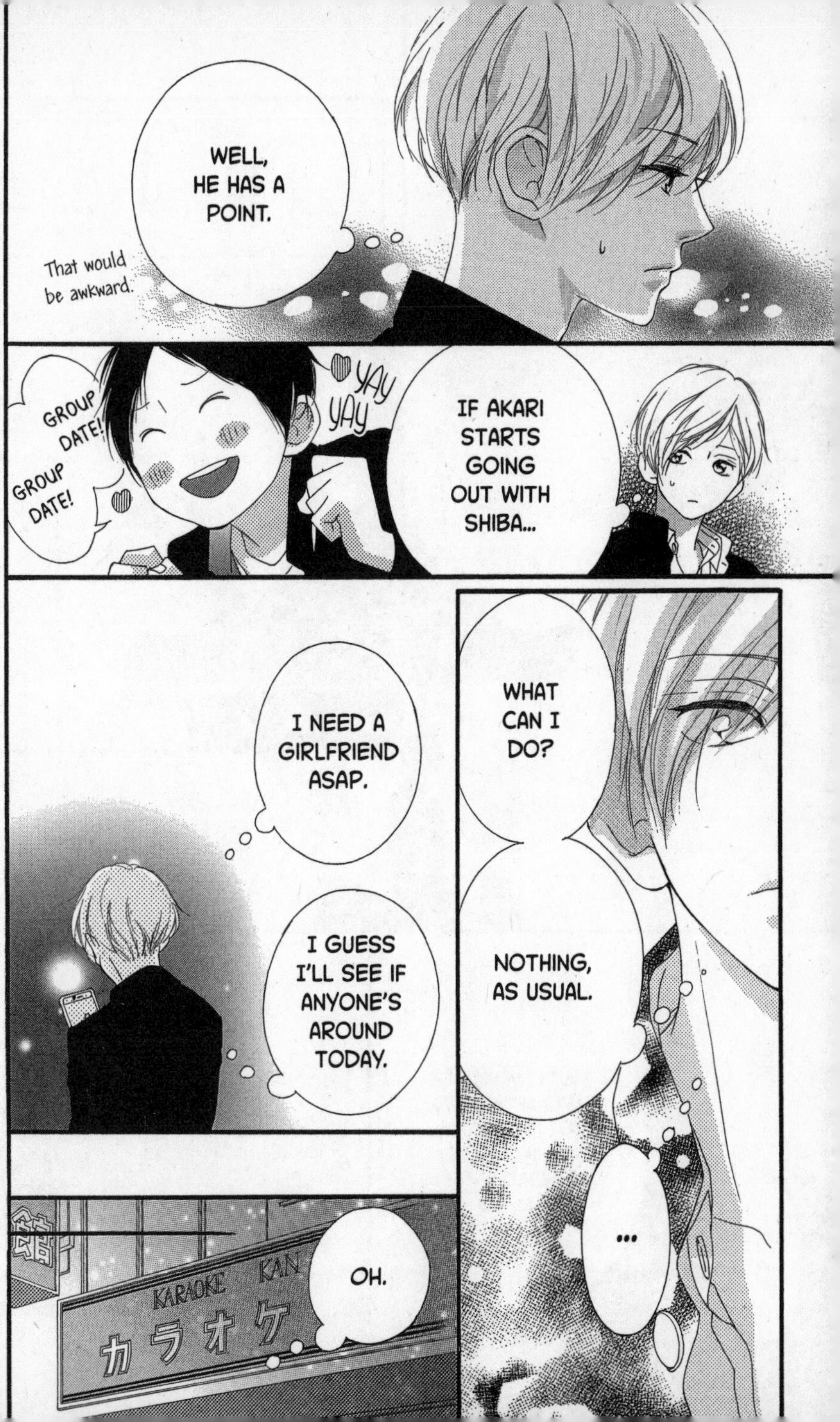
WELL, HE HAS A POINT.
That would be awkward.
IF AKARI STARTS GOING OUT WITH SHIBA...
YAY YAY
GROUP DATE!
GROUP DATE!
WHAT CAN I DO?
NOTHING, AS USUAL.
...
I NEED A GIRLFRIEND ASAP.
I GUESS I'LL SEE IF ANYONE'S AROUND TODAY.
OH.
KARAOKE KAN
カラオケ

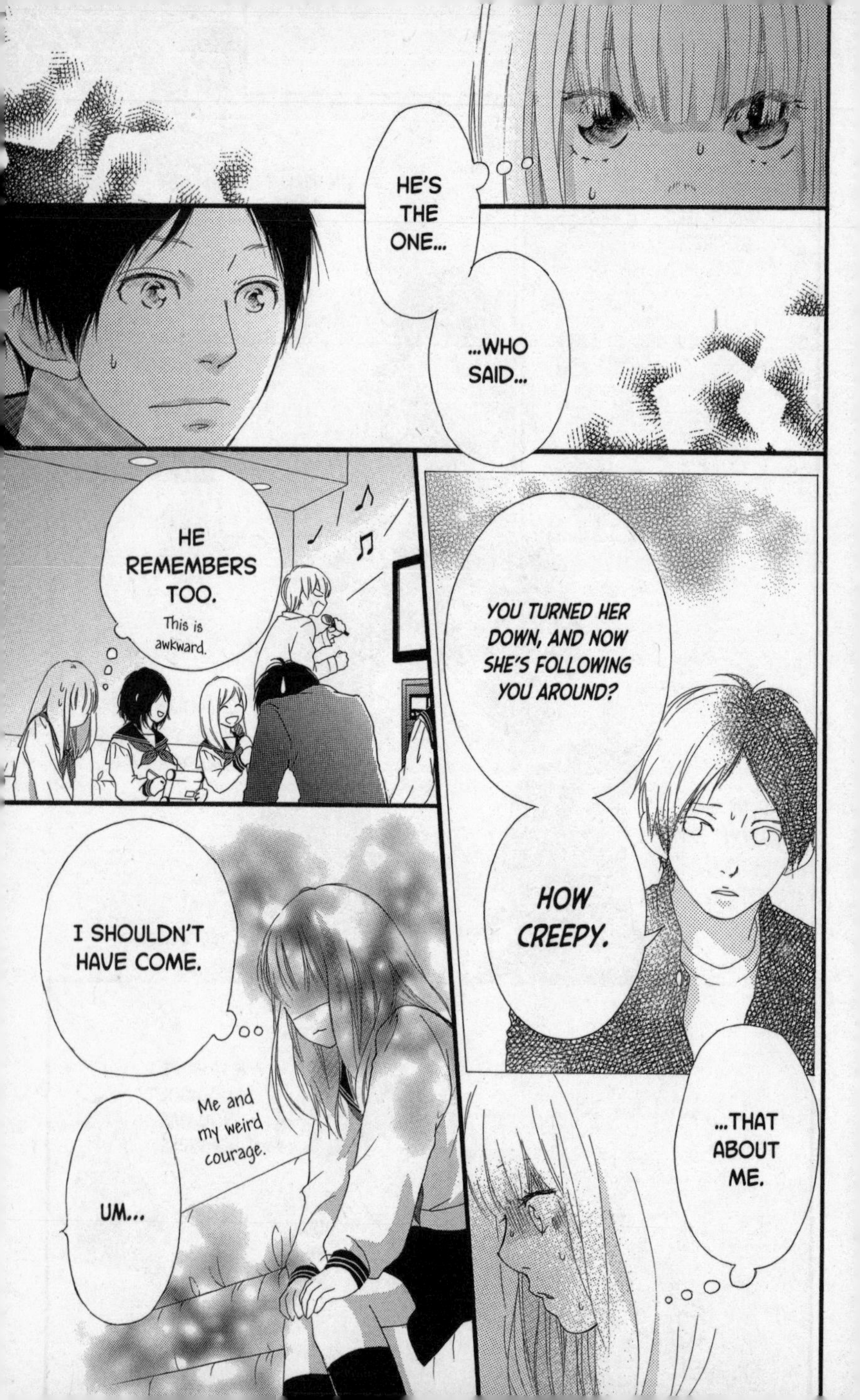
HE'S THE ONE...
...WHO SAID...
YOU TURNED HER DOWN, AND NOW SHE'S FOLLOWING YOU AROUND?
HOW CREEPY.
...THAT ABOUT ME.
HE REMEMBERS TOO.
This is awkward.
I SHOULDN'T HAVE COME.
Me and my weird courage.
UM...

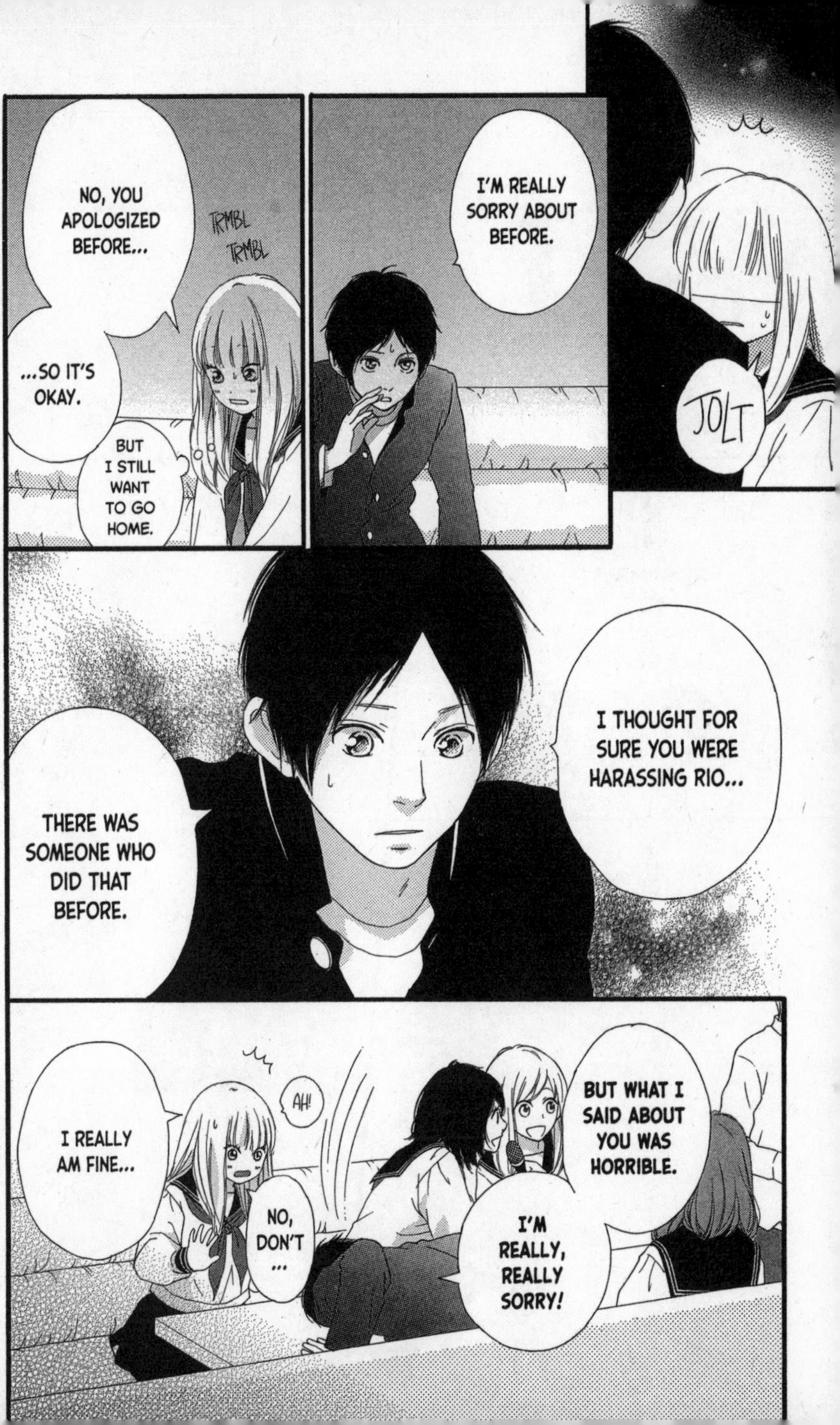
JOLT
I'M REALLY SORRY ABOUT BEFORE.
NO, YOU APOLOGIZED BEFORE...
TRMBL TRMBL
...SO IT'S OKAY.
BUT I STILL WANT TO GO HOME.
I THOUGHT FOR SURE YOU WERE HARASSING RIO...
THERE WAS SOMEONE WHO DID THAT BEFORE.
BUT WHAT I SAID ABOUT YOU WAS HORRIBLE.
I'M REALLY, REALLY SORRY!
NO, DON'T...
AH!
I REALLY AM FINE...

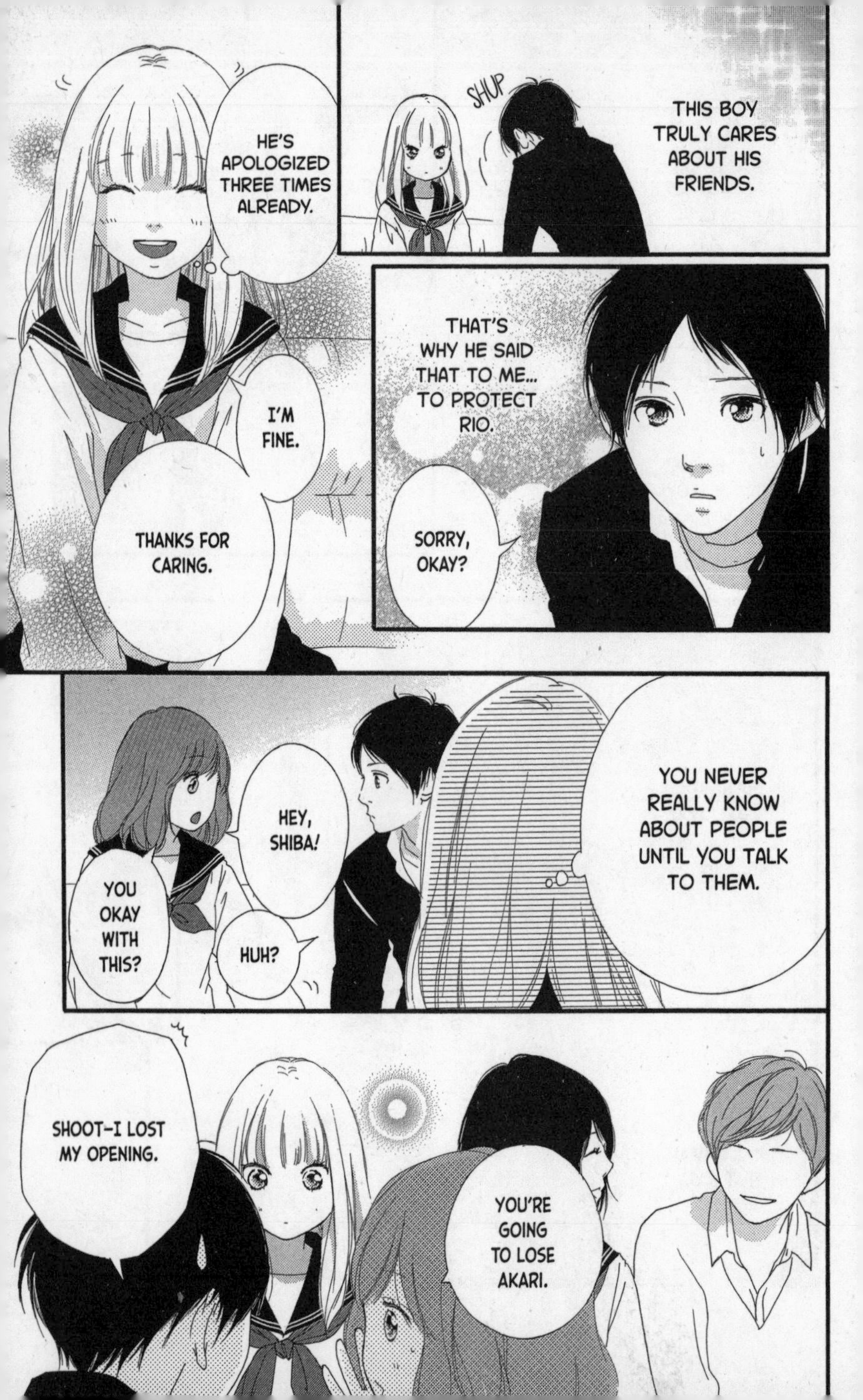
THIS BOY TRULY CARES ABOUT HIS FRIENDS.
SHUP
THAT'S WHY HE SAID THAT TO ME... TO PROTECT RIO.
SORRY, OKAY?
HE'S APOLOGIZED THREE TIMES ALREADY.
I'M FINE.
THANKS FOR CARING.
YOU NEVER REALLY KNOW ABOUT PEOPLE UNTIL YOU TALK TO THEM.
HEY, SHIBA!
HUH?
YOU OKAY WITH THIS?
YOU'RE GOING TO LOSE AKARI.
SHOOT—I LOST MY OPENING.

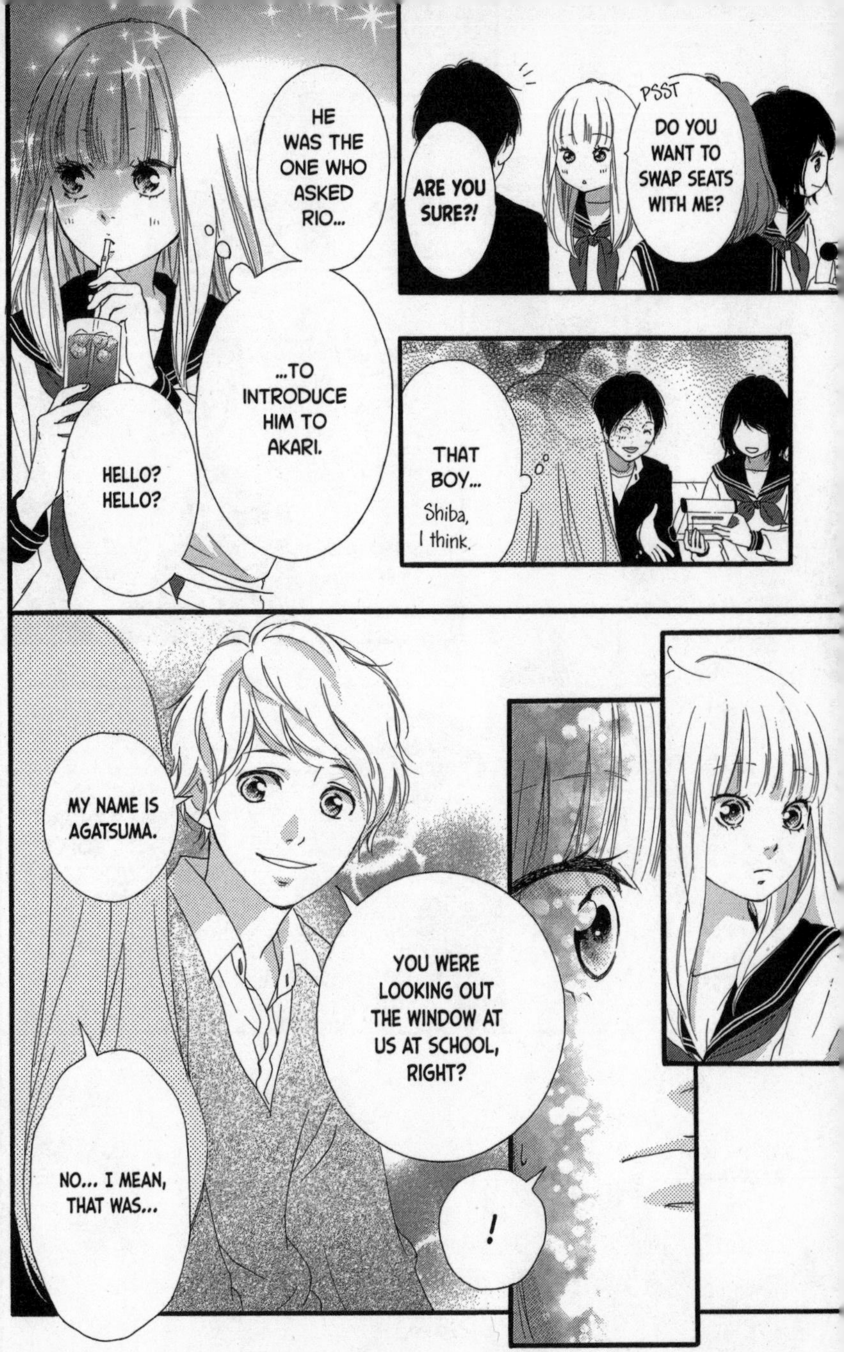
PSST
DO YOU WANT TO SWAP SEATS WITH ME?
ARE YOU SURE?!
THAT BOY...
Shiba, I think.
HE WAS THE ONE WHO ASKED RIO...
...TO INTRODUCE HIM TO AKARI.
HELLO? HELLO?
!
MY NAME IS AGATSUMA.
YOU WERE LOOKING OUT THE WINDOW AT US AT SCHOOL, RIGHT?
NO... I MEAN, THAT WAS...

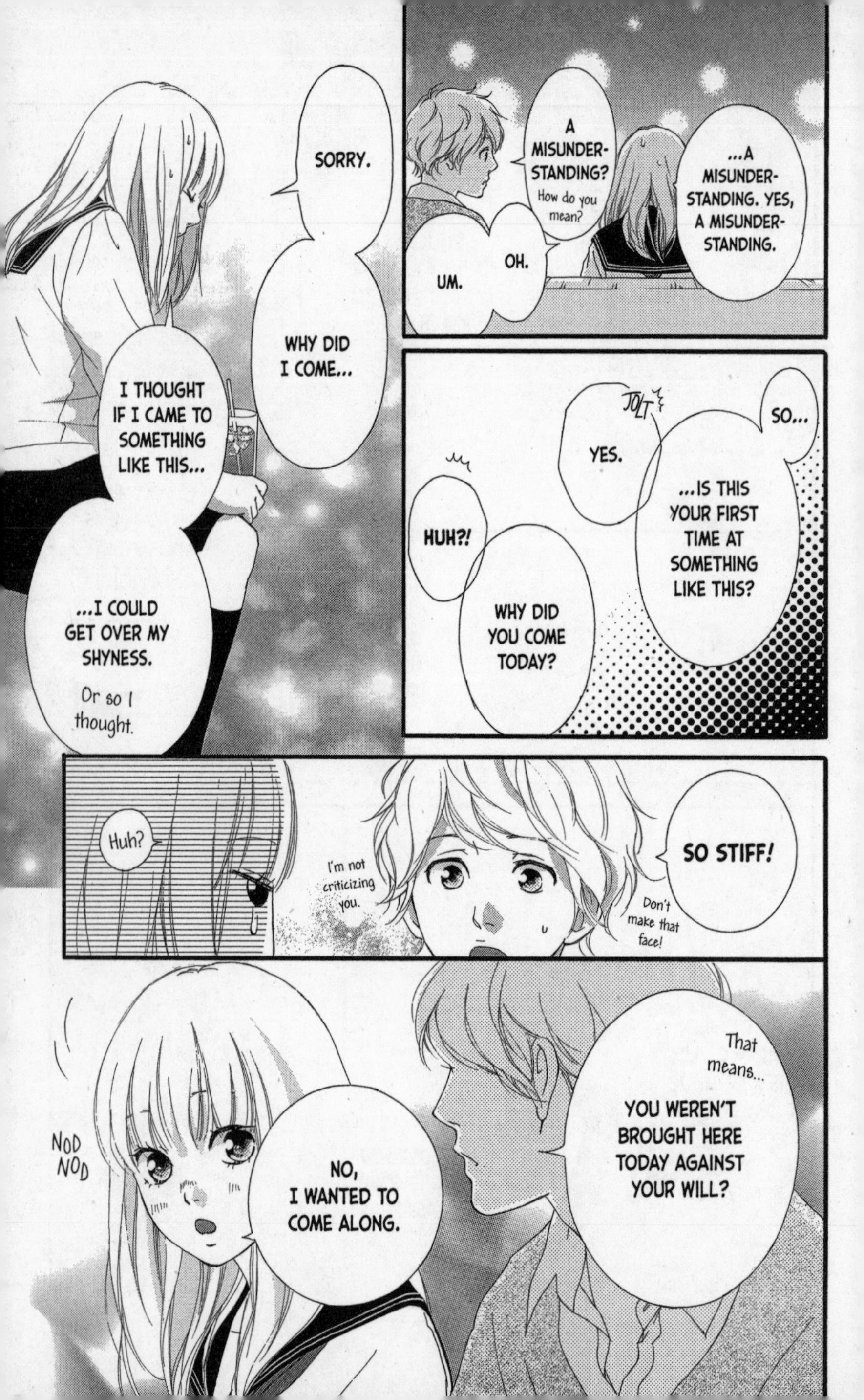
...A MISUNDER-STANDING. YES, A MISUNDER-STANDING.
A MISUNDER-STANDING? How do you mean?
OH.
UM.
SO...
...IS THIS YOUR FIRST TIME AT SOMETHING LIKE THIS?
JOLT
YES.
WHY DID YOU COME TODAY?
HUH?!
SORRY.
WHY DID I COME...
I THOUGHT IF I CAME TO SOMETHING LIKE THIS...
...I COULD GET OVER MY SHYNESS. Or so I thought.
SO STIFF!
Don't make that face!
I'm not criticizing you.
Huh?
That means... YOU WEREN'T BROUGHT HERE TODAY AGAINST YOUR WILL?
NOD NOD
NO, I WANTED TO COME ALONG.

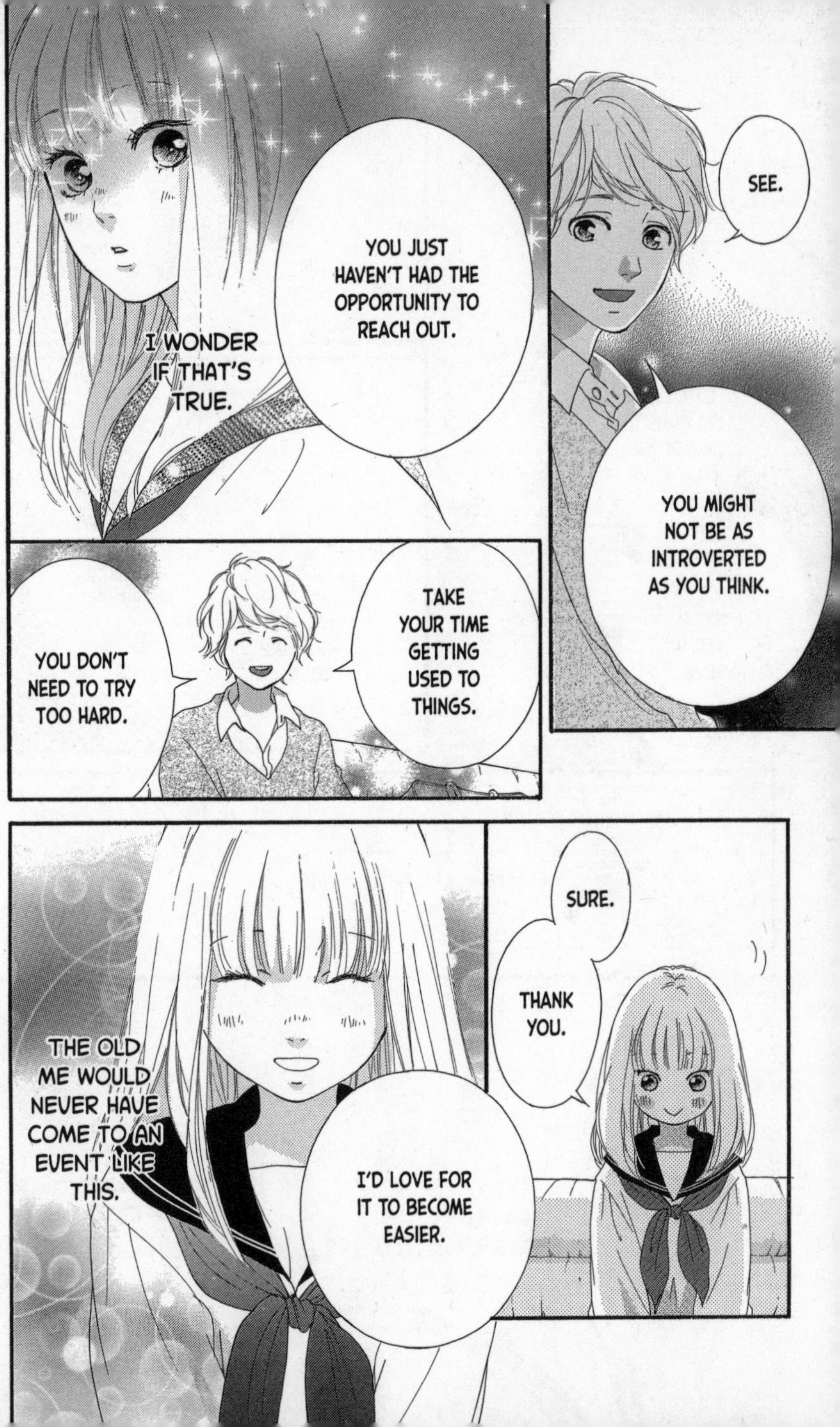
SEE.
YOU MIGHT NOT BE AS INTROVERTED AS YOU THINK.
YOU JUST HAVEN'T HAD THE OPPORTUNITY TO REACH OUT.
I WONDER IF THAT'S TRUE.
TAKE YOUR TIME GETTING USED TO THINGS.
YOU DON'T NEED TO TRY TOO HARD.
SURE.
THANK YOU.
I'D LOVE FOR IT TO BECOME EASIER.
THE OLD ME WOULD NEVER HAVE COME TO AN EVENT LIKE THIS.

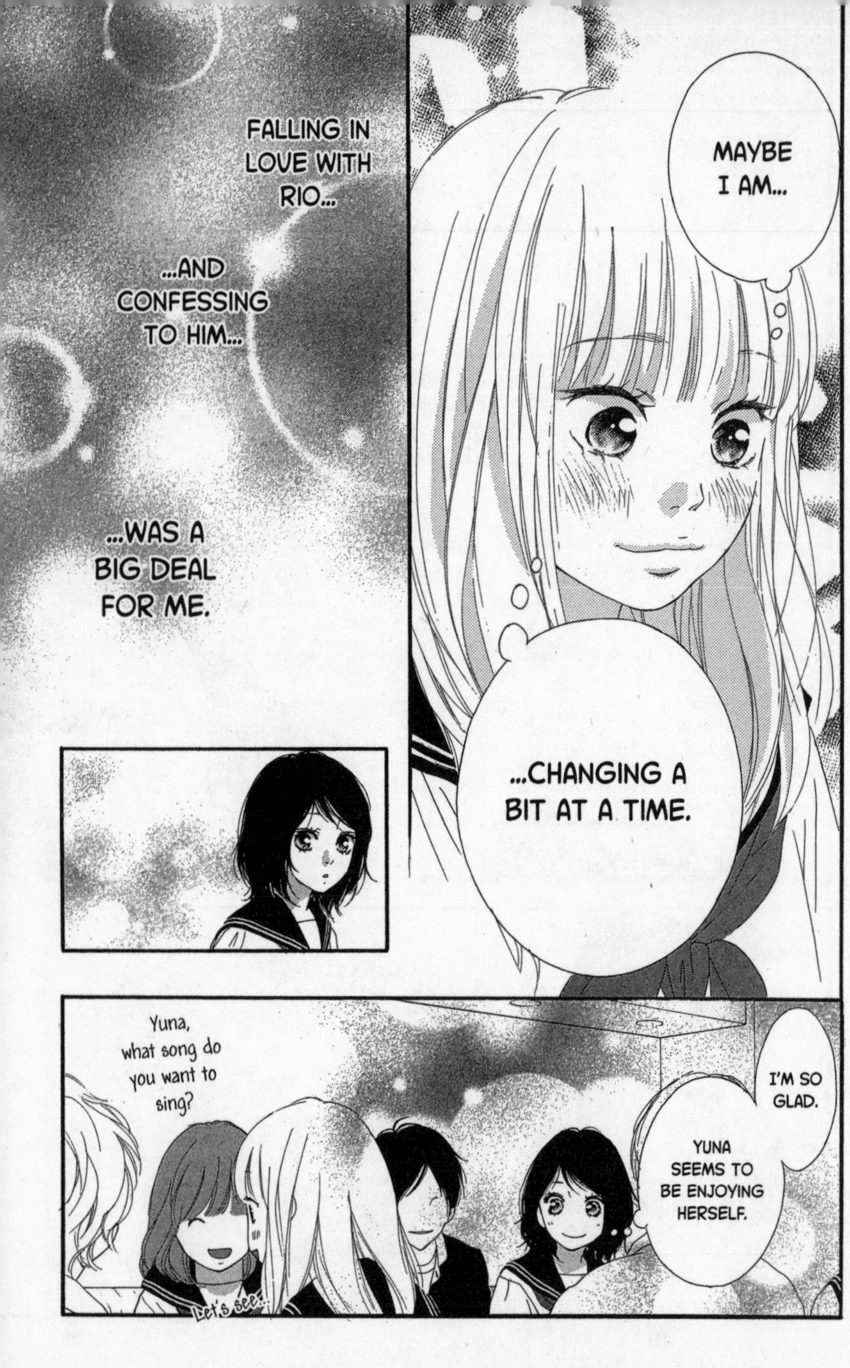
MAYBE I AM...
...CHANGING A BIT AT A TIME.
FALLING IN LOVE WITH RIO...
...AND CONFESSING TO HIM...
...WAS A BIG DEAL FOR ME.
I'M SO GLAD.
YUNA SEEMS TO BE ENJOYING HERSELF.
Yuna, what song do you want to sing?
Let's see...

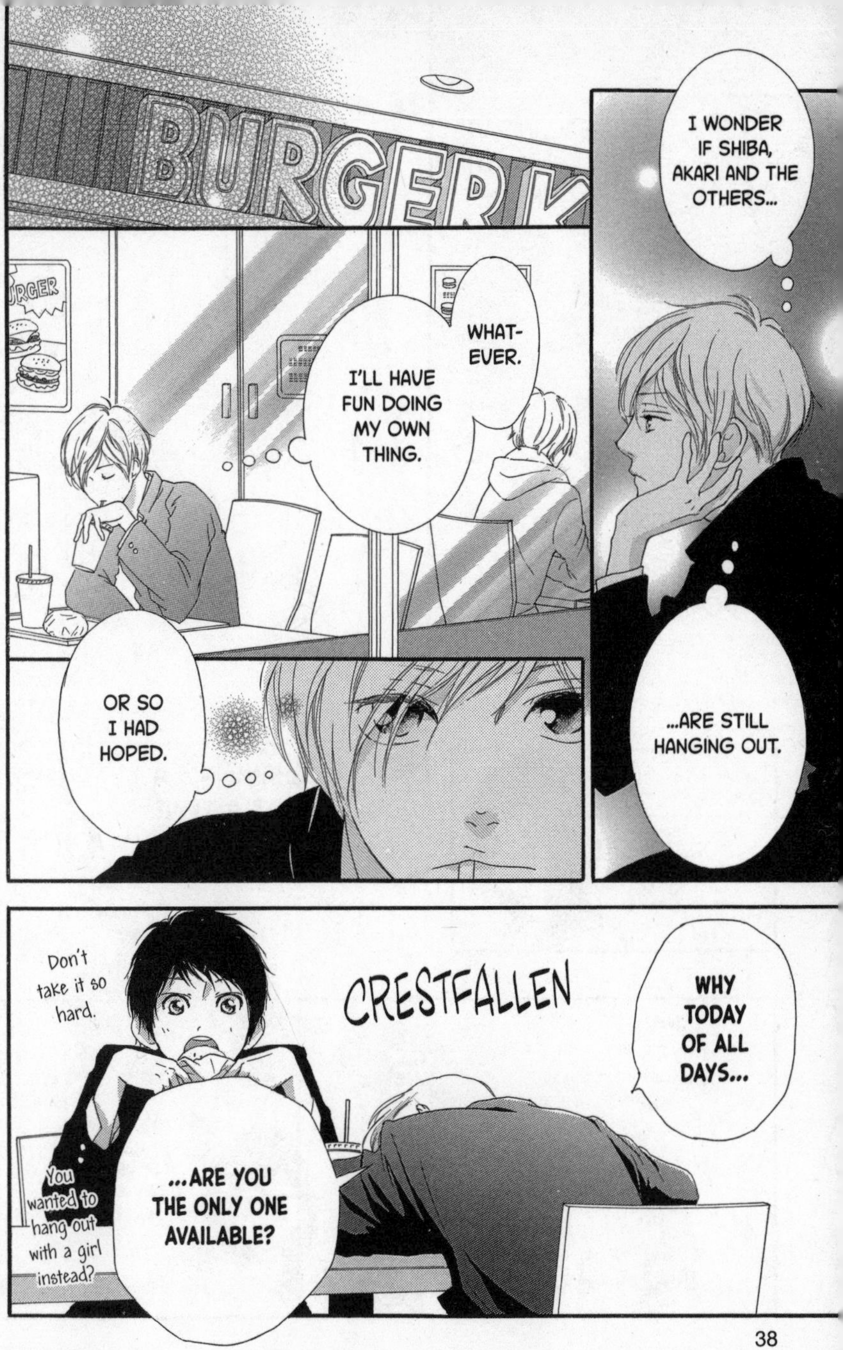
I WONDER IF SHIBA, AKARI AND THE OTHERS...
...ARE STILL HANGING OUT.
BURGER K
BURGER
WHAT-EVER.
I'LL HAVE FUN DOING MY OWN THING.
OR SO I HAD HOPED.
WHY TODAY OF ALL DAYS...
CRESTFALLEN
...ARE YOU THE ONLY ONE AVAILABLE?
Don't take it so hard.
You wanted to hang out with a girl instead?

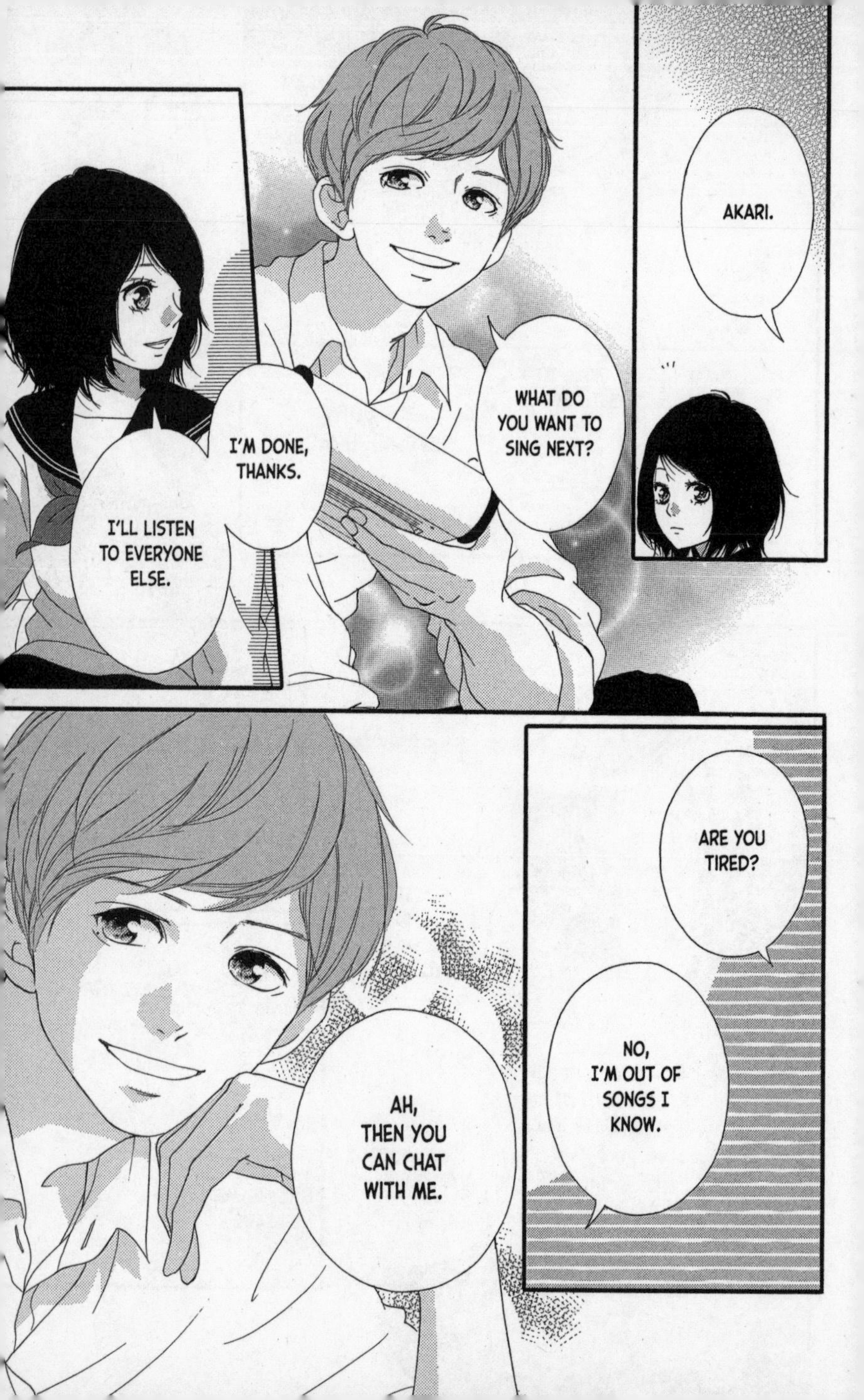
AKARI.
WHAT DO YOU WANT TO SING NEXT?
I'M DONE, THANKS.
I'LL LISTEN TO EVERYONE ELSE.
ARE YOU TIRED?
NO, I'M OUT OF SONGS I KNOW.
AH, THEN YOU CAN CHAT WITH ME.

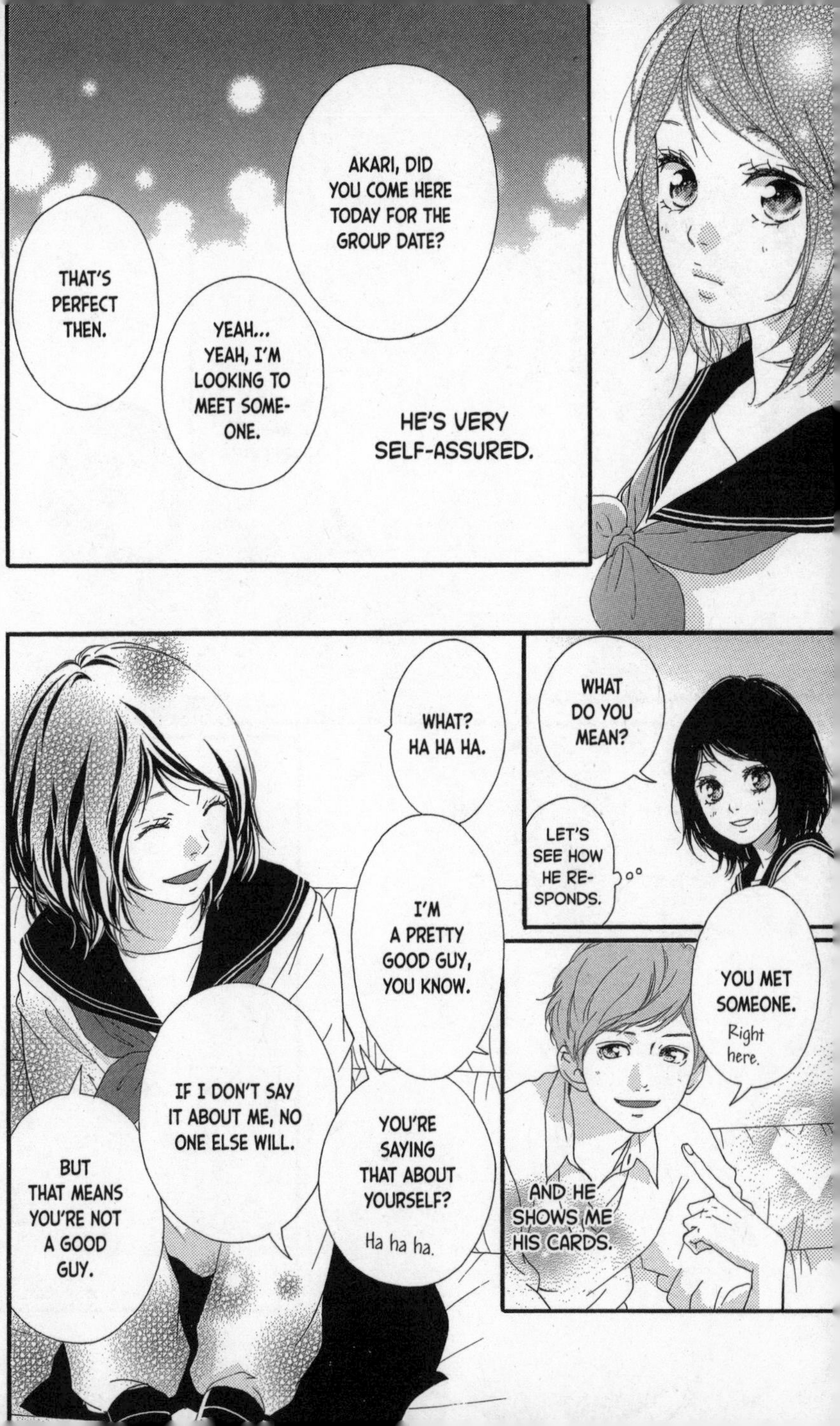
AKARI, DID YOU COME HERE TODAY FOR THE GROUP DATE?
YEAH... YEAH, I'M LOOKING TO MEET SOME-ONE.
THAT'S PERFECT THEN.
HE'S VERY SELF-ASSURED.
WHAT DO YOU MEAN?
LET'S SEE HOW HE RE-SPONDS.
YOU MET SOMEONE.
Right here.
AND HE SHOWS ME HIS CARDS.
WHAT? HA HA HA.
I'M A PRETTY GOOD GUY, YOU KNOW.
YOU'RE SAYING THAT ABOUT YOURSELF?
Ha ha ha.
IF I DON'T SAY IT ABOUT ME, NO ONE ELSE WILL.
BUT THAT MEANS YOU'RE NOT A GOOD GUY.

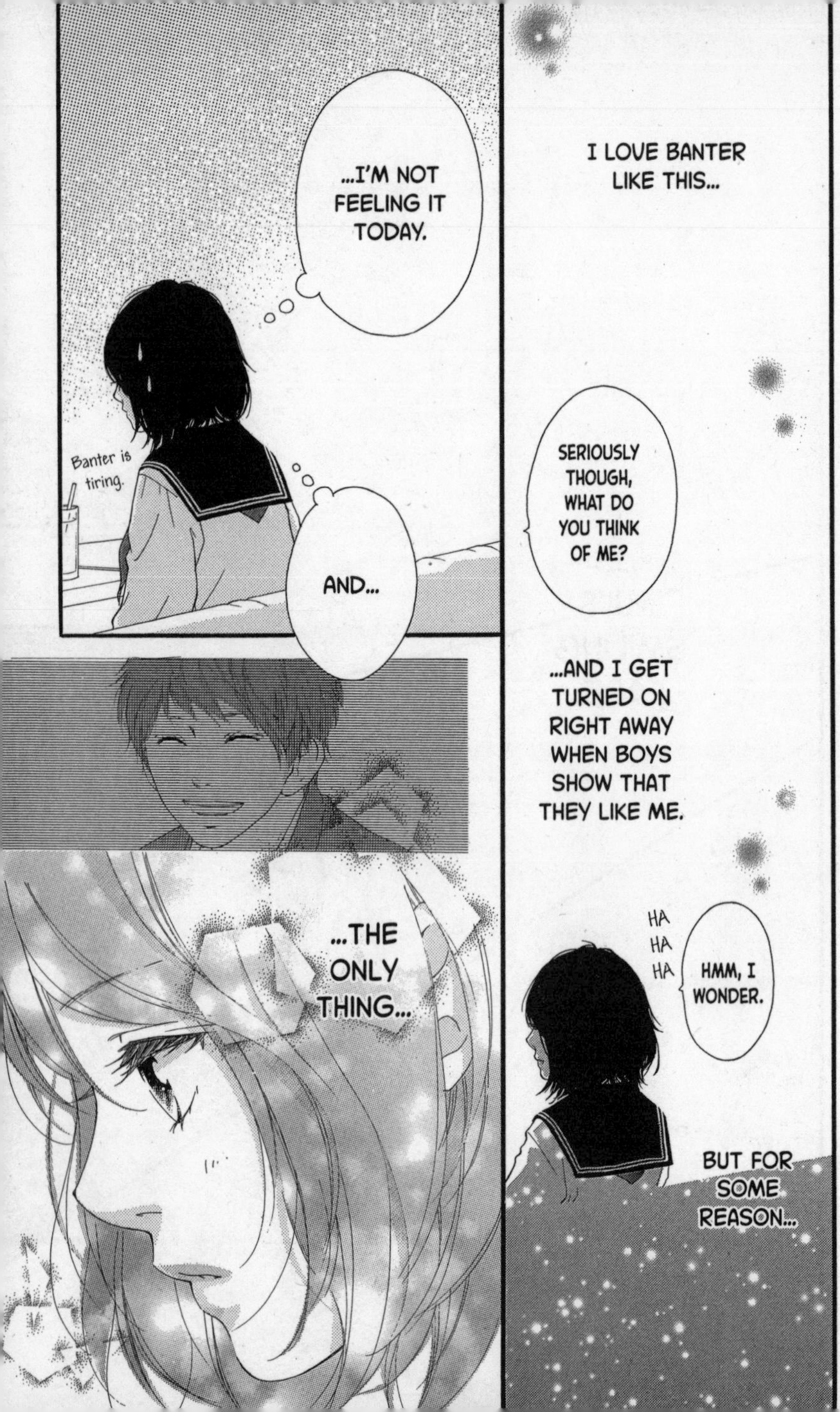
I LOVE BANTER LIKE THIS...
SERIOUSLY THOUGH, WHAT DO YOU THINK OF ME?
...AND I GET TURNED ON RIGHT AWAY WHEN BOYS SHOW THAT THEY LIKE ME.
HMM, I WONDER.
HA HA HA
BUT FOR SOME REASON...
...I'M NOT FEELING IT TODAY.
Banter is tiring.
AND...
...THE ONLY THING...

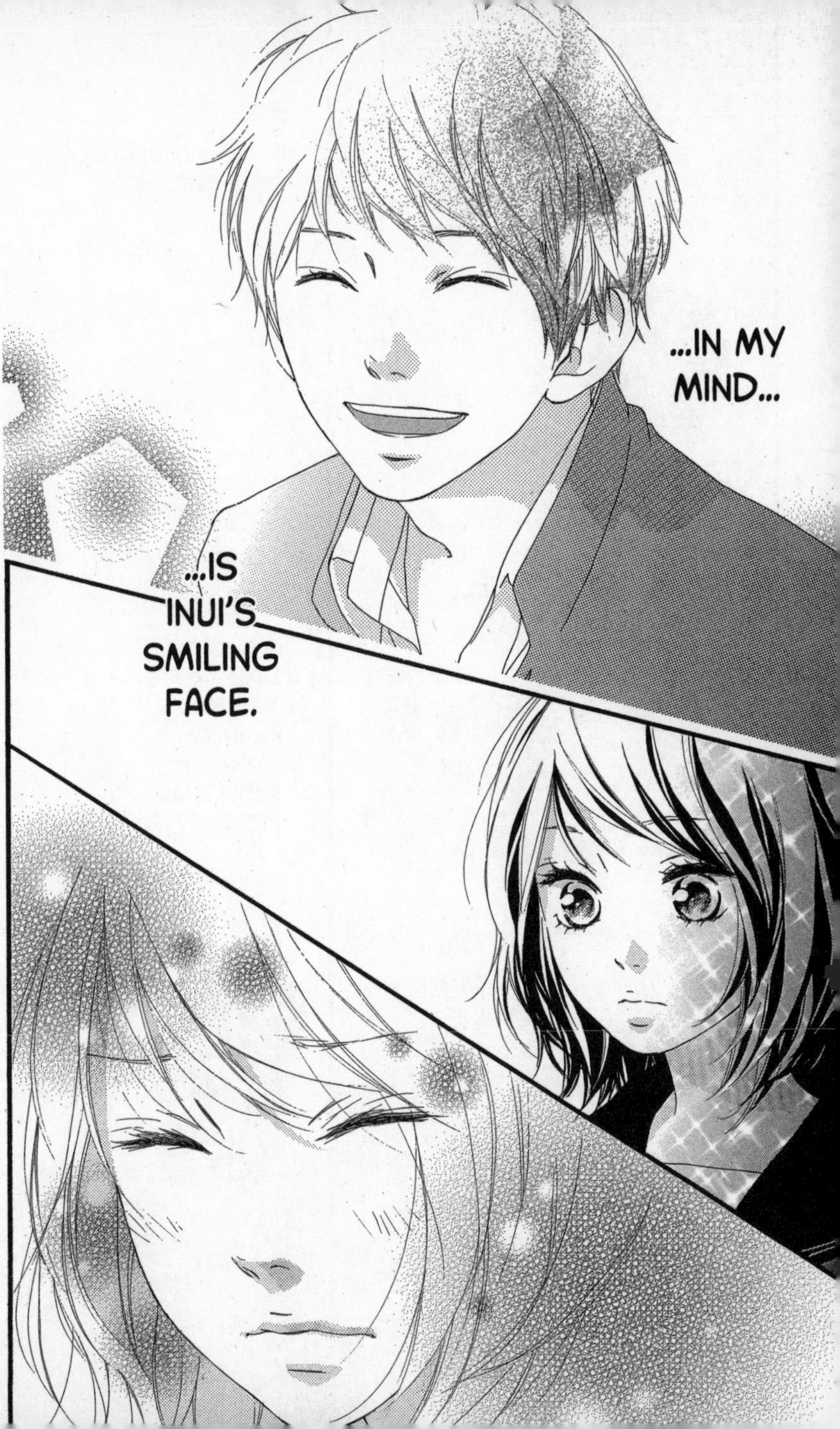
...IN MY MIND...
...IS INUI'S SMILING FACE.

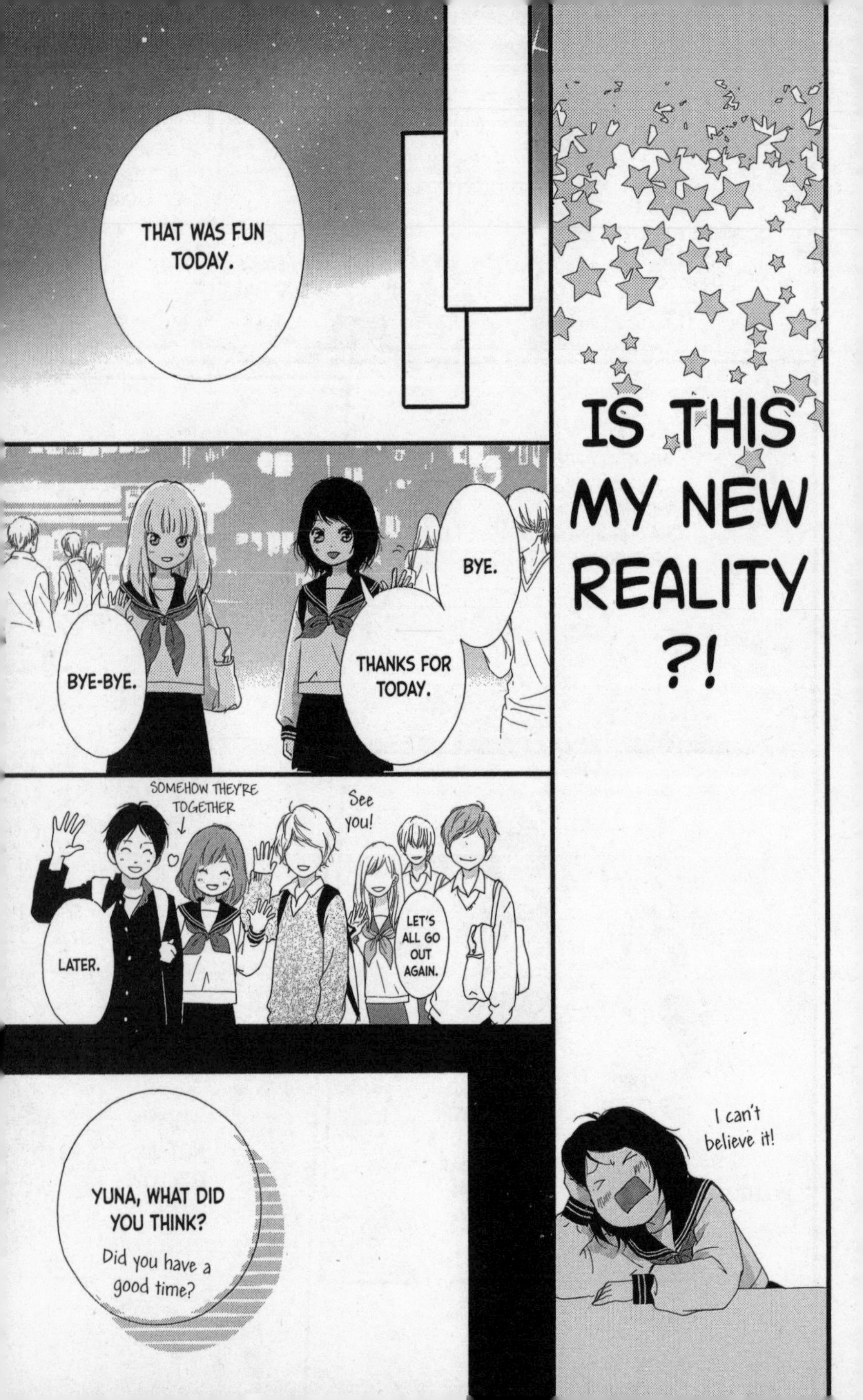
IS THIS MY NEW REALITY ?!
I can't believe it!
THAT WAS FUN TODAY.
BYE.
THANKS FOR TODAY.
BYE-BYE.
See you!
SOMEHOW THEY'RE TOGETHER
LET'S ALL GO OUT AGAIN.
LATER.
YUNA, WHAT DID YOU THINK?
Did you have a good time?

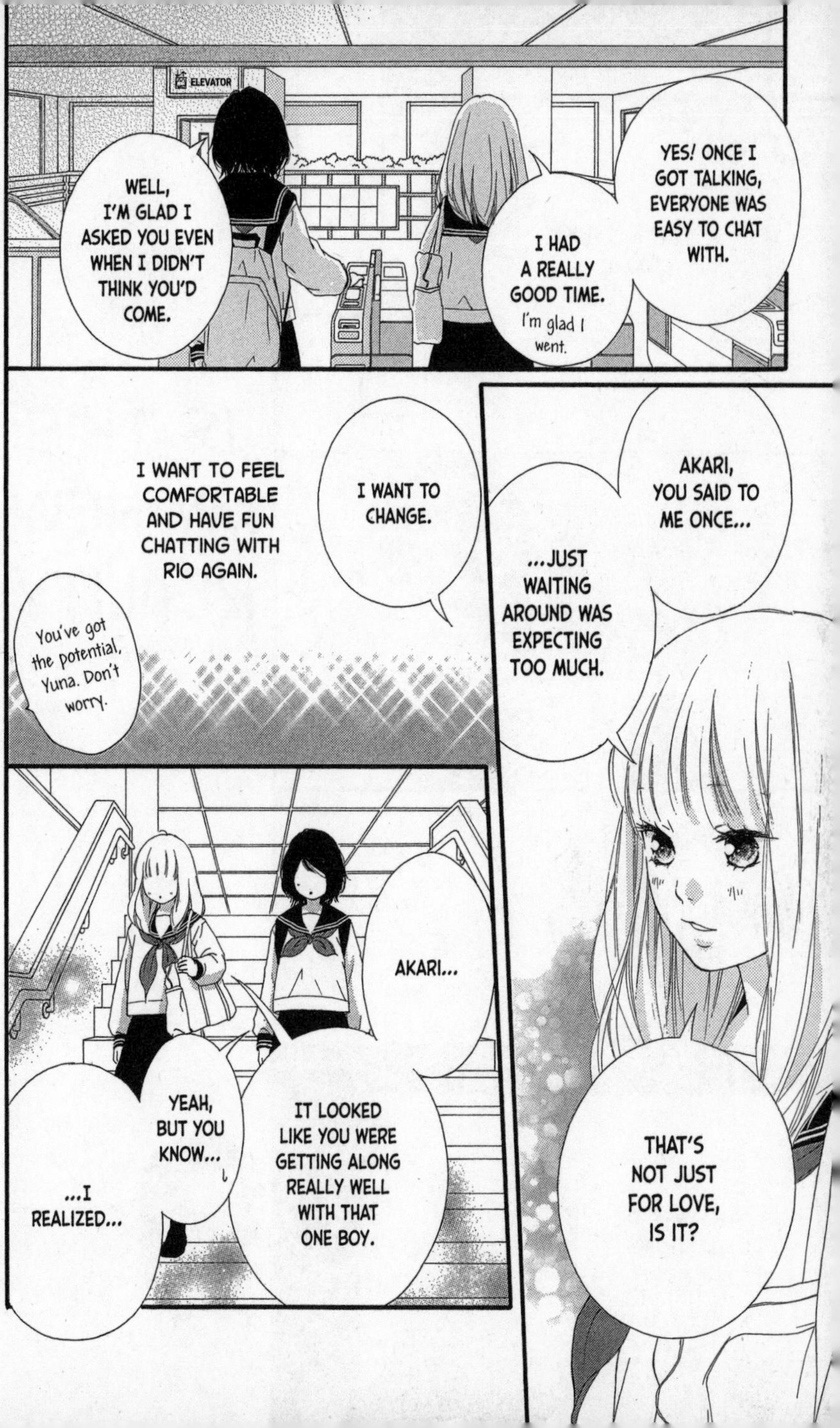
ELEVATOR
YES! ONCE I GOT TALKING, EVERYONE WAS EASY TO CHAT WITH.
I HAD A REALLY GOOD TIME. I'm glad I went.
WELL, I'M GLAD I ASKED YOU EVEN WHEN I DIDN'T THINK YOU'D COME.
AKARI, YOU SAID TO ME ONCE...
...JUST WAITING AROUND WAS EXPECTING TOO MUCH.
THAT'S NOT JUST FOR LOVE, IS IT?
I WANT TO CHANGE.
I WANT TO FEEL COMFORTABLE AND HAVE FUN CHATTING WITH RIO AGAIN.
You've got the potential, Yuna. Don't worry.
AKARI...
IT LOOKED LIKE YOU WERE GETTING ALONG REALLY WELL WITH THAT ONE BOY.
YEAH, BUT YOU KNOW...
...I REALIZED...

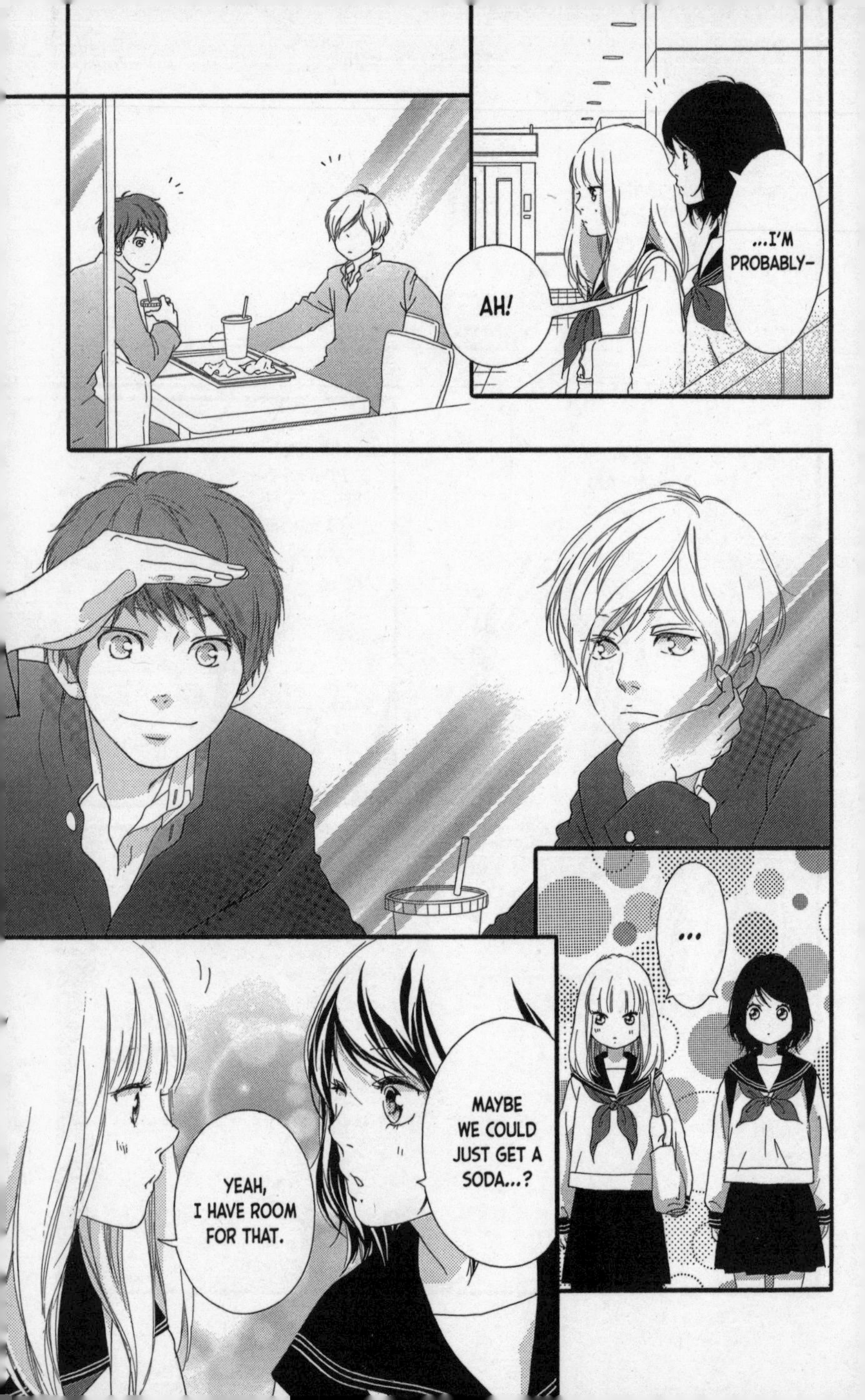
...I'M PROBABLY—
AH!
...
MAYBE WE COULD JUST GET A SODA...?
YEAH, I HAVE ROOM FOR THAT.

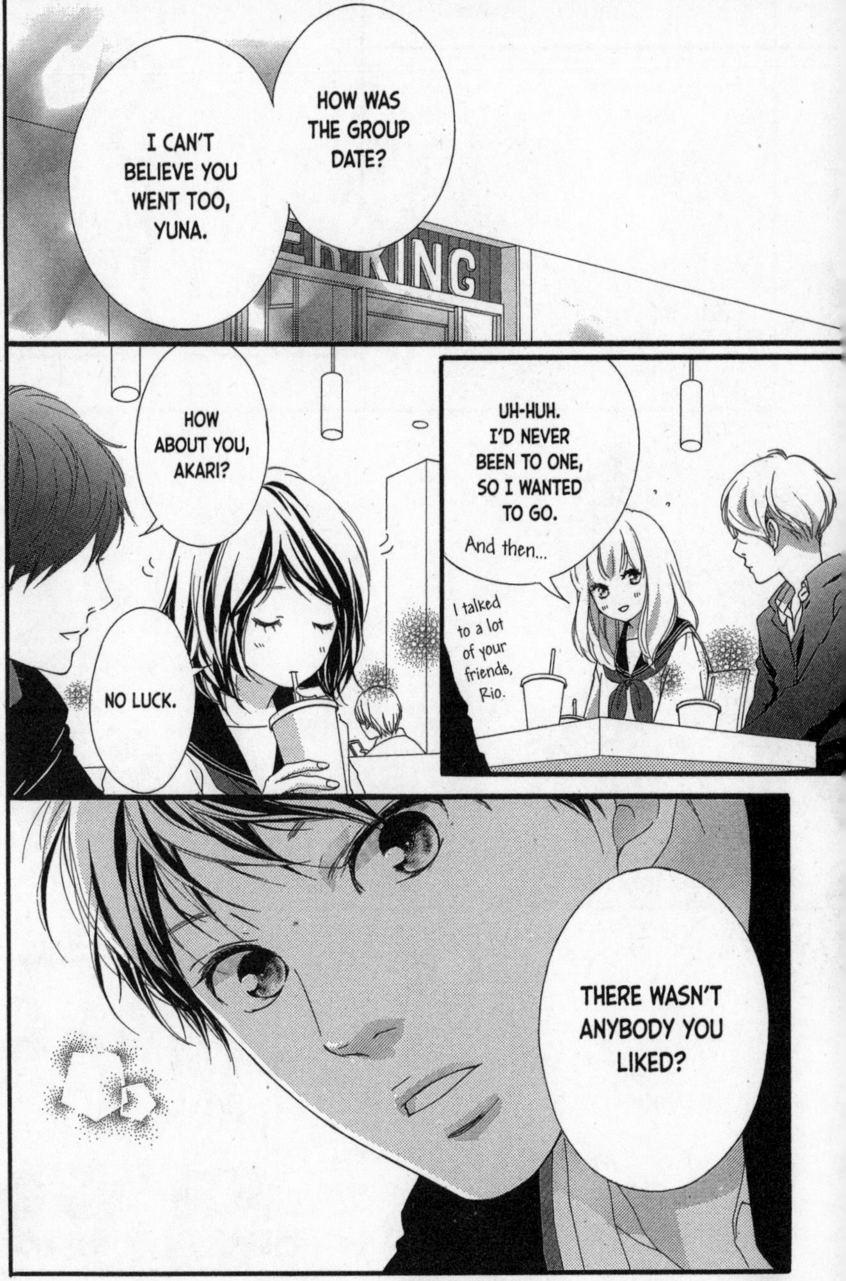
HOW WAS THE GROUP DATE?
I CAN'T BELIEVE YOU WENT TOO, YUNA.
UH-HUH. I'D NEVER BEEN TO ONE, SO I WANTED TO GO.
And then...
I talked to a lot of your friends, Rio.
HOW ABOUT YOU, AKARI?
NO LUCK.
THERE WASN'T ANYBODY YOU LIKED?

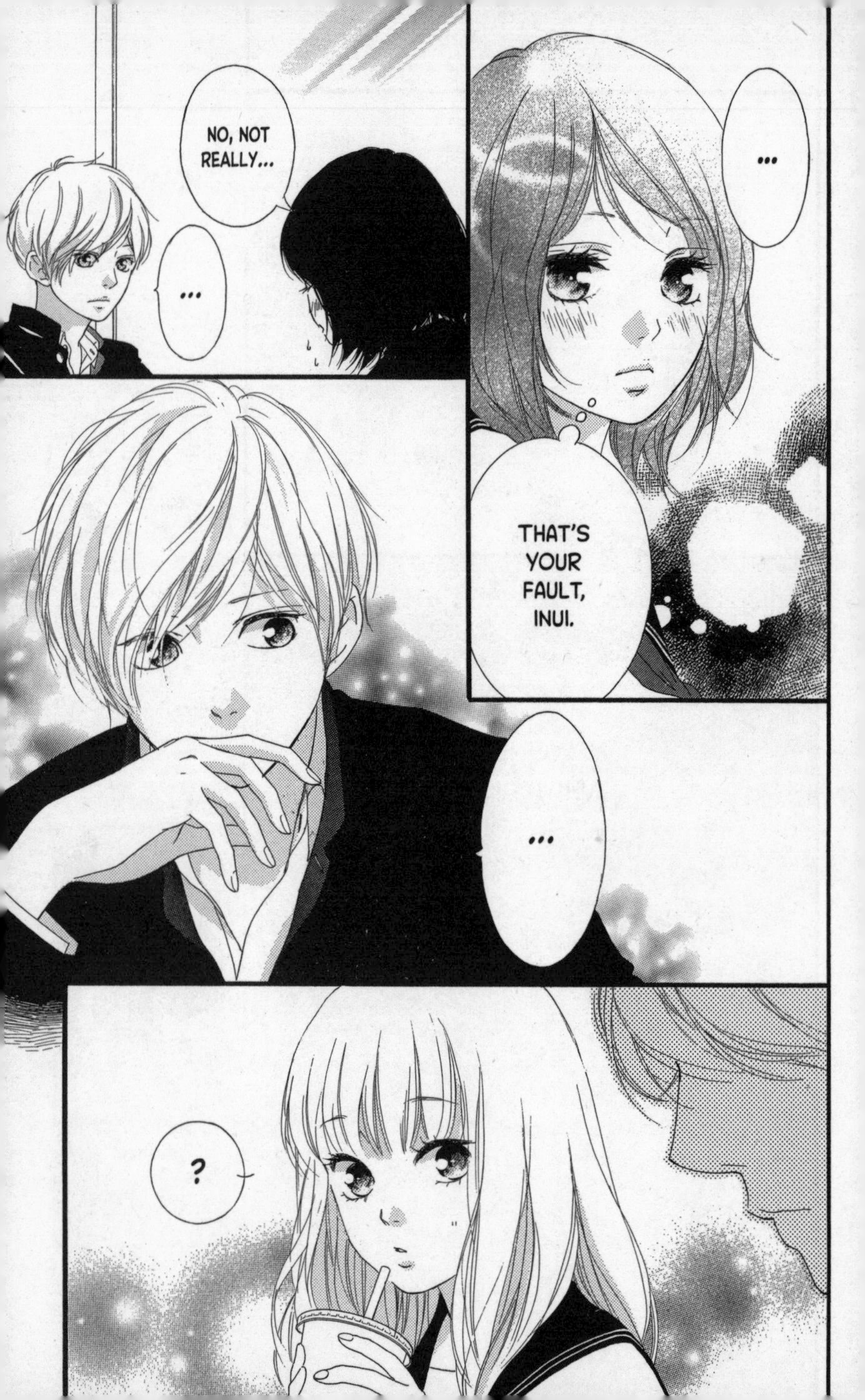
...
THAT'S YOUR FAULT, INUI.
NO, NOT REALLY...
...
...
?

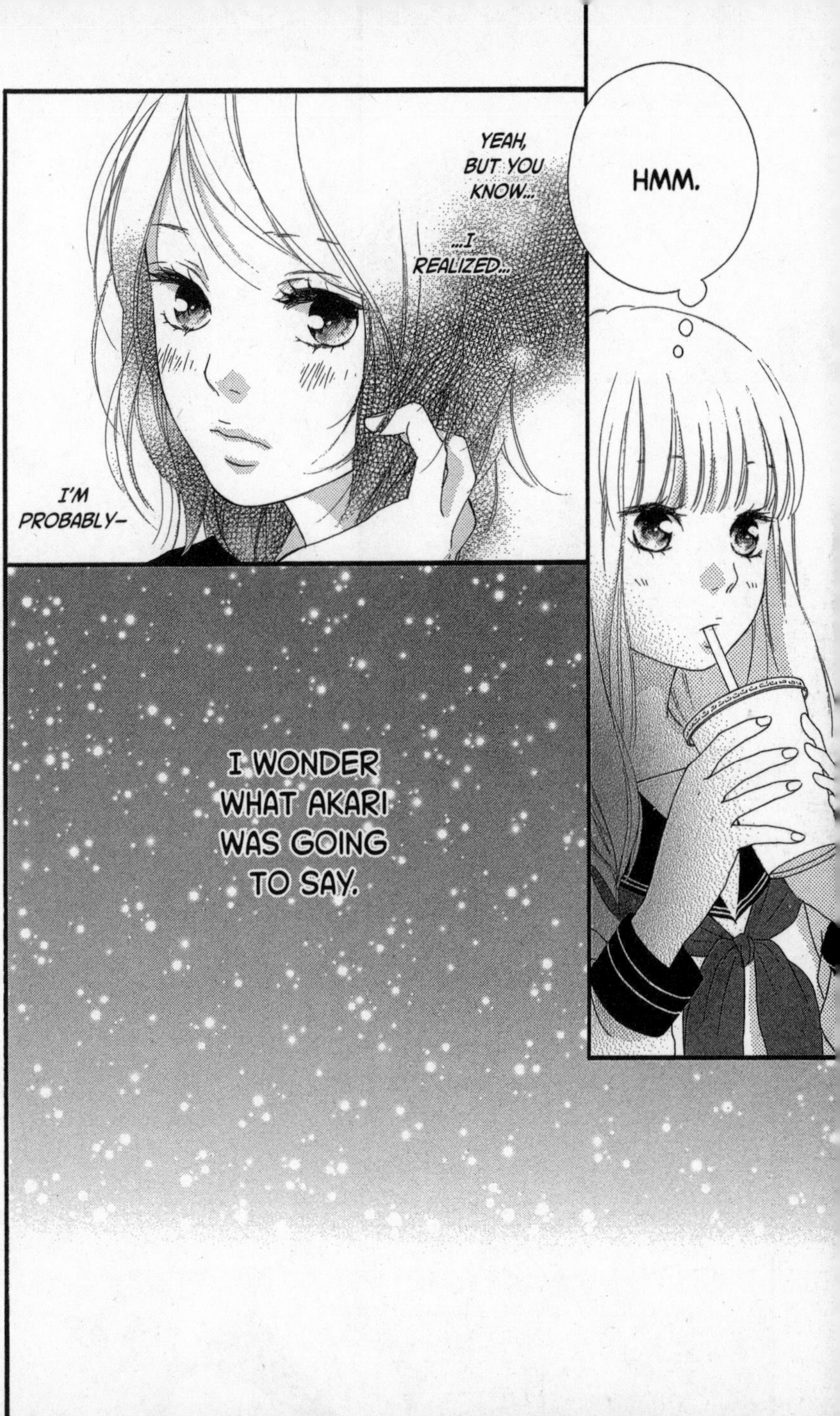
HMM.
YEAH, BUT YOU KNOW...
...I REALIZED...
I'M PROBABLY—
I WONDER WHAT AKARI WAS GOING TO SAY.

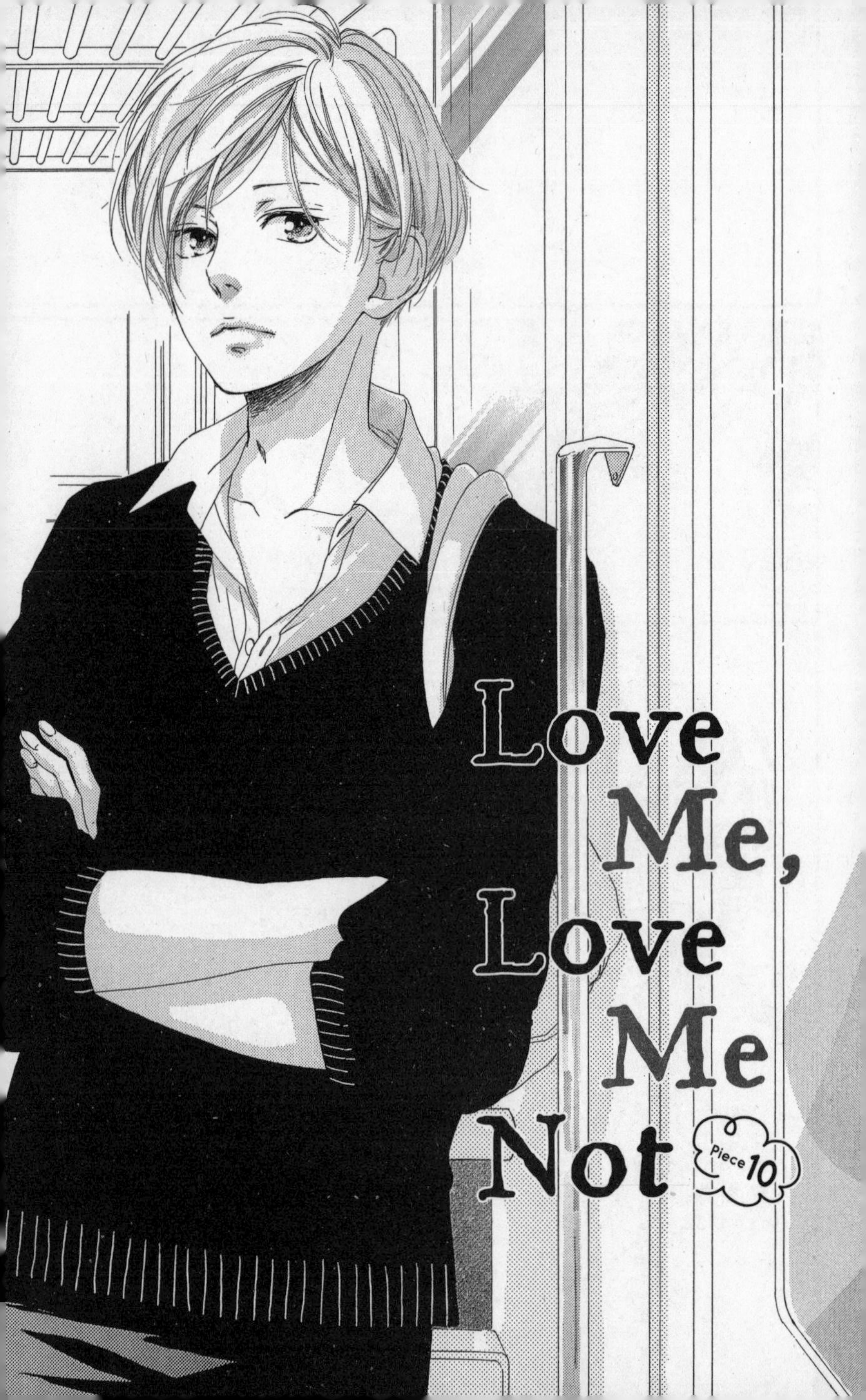
Love Me, Love Me Not
Piece 10

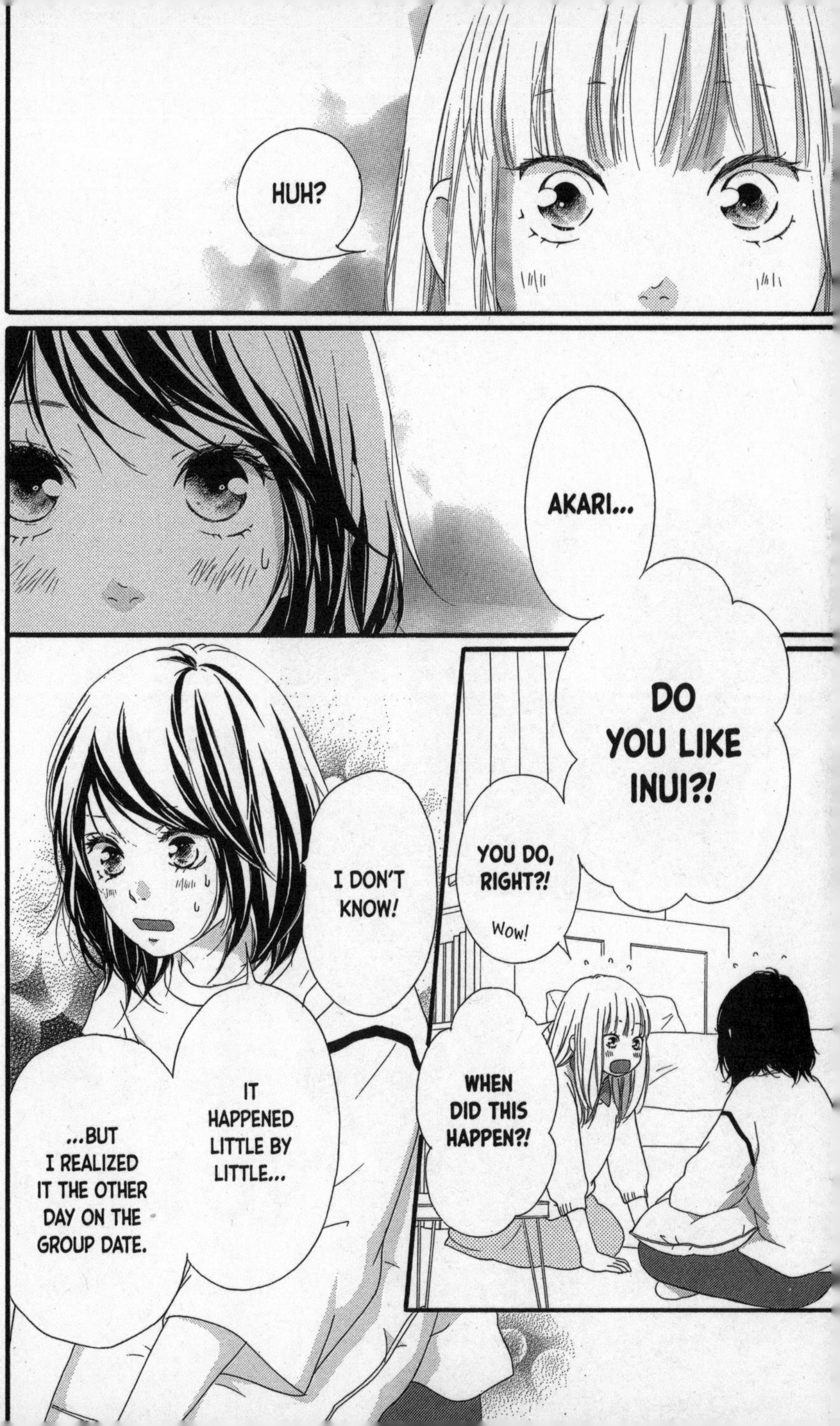
HUH?
AKARI...
DO YOU LIKE INUI?!
YOU DO, RIGHT?!
WOW!
WHEN DID THIS HAPPEN?!
I DON'T KNOW!
IT HAPPENED LITTLE BY LITTLE...
...BUT I REALIZED IT THE OTHER DAY ON THE GROUP DATE.

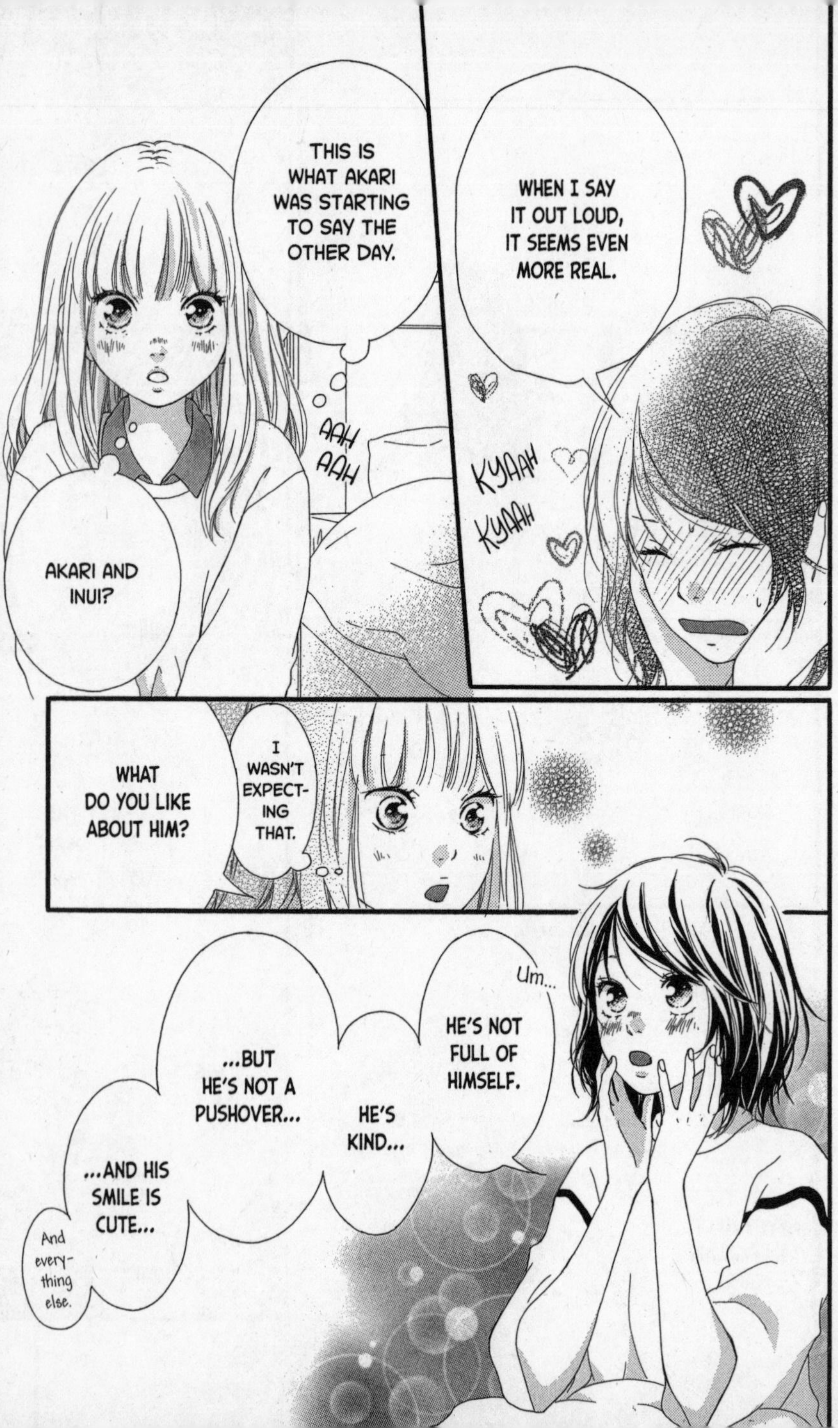
WHEN I SAY IT OUT LOUD, IT SEEMS EVEN MORE REAL.
KYAAH KYAAH
THIS IS WHAT AKARI WAS STARTING TO SAY THE OTHER DAY.
AAH AAH
AKARI AND INUI?
I WASN'T EXPECTING THAT.
WHAT DO YOU LIKE ABOUT HIM?
Um...
HE'S NOT FULL OF HIMSELF.
HE'S KIND...
...BUT HE'S NOT A PUSHOVER...
...AND HIS SMILE IS CUTE...
And everything else.

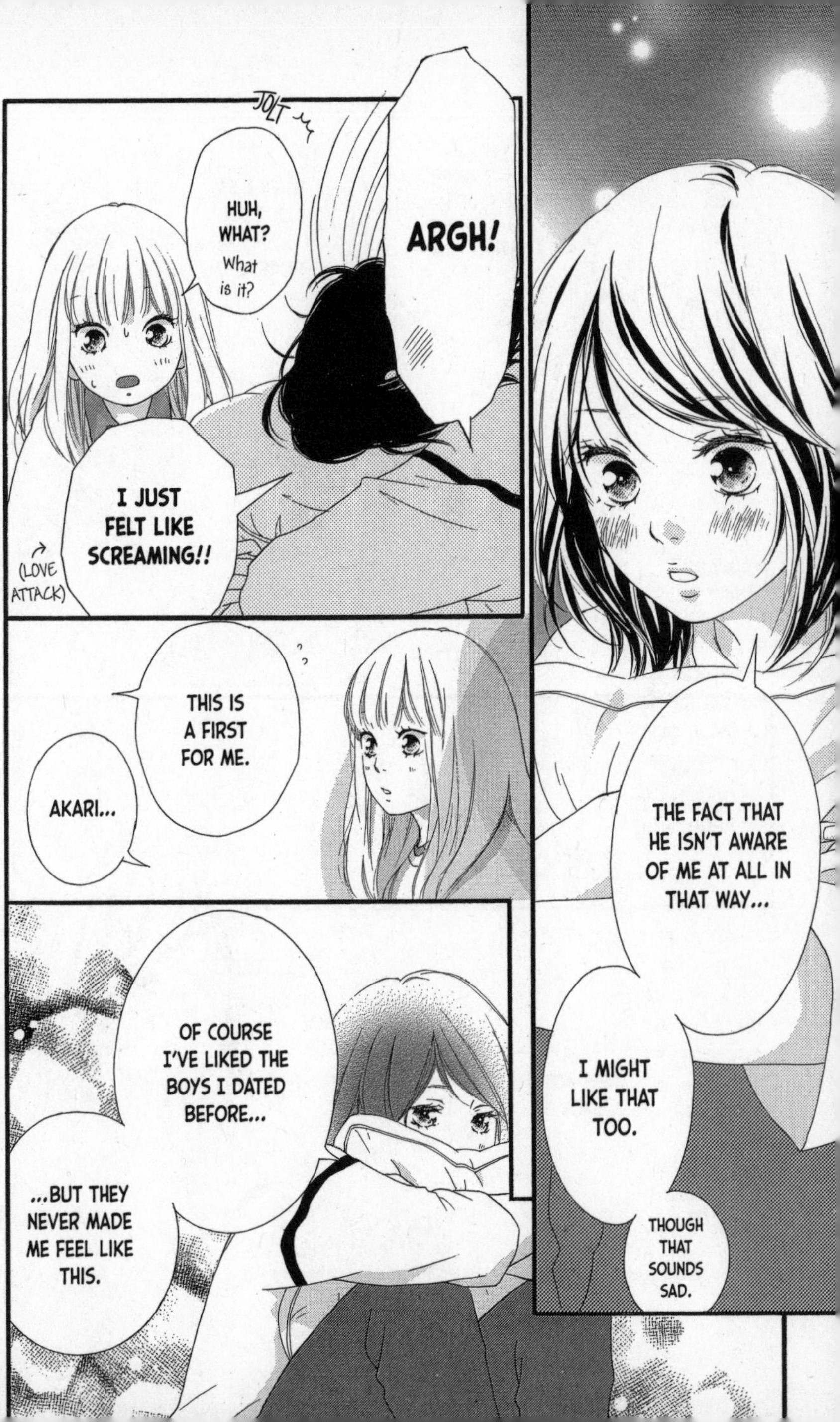
JOLT
ARGH!
HUH, WHAT? What is it?
I JUST FELT LIKE SCREAMING!!
(LOVE ATTACK)
THIS IS A FIRST FOR ME.
AKARI...
OF COURSE I'VE LIKED THE BOYS I DATED BEFORE...
...BUT THEY NEVER MADE ME FEEL LIKE THIS.
THE FACT THAT HE ISN'T AWARE OF ME AT ALL IN THAT WAY...
I MIGHT LIKE THAT TOO.
THOUGH THAT SOUNDS SAD.

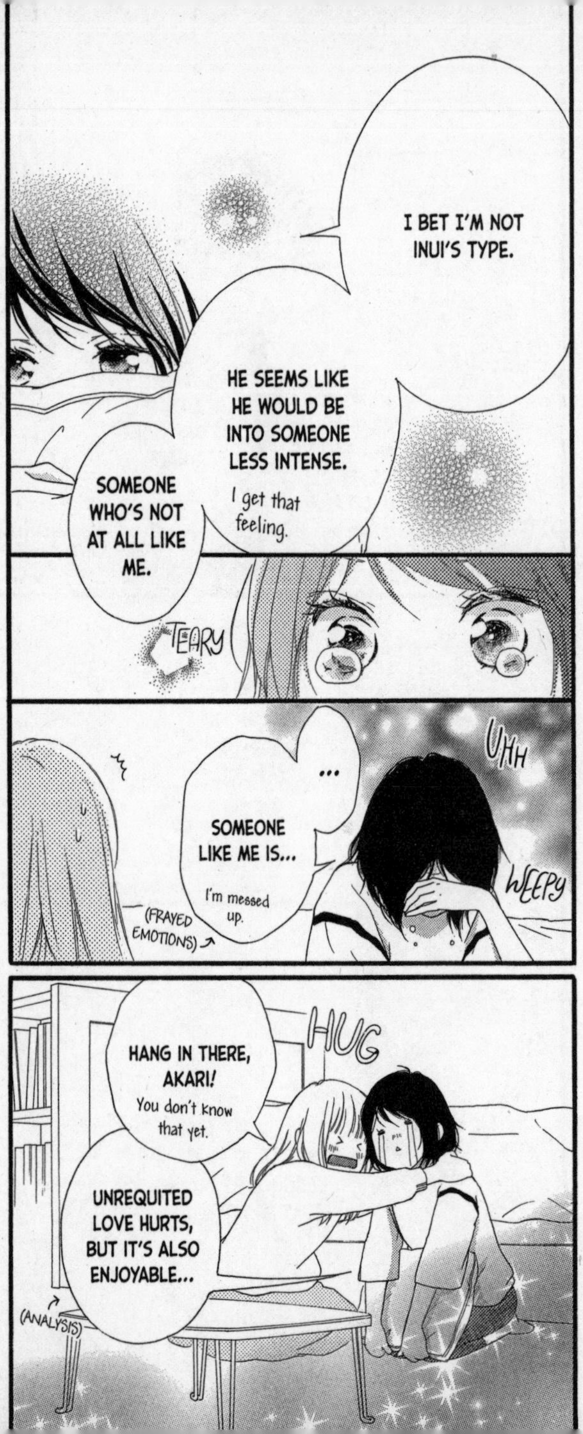
I BET I'M NOT INUI'S TYPE.
HE SEEMS LIKE HE WOULD BE INTO SOMEONE LESS INTENSE.
I get that feeling.
SOMEONE WHO'S NOT AT ALL LIKE ME.
TEARY
UHH
WEEPY
...
SOMEONE LIKE ME IS...
I'm messed up.
(FRAYED EMOTIONS)
HUG
HANG IN THERE, AKARI!
You don't know that yet.
UNREQUITED LOVE HURTS, BUT IT'S ALSO ENJOYABLE...
(ANALYSIS)

When I have to run errands, I try to plan it so I do them all at once. The other day I managed to schedule everything, and I thought, "Yes!" First stop was the dentist. Unfortunately I got on a train going the wrong way, and since it was an express, I couldn't get off for a while. I was late. When I called, they told me I could still come in, so they were able to see me that day. For a previous visit I failed spectacularly to get off at the right stop and had to cancel my appointment, so I've troubled them yet again. After that, I had an appointment at my hair-dresser. I left enough time so that I could do some shopping. The item I needed most I couldn't get, so I was thinking I'd have to go somewhere else on another day, even though I was wandering around with all this extra time to kill time. When I got to the hair-dresser, I discovered I had the wrong time and was late!

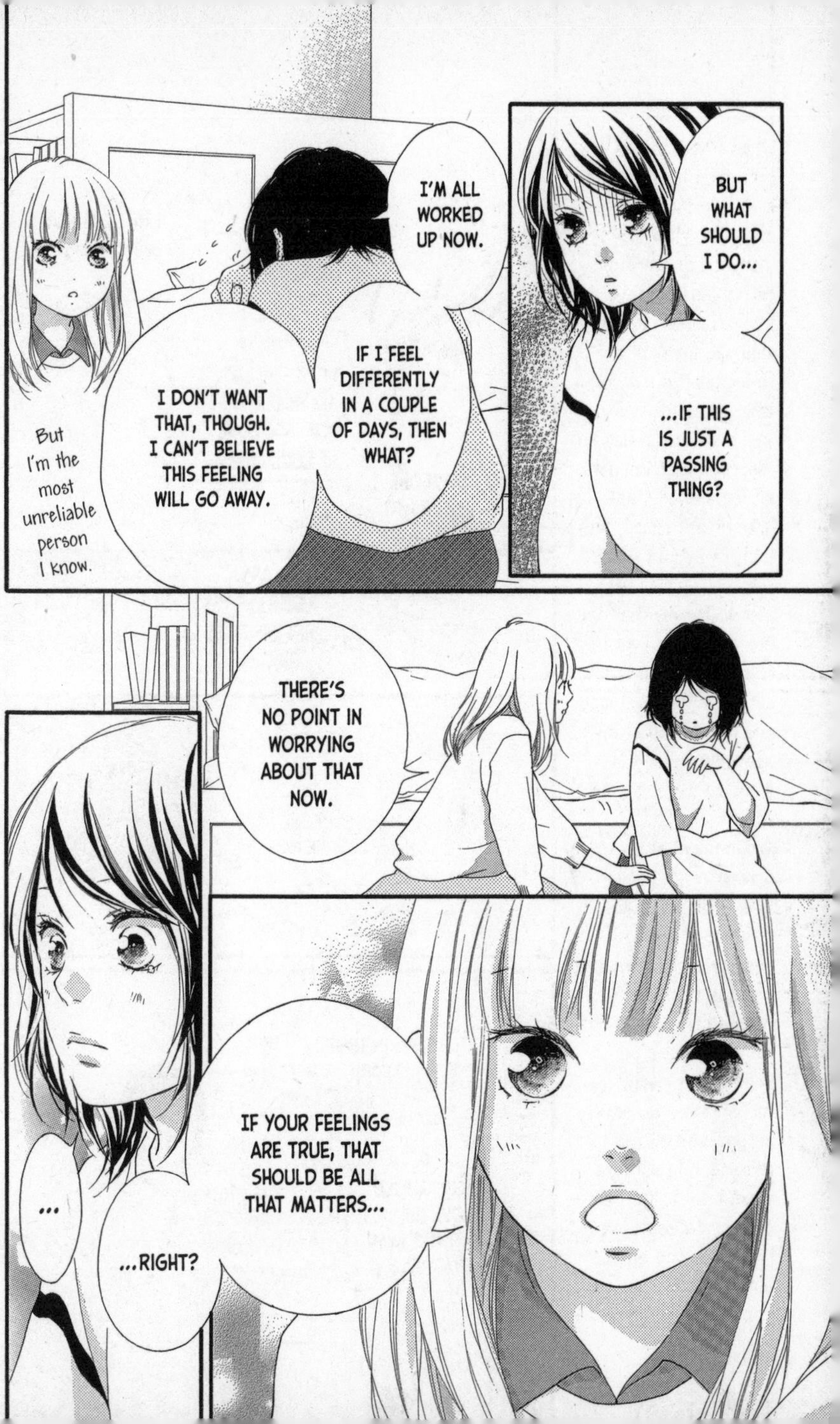
BUT WHAT SHOULD I DO...
...IF THIS IS JUST A PASSING THING?
I'M ALL WORKED UP NOW.
IF I FEEL DIFFERENTLY IN A COUPLE OF DAYS, THEN WHAT?
I DON'T WANT THAT, THOUGH. I CAN'T BELIEVE THIS FEELING WILL GO AWAY.
But I'm the most unreliable person I know.
THERE'S NO POINT IN WORRYING ABOUT THAT NOW.
IF YOUR FEELINGS ARE TRUE, THAT SHOULD BE ALL THAT MATTERS...
...RIGHT?
...

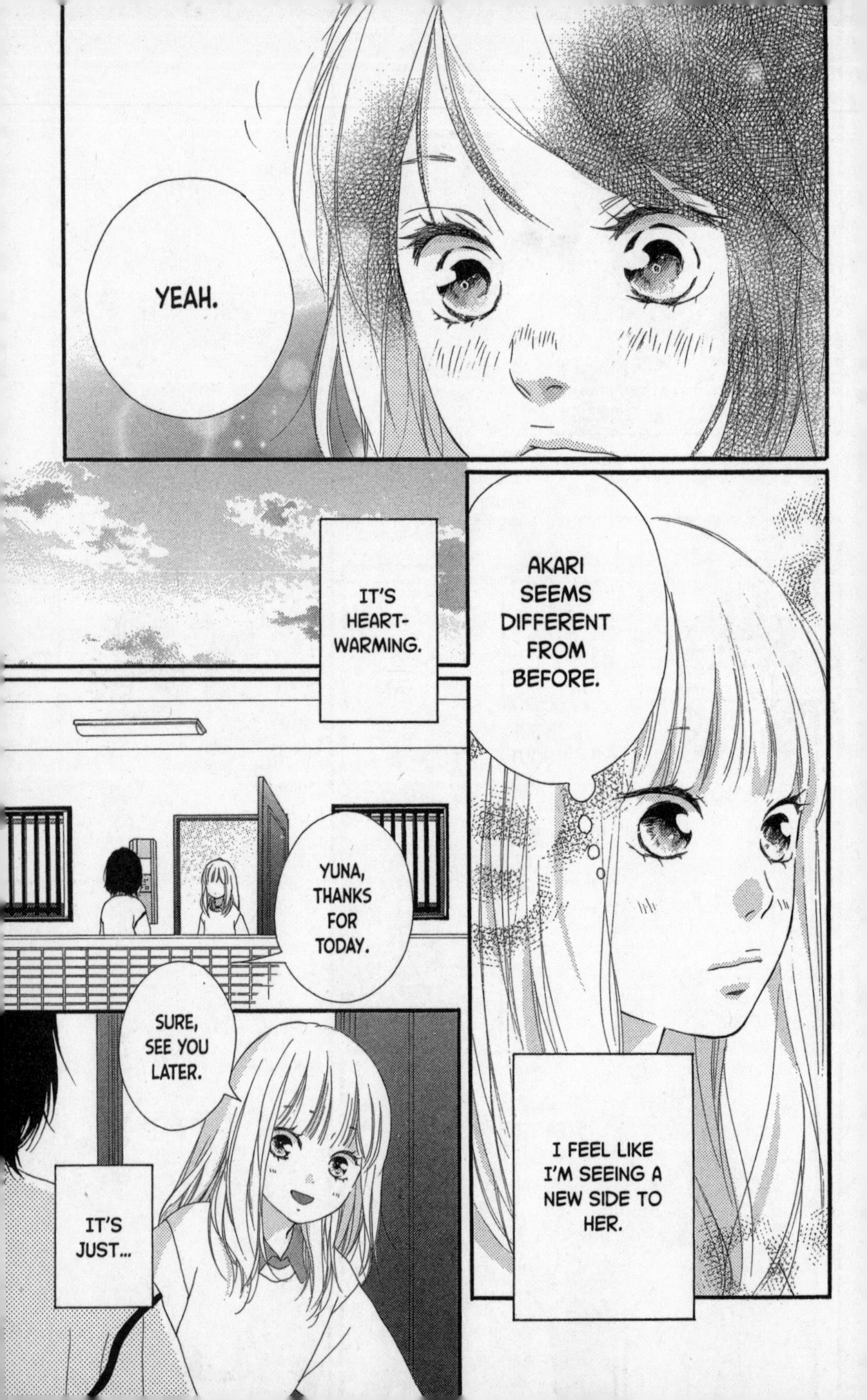
YEAH.
AKARI SEEMS DIFFERENT FROM BEFORE.
I FEEL LIKE I'M SEEING A NEW SIDE TO HER.
IT'S HEART-WARMING.
YUNA, THANKS FOR TODAY.
SURE, SEE YOU LATER.
IT'S JUST...

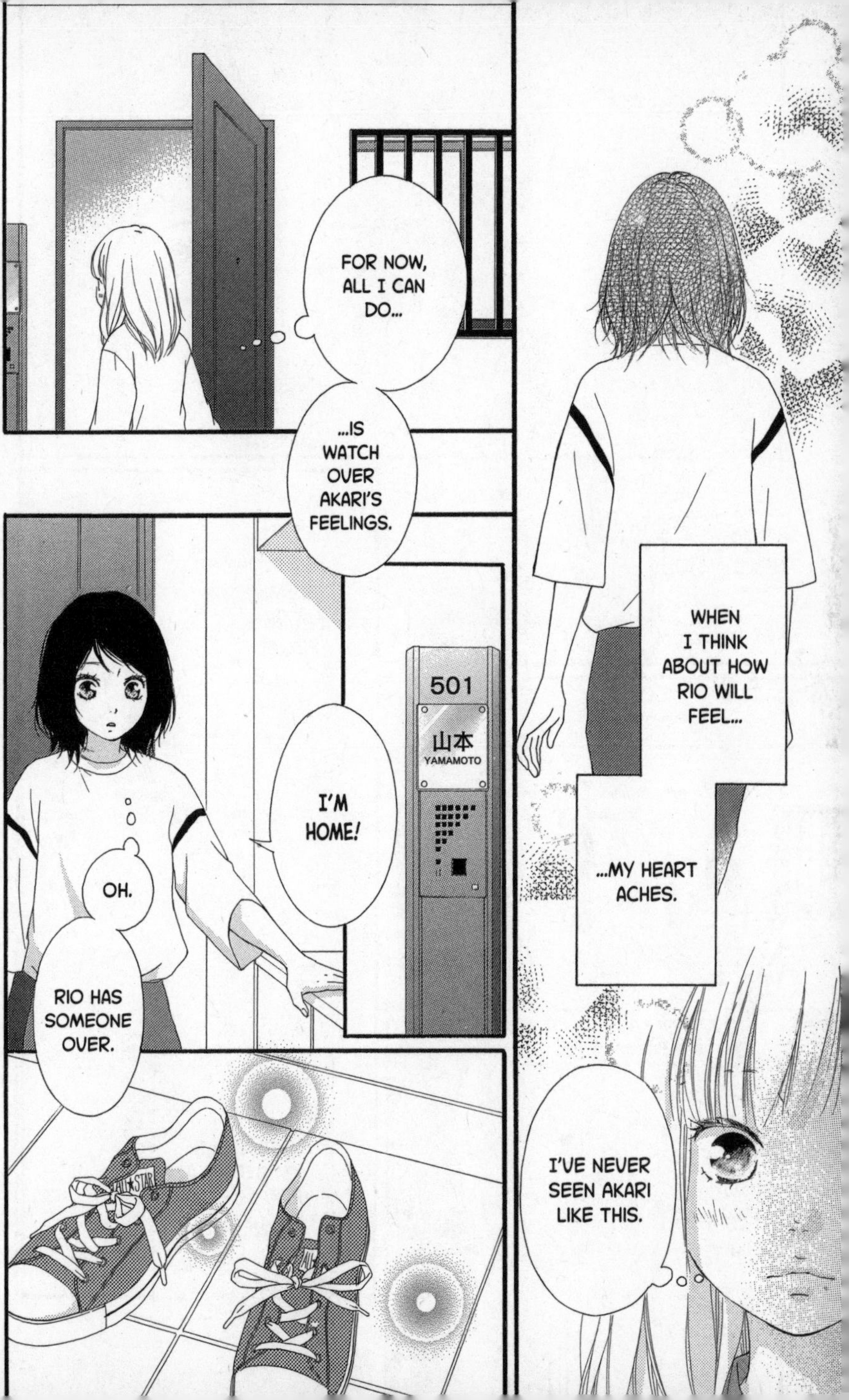

WHEN I THINK ABOUT HOW RIO WILL FEEL...
...MY HEART ACHES.
I'VE NEVER SEEN AKARI LIKE THIS.
FOR NOW, ALL I CAN DO...
...IS WATCH OVER AKARI'S FEELINGS.
501
山本
YAMAMOTO
I'M HOME!
OH.
RIO HAS SOMEONE OVER.

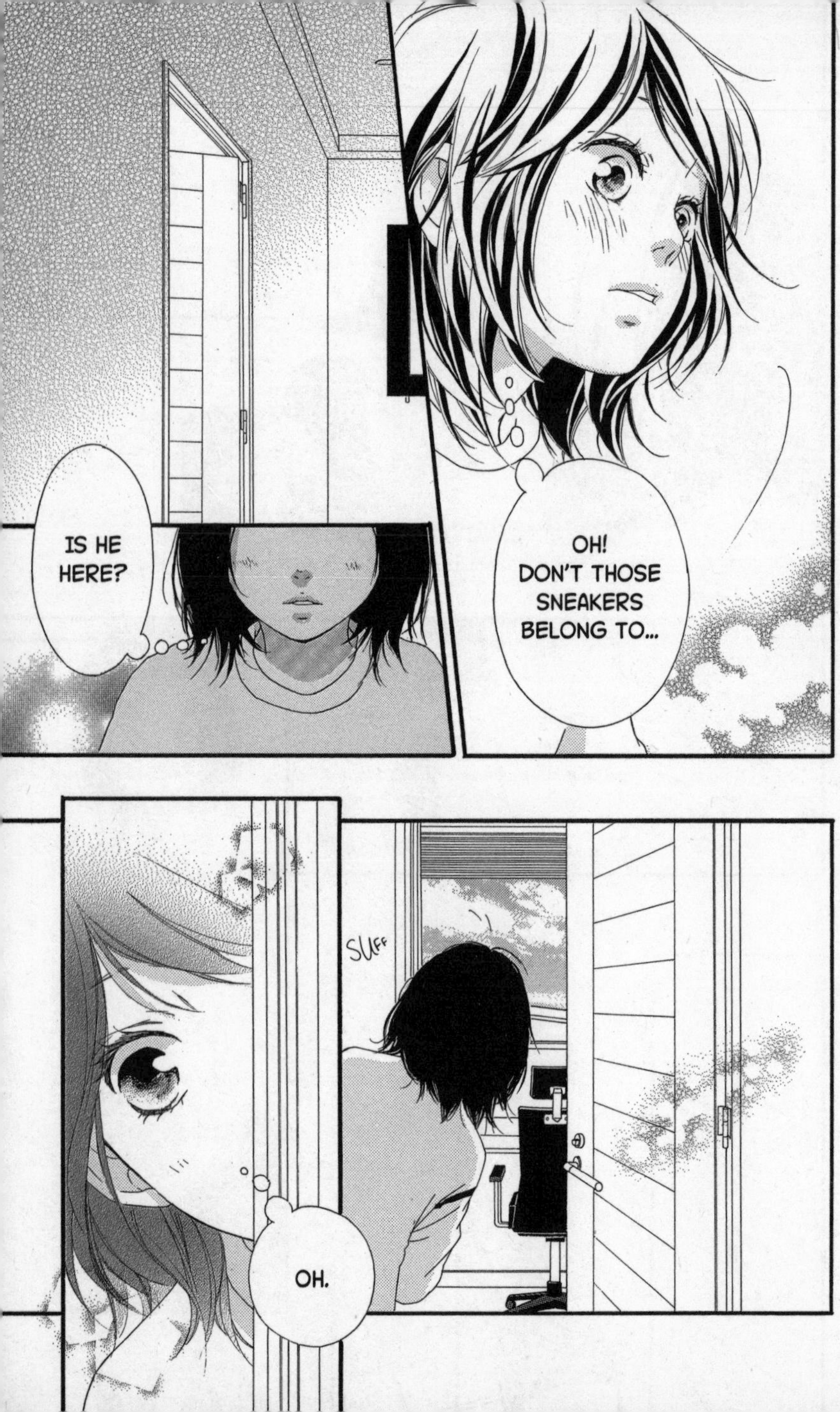
OH! DON'T THOSE SNEAKERS BELONG TO...
IS HE HERE?
SUFF
OH.

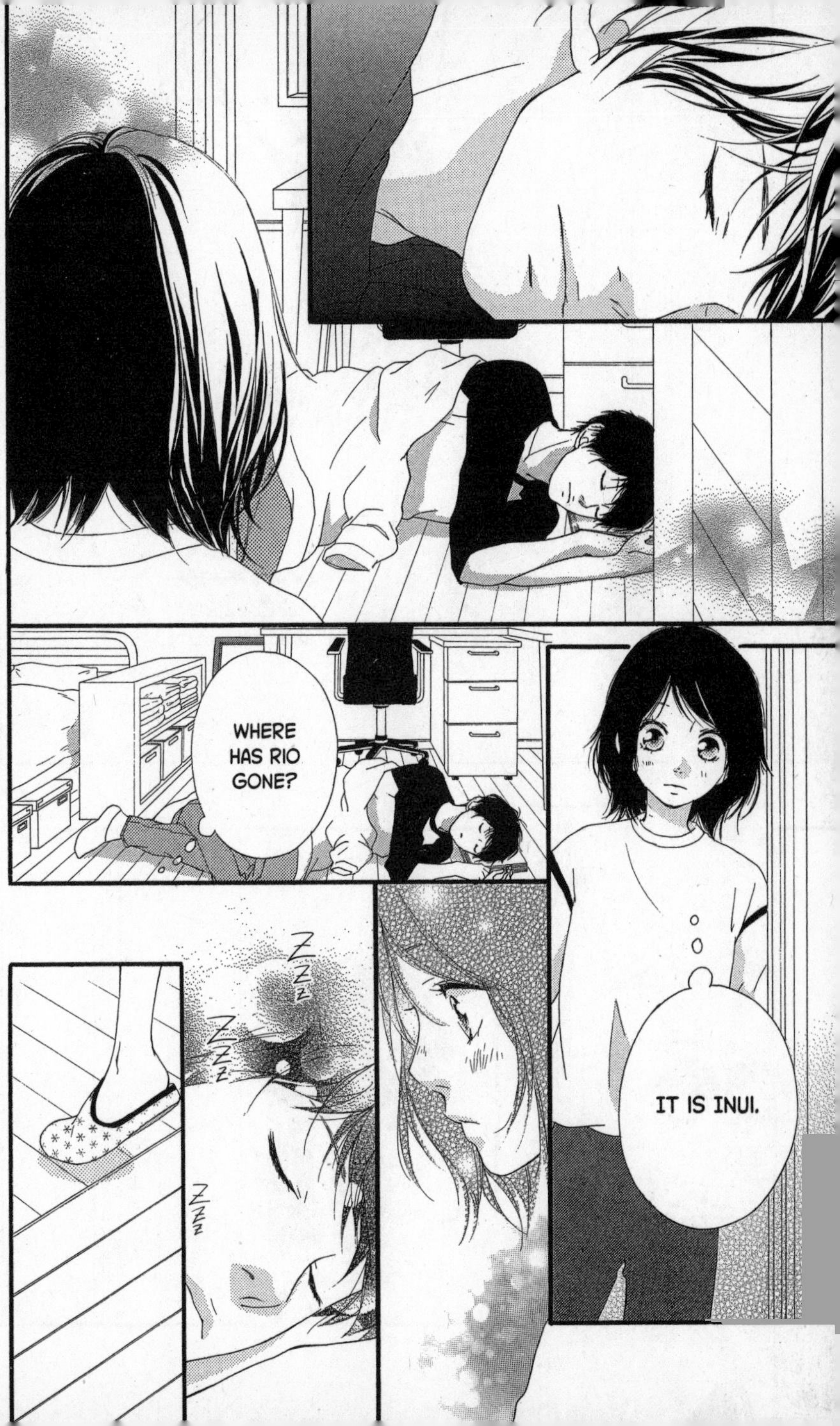
IT IS INUI.
WHERE HAS RIO GONE?
Zzz
Zzz
Zzz

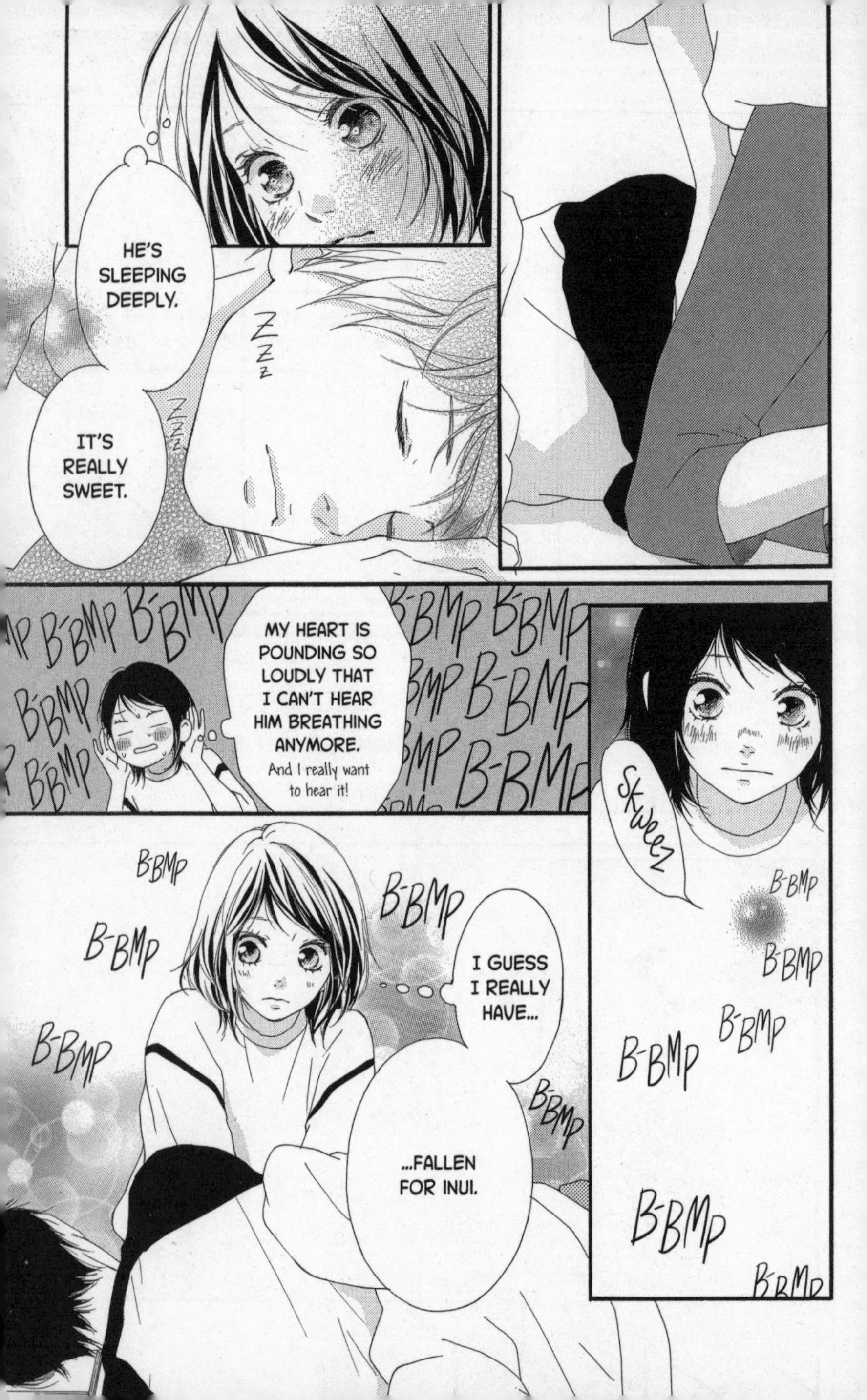

HE'S SLEEPING DEEPLY.
IT'S REALLY SWEET.
ZZZ
ZZZ
SKWEEZ
B-BMP
B-BMP
B-BMP
B-BMP
B-BMP
B-BMP
MY HEART IS POUNDING SO LOUDLY THAT I CAN'T HEAR HIM BREATHING ANYMORE.
And I really want to hear it!
B-BMP B-BMP B-BMP B-BMP B-BMP B-BMP B-BMP
B-BMP B-BMP B-BMP B-BMP
I GUESS I REALLY HAVE...
...FALLEN FOR INUI.
B-BMP
B-BMP
B-BMP
B-BMP

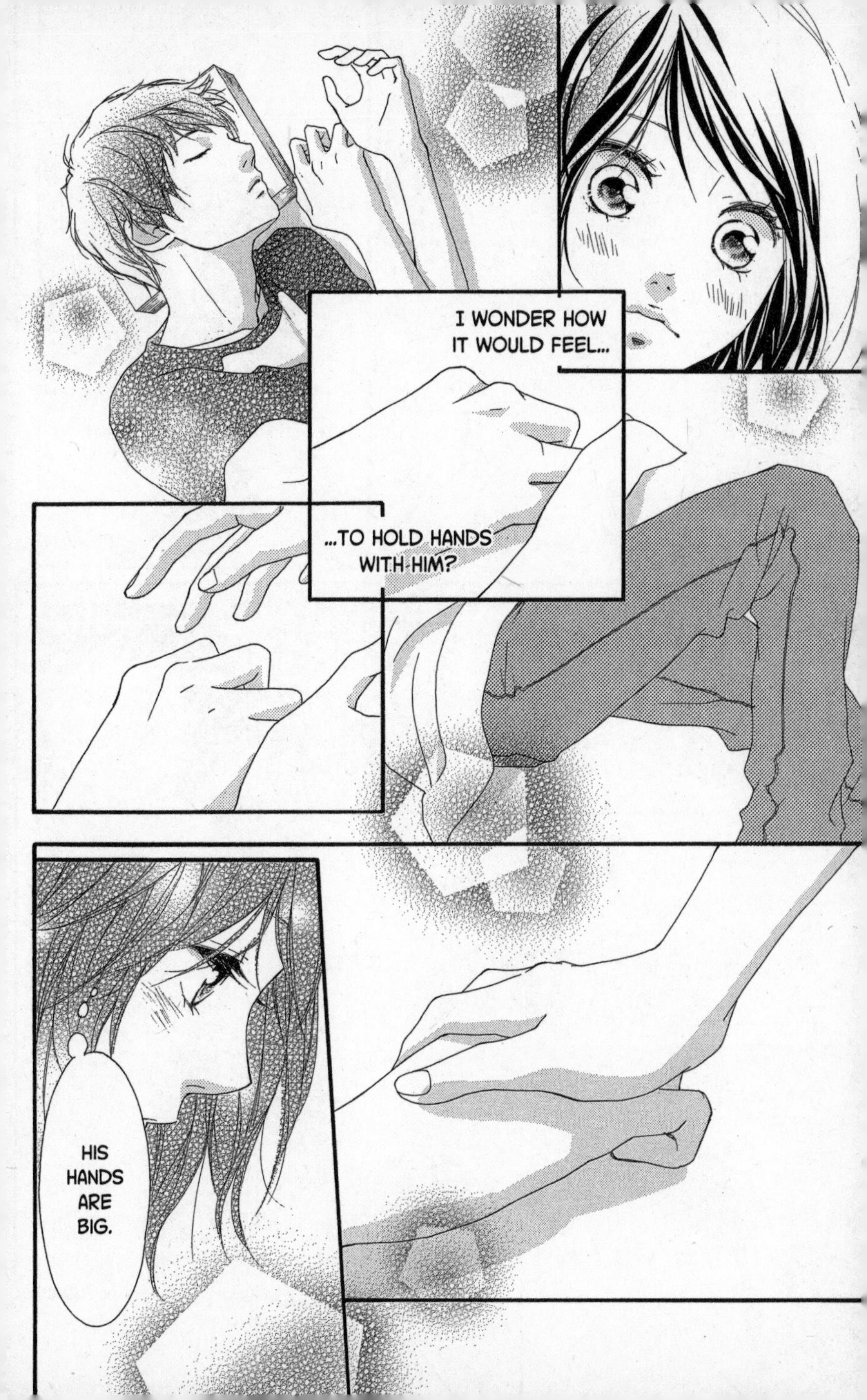
I WONDER HOW IT WOULD FEEL...
...TO HOLD HANDS WITH HIM?
HIS HANDS ARE BIG.

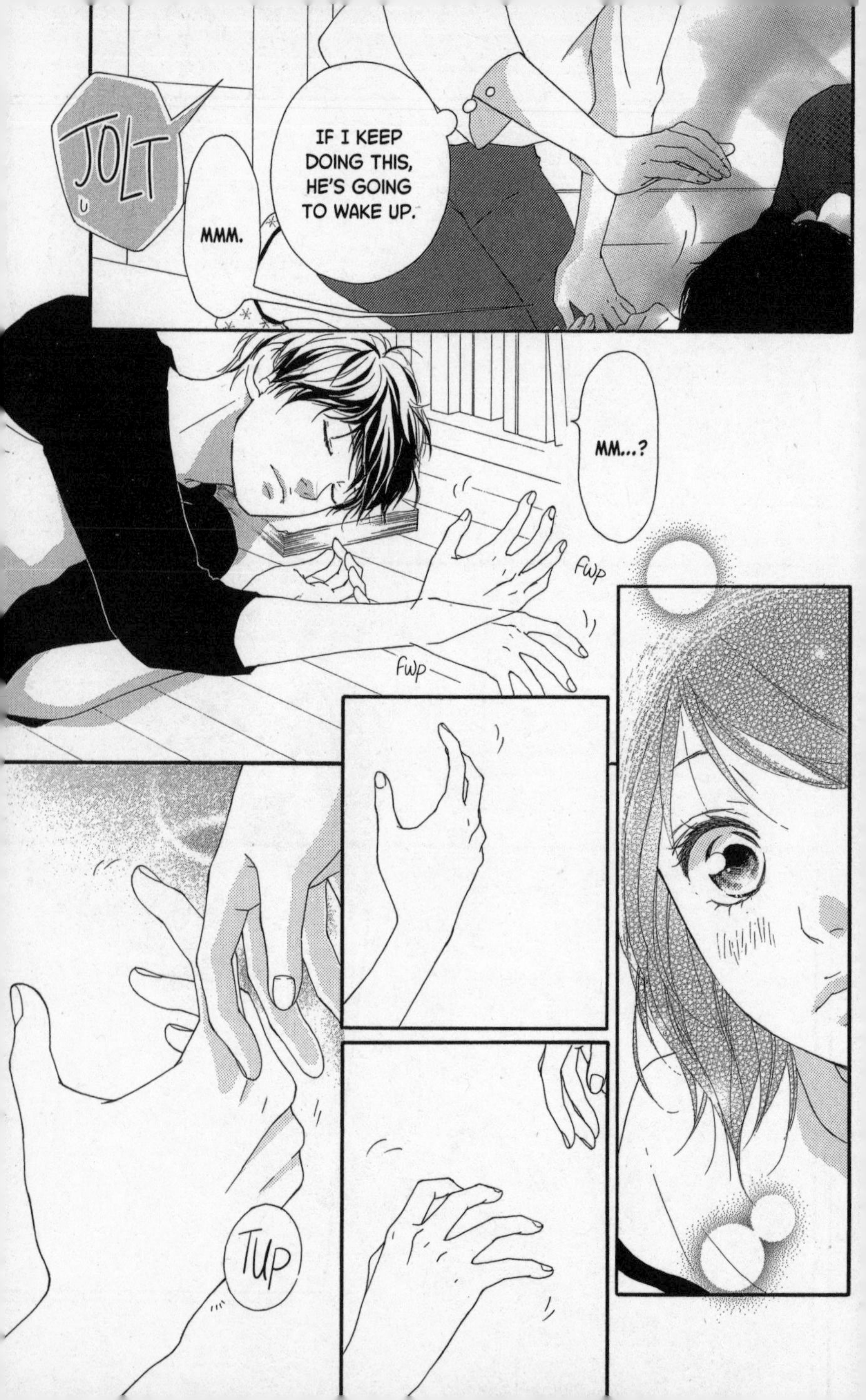
IF I KEEP DOING THIS, HE'S GOING TO WAKE UP.
MMM.
JOLT
MM...?
FWP
FWP
TUP

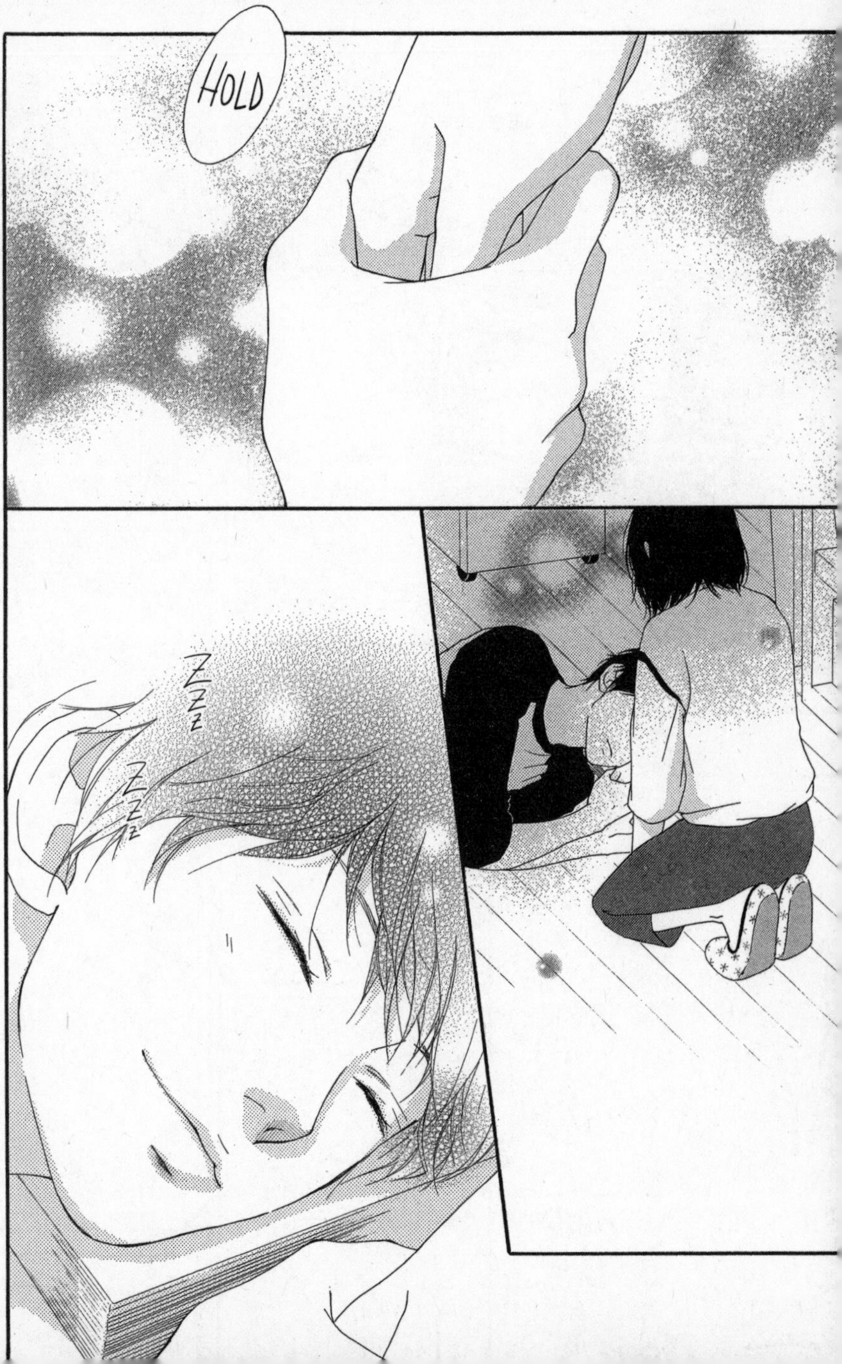
HOLD
ZZZ
ZZZ

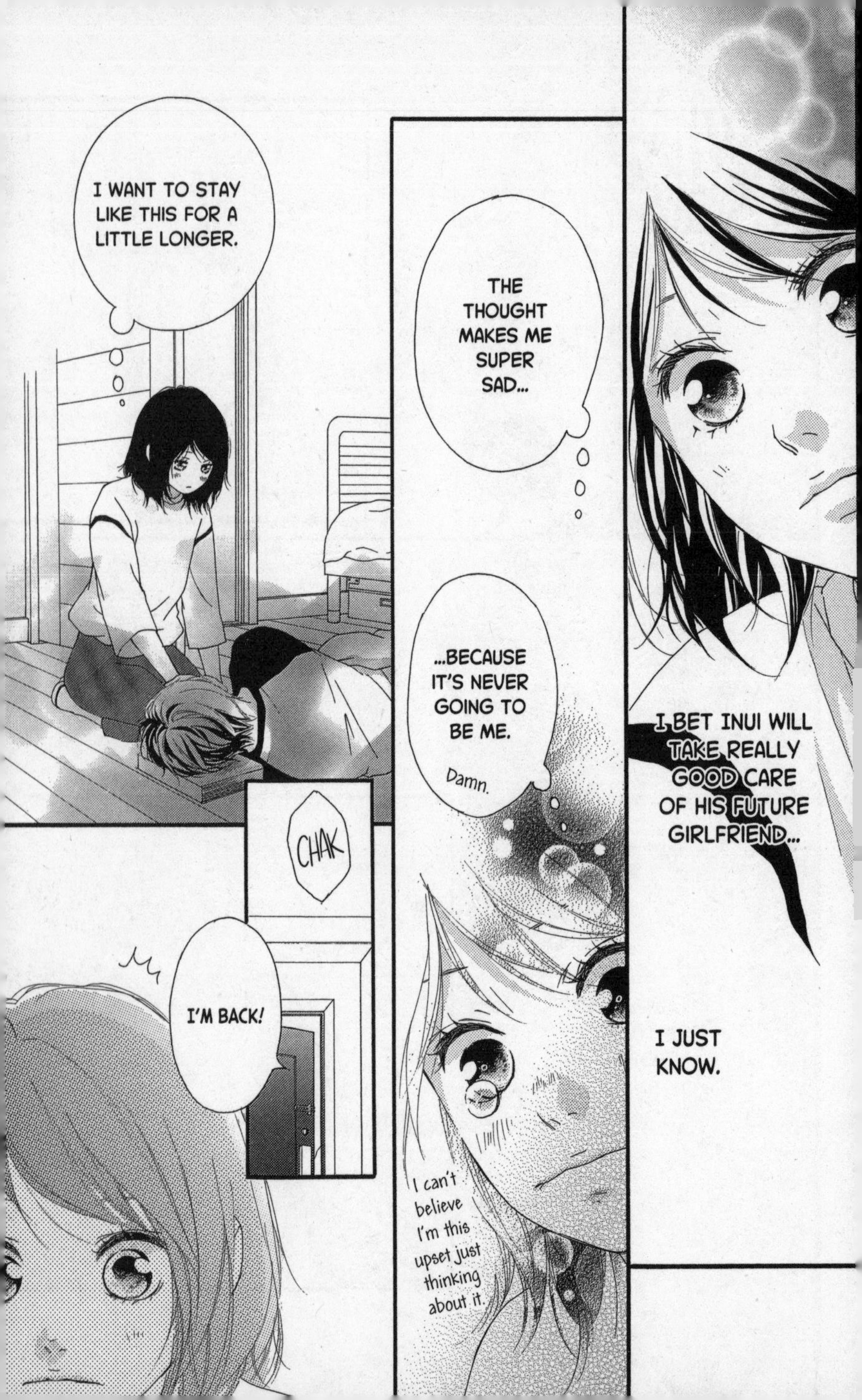
I BET INUI WILL TAKE REALLY GOOD CARE OF HIS FUTURE GIRLFRIEND...
I JUST KNOW.
THE THOUGHT MAKES ME SUPER SAD...
...BECAUSE IT'S NEVER GOING TO BE ME.
Damn.
I can't believe I'm this upset just thinking about it.
I WANT TO STAY LIKE THIS FOR A LITTLE LONGER.
CHAK
I'M BACK!

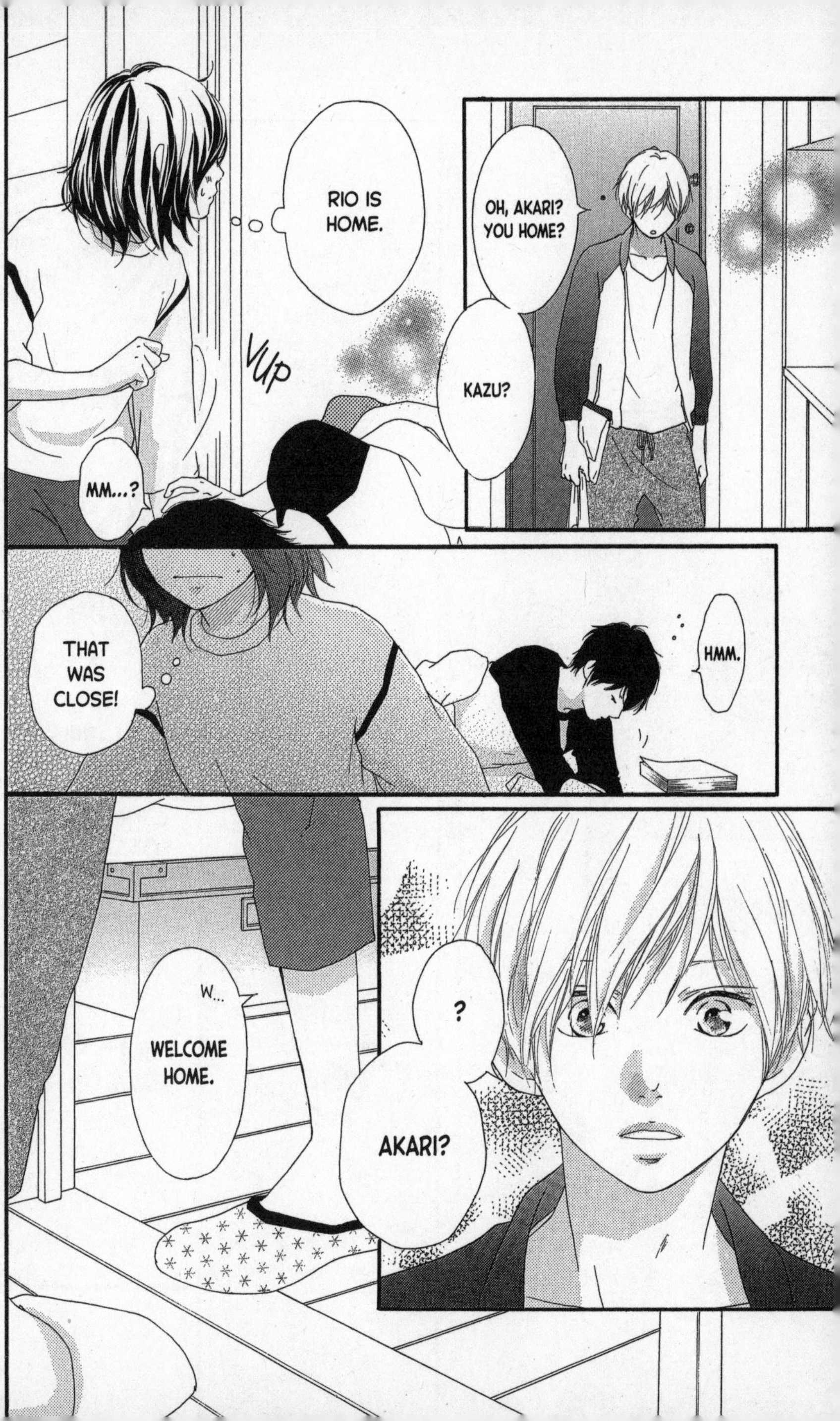
OH, AKARI? YOU HOME?
KAZU?
RIO IS HOME.
VUP
MM...?
HMM.
THAT WAS CLOSE!
?
AKARI?
W...
WELCOME HOME.

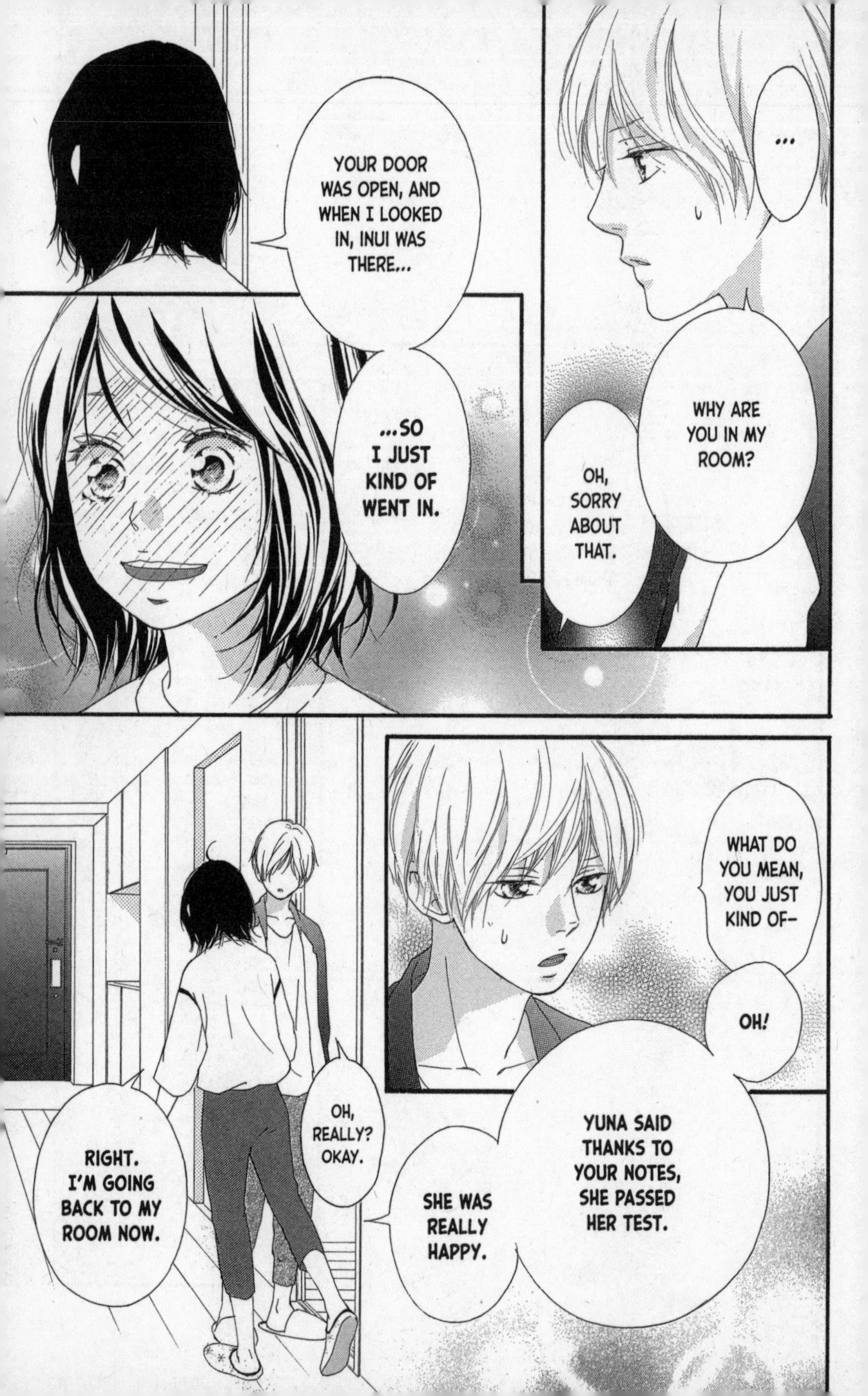
...
WHY ARE YOU IN MY ROOM?
OH, SORRY ABOUT THAT.
YOUR DOOR WAS OPEN, AND WHEN I LOOKED IN, INUI WAS THERE...
...SO I JUST KIND OF WENT IN.
WHAT DO YOU MEAN, YOU JUST KIND OF–
OH!
YUNA SAID THANKS TO YOUR NOTES, SHE PASSED HER TEST.
SHE WAS REALLY HAPPY.
OH, REALLY? OKAY.
RIGHT. I'M GOING BACK TO MY ROOM NOW.

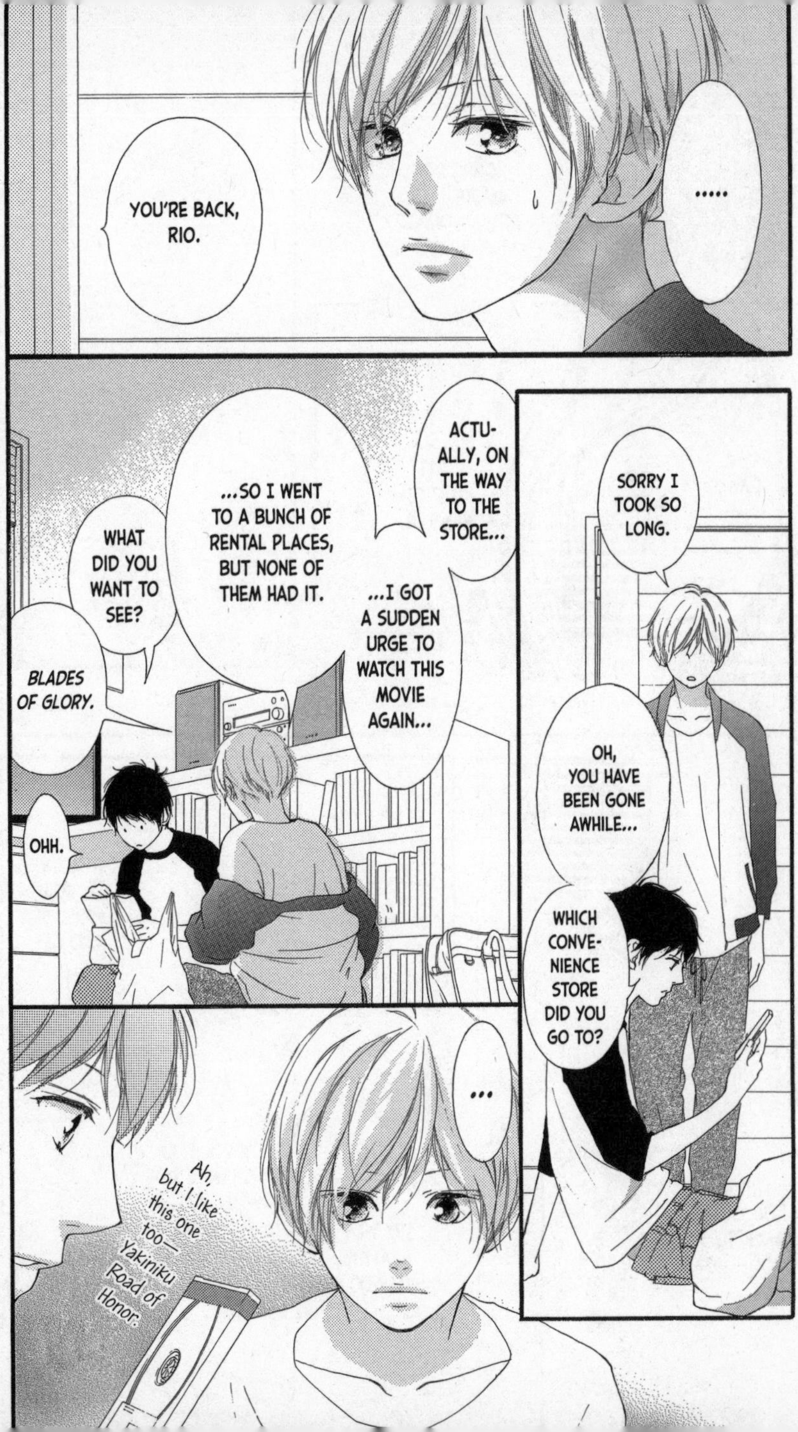
.....
YOU'RE BACK, RIO.
SORRY I TOOK SO LONG.
OH, YOU HAVE BEEN GONE AWHILE...
WHICH CONVENIENCE STORE DID YOU GO TO?
ACTUALLY, ON THE WAY TO THE STORE...
...I GOT A SUDDEN URGE TO WATCH THIS MOVIE AGAIN...
...SO I WENT TO A BUNCH OF RENTAL PLACES, BUT NONE OF THEM HAD IT.
WHAT DID YOU WANT TO SEE?
BLADES OF GLORY.
OHH.
...
Ah, but I like this one too—Yakiniku Road of Honor.

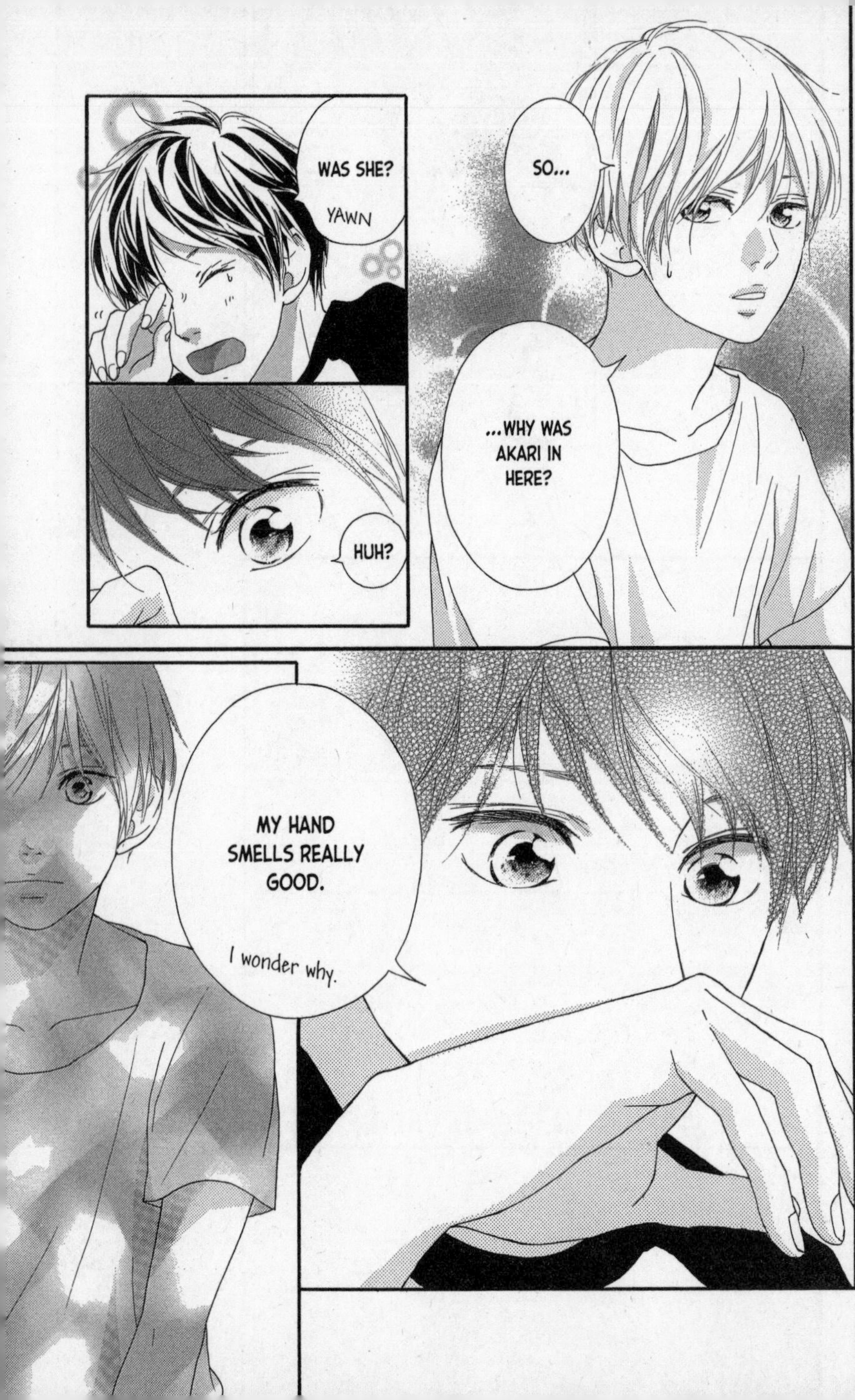
SO...
...WHY WAS AKARI IN HERE?
WAS SHE?
YAWN
HUH?
MY HAND SMELLS REALLY GOOD.
I wonder why.

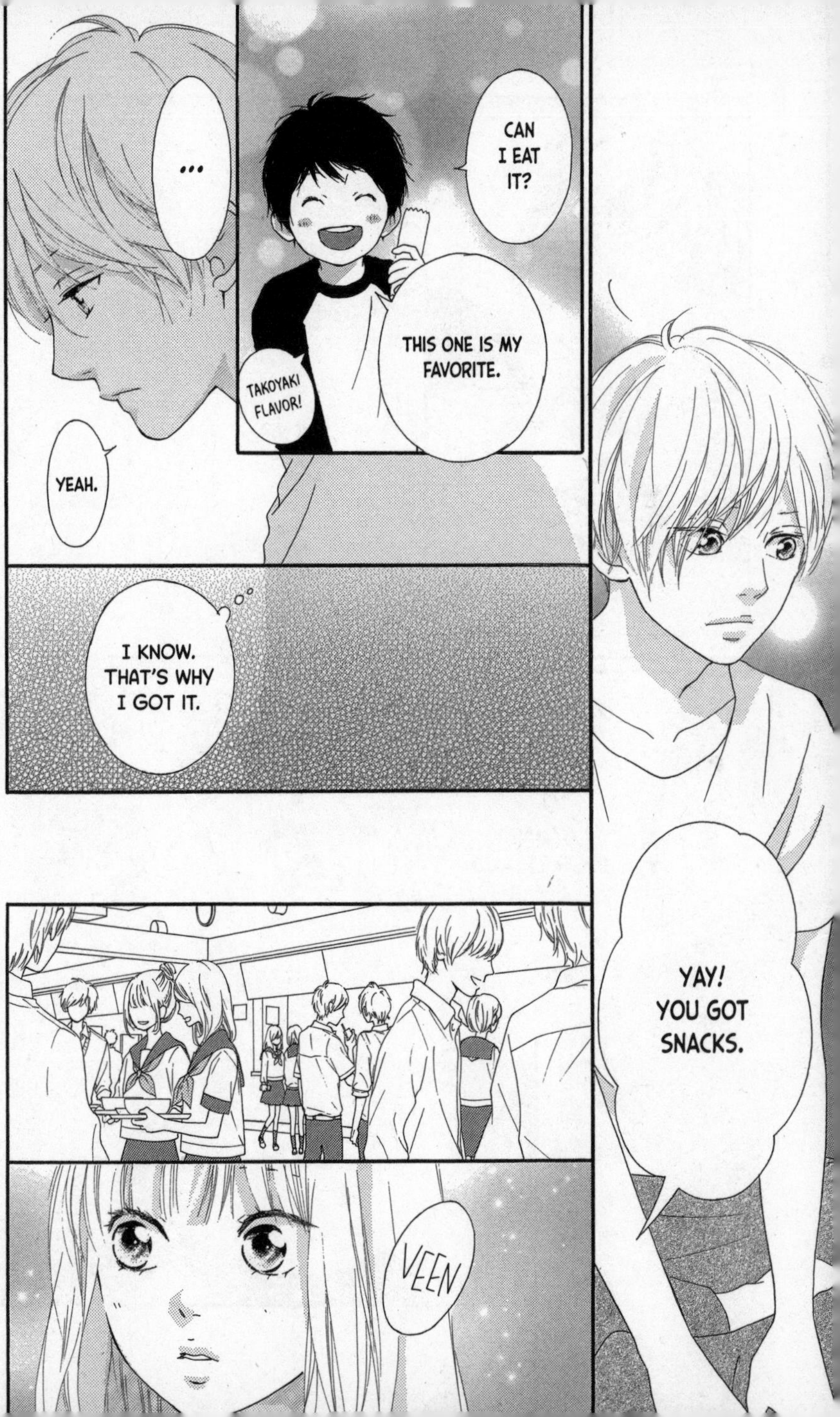
YAY! YOU GOT SNACKS.
...
CAN I EAT IT?
THIS ONE IS MY FAVORITE.
TAKOYAKI FLAVOR!
YEAH.
I KNOW. THAT'S WHY I GOT IT.
VEEN

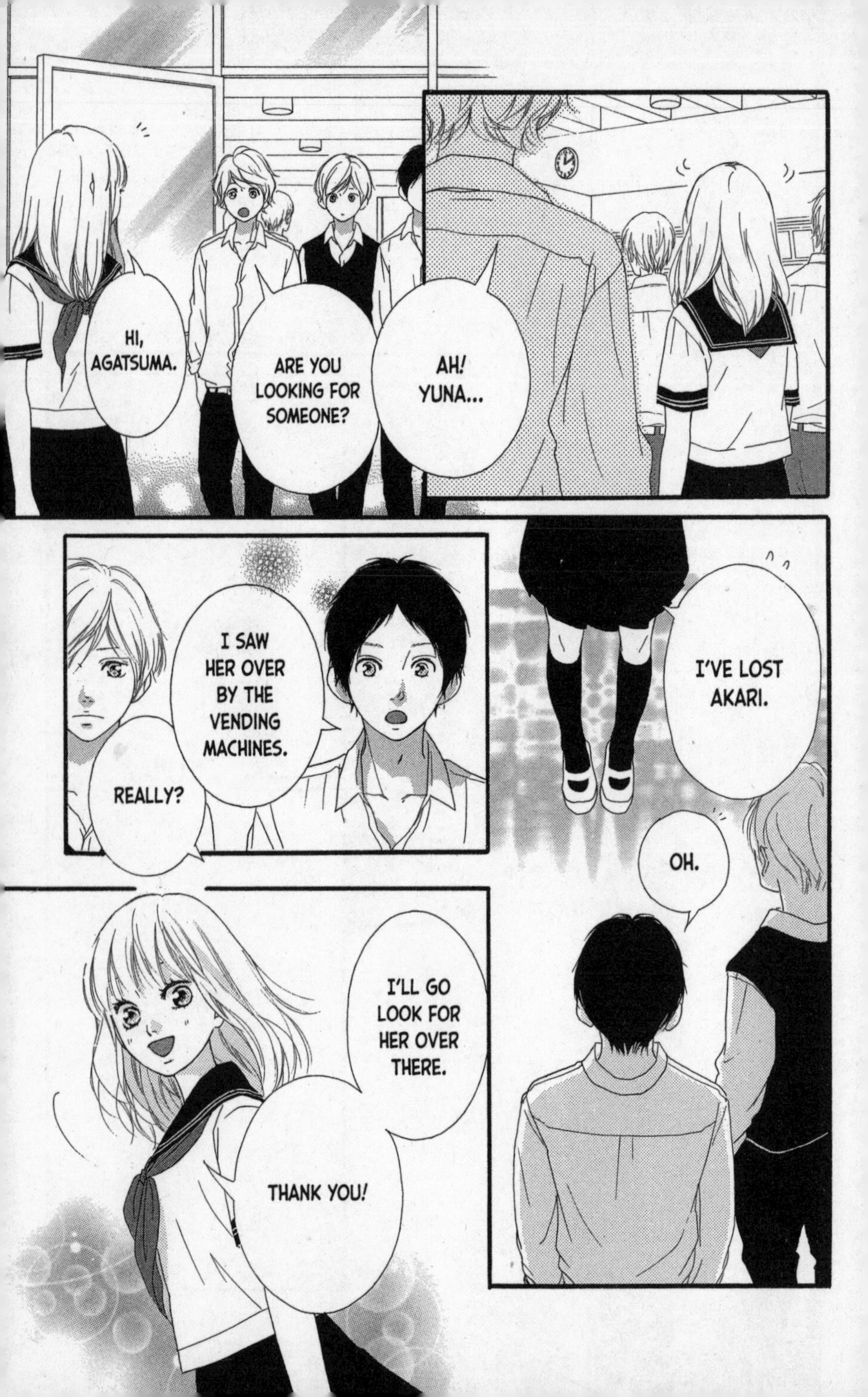
AH! YUNA...
ARE YOU LOOKING FOR SOMEONE?
HI, AGATSUMA.
I'VE LOST AKARI.
OH.
I SAW HER OVER BY THE VENDING MACHINES.
REALLY?
I'LL GO LOOK FOR HER OVER THERE.
THANK YOU!

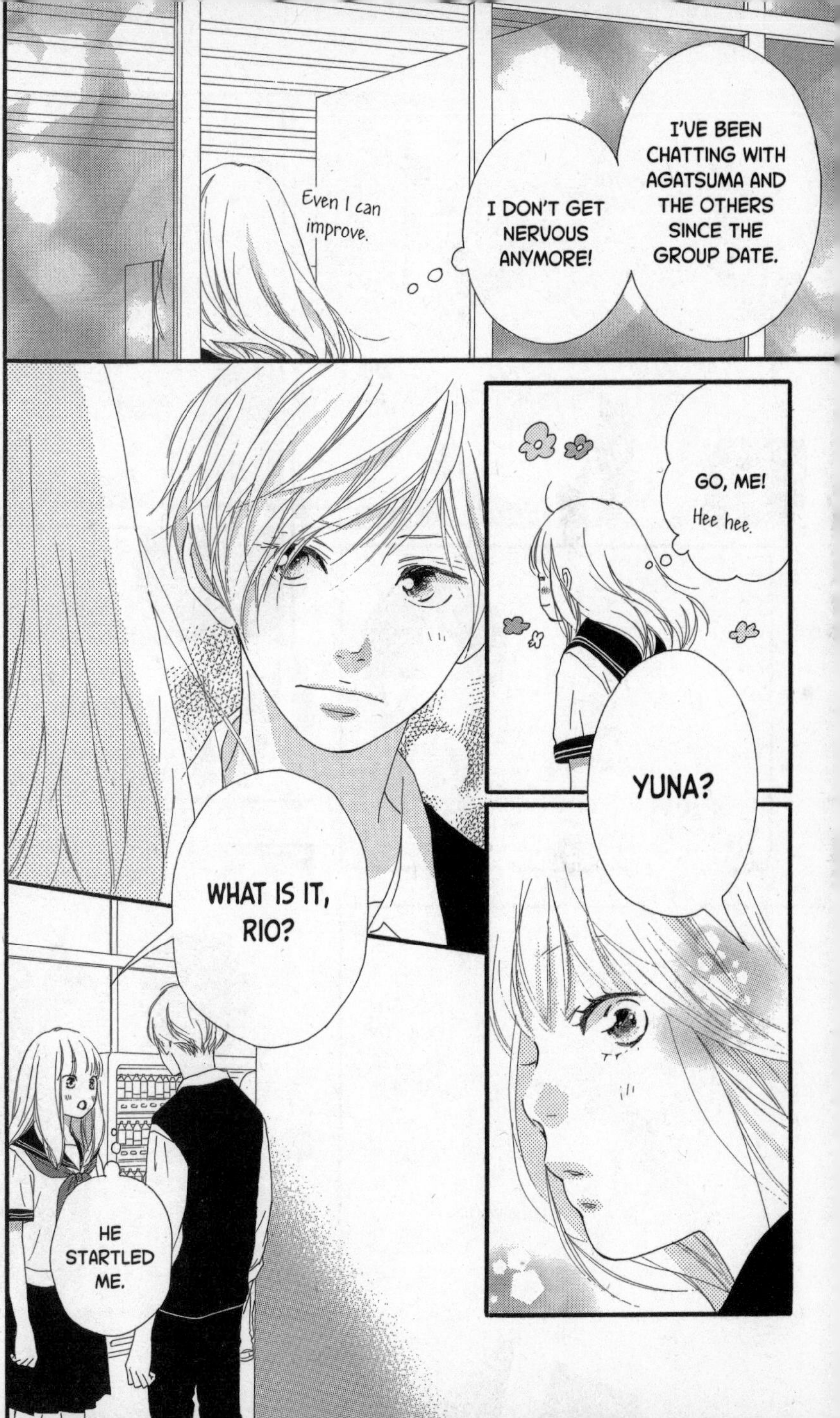
I'VE BEEN CHATTING WITH AGATSUMA AND THE OTHERS SINCE THE GROUP DATE.
I DON'T GET NERVOUS ANYMORE!
Even I can improve.
GO, ME!
Hee hee.
YUNA?
WHAT IS IT, RIO?
HE STARTLED ME.

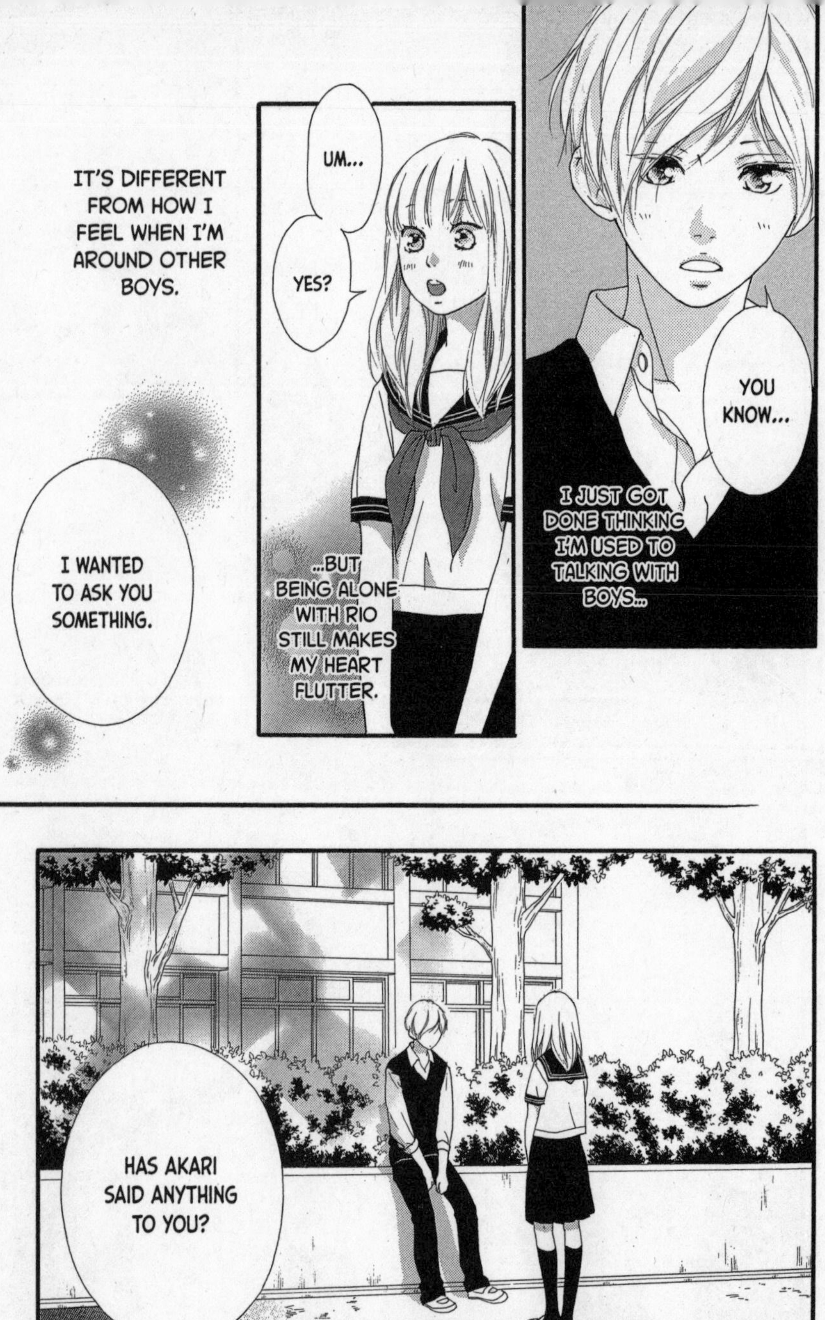
YOU KNOW...
I JUST GOT DONE THINKING I'M USED TO TALKING WITH BOYS...
UM... YES?
...BUT BEING ALONE WITH RIO STILL MAKES MY HEART FLUTTER.
IT'S DIFFERENT FROM HOW I FEEL WHEN I'M AROUND OTHER BOYS.
I WANTED TO ASK YOU SOMETHING.
HAS AKARI SAID ANYTHING TO YOU?

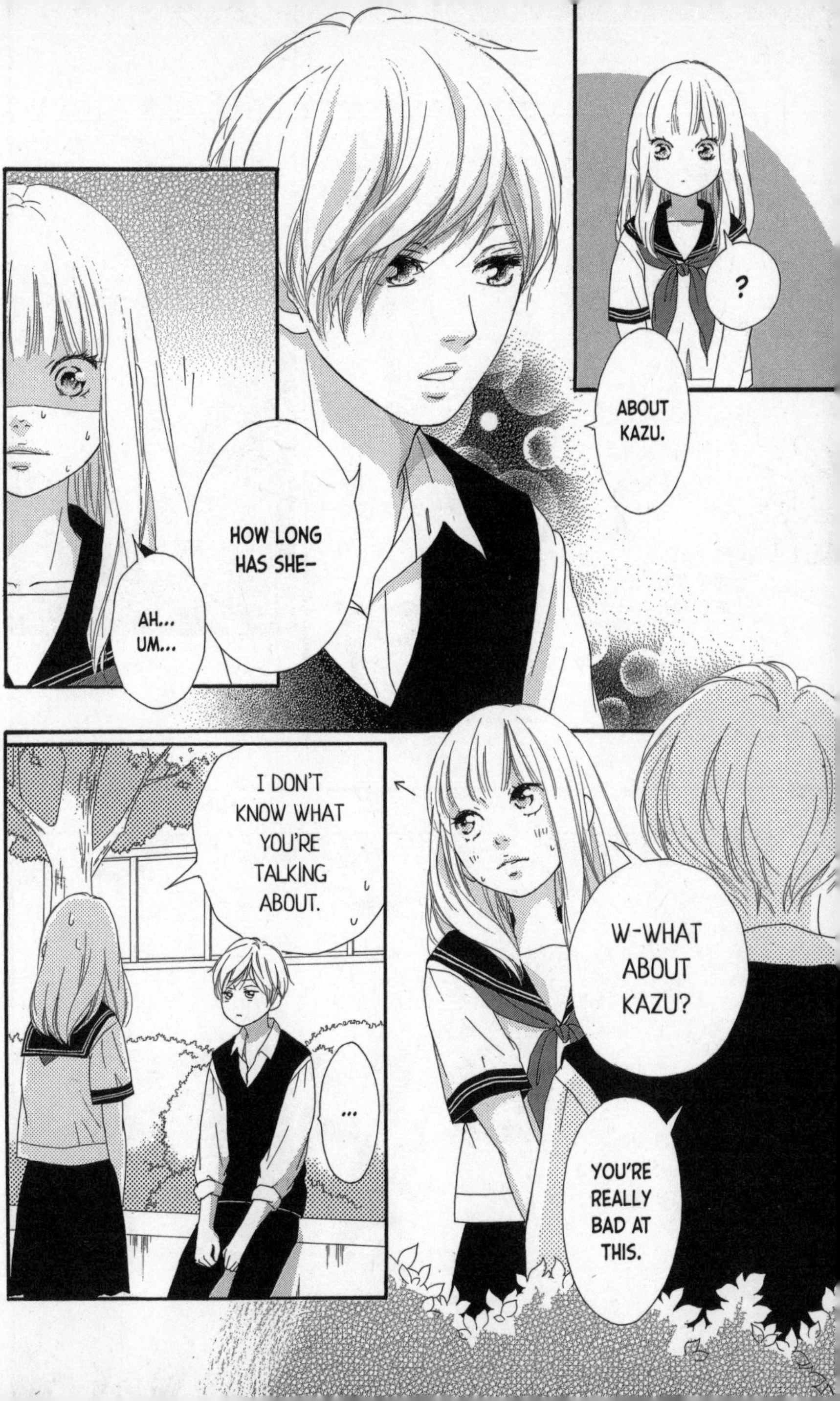

?
ABOUT KAZU.
HOW LONG HAS SHE-
AH... UM...
W-WHAT ABOUT KAZU?
YOU'RE REALLY BAD AT THIS.
I DON'T KNOW WHAT YOU'RE TALKING ABOUT.
...

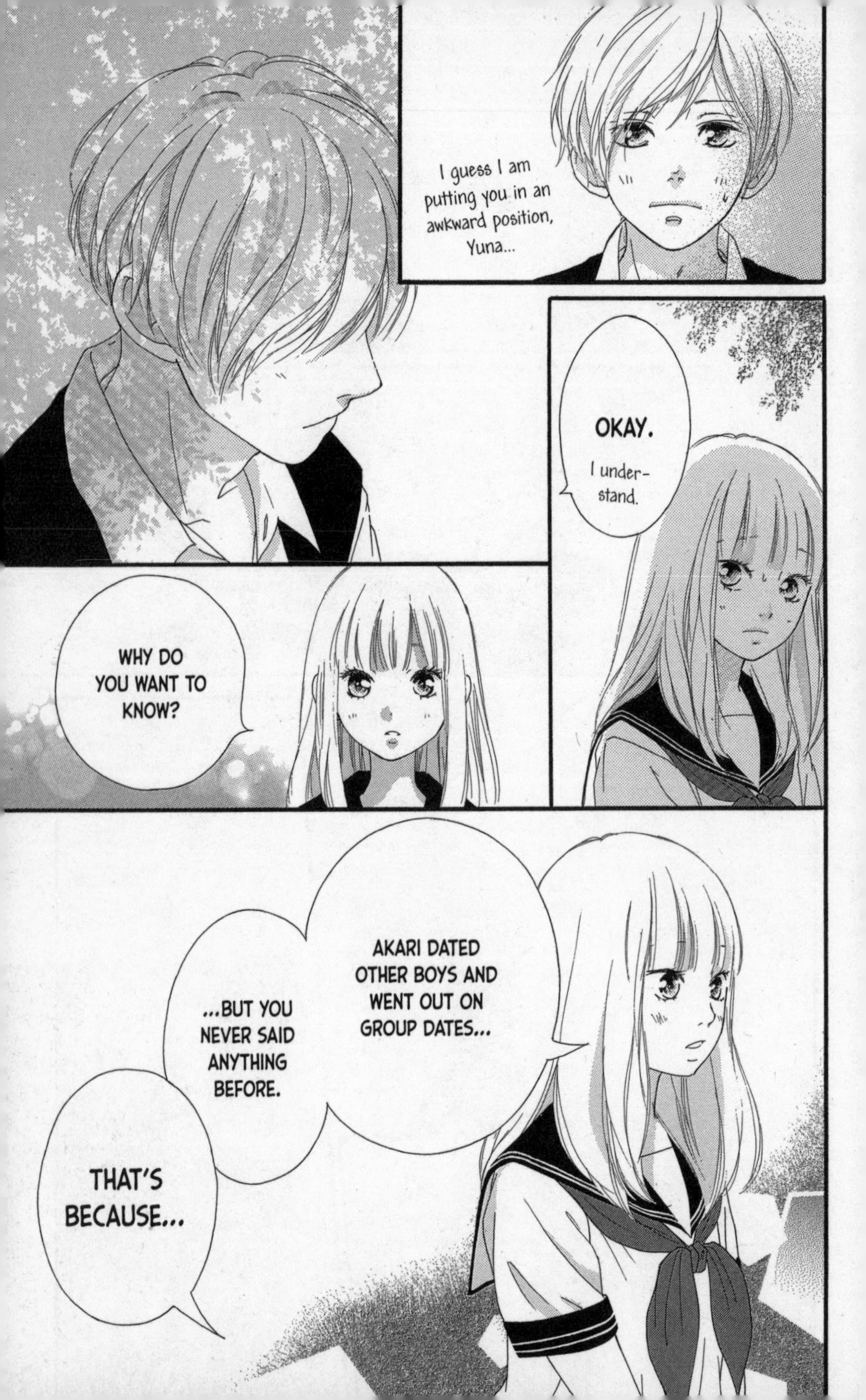
I guess I am putting you in an awkward position, Yuna...
OKAY. I under-stand.
WHY DO YOU WANT TO KNOW?
AKARI DATED OTHER BOYS AND WENT OUT ON GROUP DATES...
...BUT YOU NEVER SAID ANYTHING BEFORE.
THAT'S BECAUSE...

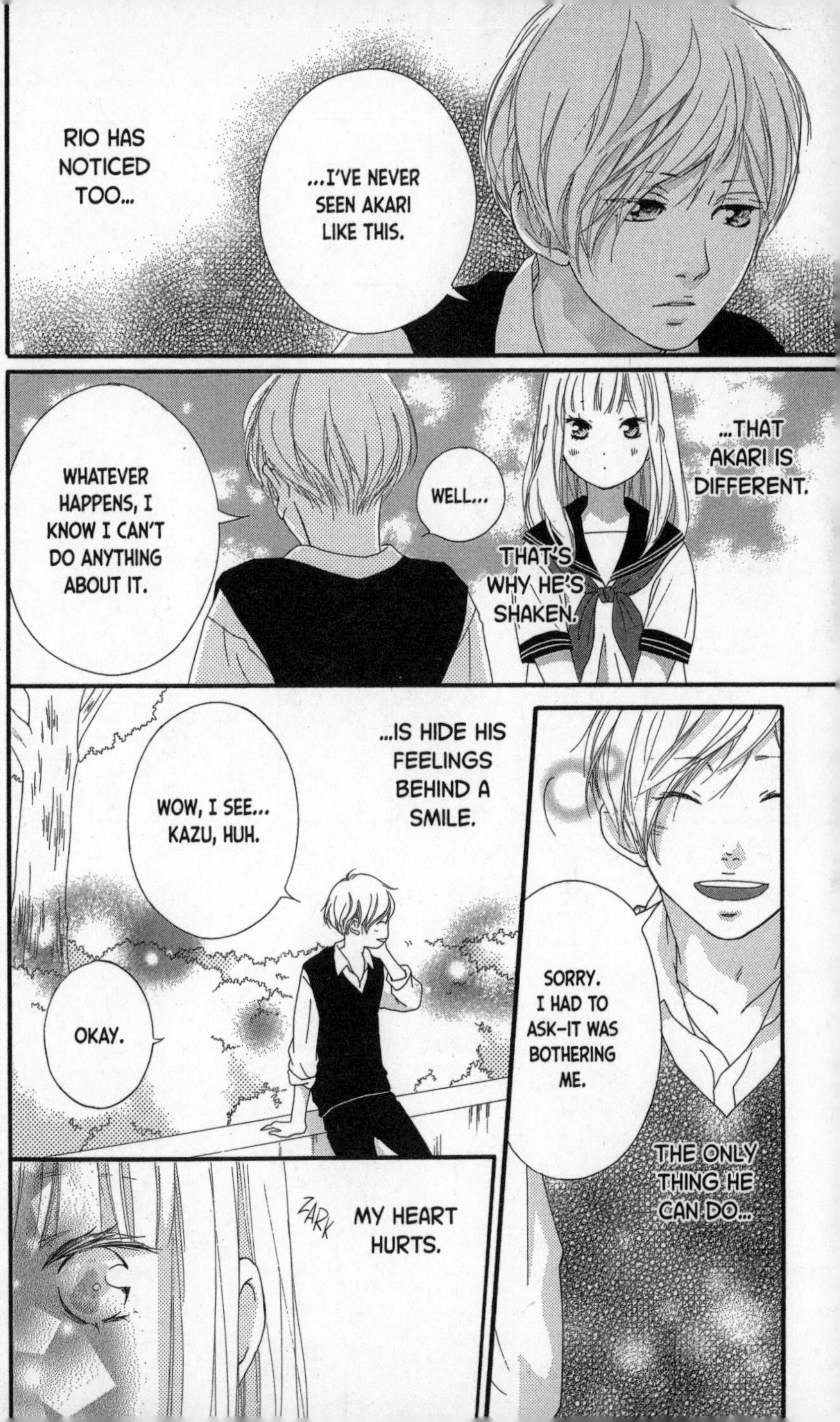
...I'VE NEVER SEEN AKARI LIKE THIS.
RIO HAS NOTICED TOO...
...THAT AKARI IS DIFFERENT.
THAT'S WHY HE'S SHAKEN.
WELL...
WHATEVER HAPPENS, I KNOW I CAN'T DO ANYTHING ABOUT IT.
SORRY. I HAD TO ASK—IT WAS BOTHERING ME.
THE ONLY THING HE CAN DO...
...IS HIDE HIS FEELINGS BEHIND A SMILE.
WOW, I SEE... KAZU, HUH.
OKAY.
ZARK
MY HEART HURTS.

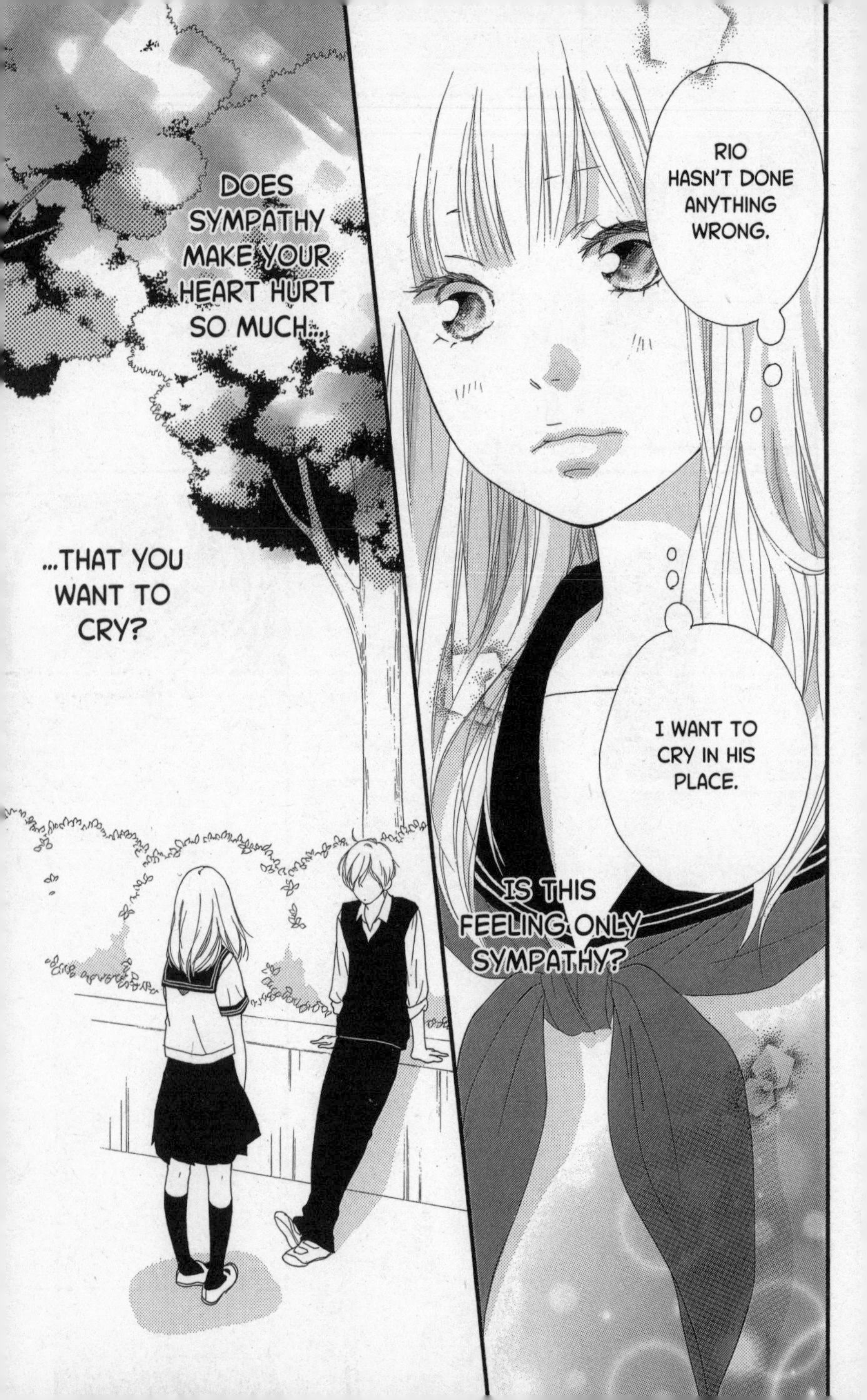
RIO HASN'T DONE ANYTHING WRONG.
I WANT TO CRY IN HIS PLACE.
IS THIS FEELING ONLY SYMPATHY?
DOES SYMPATHY MAKE YOUR HEART HURT SO MUCH...
...THAT YOU WANT TO CRY?

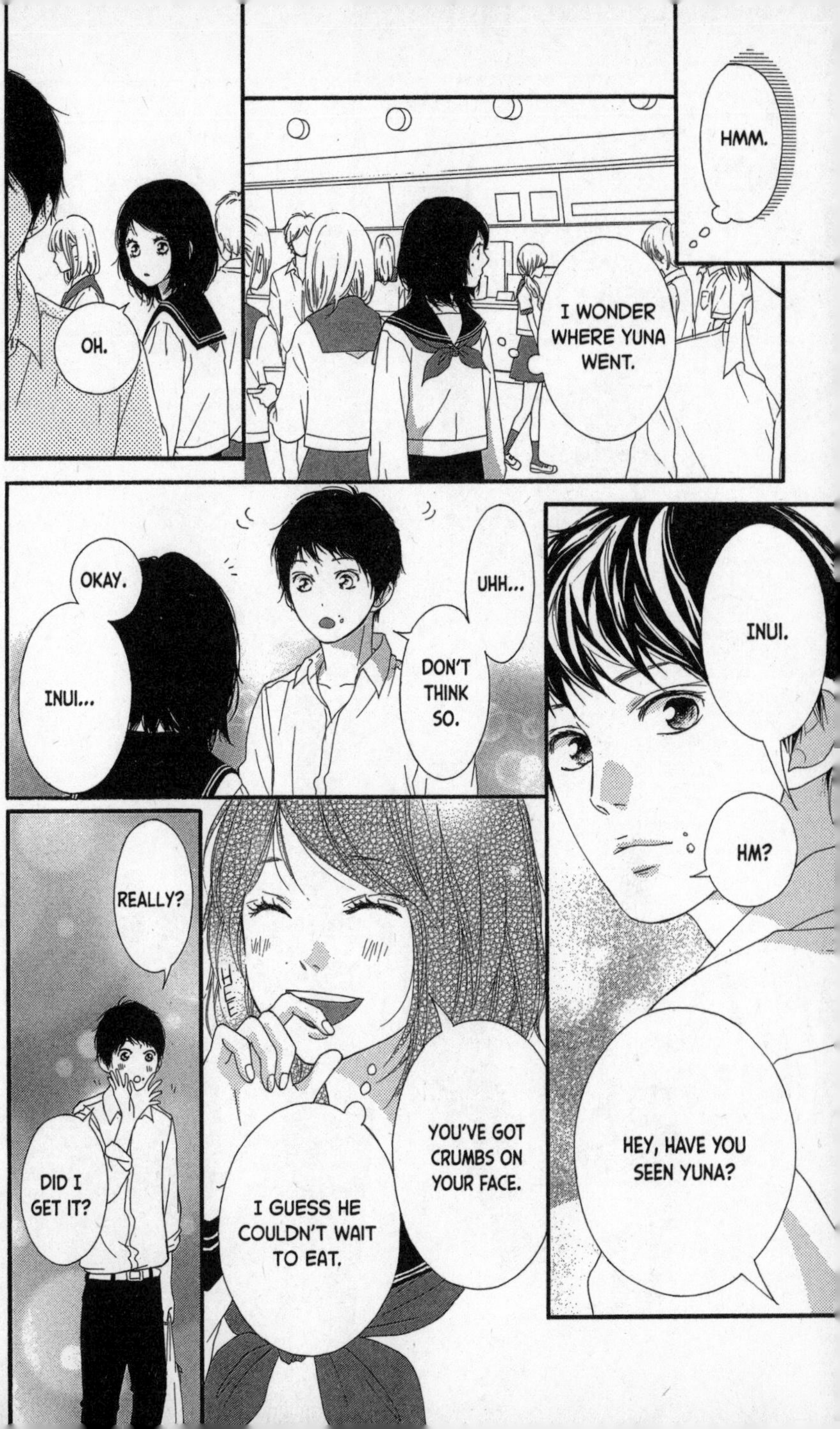
HMM.
I WONDER WHERE YUNA WENT.
OH.
INUI.
HM?
HEY, HAVE YOU SEEN YUNA?
UHH...
DON'T THINK SO.
OKAY.
INUI...
YOU'VE GOT CRUMBS ON YOUR FACE.
I GUESS HE COULDN'T WAIT TO EAT.
REALLY?
DID I GET IT?

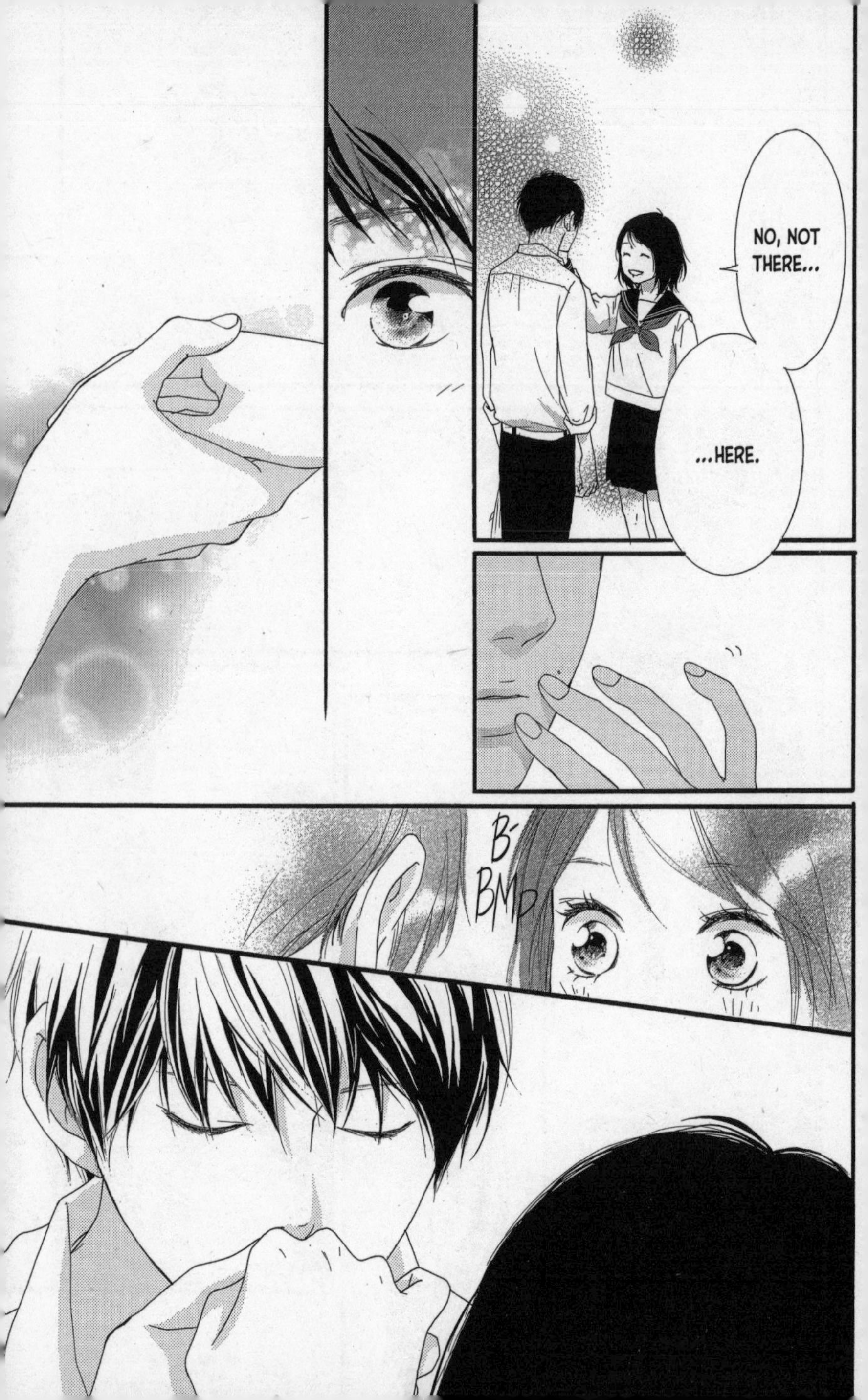
NO, NOT THERE...
...HERE.
B-BMP

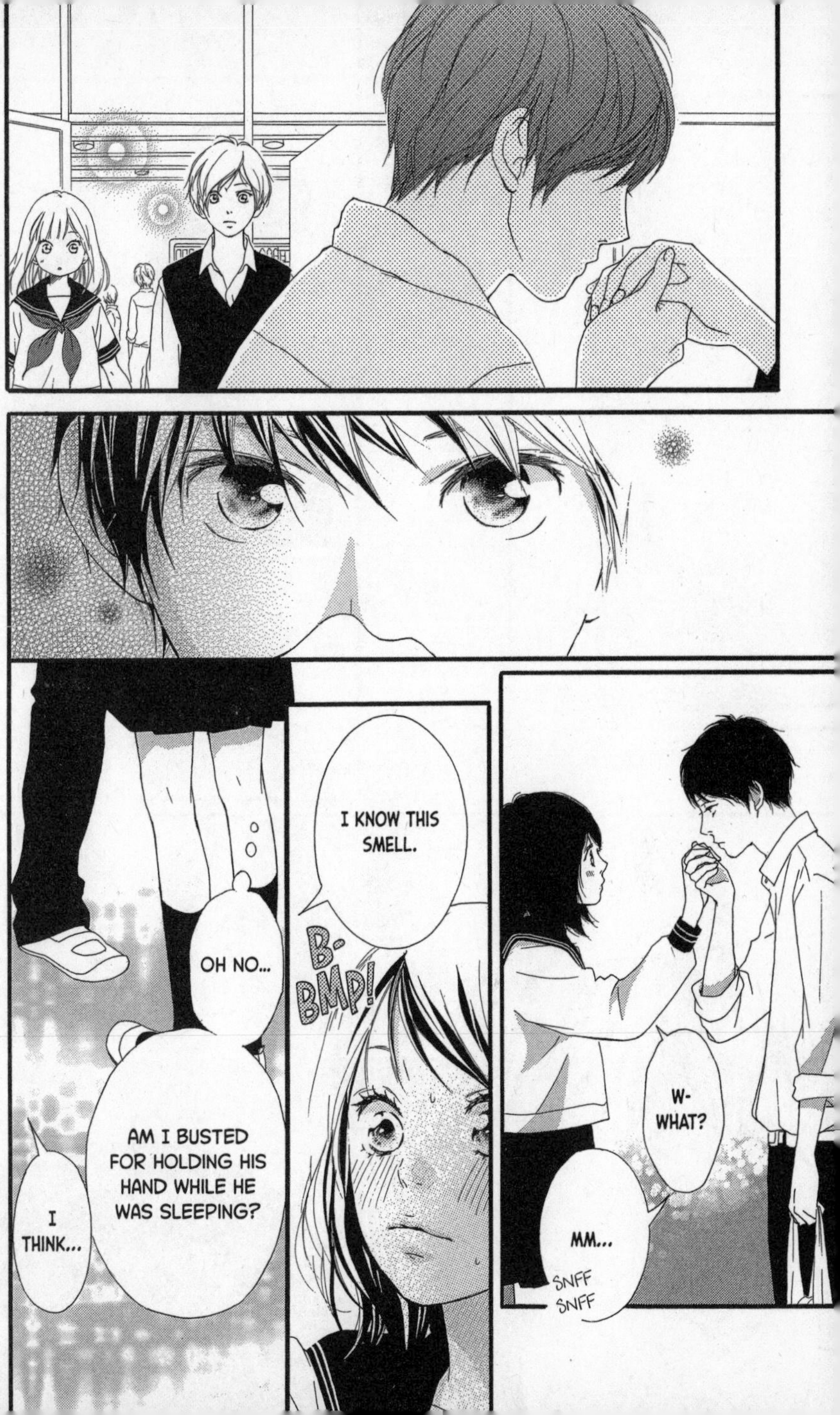
W-WHAT?
MM...
SNFF SNFF
I KNOW THIS SMELL.
B-BMP!
OH NO...
AM I BUSTED FOR HOLDING HIS HAND WHILE HE WAS SLEEPING?
I THINK...

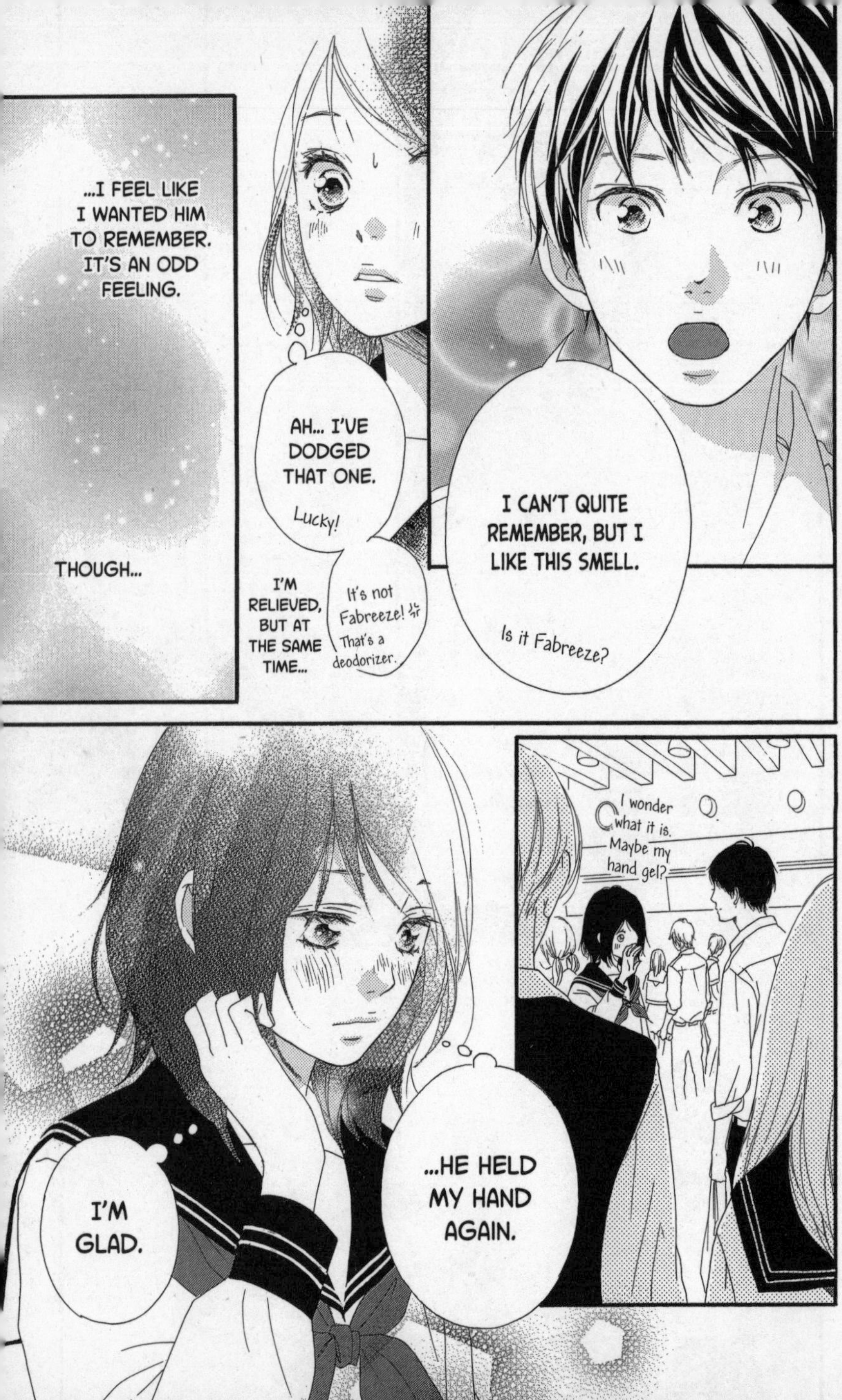
I CAN'T QUITE REMEMBER, BUT I LIKE THIS SMELL.
Is it Fabreeze?
AH... I'VE DODGED THAT ONE.
Lucky!
It's not Fabreeze! That's a deodorizer.
I'M RELIEVED, BUT AT THE SAME TIME...
...I FEEL LIKE I WANTED HIM TO REMEMBER. IT'S AN ODD FEELING.
THOUGH...
I wonder what it is. Maybe my hand gel?
...HE HELD MY HAND AGAIN.
I'M GLAD.

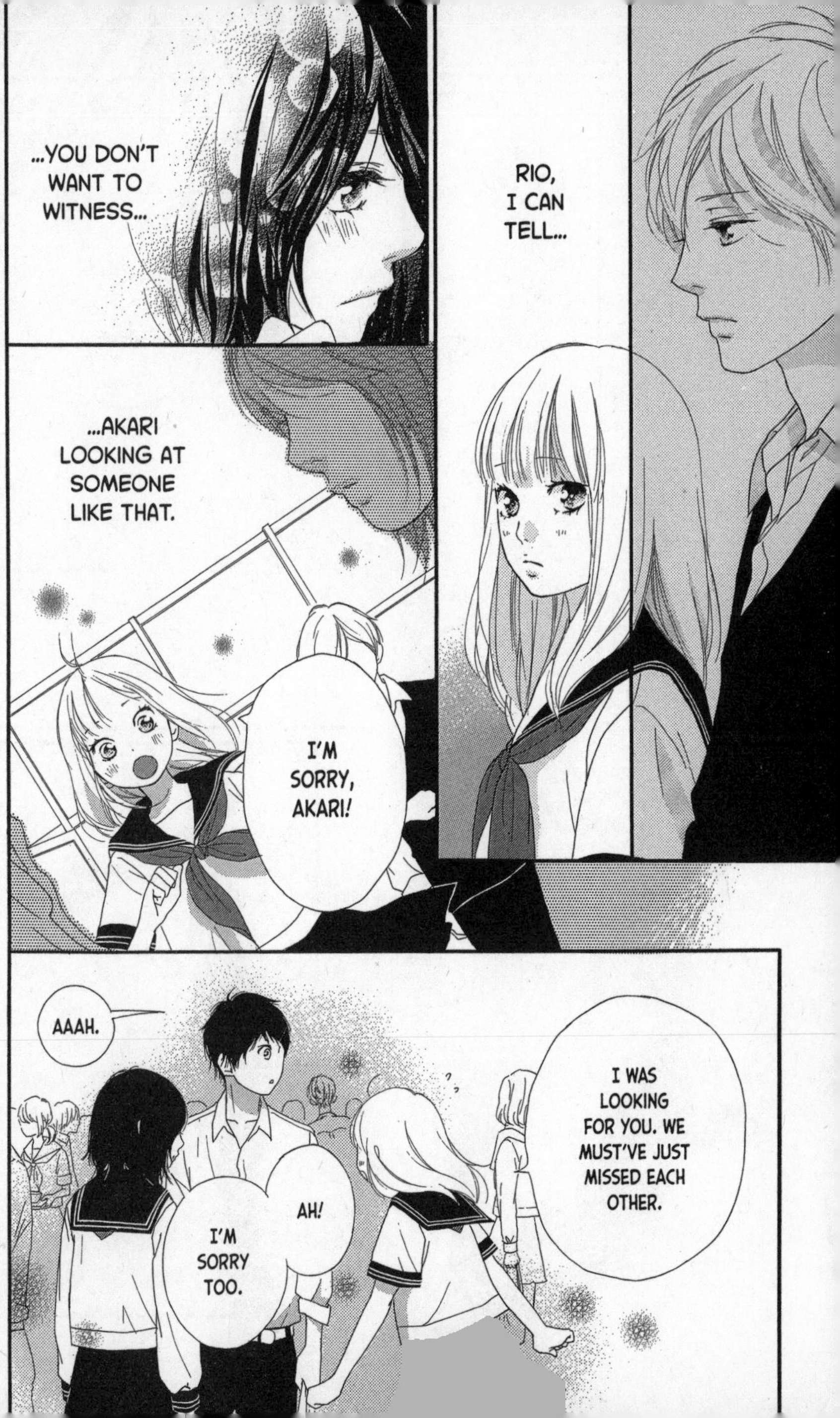
RIO, I CAN TELL...
...YOU DON'T WANT TO WITNESS...
...AKARI LOOKING AT SOMEONE LIKE THAT.
I'M SORRY, AKARI!
AAAH.
I WAS LOOKING FOR YOU. WE MUST'VE JUST MISSED EACH OTHER.
AH!
I'M SORRY TOO.

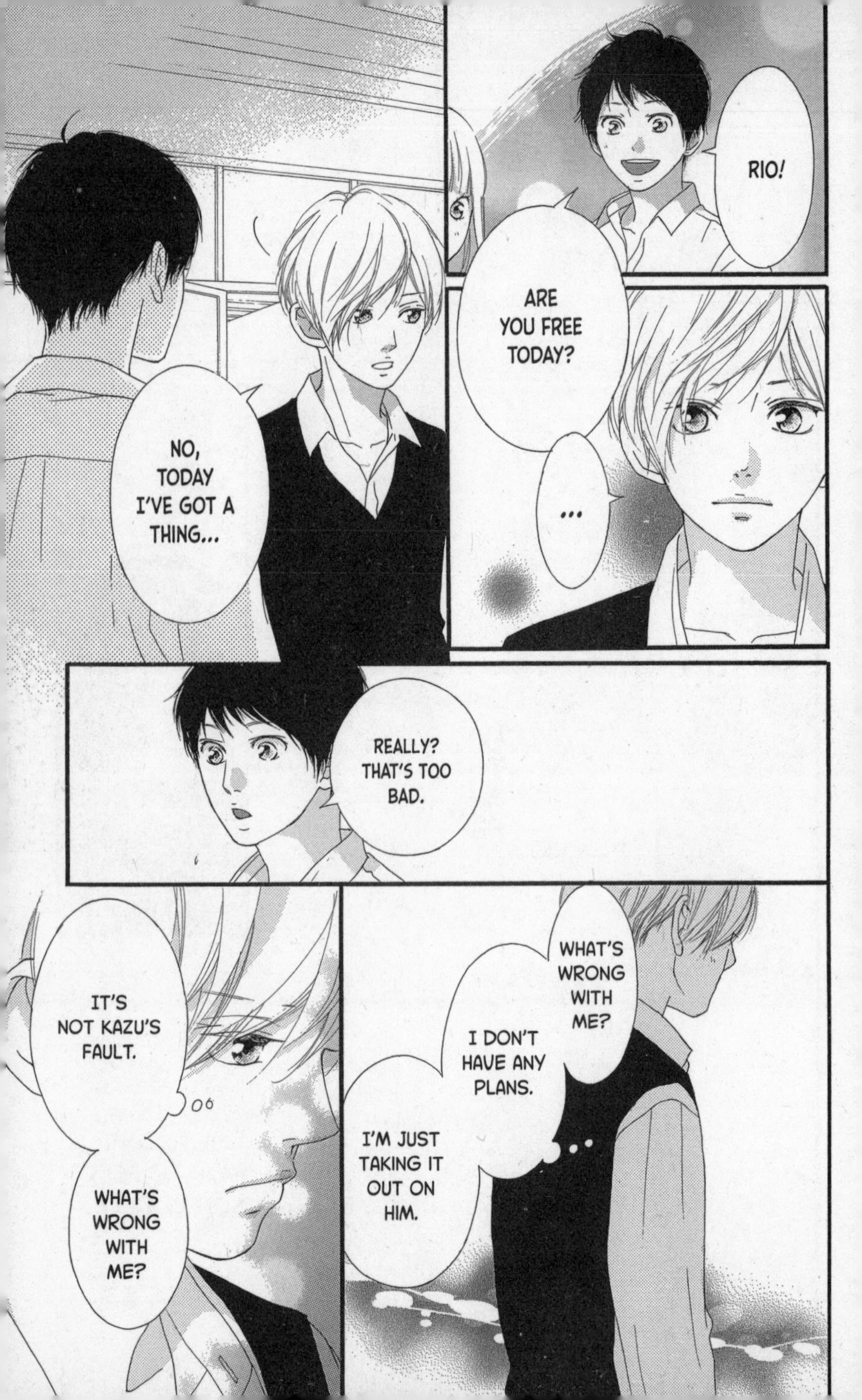
RIO!
ARE YOU FREE TODAY?
...
NO, TODAY I'VE GOT A THING...
REALLY? THAT'S TOO BAD.
WHAT'S WRONG WITH ME?
I DON'T HAVE ANY PLANS.
I'M JUST TAKING IT OUT ON HIM.
IT'S NOT KAZU'S FAULT.
WHAT'S WRONG WITH ME?

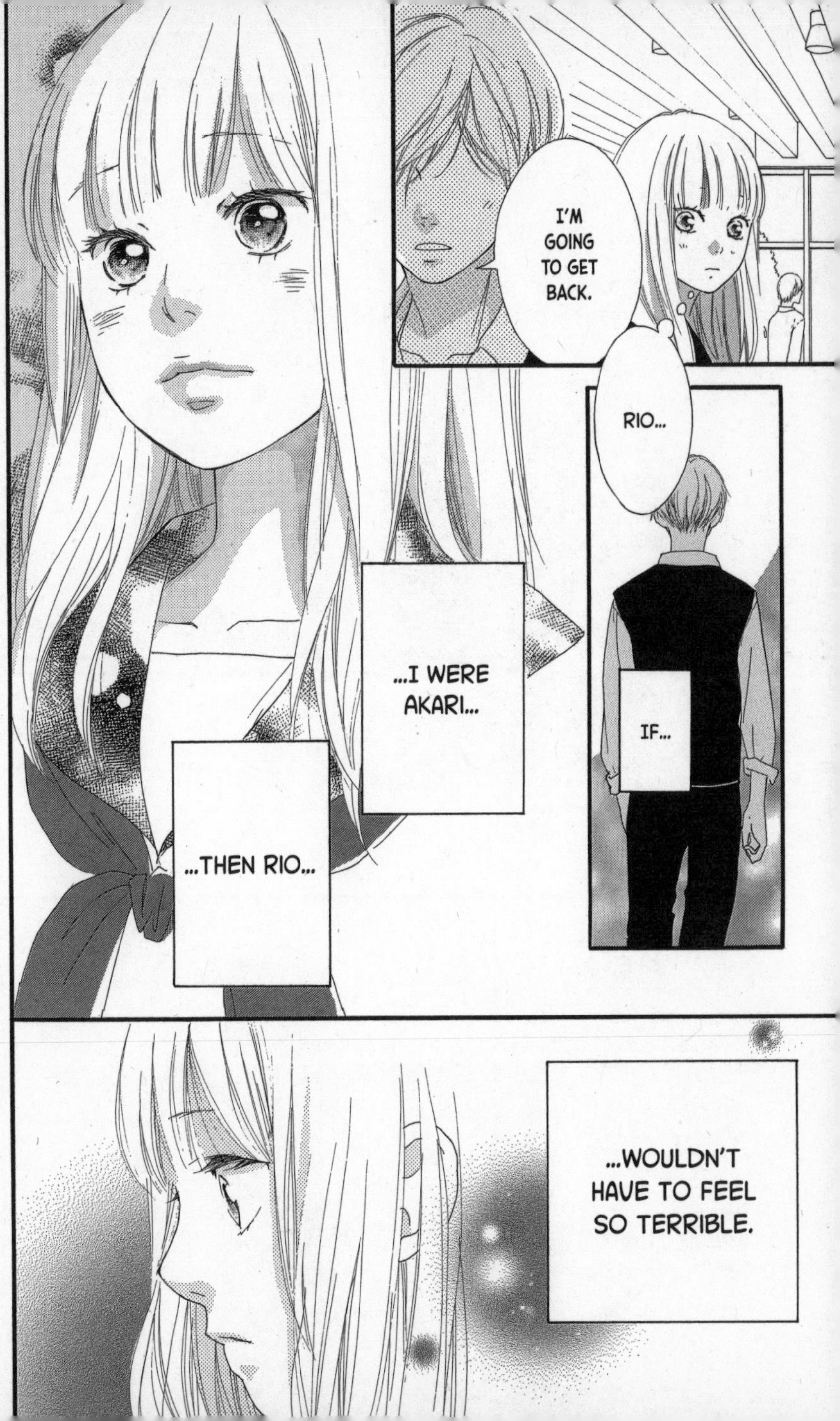
I'M GOING TO GET BACK.
RIO...
IF...
...I WERE AKARI...
...THEN RIO...
...WOULDN'T HAVE TO FEEL SO TERRIBLE.

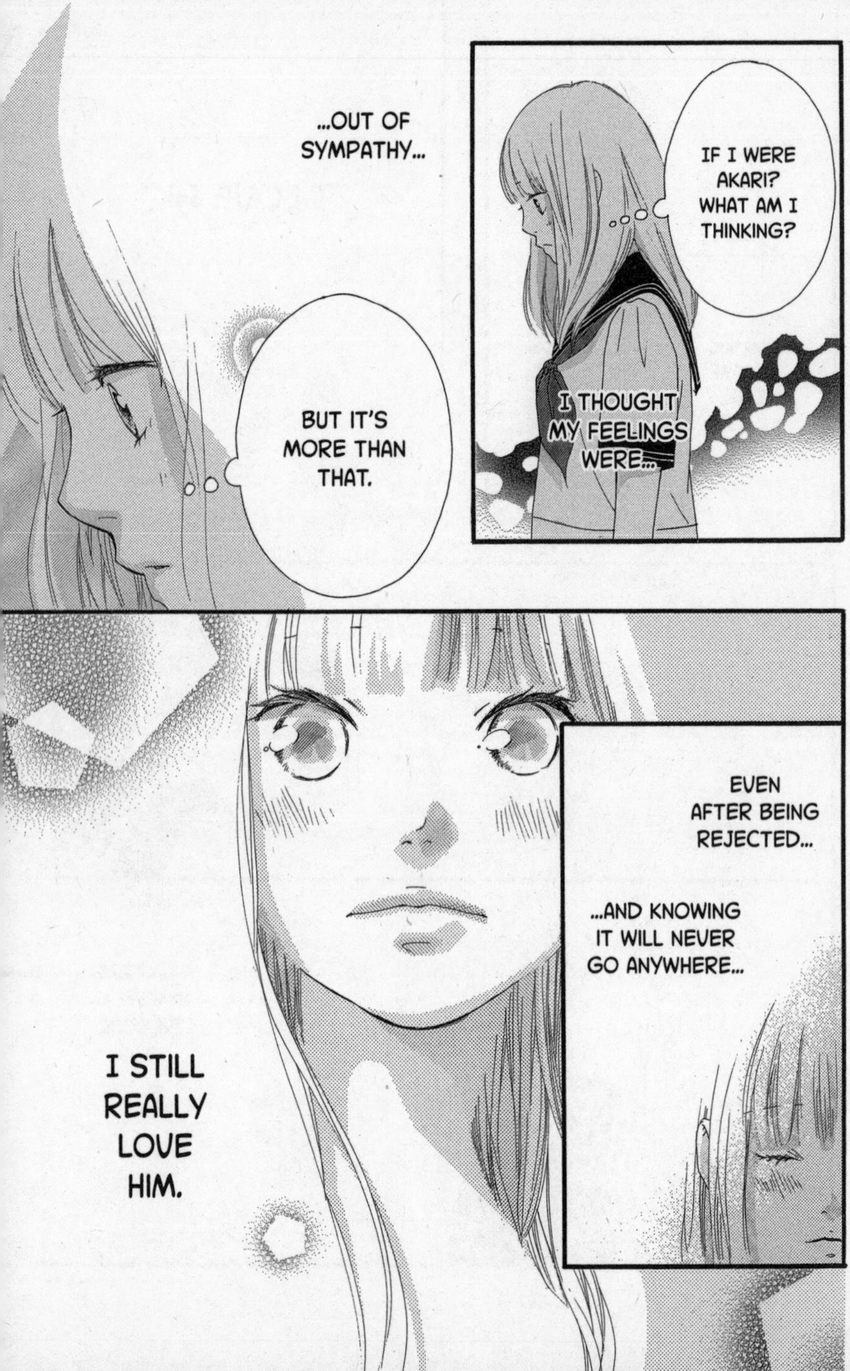
IF I WERE AKARI? WHAT AM I THINKING?
I THOUGHT MY FEELINGS WERE...
...OUT OF SYMPATHY...
BUT IT'S MORE THAN THAT.
EVEN AFTER BEING REJECTED...
...AND KNOWING IT WILL NEVER GO ANYWHERE...
I STILL REALLY LOVE HIM.

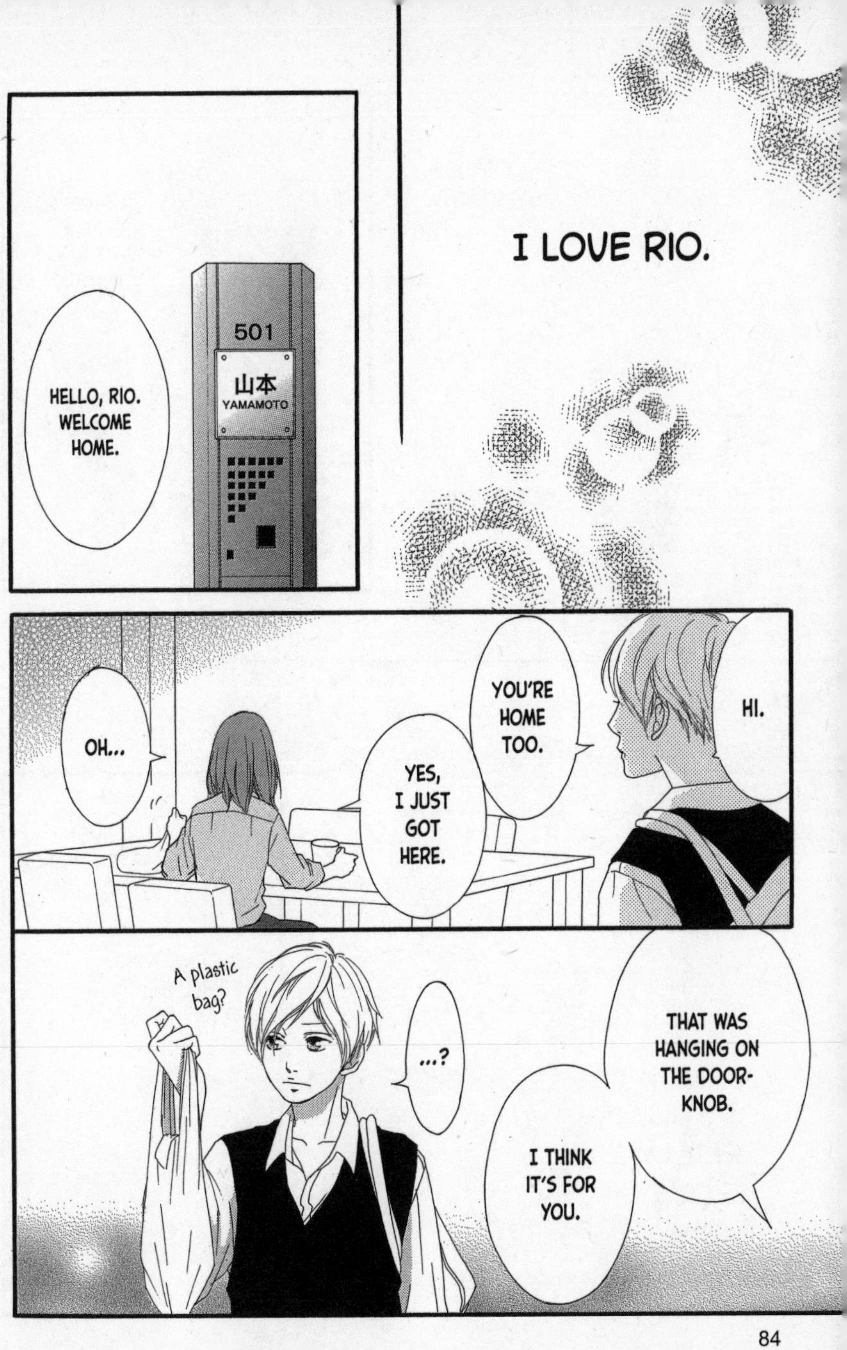

I LOVE RIO.
501
山本
YAMAMOTO
HELLO, RIO. WELCOME HOME.
HI.
YOU'RE HOME TOO.
YES, I JUST GOT HERE.
OH...
THAT WAS HANGING ON THE DOOR-KNOB.
I THINK IT'S FOR YOU.
...?
A plastic bag?

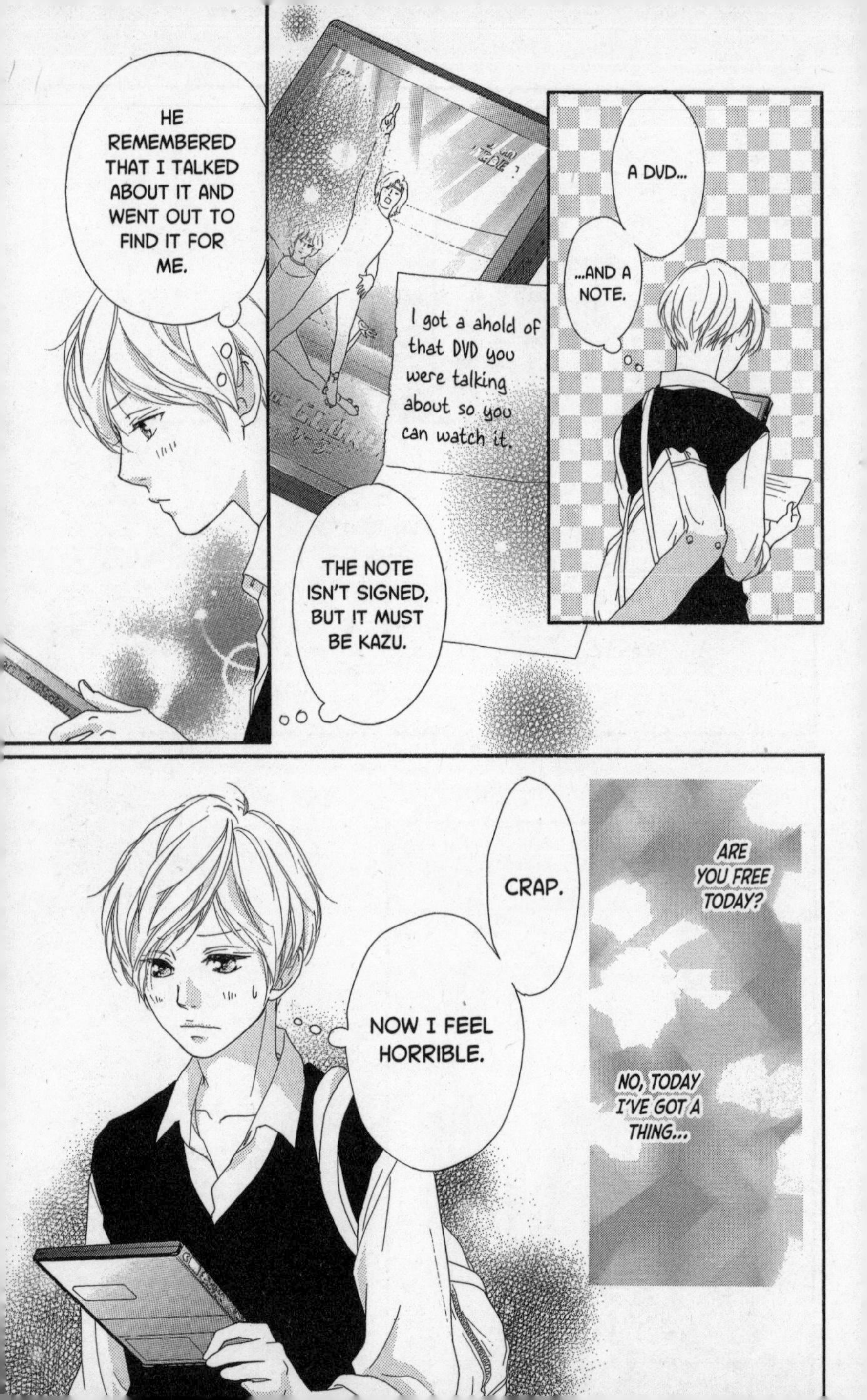
A DVD...
...AND A NOTE.
I got a ahold of that DVD you were talking about so you can watch it.
THE NOTE ISN'T SIGNED, BUT IT MUST BE KAZU.
HE REMEMBERED THAT I TALKED ABOUT IT AND WENT OUT TO FIND IT FOR ME.
ARE YOU FREE TODAY?
NO, TODAY I'VE GOT A THING...
CRAP.
NOW I FEEL HORRIBLE.

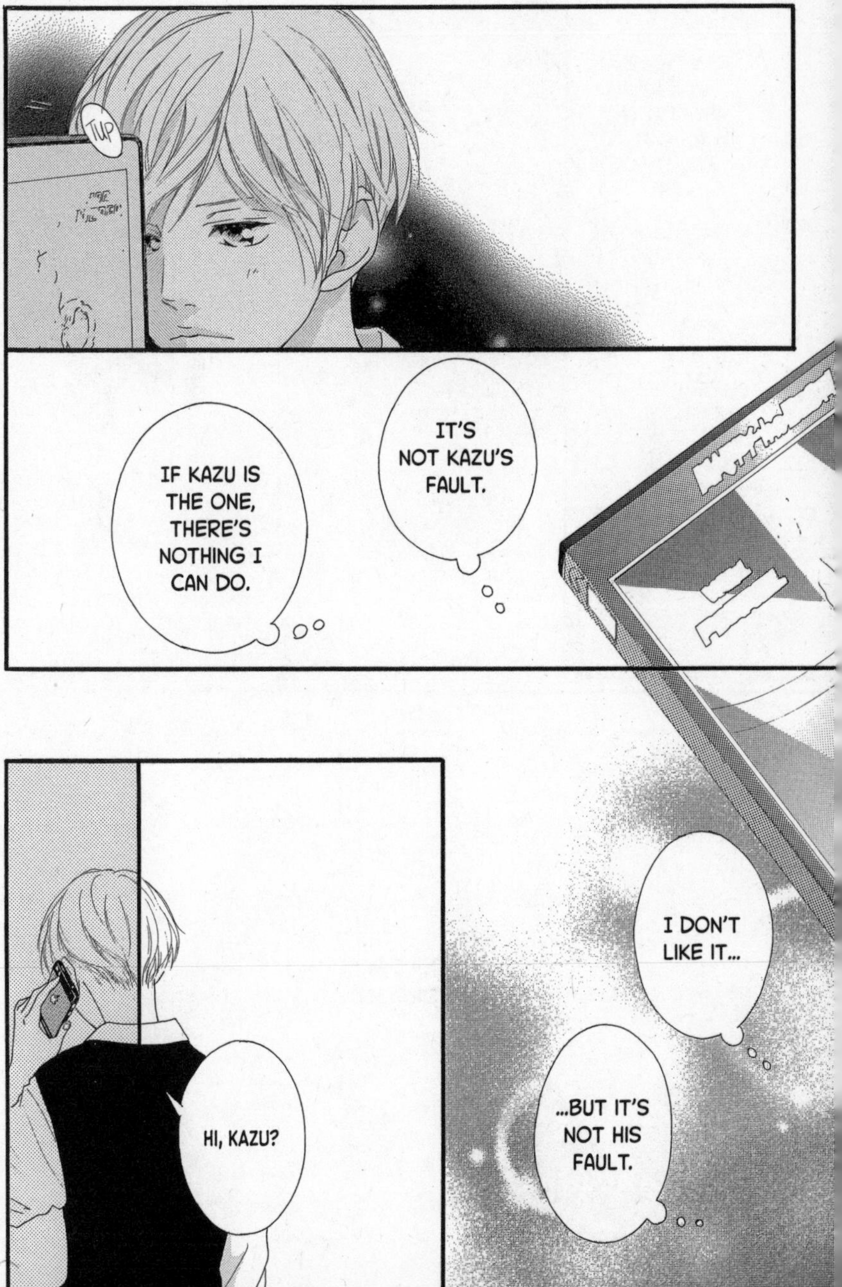
TUP
IT'S NOT KAZU'S FAULT.
IF KAZU IS THE ONE, THERE'S NOTHING I CAN DO.
I DON'T LIKE IT...
...BUT IT'S NOT HIS FAULT.
HI, KAZU?

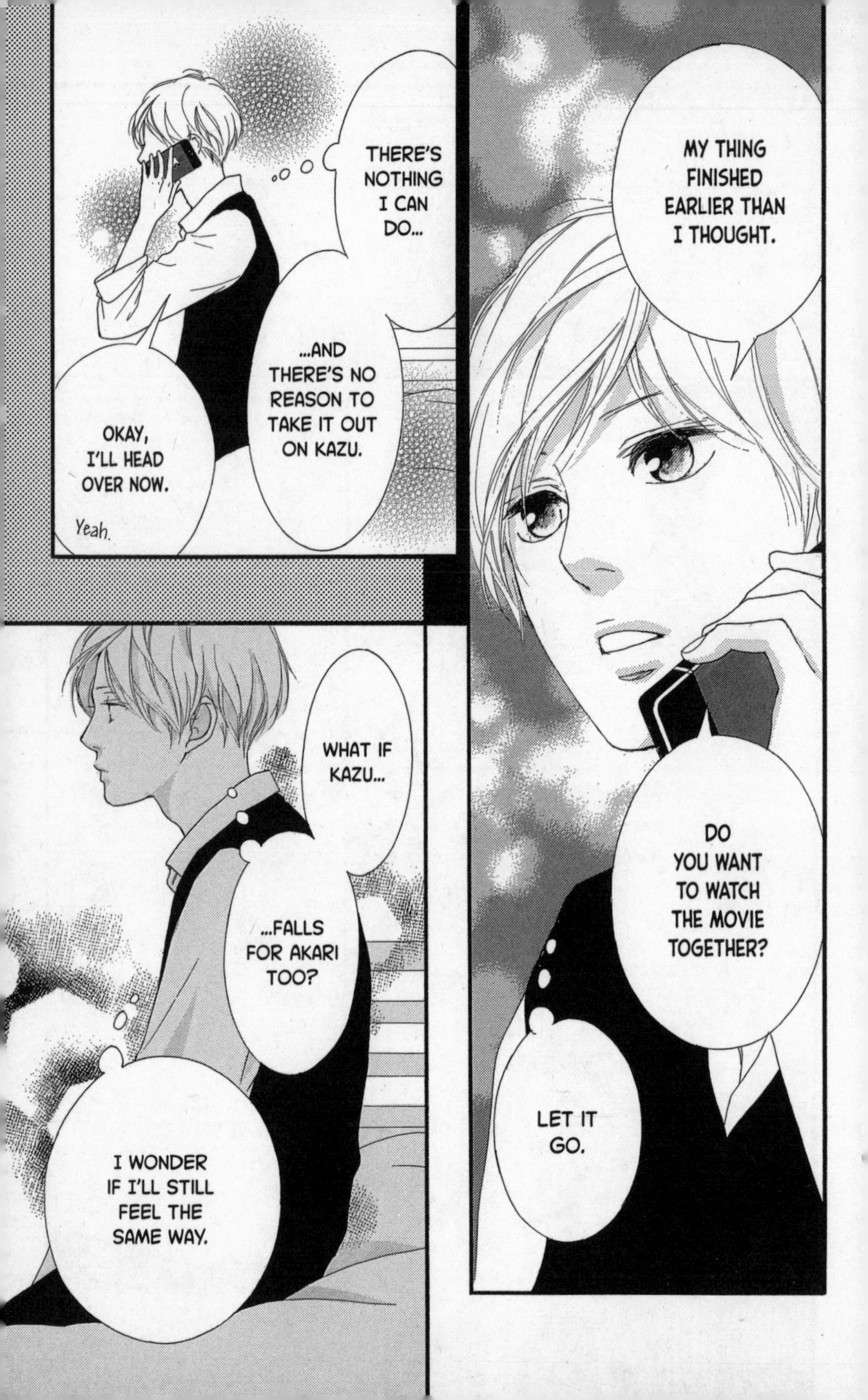
MY THING FINISHED EARLIER THAN I THOUGHT.
DO YOU WANT TO WATCH THE MOVIE TOGETHER?
LET IT GO.
THERE'S NOTHING I CAN DO...
...AND THERE'S NO REASON TO TAKE IT OUT ON KAZU.
OKAY, I'LL HEAD OVER NOW.
Yeah.
WHAT IF KAZU...
...FALLS FOR AKARI TOO?
I WONDER IF I'LL STILL FEEL THE SAME WAY.

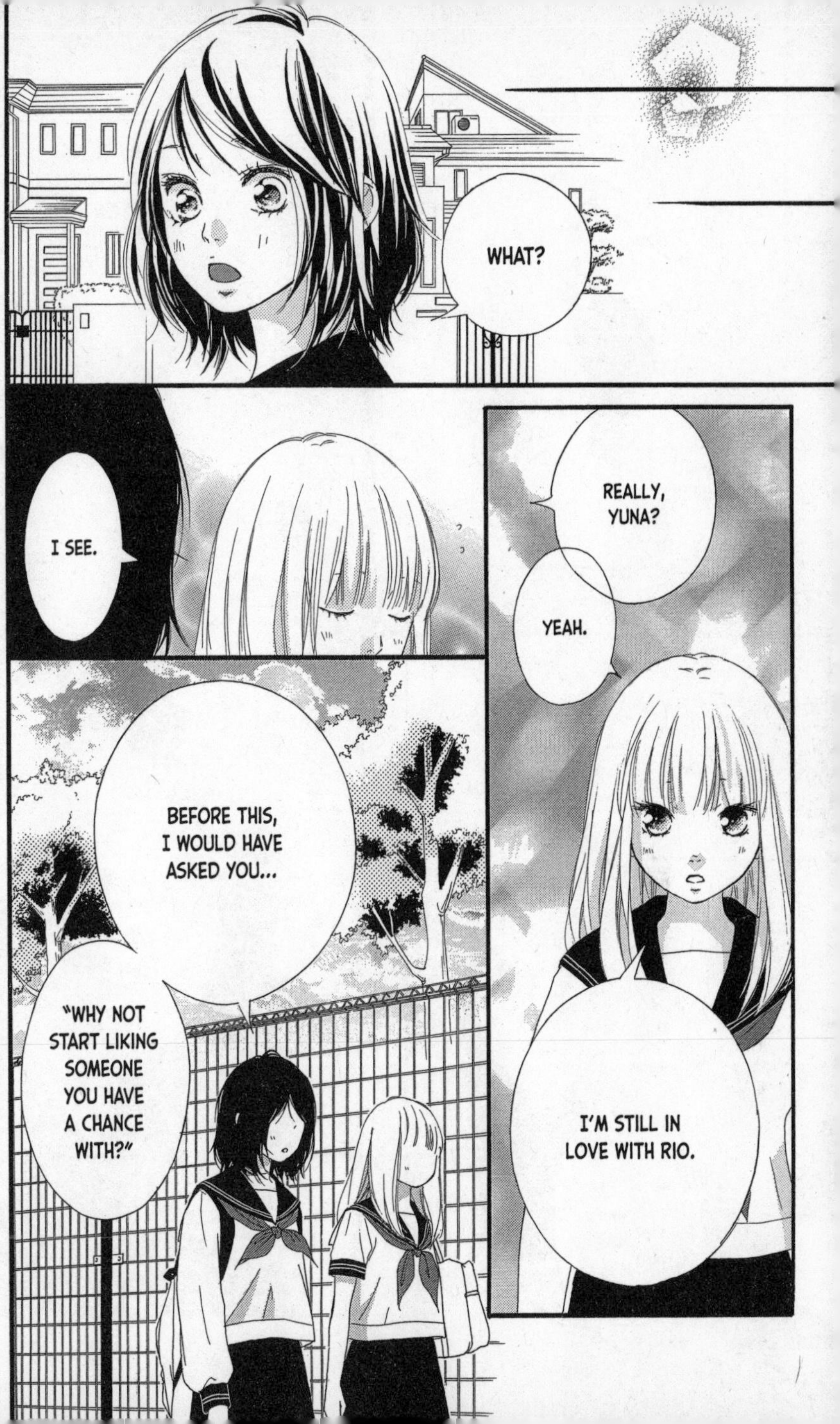
WHAT?
REALLY, YUNA?
YEAH.
I'M STILL IN LOVE WITH RIO.
I SEE.
BEFORE THIS, I WOULD HAVE ASKED YOU...
"WHY NOT START LIKING SOMEONE YOU HAVE A CHANCE WITH?"

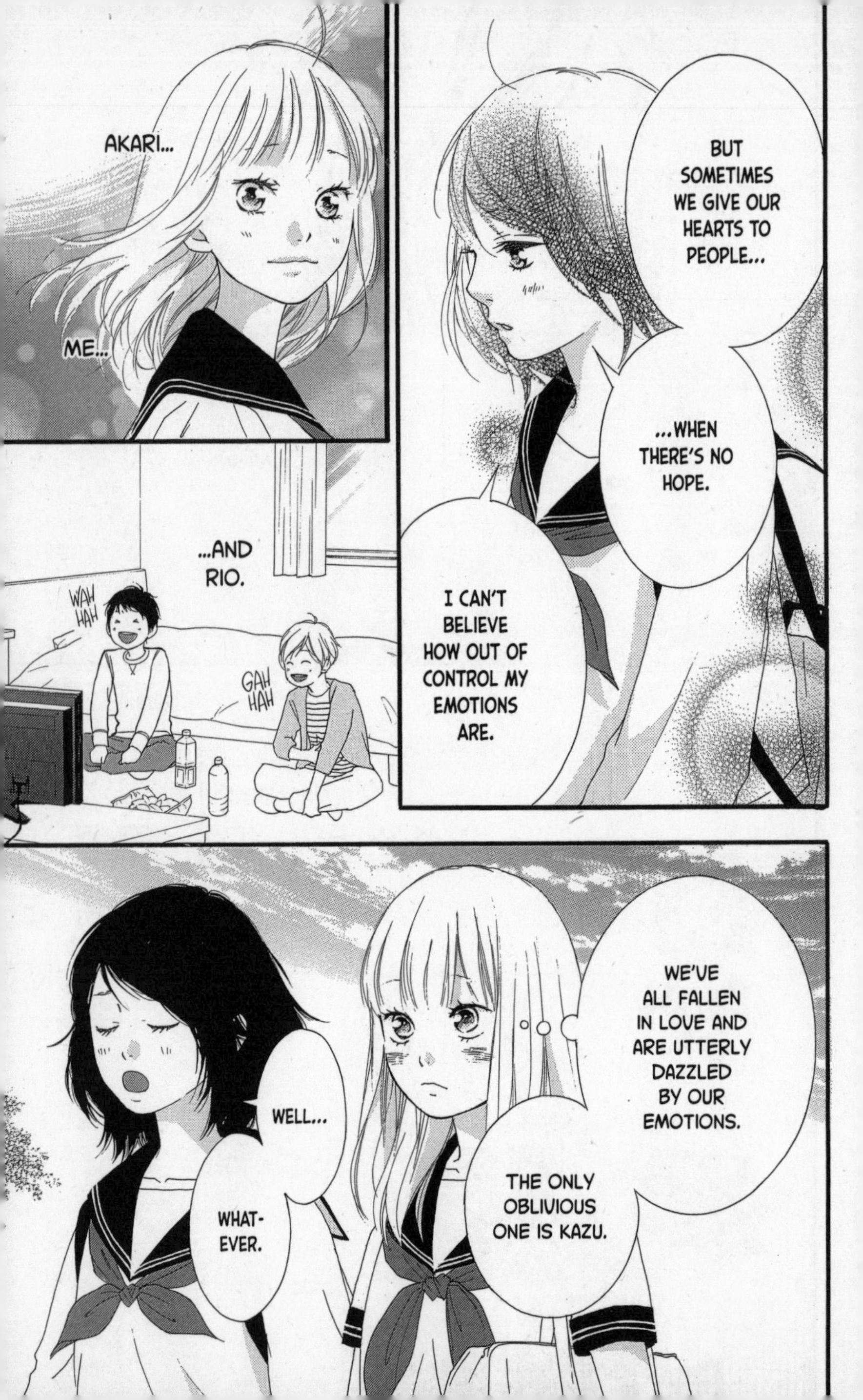
BUT SOMETIMES WE GIVE OUR HEARTS TO PEOPLE...
...WHEN THERE'S NO HOPE.
I CAN'T BELIEVE HOW OUT OF CONTROL MY EMOTIONS ARE.
AKARI...
ME...
...AND RIO.
WAH HAH
GAH HAH
WE'VE ALL FALLEN IN LOVE AND ARE UTTERLY DAZZLED BY OUR EMOTIONS.
THE ONLY OBLIVIOUS ONE IS KAZU.
WELL...
WHAT-EVER.

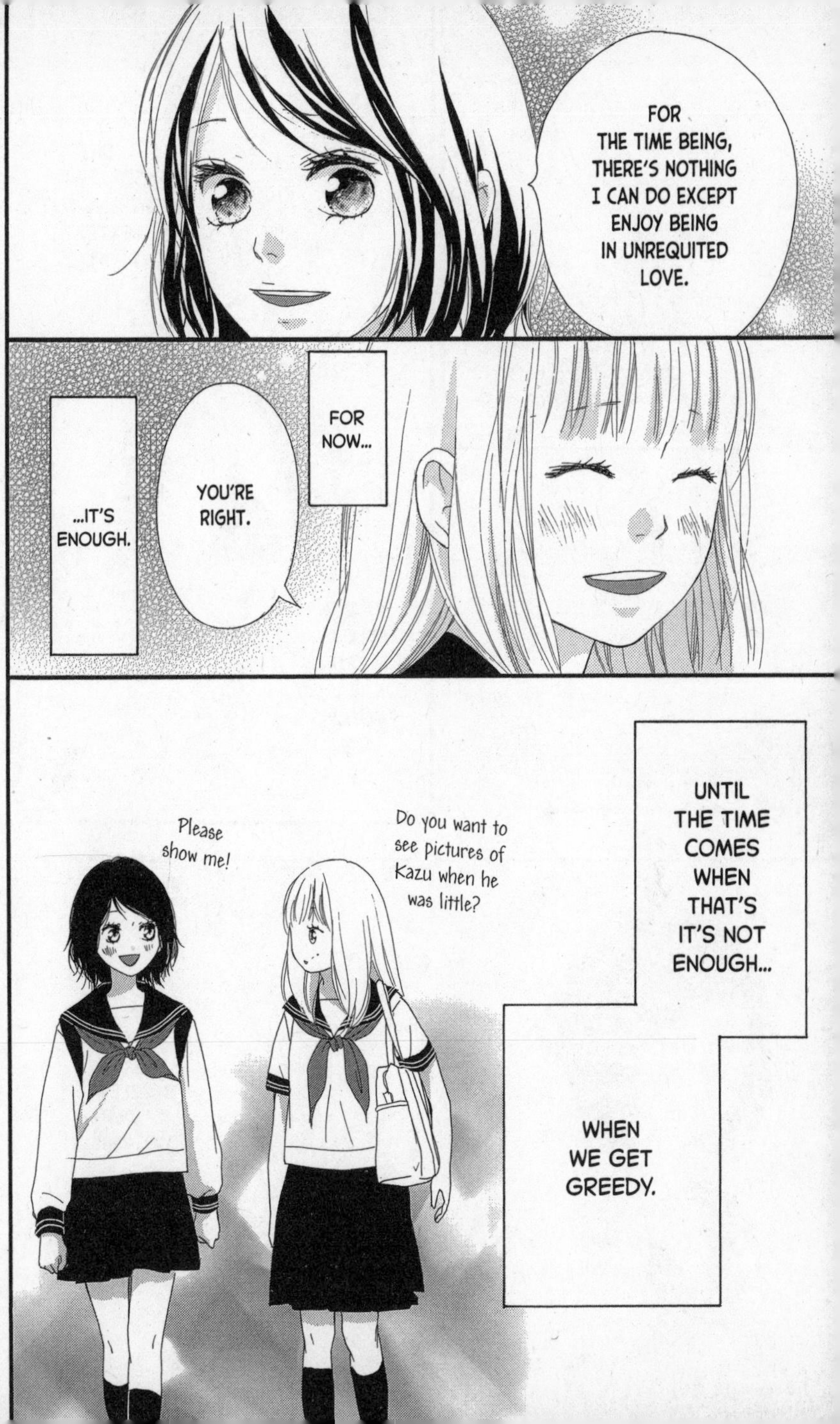
FOR THE TIME BEING, THERE'S NOTHING I CAN DO EXCEPT ENJOY BEING IN UNREQUITED LOVE.
FOR NOW...
YOU'RE RIGHT.
...IT'S ENOUGH.
UNTIL THE TIME COMES WHEN THAT'S IT'S NOT ENOUGH...
WHEN WE GET GREEDY.
Do you want to see pictures of Kazu when he was little?
Please show me!

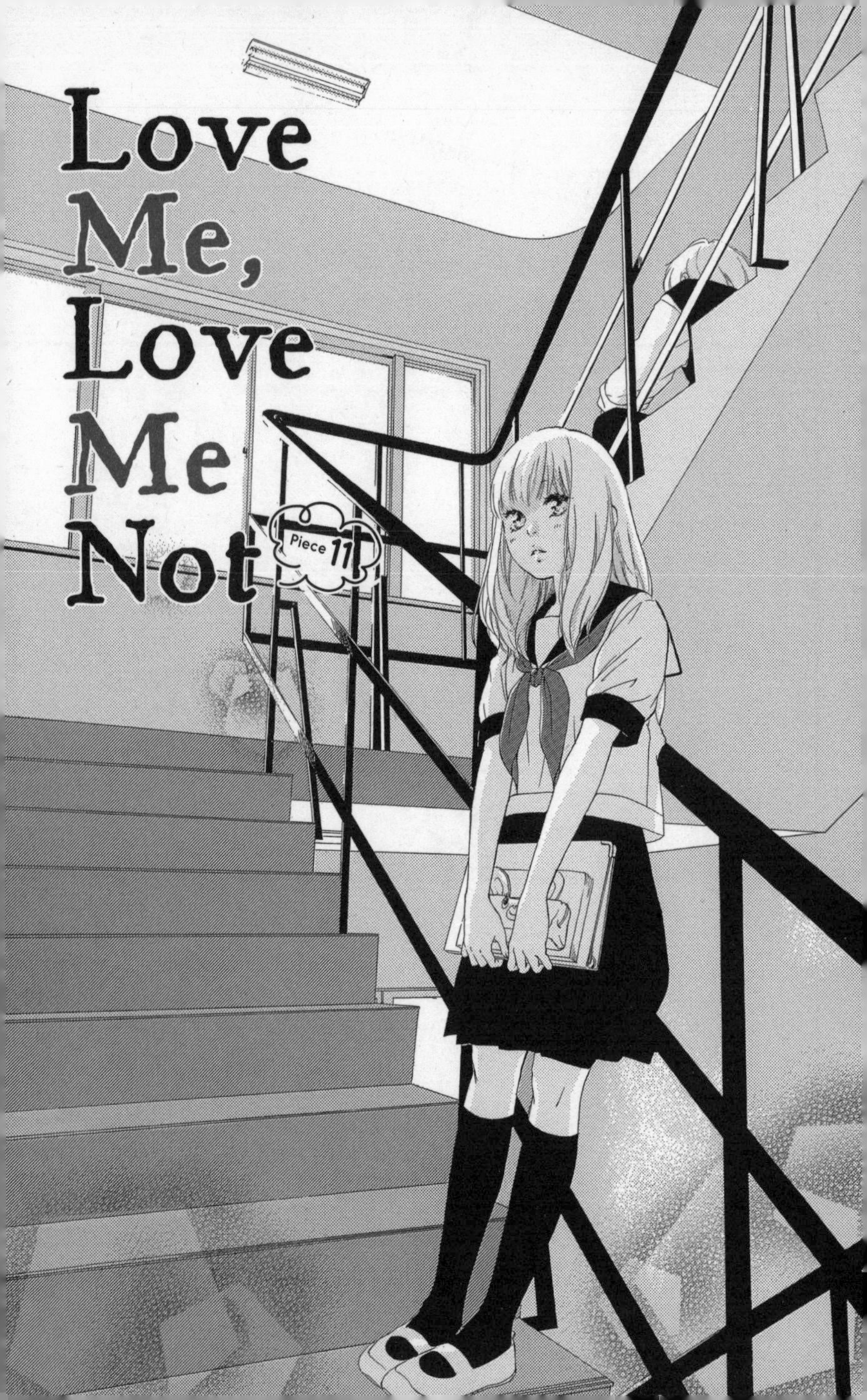
Love Me, Love Me Not
Piece 11

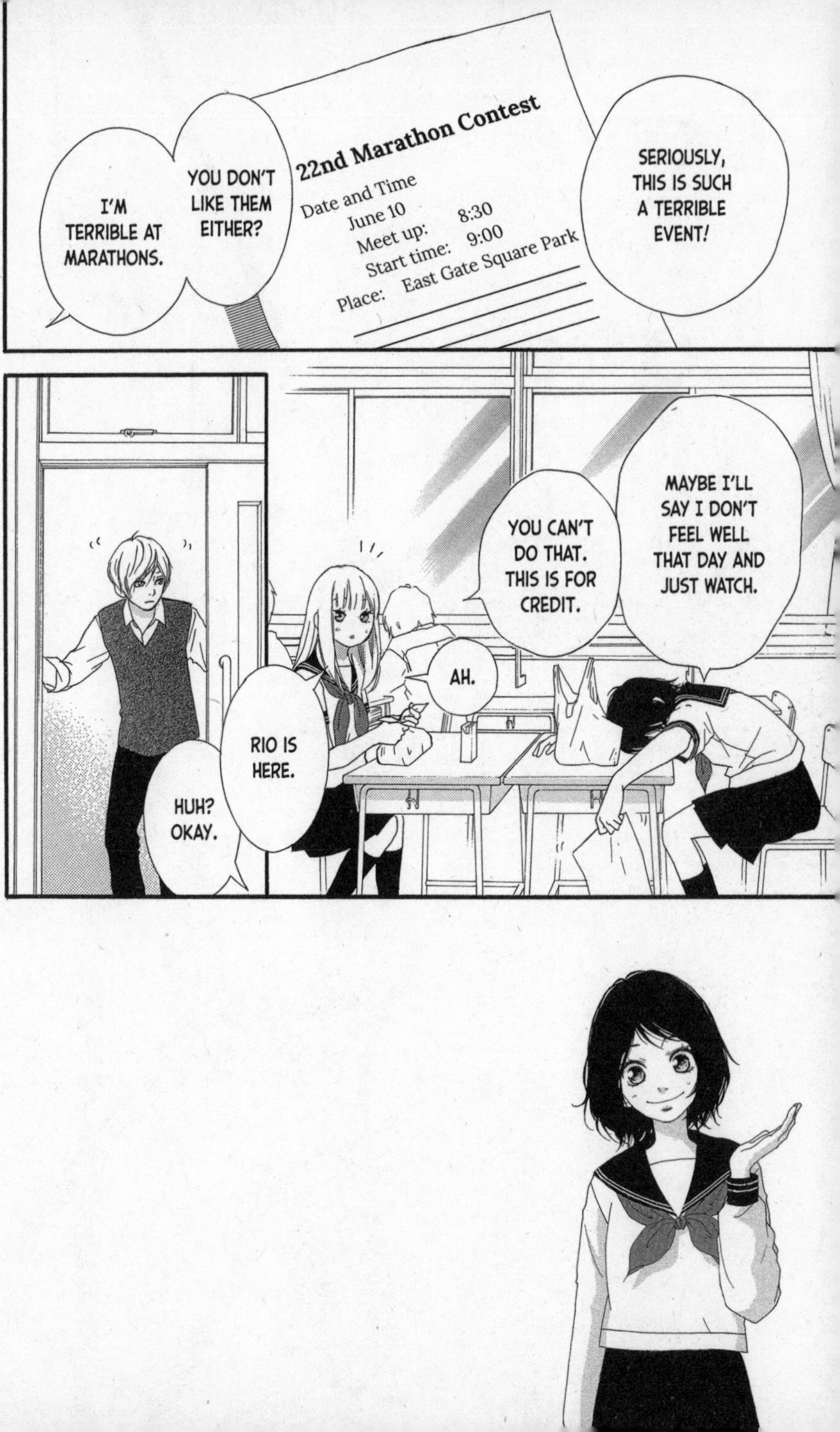
SERIOUSLY, THIS IS SUCH A TERRIBLE EVENT!
22nd Marathon Contest
Date and Time
June 10
Meet up: 8:30
Start time: 9:00
Place: East Gate Square Park
YOU DON'T LIKE THEM EITHER?
I'M TERRIBLE AT MARATHONS.
MAYBE I'LL SAY I DON'T FEEL WELL THAT DAY AND JUST WATCH.
YOU CAN'T DO THAT. THIS IS FOR CREDIT.
AH.
RIO IS HERE.
HUH? OKAY.

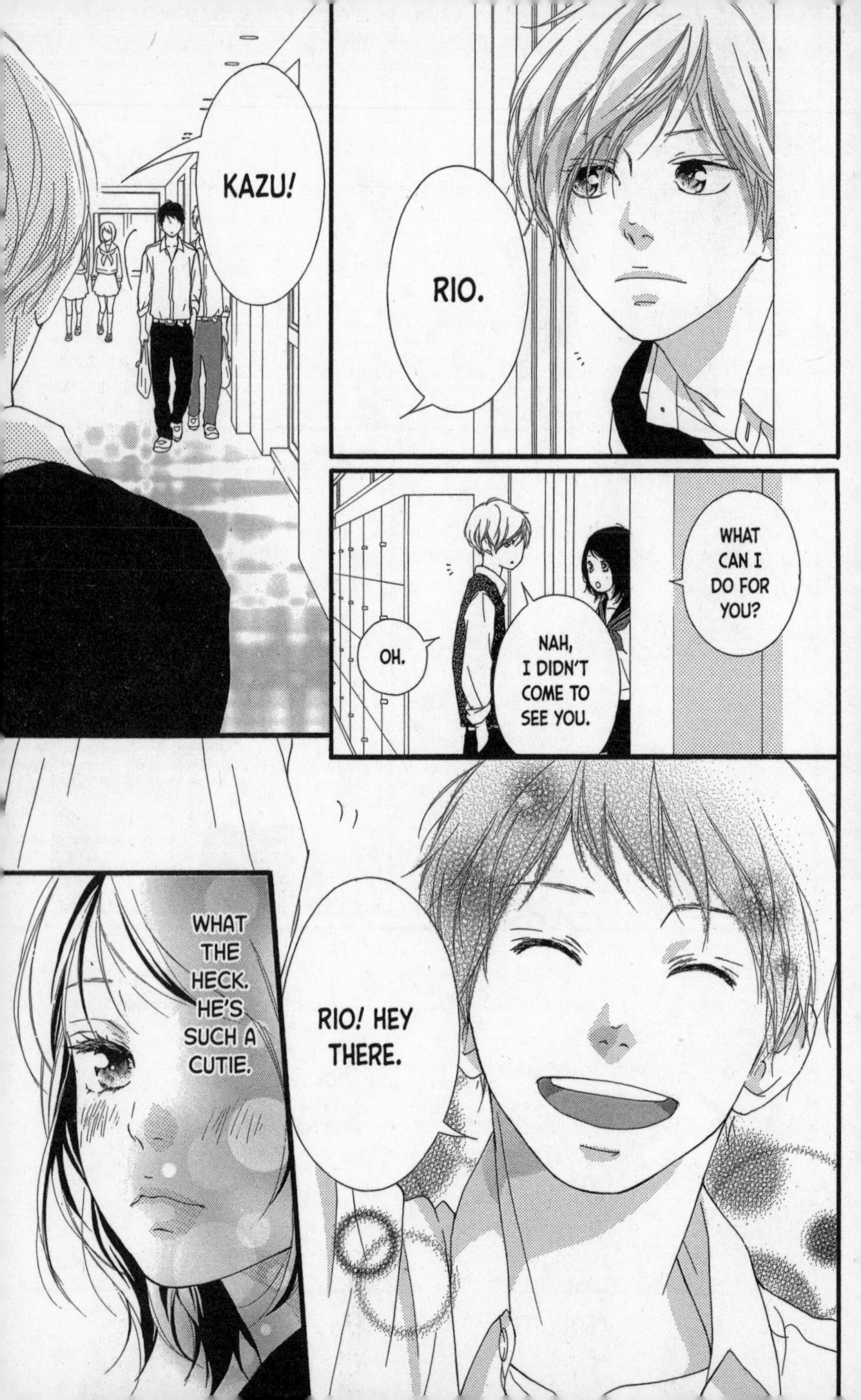
RIO.
WHAT CAN I DO FOR YOU?
NAH, I DIDN'T COME TO SEE YOU.
OH.
KAZU!
RIO! HEY THERE.
WHAT THE HECK. HE'S SUCH A CUTIE.

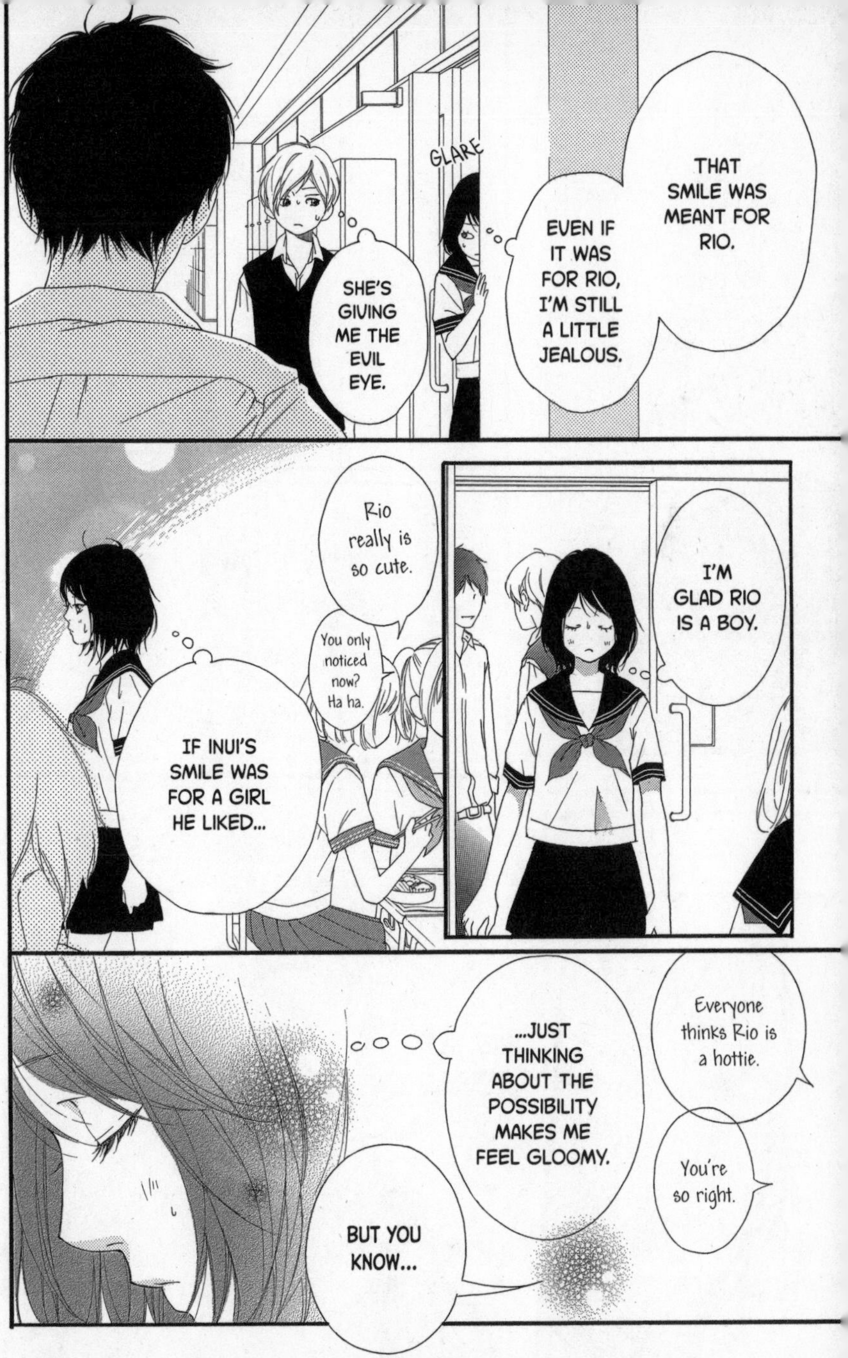
THAT SMILE WAS MEANT FOR RIO.
EVEN IF IT WAS FOR RIO, I'M STILL A LITTLE JEALOUS.
GLARE
SHE'S GIVING ME THE EVIL EYE.
I'M GLAD RIO IS A BOY.
Rio really is so cute.
You only noticed now? Ha ha.
IF INUI'S SMILE WAS FOR A GIRL HE LIKED...
Everyone thinks Rio is a hottie.
You're so right.
...JUST THINKING ABOUT THE POSSIBILITY MAKES ME FEEL GLOOMY.
BUT YOU KNOW...

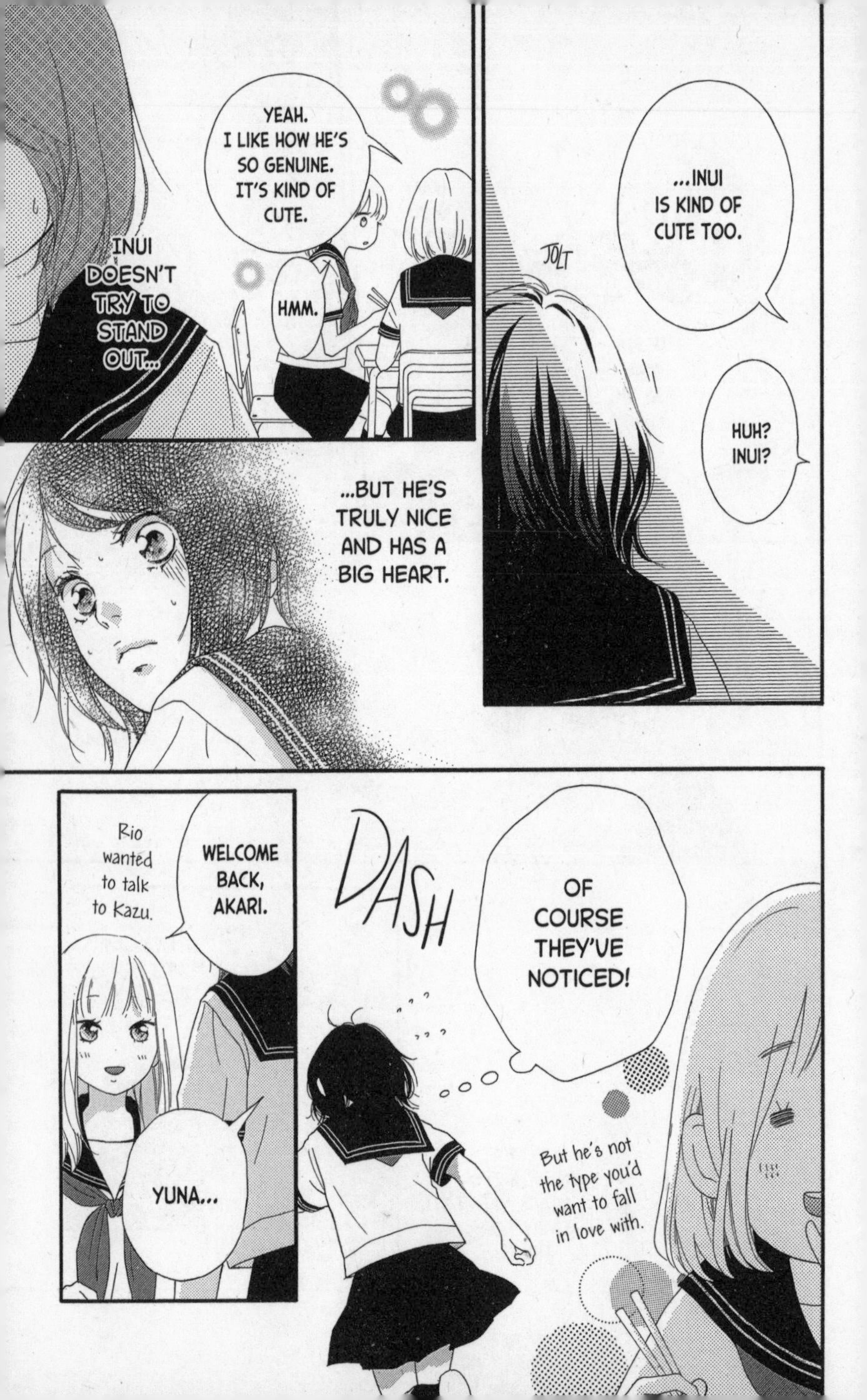
...INUI IS KIND OF CUTE TOO.
JOLT
HUH? INUI?
YEAH. I LIKE HOW HE'S SO GENUINE. IT'S KIND OF CUTE.
HMM.
INUI DOESN'T TRY TO STAND OUT...
...BUT HE'S TRULY NICE AND HAS A BIG HEART.
OF COURSE THEY'VE NOTICED!
But he's not the type you'd want to fall in love with.
DASH
WELCOME BACK, AKARI.
Rio wanted to talk to Kazu.
YUNA...

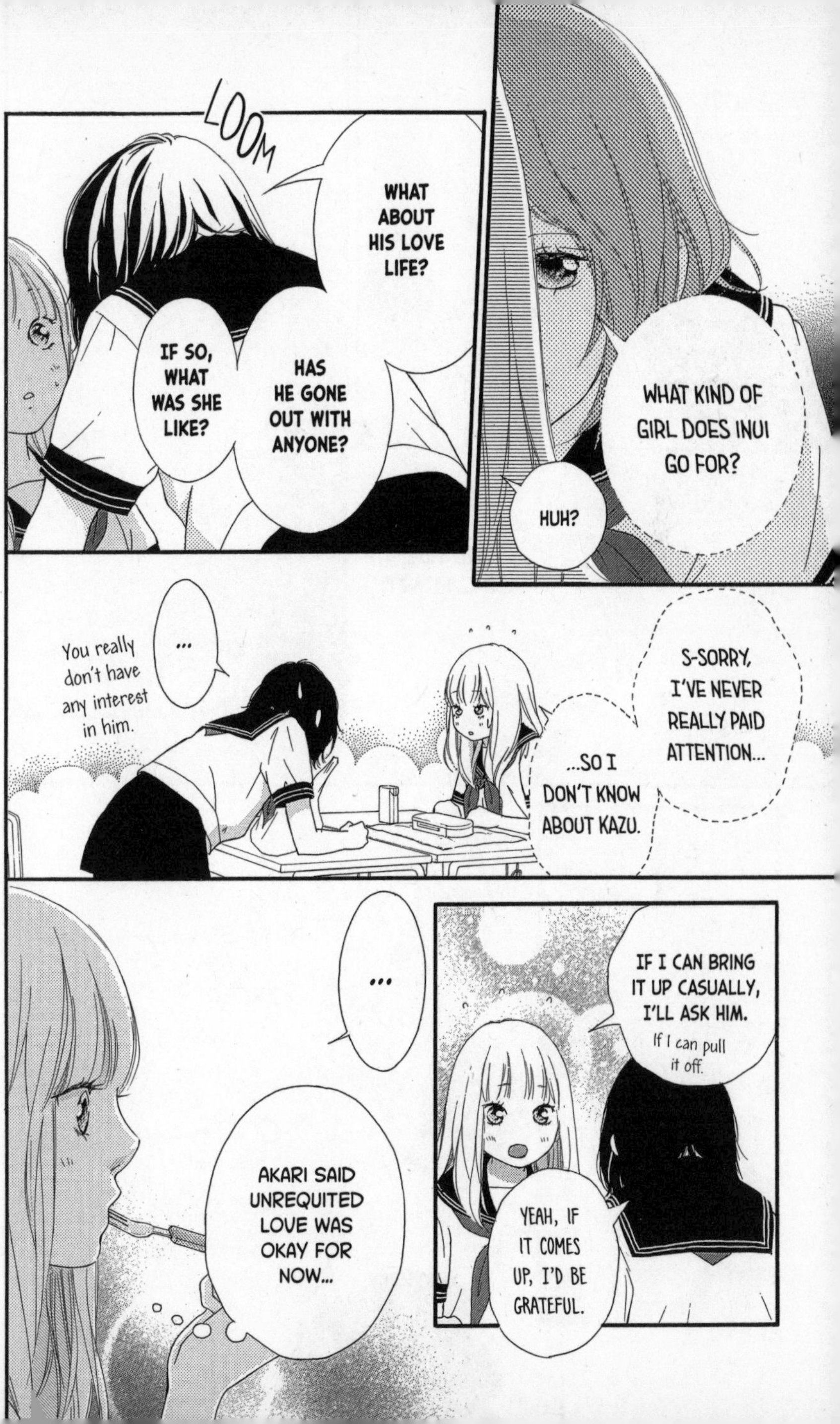
WHAT KIND OF GIRL DOES INUI GO FOR?
HUH?
LOOM
WHAT ABOUT HIS LOVE LIFE?
HAS HE GONE OUT WITH ANYONE?
IF SO, WHAT WAS SHE LIKE?
S-SORRY, I'VE NEVER REALLY PAID ATTENTION...
...SO I DON'T KNOW ABOUT KAZU.
...
You really don't have any interest in him.
IF I CAN BRING IT UP CASUALLY, I'LL ASK HIM.
If I can pull it off.
YEAH, IF IT COMES UP, I'D BE GRATEFUL.
...
AKARI SAID UNREQUITED LOVE WAS OKAY FOR NOW...

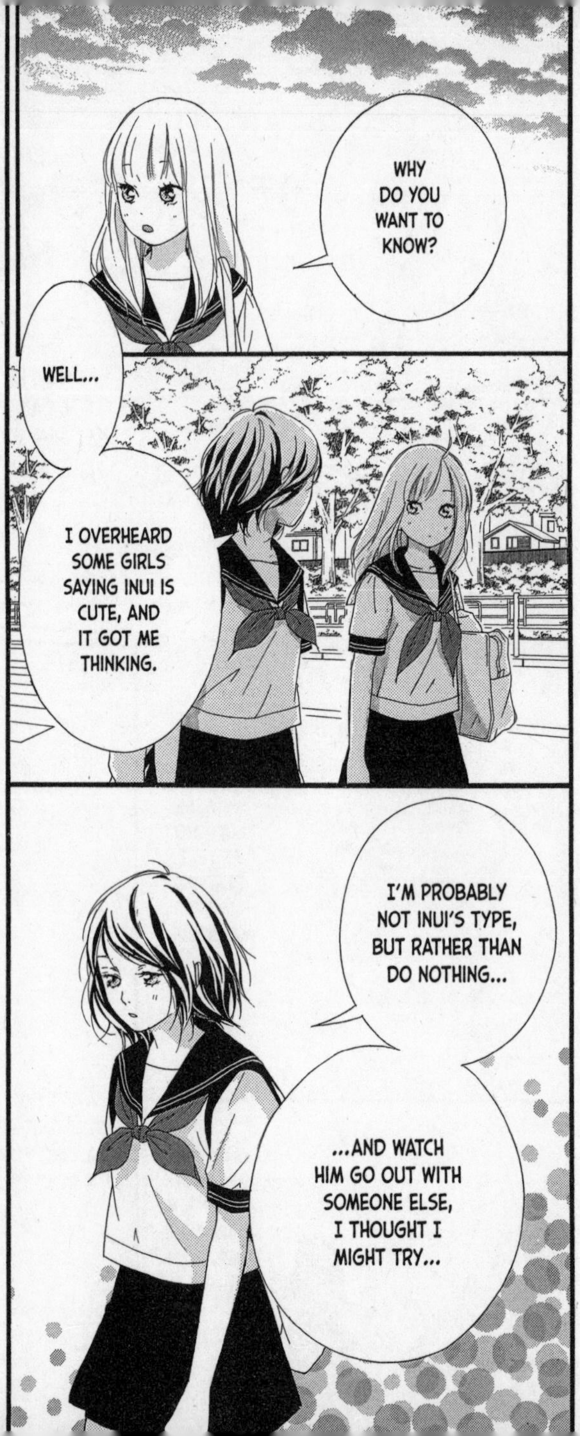
WHY DO YOU WANT TO KNOW?
WELL...
I OVERHEARD SOME GIRLS SAYING INUI IS CUTE, AND IT GOT ME THINKING.
I'M PROBABLY NOT INUI'S TYPE, BUT RATHER THAN DO NOTHING...
...AND WATCH HIM GO OUT WITH SOMEONE ELSE, I THOUGHT I MIGHT TRY...

I used a school marathon as material for this. I was in a marathon only when I was in elementary school, so I had to ask people who did one in high school. (How was it set up? Did you run around the school or at a big park? Did you all meet there?) I managed to come up with an image I could draw. (Thank you, Ase Umi-chan.) Even in elementary school I thought it was pretty tedious, so it must be terrible in high school. It seems lots of high schools have these events, and many other writers have said, "Oh, we did that." One person picked a high school based on the shortest distance they had to run. It seems it wasn't a very popular event for anyone. If you decide to go to a school that does a marathon... Go for it—I'm behind you all the way!!

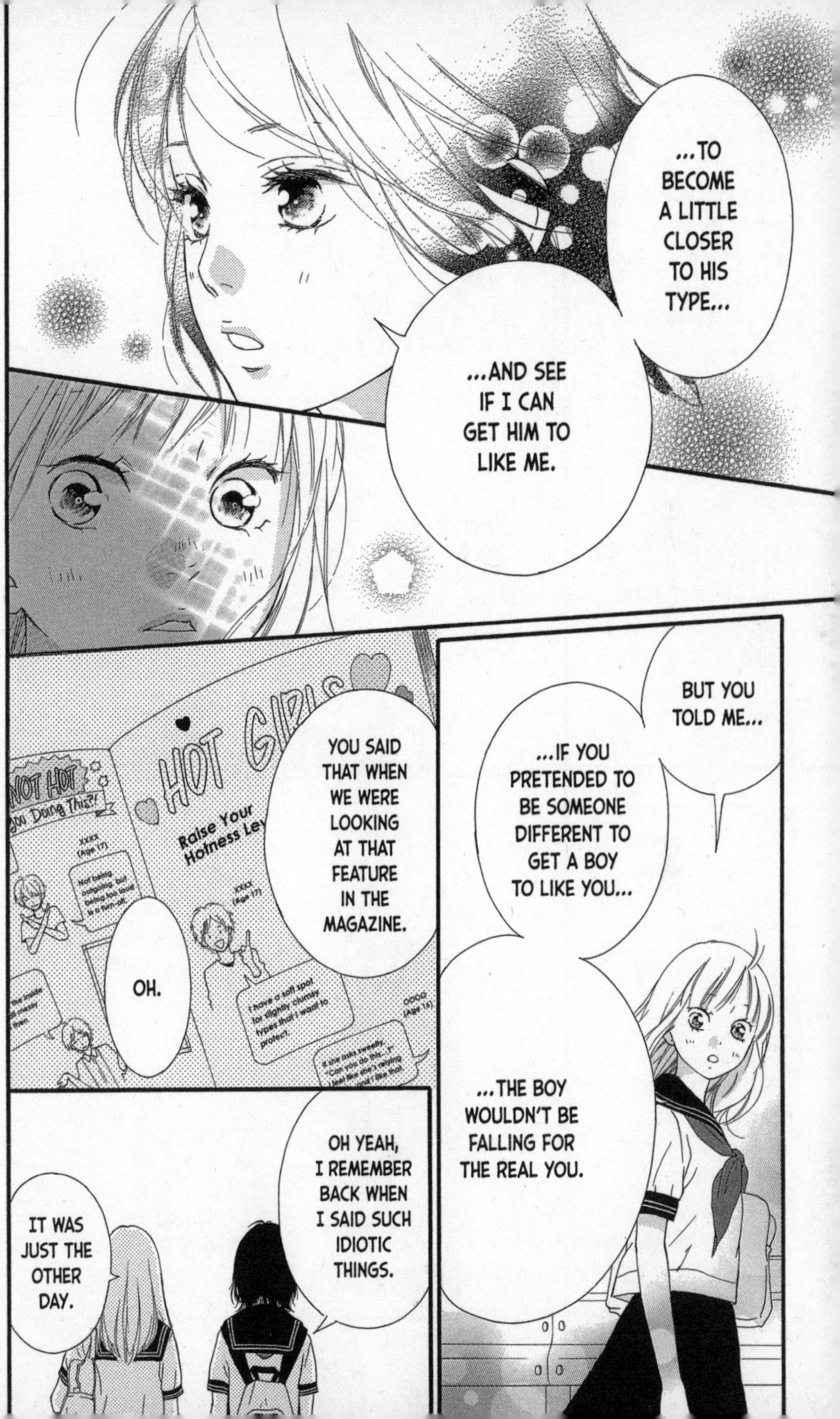
...TO BECOME A LITTLE CLOSER TO HIS TYPE...
...AND SEE IF I CAN GET HIM TO LIKE ME.
BUT YOU TOLD ME...
...IF YOU PRETENDED TO BE SOMEONE DIFFERENT TO GET A BOY TO LIKE YOU...
...THE BOY WOULDN'T BE FALLING FOR THE REAL YOU.
YOU SAID THAT WHEN WE WERE LOOKING AT THAT FEATURE IN THE MAGAZINE.
NOT HOT
Not being outgoing, but being too loud is a turn-off.
I have a soft spot for slightly clumsy types that I want to protect.
OH.
OH YEAH, I REMEMBER BACK WHEN I SAID SUCH IDIOTIC THINGS.
IT WAS JUST THE OTHER DAY.

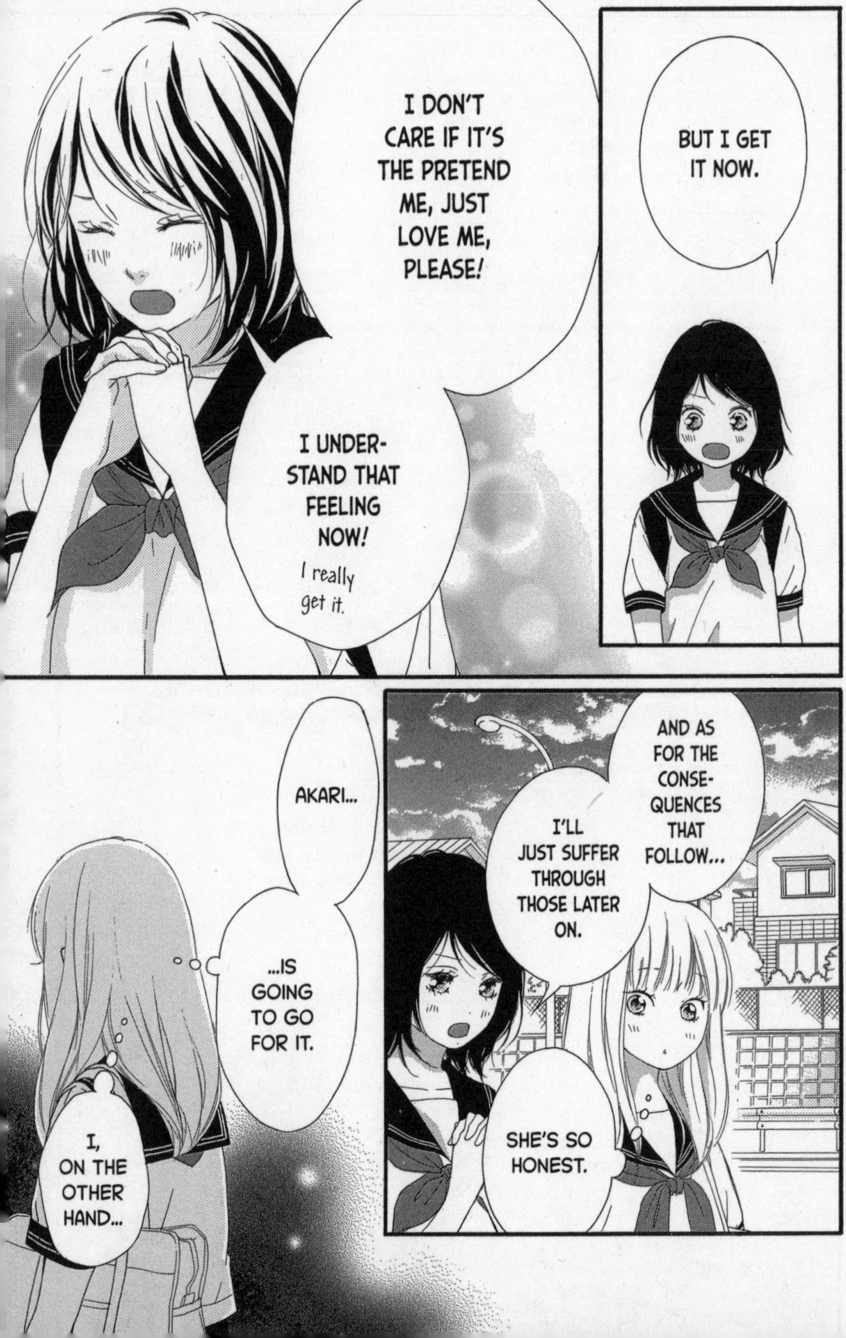
BUT I GET IT NOW.
I DON'T CARE IF IT'S THE PRETEND ME, JUST LOVE ME, PLEASE!
I UNDER-STAND THAT FEELING NOW!
I really get it.
AND AS FOR THE CONSE-QUENCES THAT FOLLOW...
I'LL JUST SUFFER THROUGH THOSE LATER ON.
SHE'S SO HONEST.
AKARI...
...IS GOING TO GO FOR IT.
I, ON THE OTHER HAND...

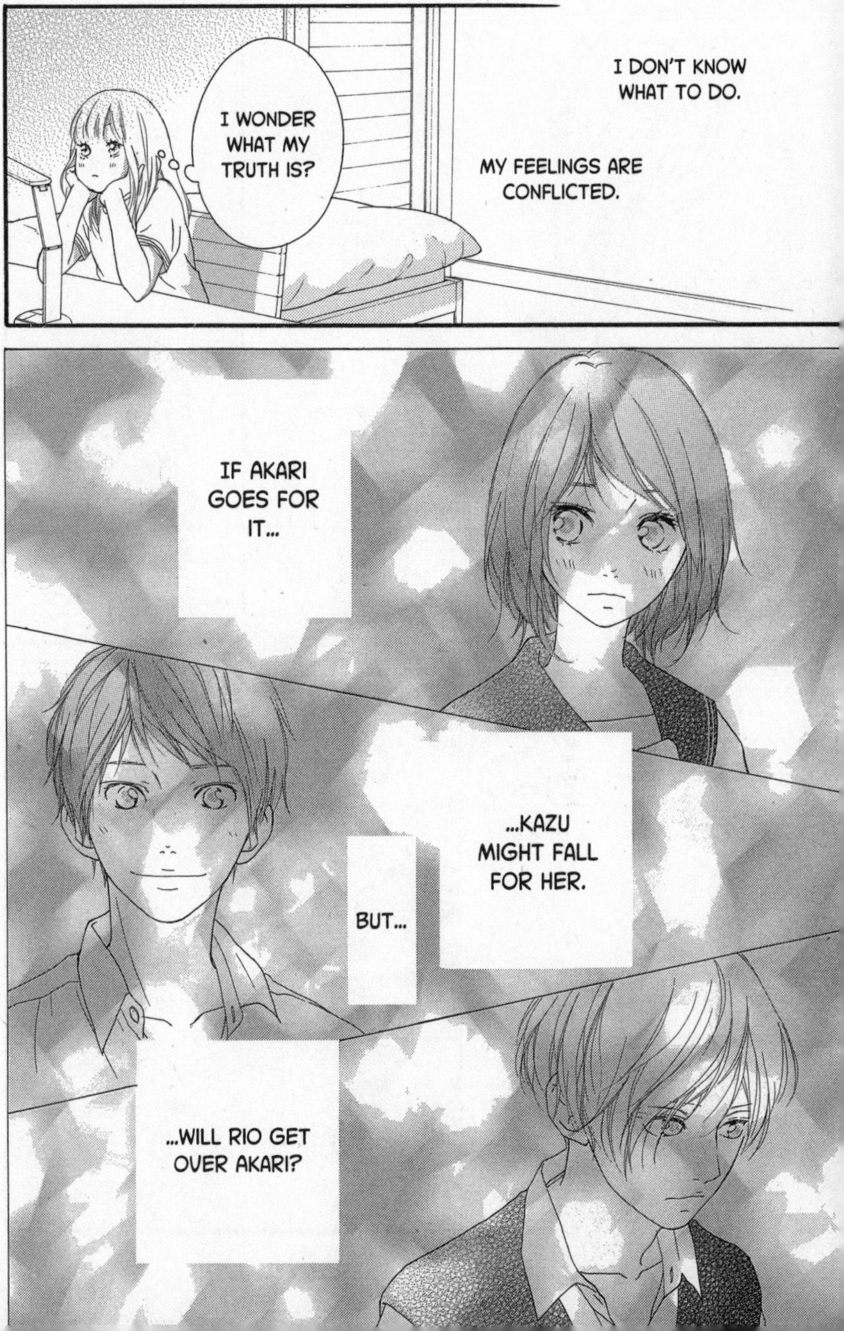
I DON'T KNOW WHAT TO DO.
MY FEELINGS ARE CONFLICTED.
I WONDER WHAT MY TRUTH IS?
IF AKARI GOES FOR IT...
...KAZU MIGHT FALL FOR HER.
BUT...
...WILL RIO GET OVER AKARI?

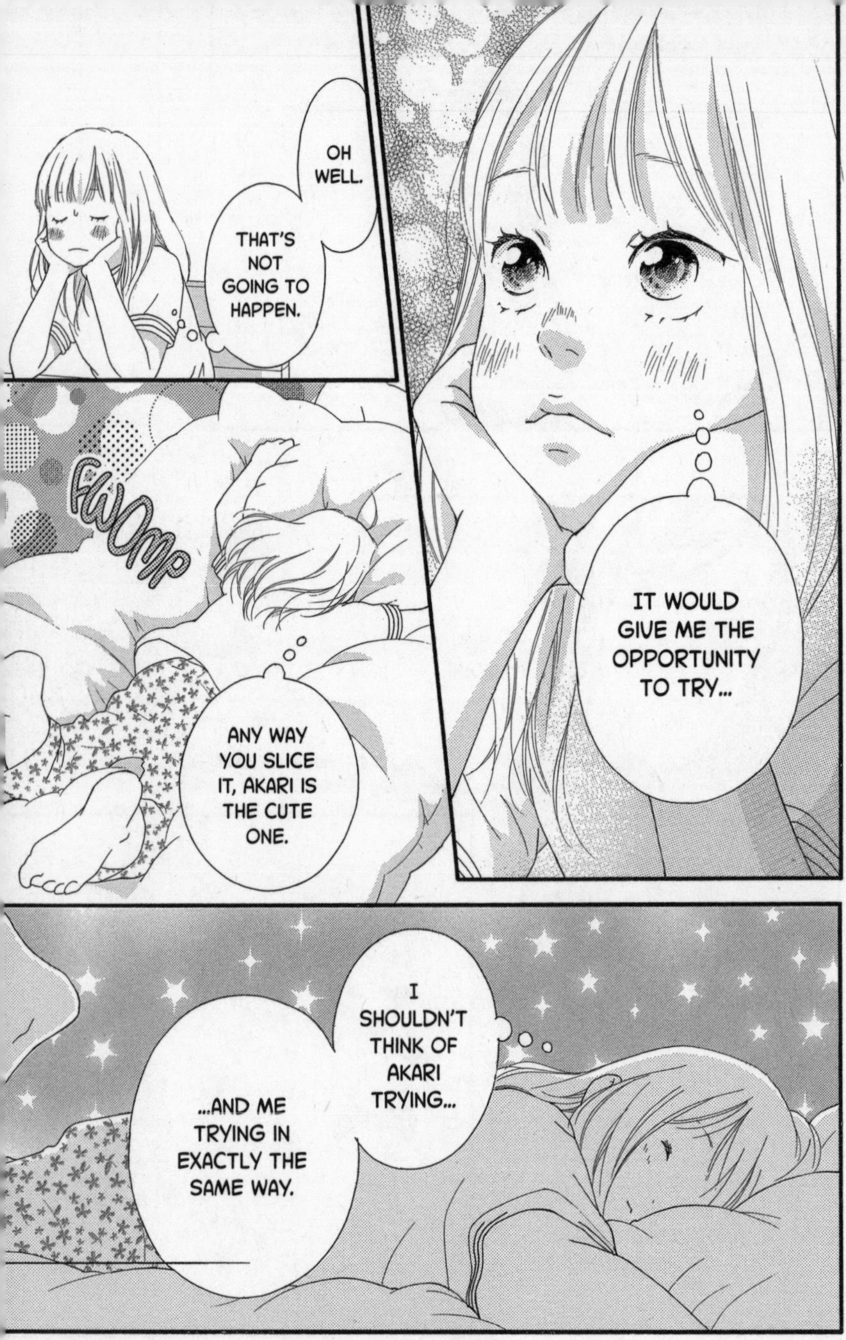
IT WOULD GIVE ME THE OPPORTUNITY TO TRY...
OH WELL.
THAT'S NOT GOING TO HAPPEN.
FWOMP
ANY WAY YOU SLICE IT, AKARI IS THE CUTE ONE.
I SHOULDN'T THINK OF AKARI TRYING...
...AND ME TRYING IN EXACTLY THE SAME WAY.

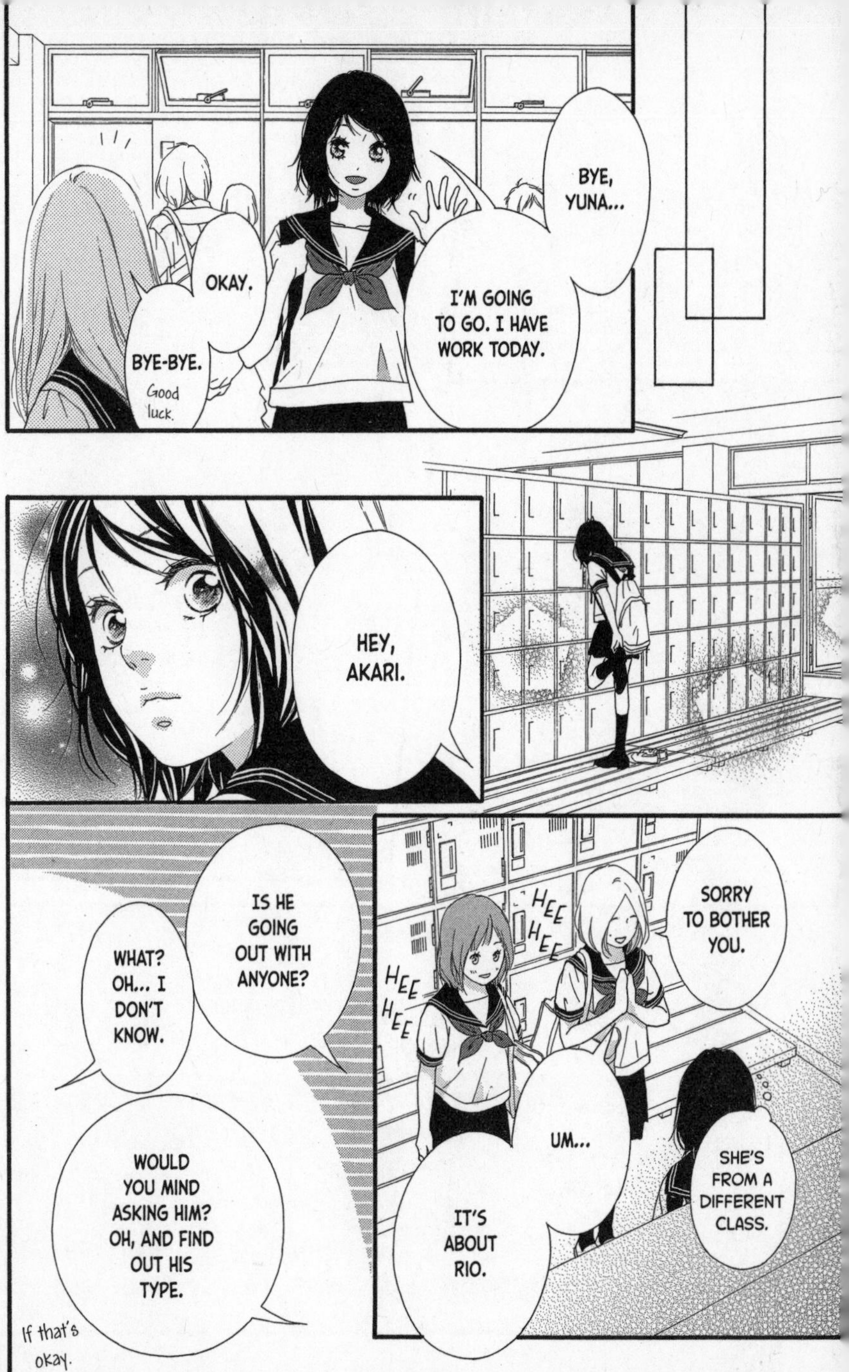
BYE, YUNA...
I'M GOING TO GO. I HAVE WORK TODAY.
OKAY.
BYE-BYE.
Good luck.
HEY, AKARI.
SORRY TO BOTHER YOU.
HEE HEE
HEE HEE
SHE'S FROM A DIFFERENT CLASS.
UM...
IT'S ABOUT RIO.
IS HE GOING OUT WITH ANYONE?
WHAT? OH... I DON'T KNOW.
WOULD YOU MIND ASKING HIM? OH, AND FIND OUT HIS TYPE.
If that's okay.

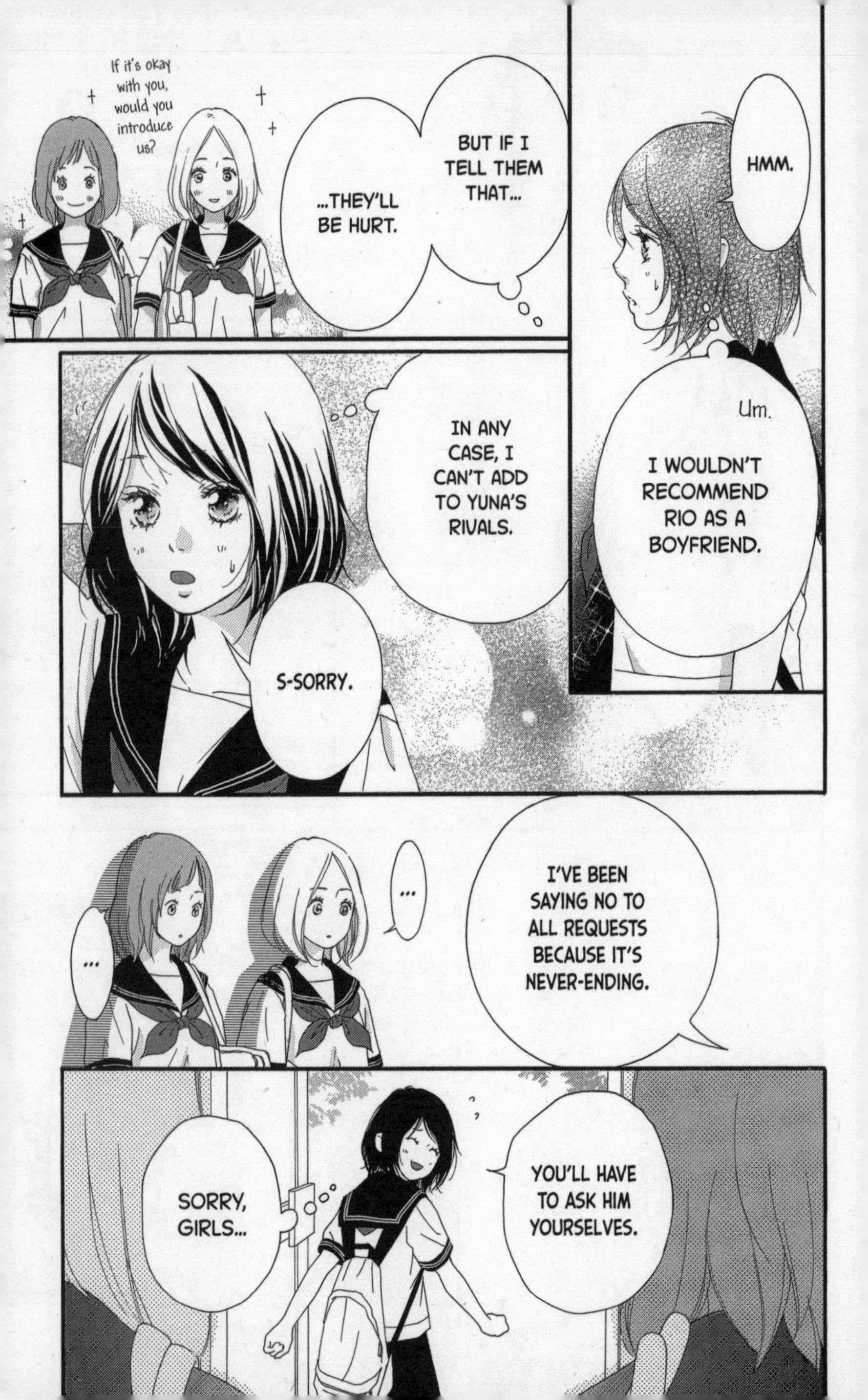
HMM.
Um.
I WOULDN'T RECOMMEND RIO AS A BOYFRIEND.
If it's okay with you, would you introduce us?
BUT IF I TELL THEM THAT...
...THEY'LL BE HURT.
IN ANY CASE, I CAN'T ADD TO YUNA'S RIVALS.
S-SORRY.
I'VE BEEN SAYING NO TO ALL REQUESTS BECAUSE IT'S NEVER-ENDING.
...
...
YOU'LL HAVE TO ASK HIM YOURSELVES.
SORRY, GIRLS...

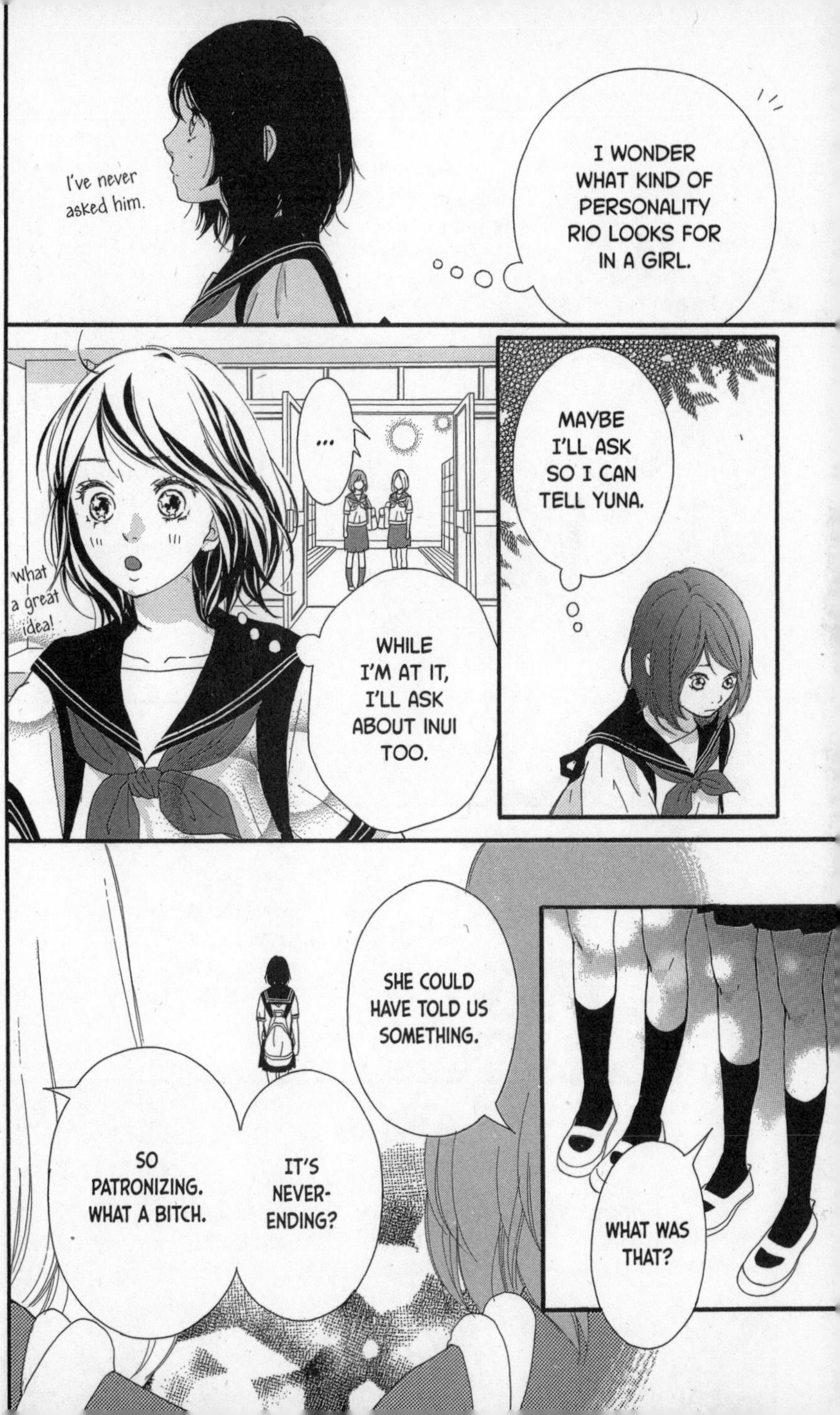
I WONDER WHAT KIND OF PERSONALITY RIO LOOKS FOR IN A GIRL.
I've never asked him.
MAYBE I'LL ASK SO I CAN TELL YUNA.
...
WHILE I'M AT IT, I'LL ASK ABOUT INUI TOO.
What a great idea!
WHAT WAS THAT?
SHE COULD HAVE TOLD US SOMETHING.
IT'S NEVER-ENDING?
SO PATRONIZING. WHAT A BITCH.

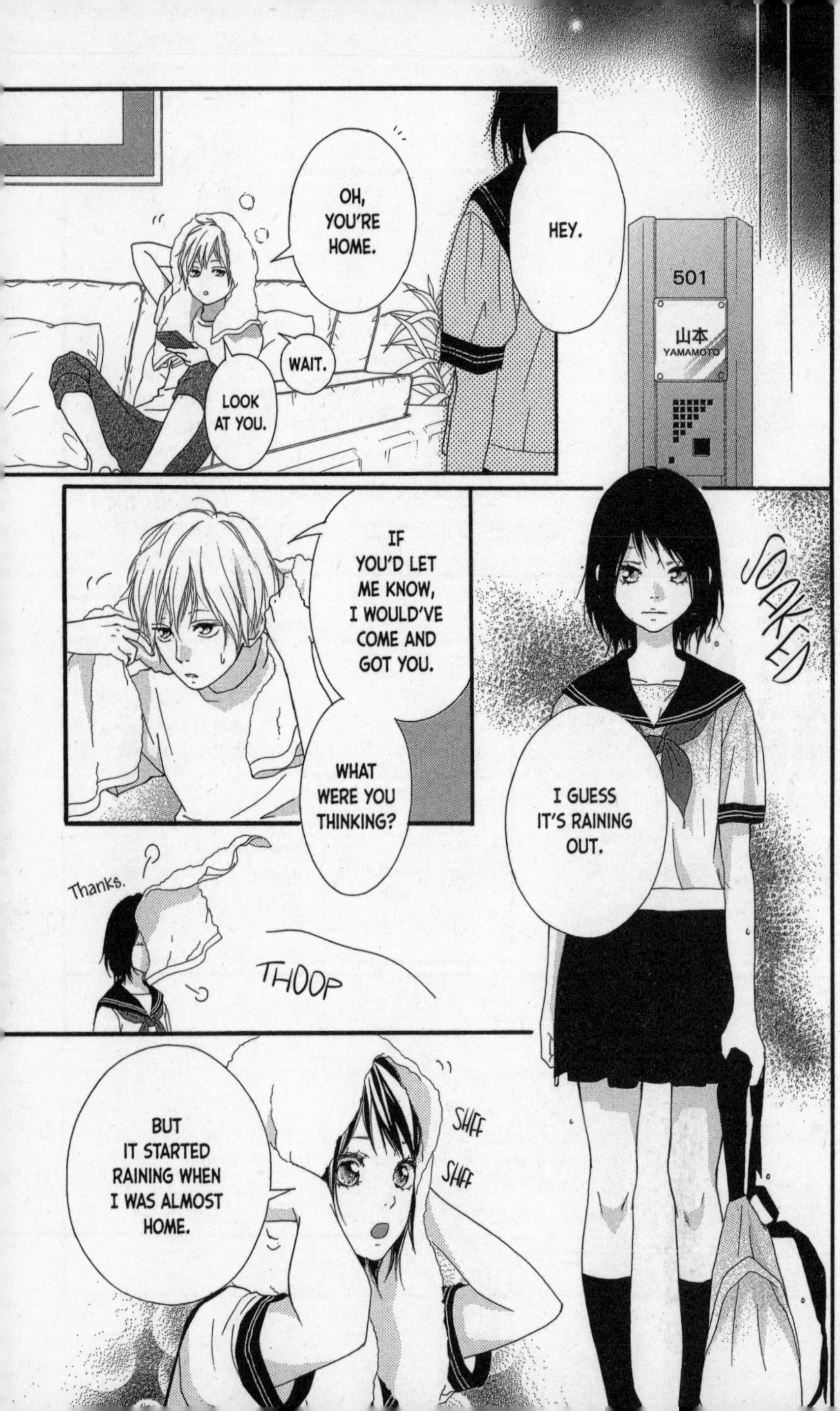
501
山本
YAMAMOTO
HEY.
OH, YOU'RE HOME.
WAIT.
LOOK AT YOU.
SOAKED
I GUESS IT'S RAINING OUT.
IF YOU'D LET ME KNOW, I WOULD'VE COME AND GOT YOU.
WHAT WERE YOU THINKING?
Thanks.
THOOP
BUT IT STARTED RAINING WHEN I WAS ALMOST HOME.
SHFF
SHFF

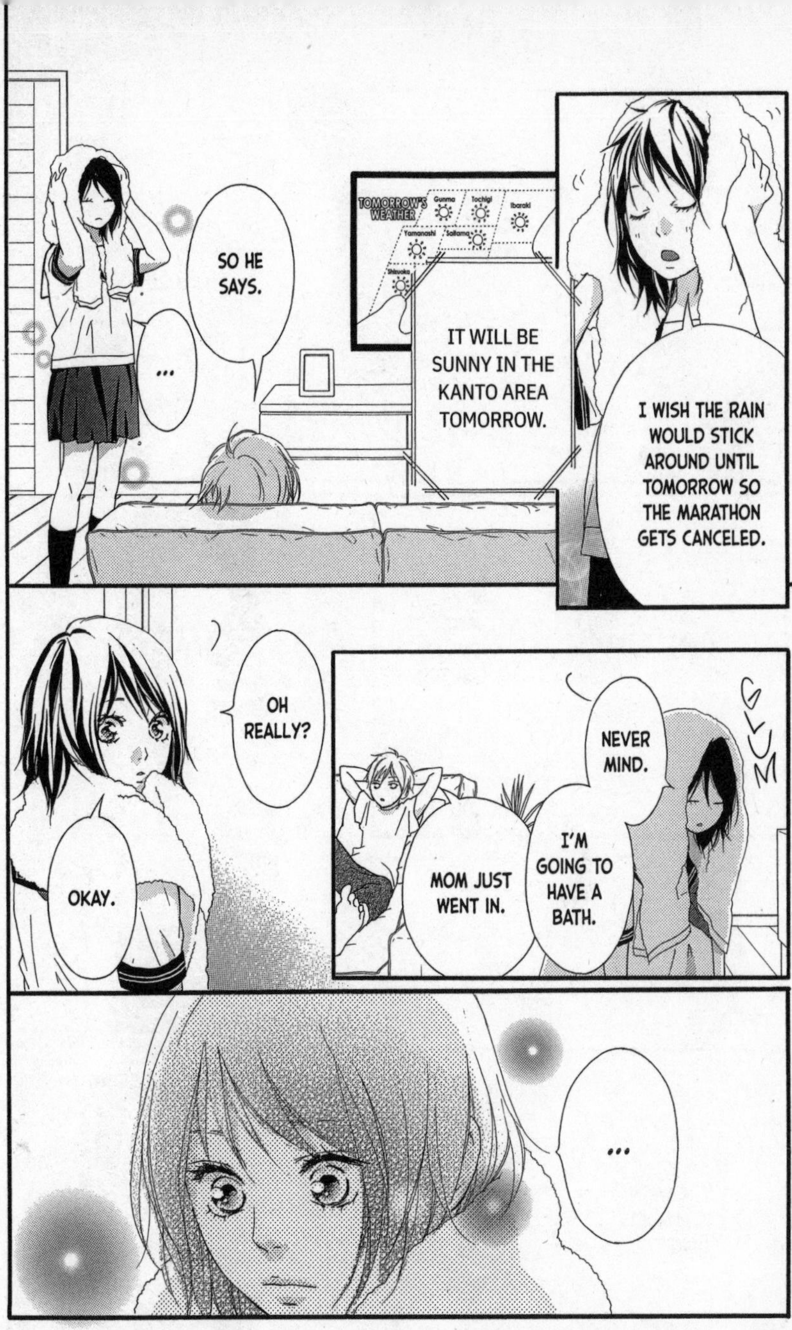
I WISH THE RAIN WOULD STICK AROUND UNTIL TOMORROW SO THE MARATHON GETS CANCELED.
TOMORROW'S WEATHER
Gunma
Tochigi
Ibaraki
Yamanashi
Saitama
Shizuoka
IT WILL BE SUNNY IN THE KANTO AREA TOMORROW.
SO HE SAYS.
...
GLUM
NEVER MIND.
I'M GOING TO HAVE A BATH.
MOM JUST WENT IN.
OH REALLY?
OKAY.
...

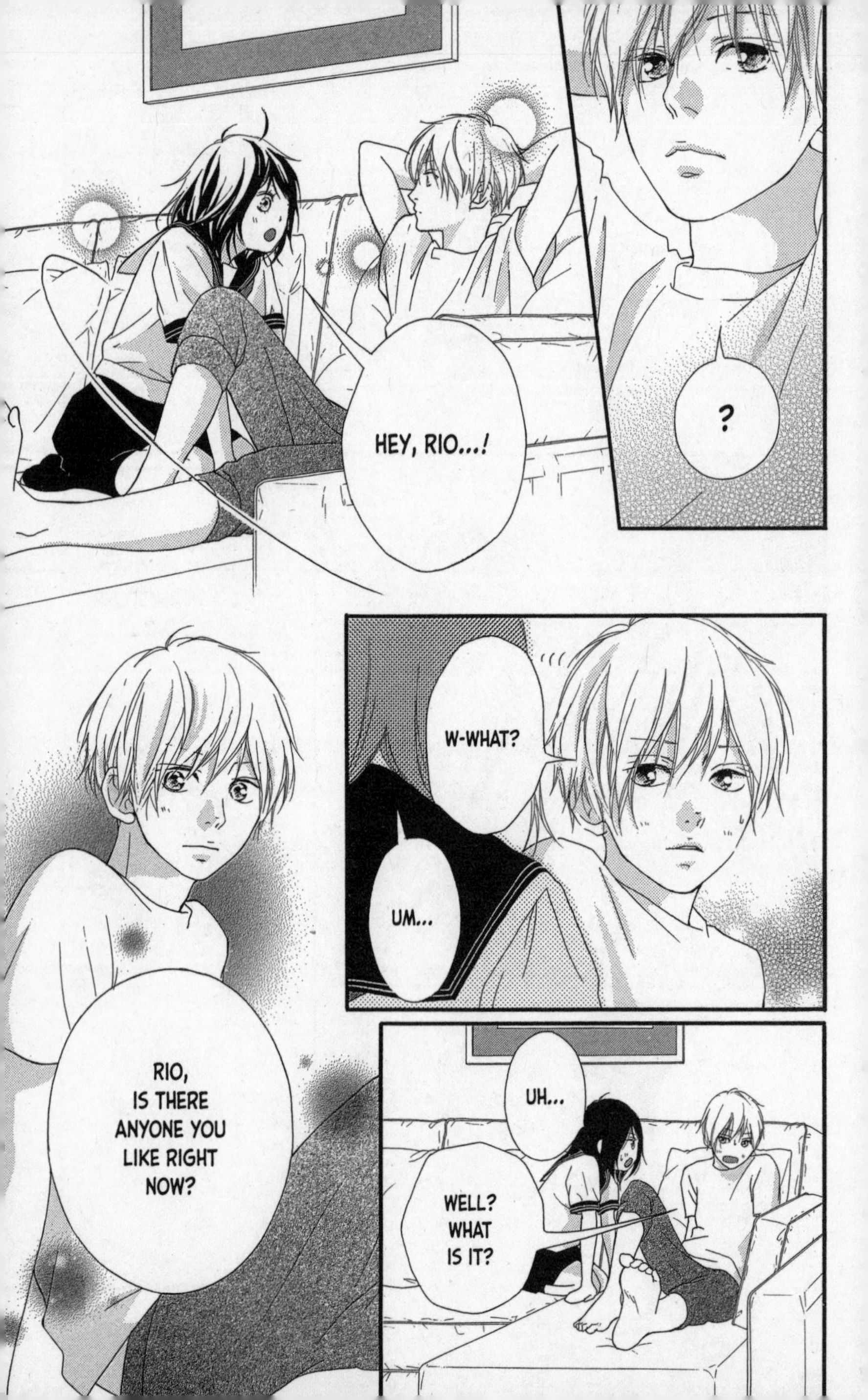
?
HEY, RIO...!
W-WHAT?
UM...
UH...
WELL? WHAT IS IT?
RIO, IS THERE ANYONE YOU LIKE RIGHT NOW?

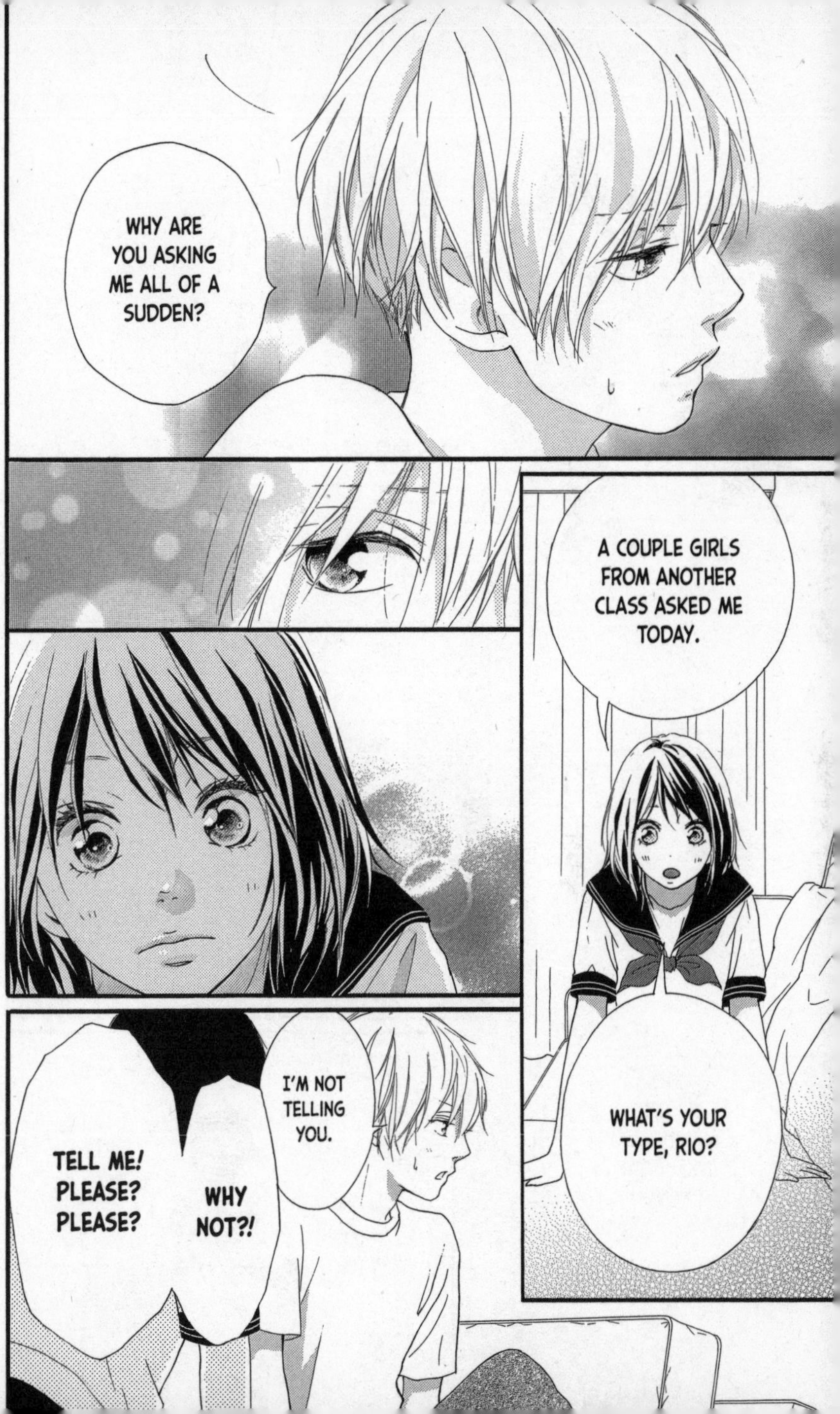
WHY ARE YOU ASKING ME ALL OF A SUDDEN?
A COUPLE GIRLS FROM ANOTHER CLASS ASKED ME TODAY.
WHAT'S YOUR TYPE, RIO?
I'M NOT TELLING YOU.
WHY NOT?!
TELL ME! PLEASE? PLEASE?

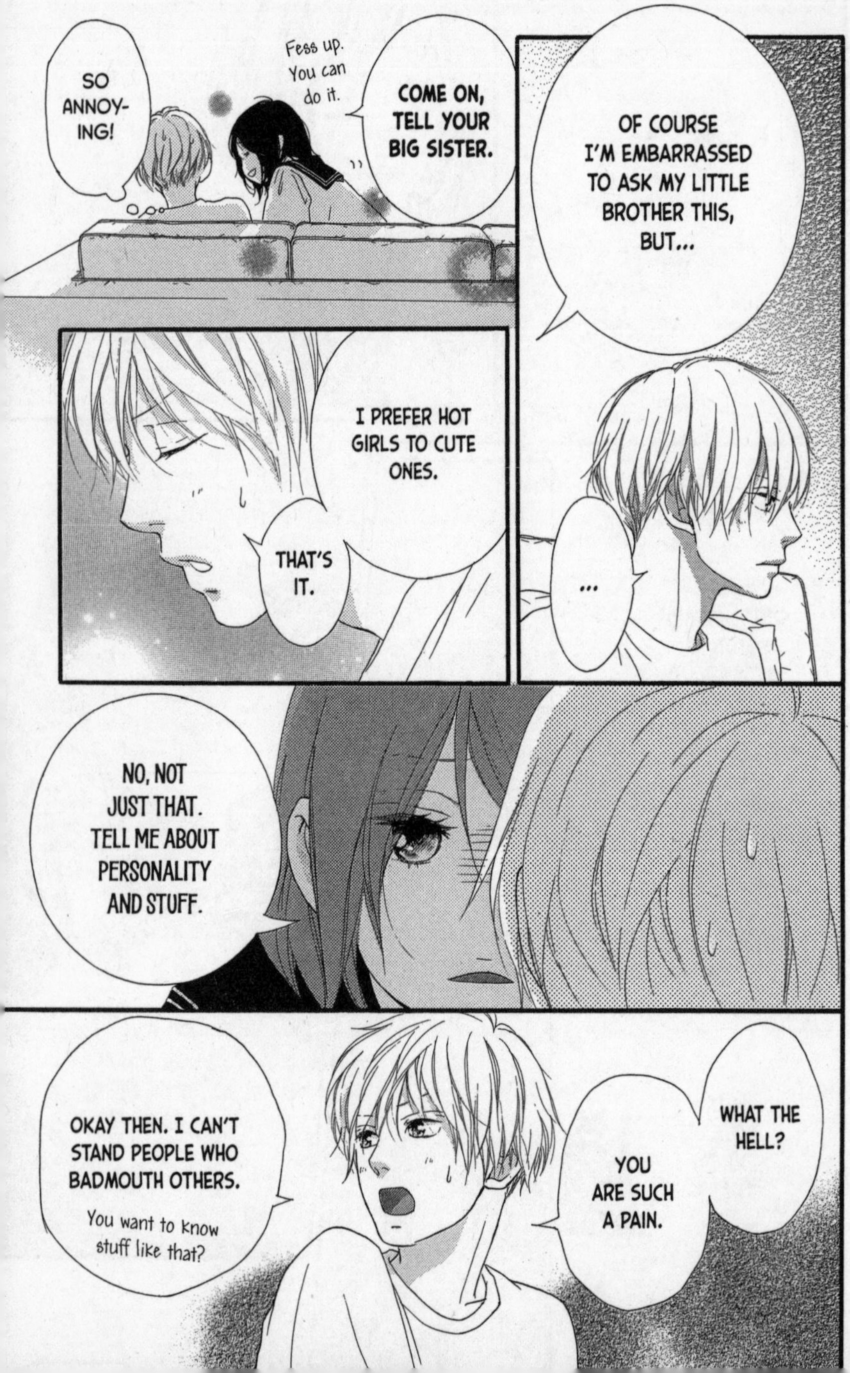
OF COURSE I'M EMBARRASSED TO ASK MY LITTLE BROTHER THIS, BUT...
...
COME ON, TELL YOUR BIG SISTER.
Fess up. You can do it.
SO ANNOY-ING!
I PREFER HOT GIRLS TO CUTE ONES.
THAT'S IT.
NO, NOT JUST THAT. TELL ME ABOUT PERSONALITY AND STUFF.
WHAT THE HELL?
YOU ARE SUCH A PAIN.
OKAY THEN. I CAN'T STAND PEOPLE WHO BADMOUTH OTHERS.
You want to know stuff like that?

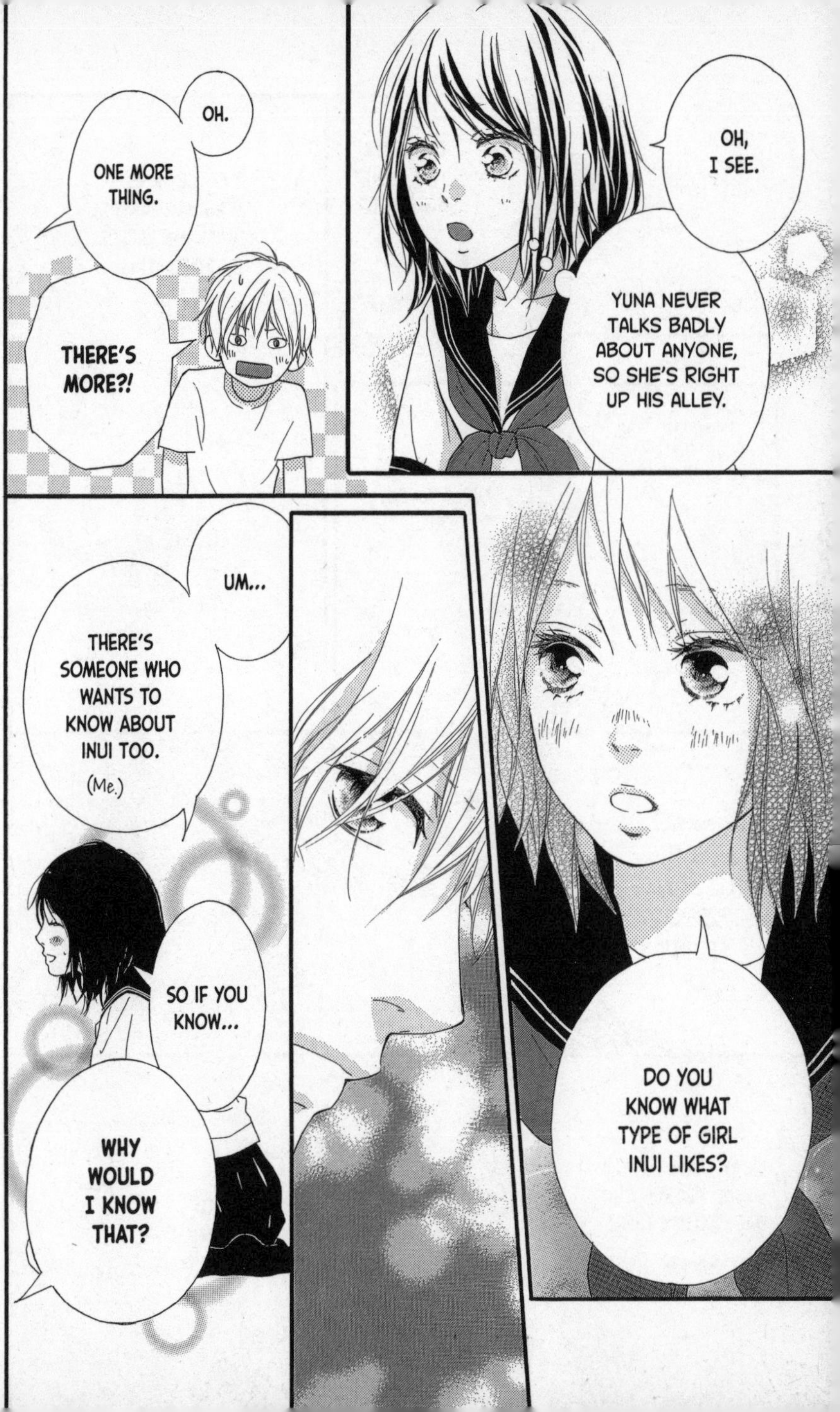
OH, I SEE.
YUNA NEVER TALKS BADLY ABOUT ANYONE, SO SHE'S RIGHT UP HIS ALLEY.
OH.
ONE MORE THING.
THERE'S MORE?!
DO YOU KNOW WHAT TYPE OF GIRL INUI LIKES?
UM...
THERE'S SOMEONE WHO WANTS TO KNOW ABOUT INUI TOO.
(Me.)
SO IF YOU KNOW...
WHY WOULD I KNOW THAT?

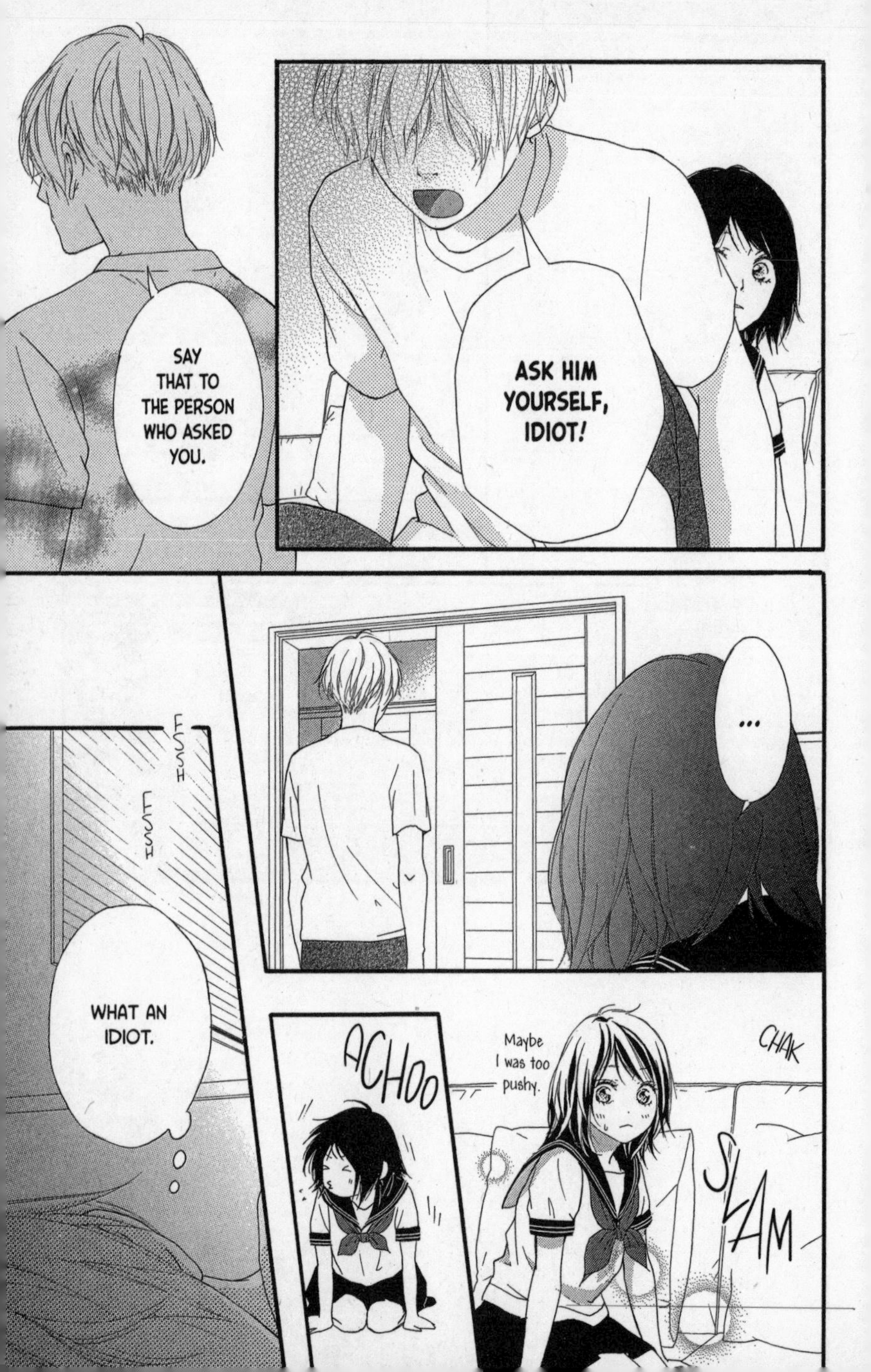
ASK HIM YOURSELF, IDIOT!
SAY THAT TO THE PERSON WHO ASKED YOU.
...
CHAK
SLAM
Maybe I was too pushy.
ACHOO
FSSH
FSSH
WHAT AN IDIOT.

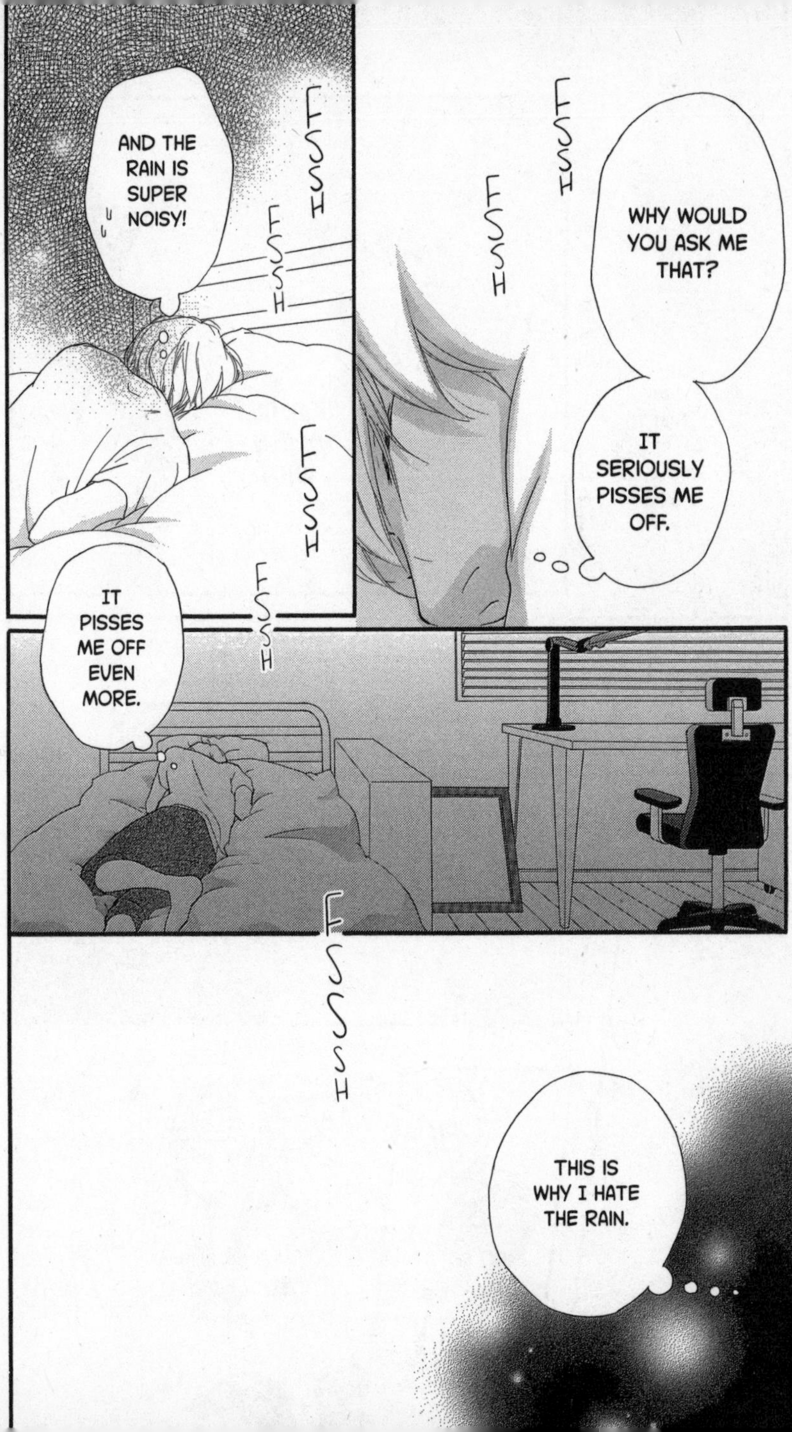
FSSH
FSSH
WHY WOULD YOU ASK ME THAT?
IT SERIOUSLY PISSES ME OFF.
FSSH
FSSH
AND THE RAIN IS SUPER NOISY!
FSSH
FSSH
IT PISSES ME OFF EVEN MORE.
FSSH
THIS IS WHY I HATE THE RAIN.

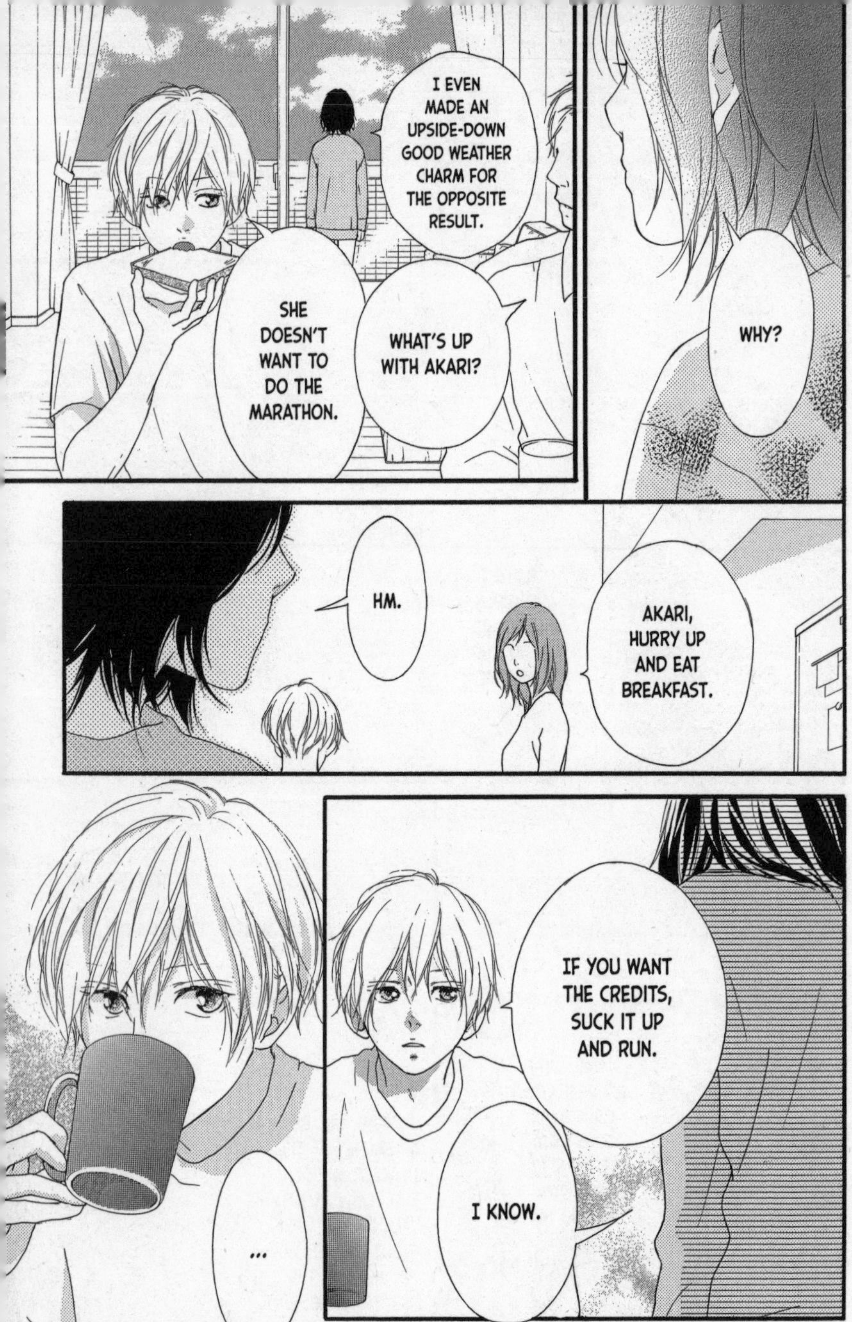
WHY?
I EVEN MADE AN UPSIDE-DOWN GOOD WEATHER CHARM FOR THE OPPOSITE RESULT.
WHAT'S UP WITH AKARI?
SHE DOESN'T WANT TO DO THE MARATHON.
AKARI, HURRY UP AND EAT BREAKFAST.
HM.
IF YOU WANT THE CREDITS, SUCK IT UP AND RUN.
I KNOW.
...

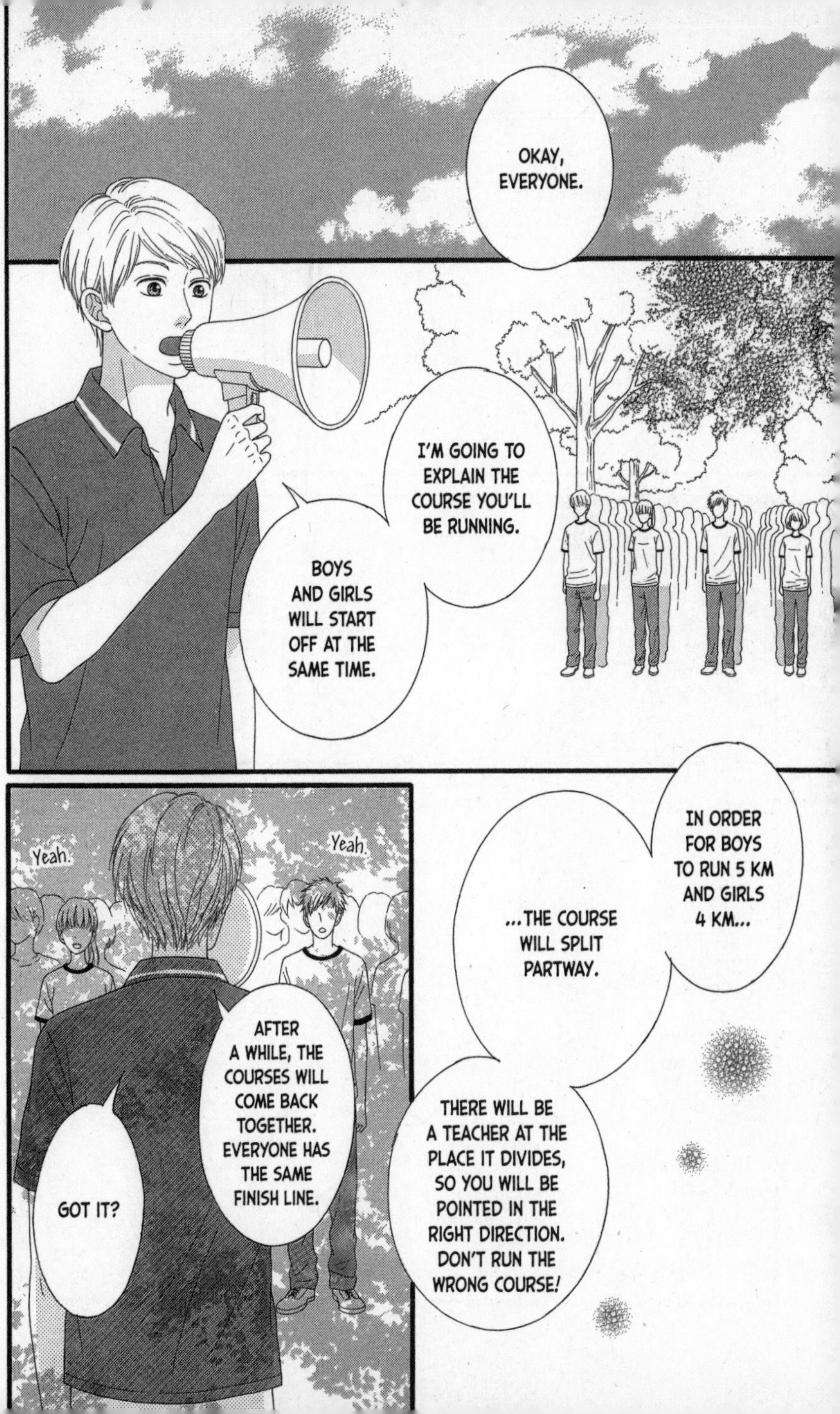
OKAY, EVERYONE.
I'M GOING TO EXPLAIN THE COURSE YOU'LL BE RUNNING.
BOYS AND GIRLS WILL START OFF AT THE SAME TIME.
IN ORDER FOR BOYS TO RUN 5 KM AND GIRLS 4 KM...
...THE COURSE WILL SPLIT PARTWAY.
THERE WILL BE A TEACHER AT THE PLACE IT DIVIDES, SO YOU WILL BE POINTED IN THE RIGHT DIRECTION. DON'T RUN THE WRONG COURSE!
Yeah.
Yeah.
AFTER A WHILE, THE COURSES WILL COME BACK TOGETHER. EVERYONE HAS THE SAME FINISH LINE.
GOT IT?

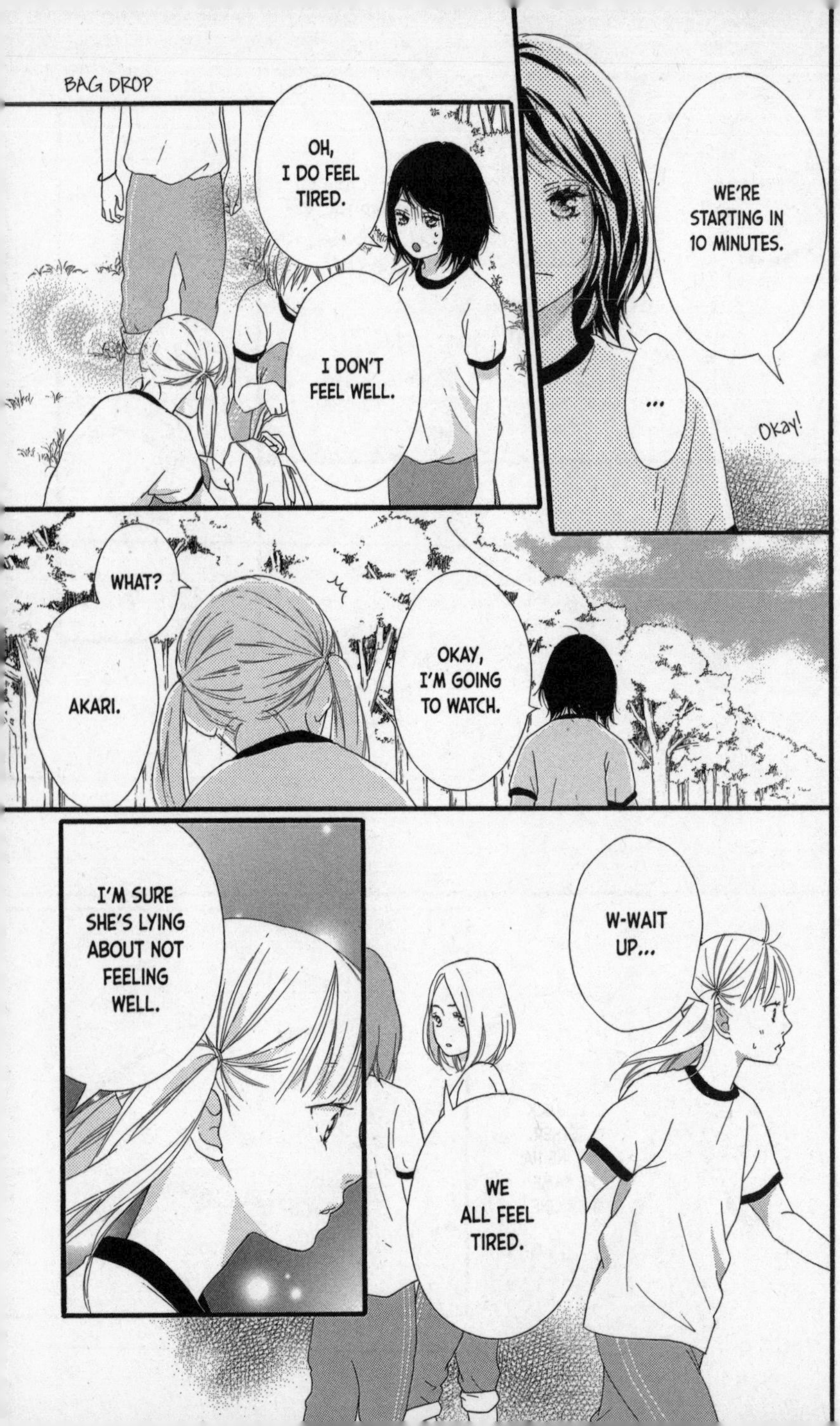
WE'RE STARTING IN 10 MINUTES.
...
Okay!
BAG DROP
OH, I DO FEEL TIRED.
I DON'T FEEL WELL.
OKAY, I'M GOING TO WATCH.
WHAT?
AKARI.
W-WAIT UP...
WE ALL FEEL TIRED.
I'M SURE SHE'S LYING ABOUT NOT FEELING WELL.

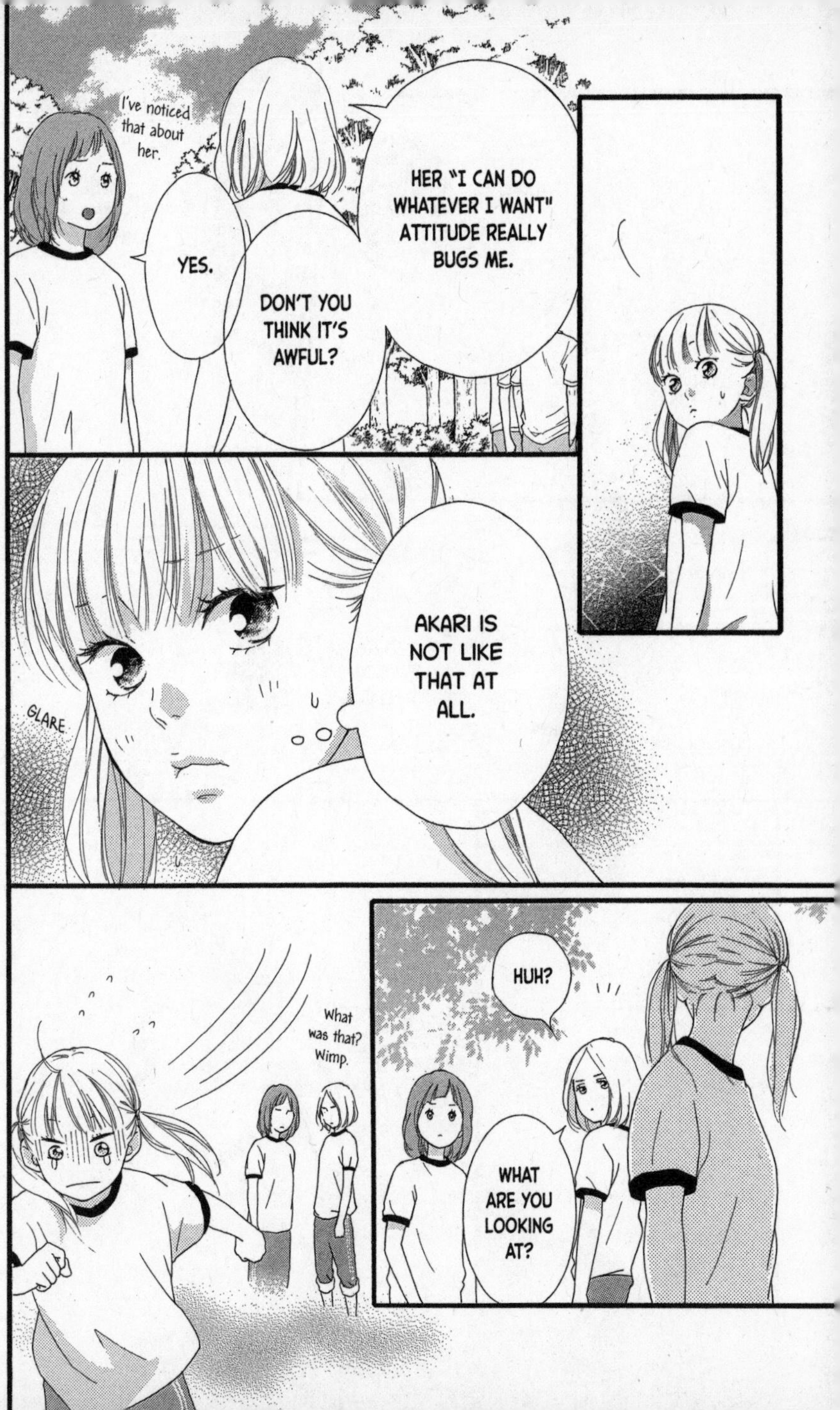
HER "I CAN DO WHATEVER I WANT" ATTITUDE REALLY BUGS ME.
DON'T YOU THINK IT'S AWFUL?
YES.
I've noticed that about her.
AKARI IS NOT LIKE THAT AT ALL.
GLARE
HUH?
WHAT ARE YOU LOOKING AT?
What was that? Wimp.

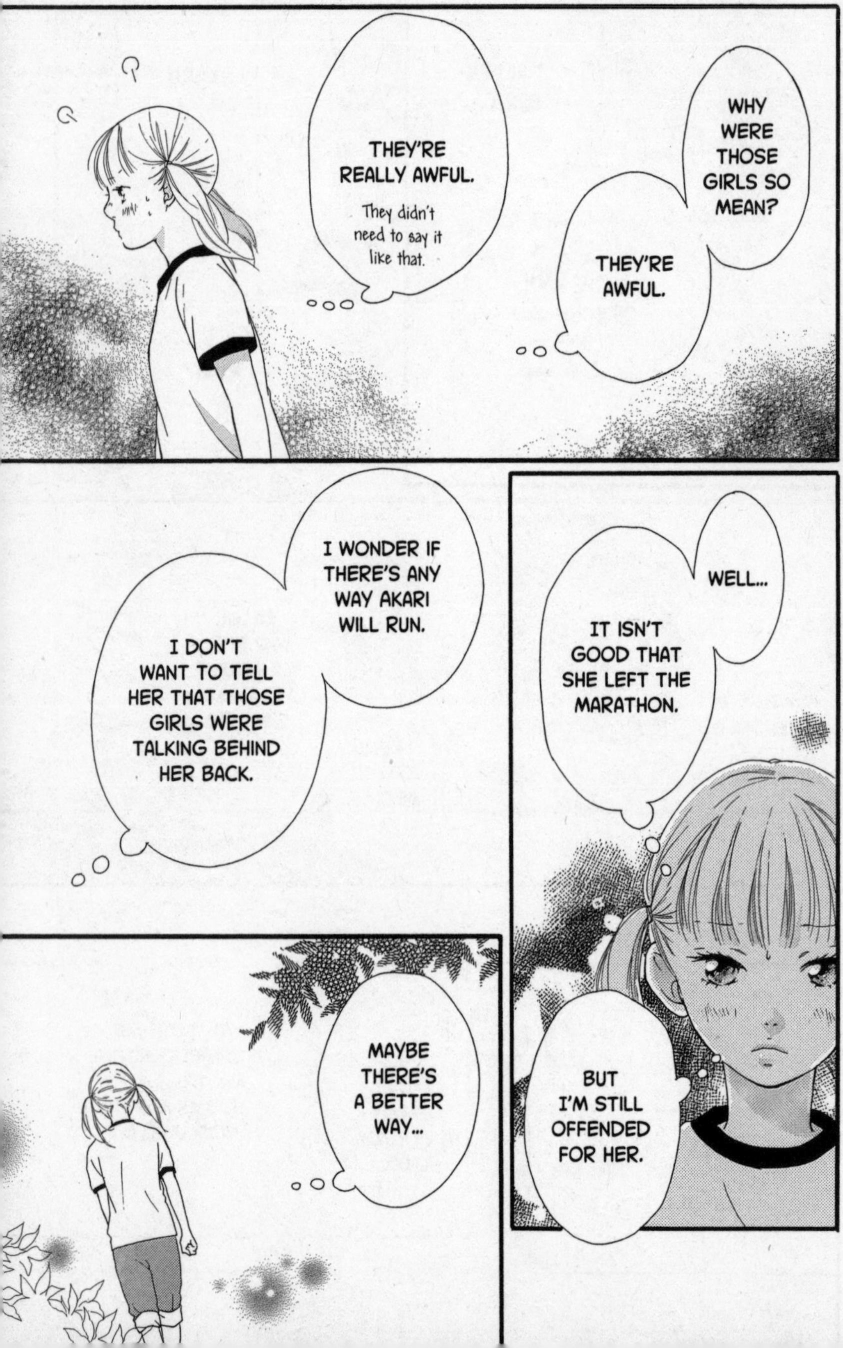
WHY WERE THOSE GIRLS SO MEAN?
THEY'RE AWFUL.
THEY'RE REALLY AWFUL.
They didn't need to say it like that.
WELL...
IT ISN'T GOOD THAT SHE LEFT THE MARATHON.
BUT I'M STILL OFFENDED FOR HER.
I WONDER IF THERE'S ANY WAY AKARI WILL RUN.
I DON'T WANT TO TELL HER THAT THOSE GIRLS WERE TALKING BEHIND HER BACK.
MAYBE THERE'S A BETTER WAY...

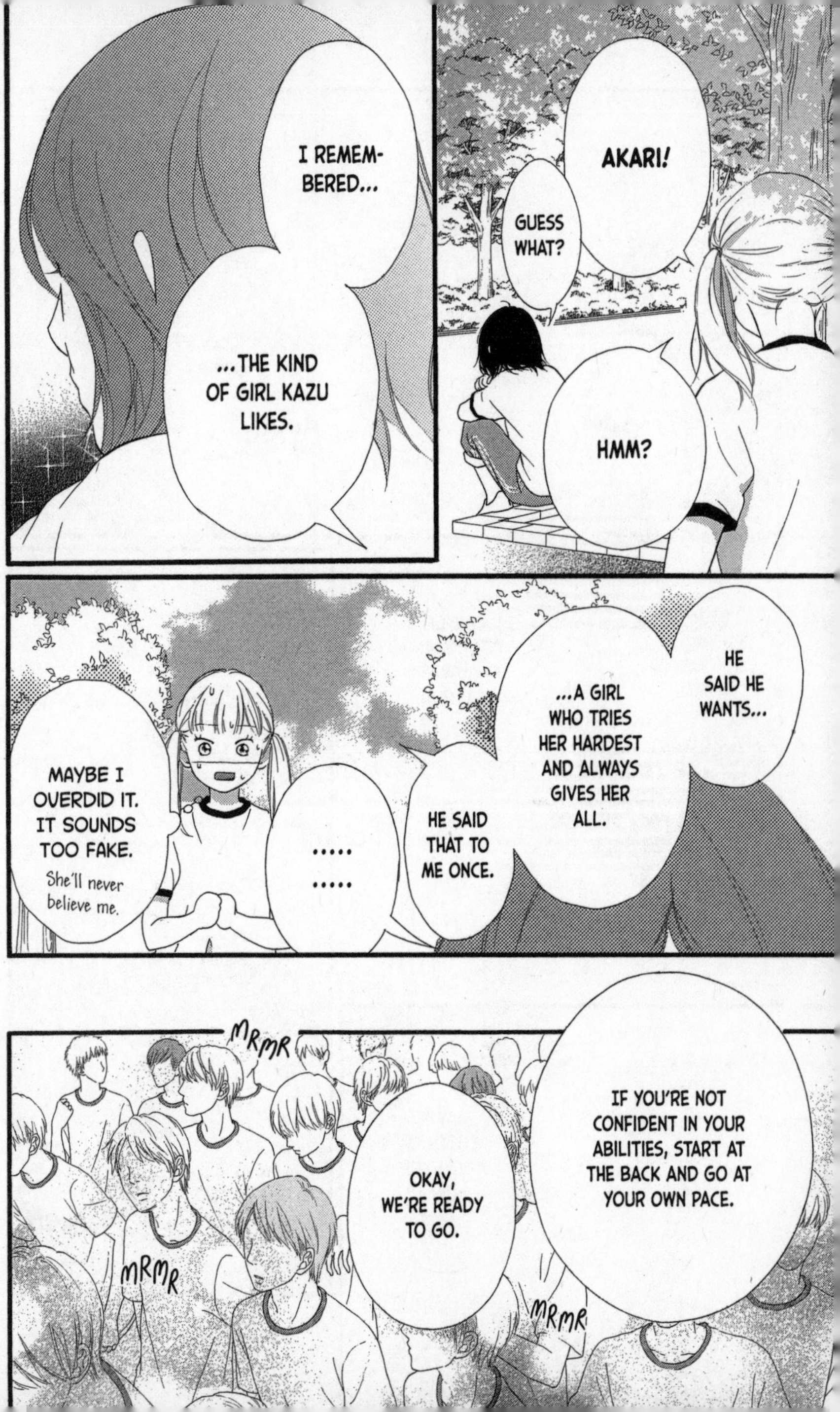
AKARI!
GUESS WHAT?
HMM?
I REMEM-BERED...
...THE KIND OF GIRL KAZU LIKES.
HE SAID HE WANTS...
...A GIRL WHO TRIES HER HARDEST AND ALWAYS GIVES HER ALL.
HE SAID THAT TO ME ONCE.
....
MAYBE I OVERDID IT. IT SOUNDS TOO FAKE.
She'll never believe me.
MRMR
IF YOU'RE NOT CONFIDENT IN YOUR ABILITIES, START AT THE BACK AND GO AT YOUR OWN PACE.
OKAY, WE'RE READY TO GO.
MRMR
MRMR

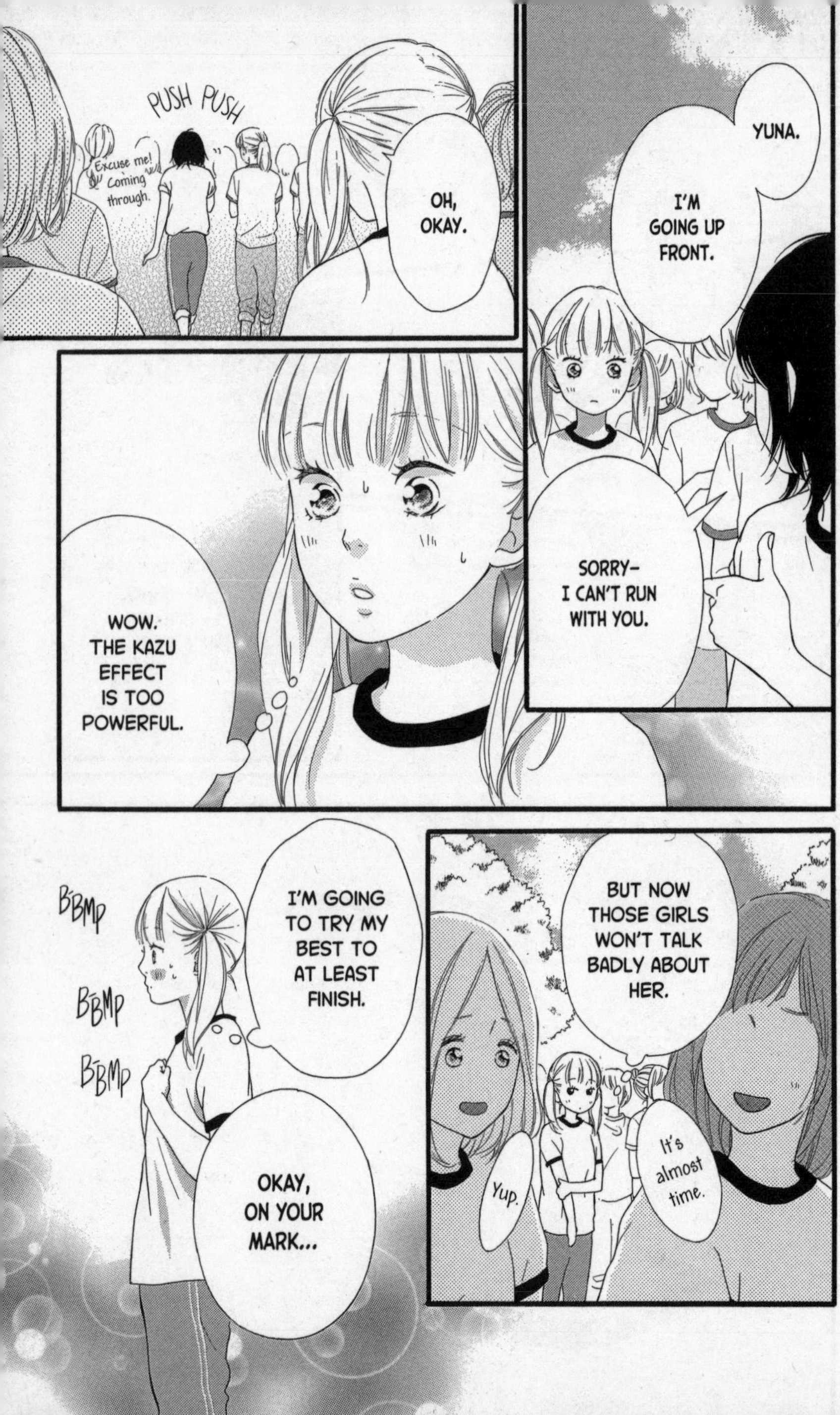
YUNA.
I'M GOING UP FRONT.
SORRY— I CAN'T RUN WITH YOU.
PUSH PUSH
Excuse me! Coming through.
OH, OKAY.
WOW. THE KAZU EFFECT IS TOO POWERFUL.
BUT NOW THOSE GIRLS WON'T TALK BADLY ABOUT HER.
It's almost time.
Yup.
B-BMP
B-BMP
B-BMP
I'M GOING TO TRY MY BEST TO AT LEAST FINISH.
OKAY, ON YOUR MARK...

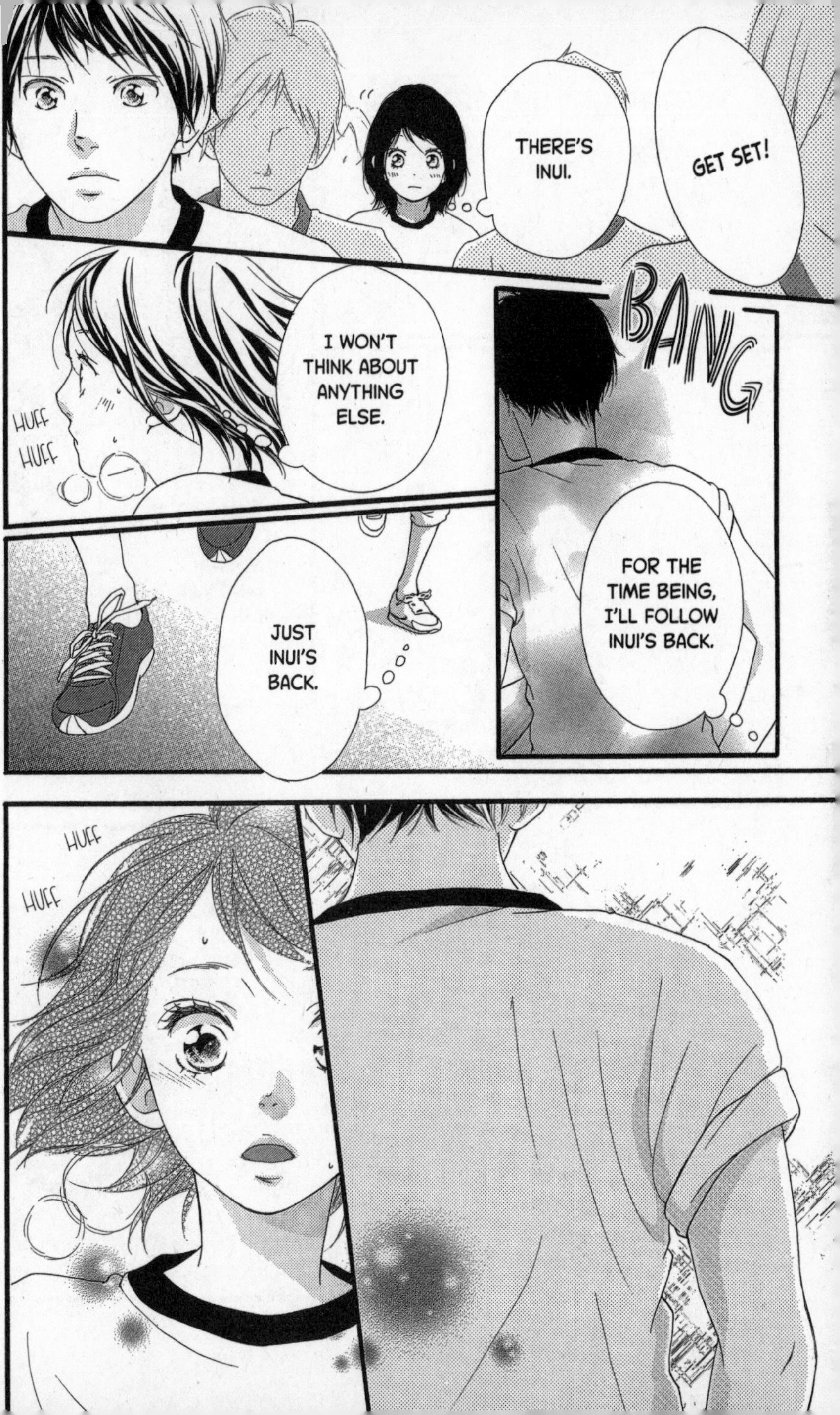
GET SET!
THERE'S INUI.
BANG
FOR THE TIME BEING, I'LL FOLLOW INUI'S BACK.
I WON'T THINK ABOUT ANYTHING ELSE.
HUFF HUFF
JUST INUI'S BACK.
HUFF HUFF

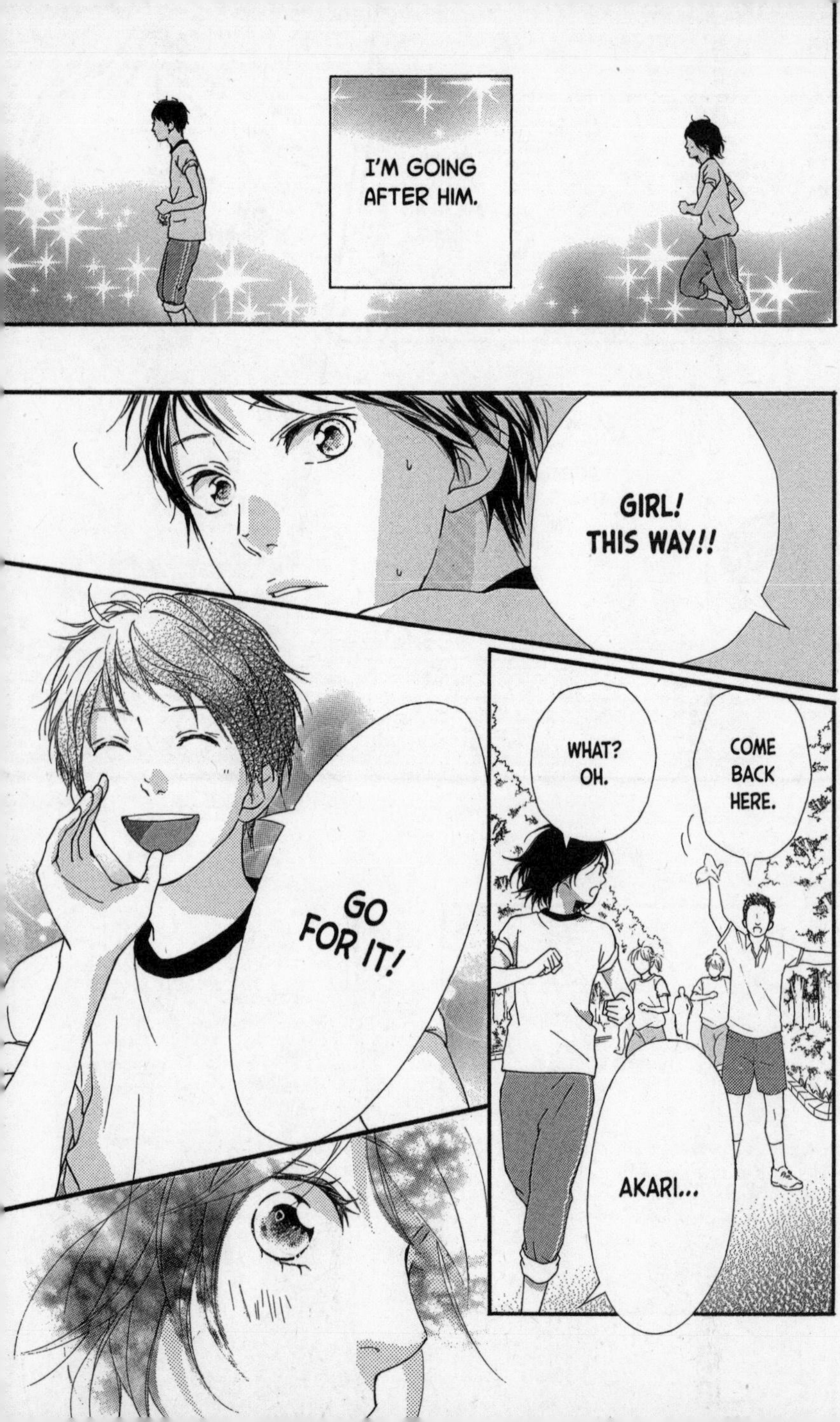
I'M GOING AFTER HIM.
GIRL! THIS WAY!!
COME BACK HERE.
WHAT? OH.
AKARI...
GO FOR IT!

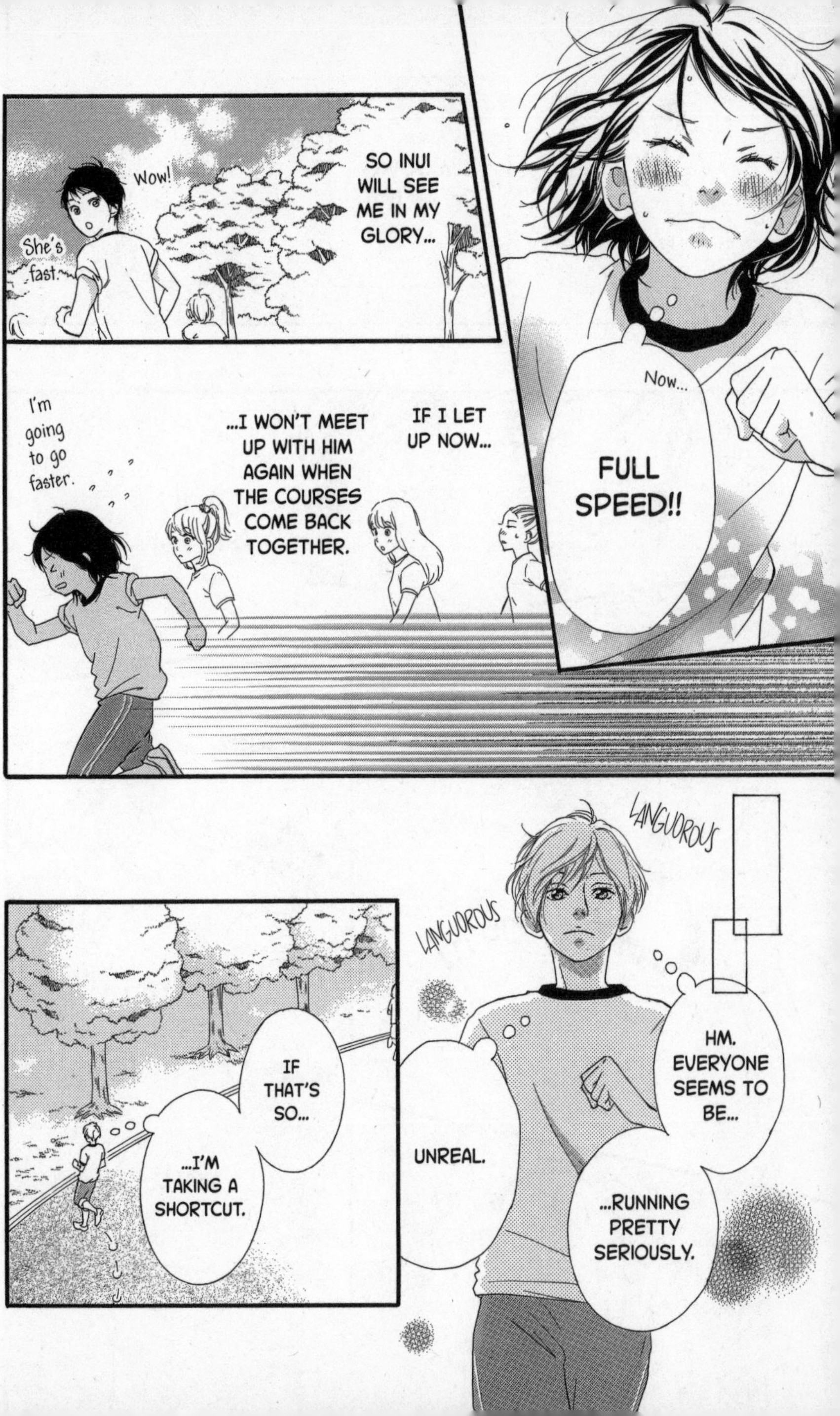
Now...
FULL SPEED!!
SO INUI WILL SEE ME IN MY GLORY...
Wow!
She's fast.
IF I LET UP NOW...
...I WON'T MEET UP WITH HIM AGAIN WHEN THE COURSES COME BACK TOGETHER.
I'm going to go faster.
LANGUOROUS
LANGUOROUS
HM. EVERYONE SEEMS TO BE...
...RUNNING PRETTY SERIOUSLY.
UNREAL.
IF THAT'S SO...
...I'M TAKING A SHORTCUT.

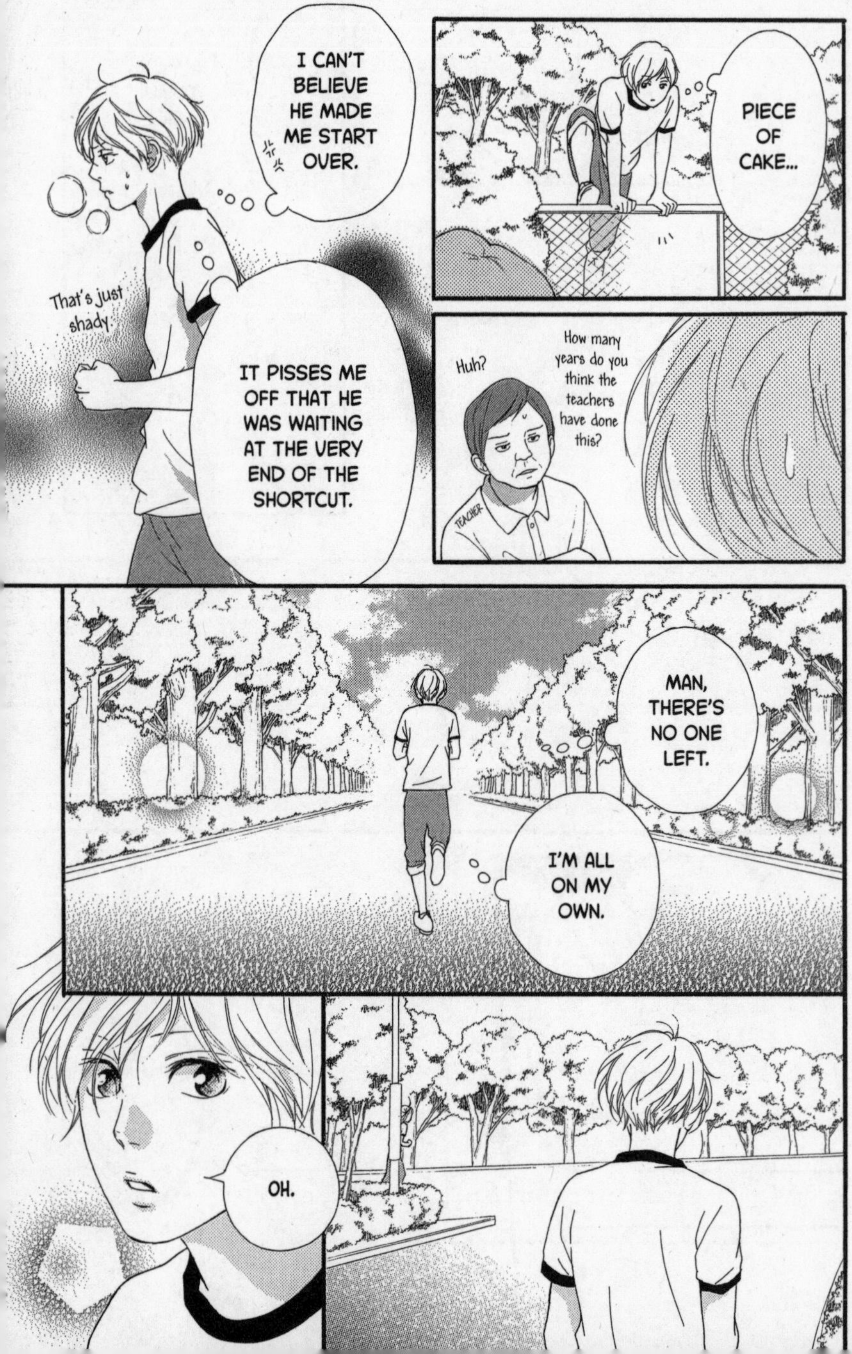
PIECE OF CAKE...
How many years do you think the teachers have done this?
Huh?
TEACHER
I CAN'T BELIEVE HE MADE ME START OVER.
IT PISSES ME OFF THAT HE WAS WAITING AT THE VERY END OF THE SHORTCUT.
That's just shady.
MAN, THERE'S NO ONE LEFT.
I'M ALL ON MY OWN.
OH.

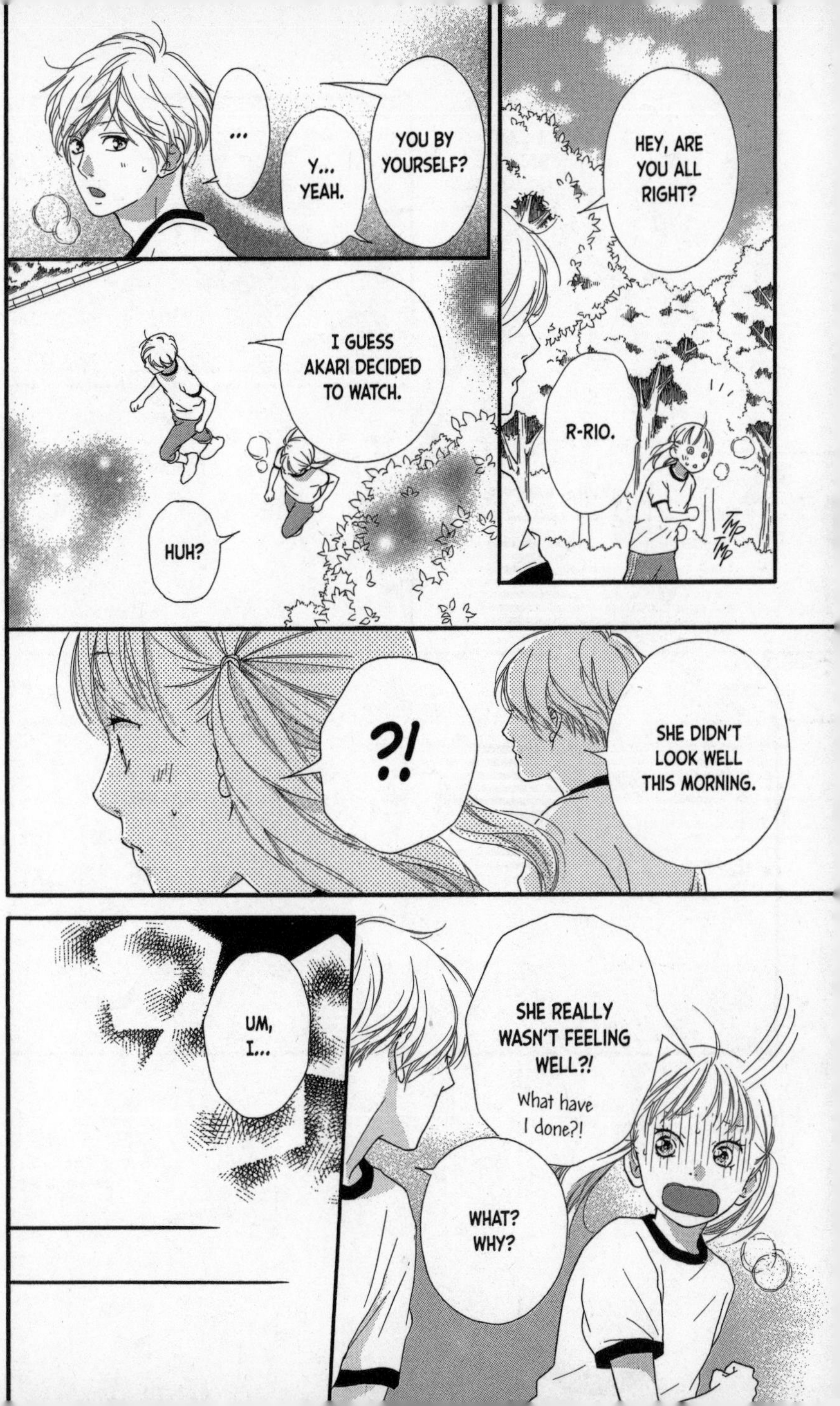
HEY, ARE YOU ALL RIGHT?
R-RIO.
TMP TMP
YOU BY YOURSELF?
Y... YEAH.
...
I GUESS AKARI DECIDED TO WATCH.
HUH?
SHE DIDN'T LOOK WELL THIS MORNING.
?!
SHE REALLY WASN'T FEELING WELL?!
What have I done?!
WHAT? WHY?
UM, I...

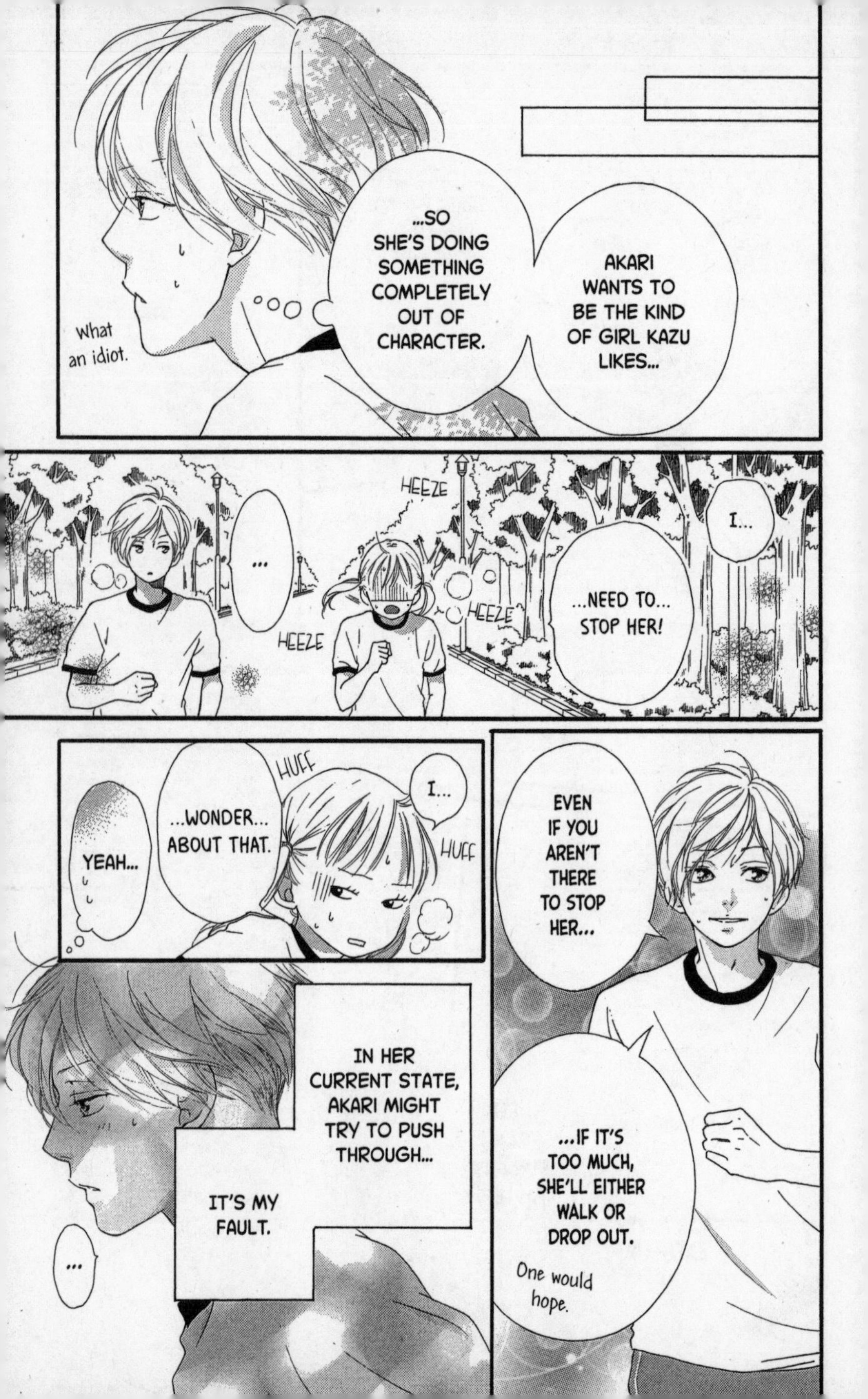
AKARI WANTS TO BE THE KIND OF GIRL KAZU LIKES...
...SO SHE'S DOING SOMETHING COMPLETELY OUT OF CHARACTER.
What an idiot.
I...
...NEED TO... STOP HER!
HEEZE
HEEZE
HEEZE
...
EVEN IF YOU AREN'T THERE TO STOP HER...
...IF IT'S TOO MUCH, SHE'LL EITHER WALK OR DROP OUT.
One would hope.
I...
HUFF
HUFF
...WONDER... ABOUT THAT.
YEAH...
IN HER CURRENT STATE, AKARI MIGHT TRY TO PUSH THROUGH...
IT'S MY FAULT.
...

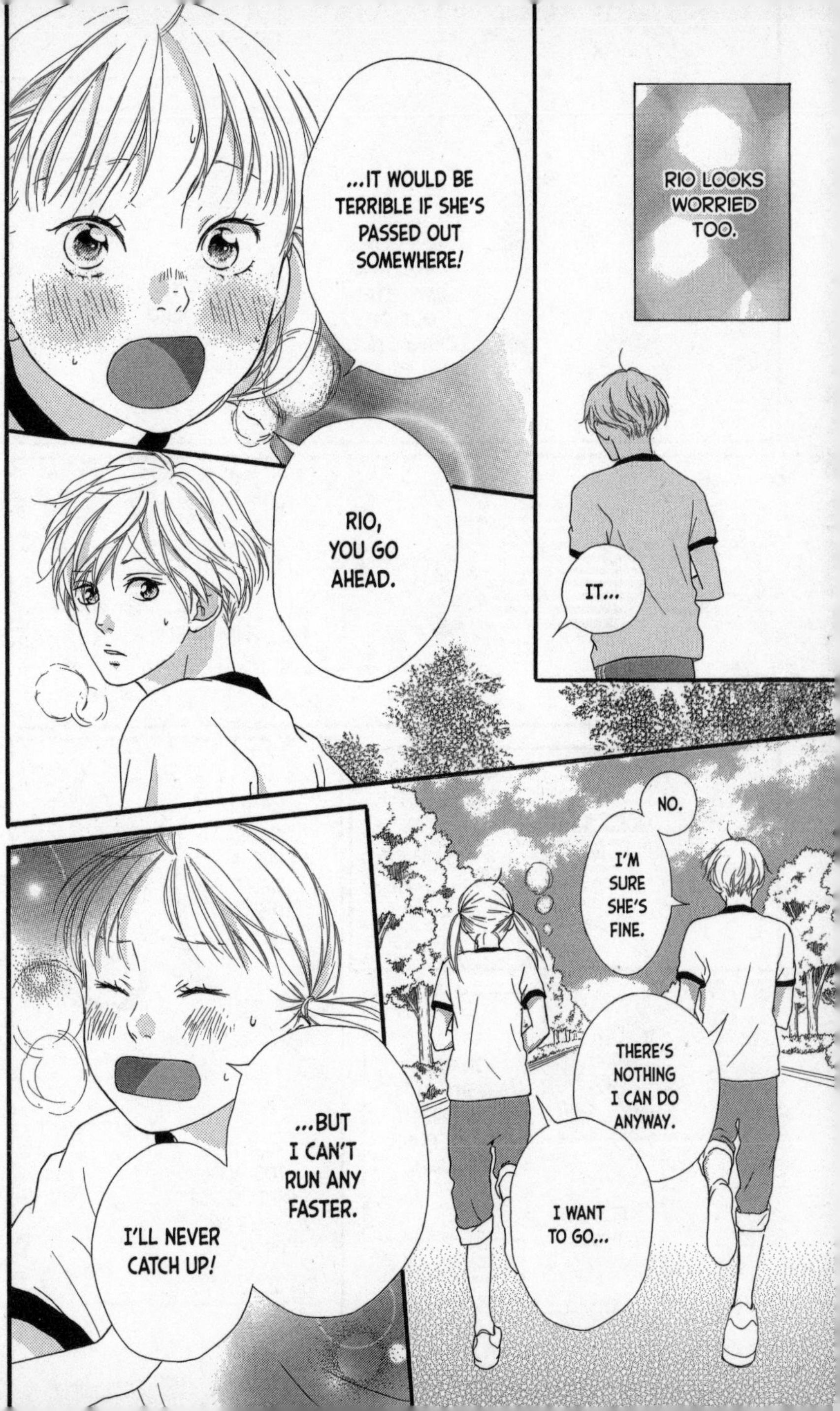
RIO LOOKS WORRIED TOO.
IT...
...IT WOULD BE TERRIBLE IF SHE'S PASSED OUT SOMEWHERE!
RIO, YOU GO AHEAD.
NO.
I'M SURE SHE'S FINE.
THERE'S NOTHING I CAN DO ANYWAY.
I WANT TO GO...
...BUT I CAN'T RUN ANY FASTER.
I'LL NEVER CATCH UP!

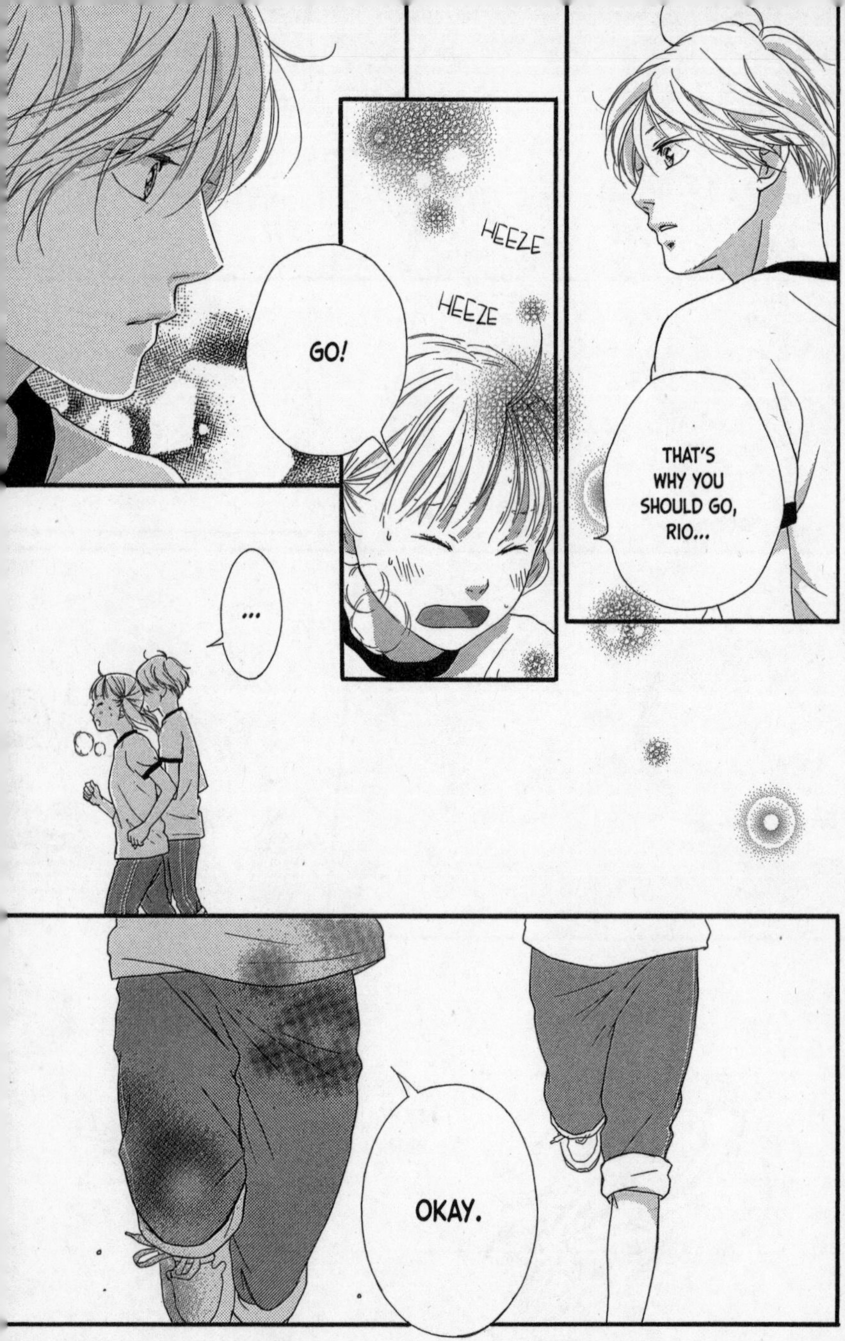
THAT'S WHY YOU SHOULD GO, RIO...
HEEZE
HEEZE
GO!
...
OKAY.

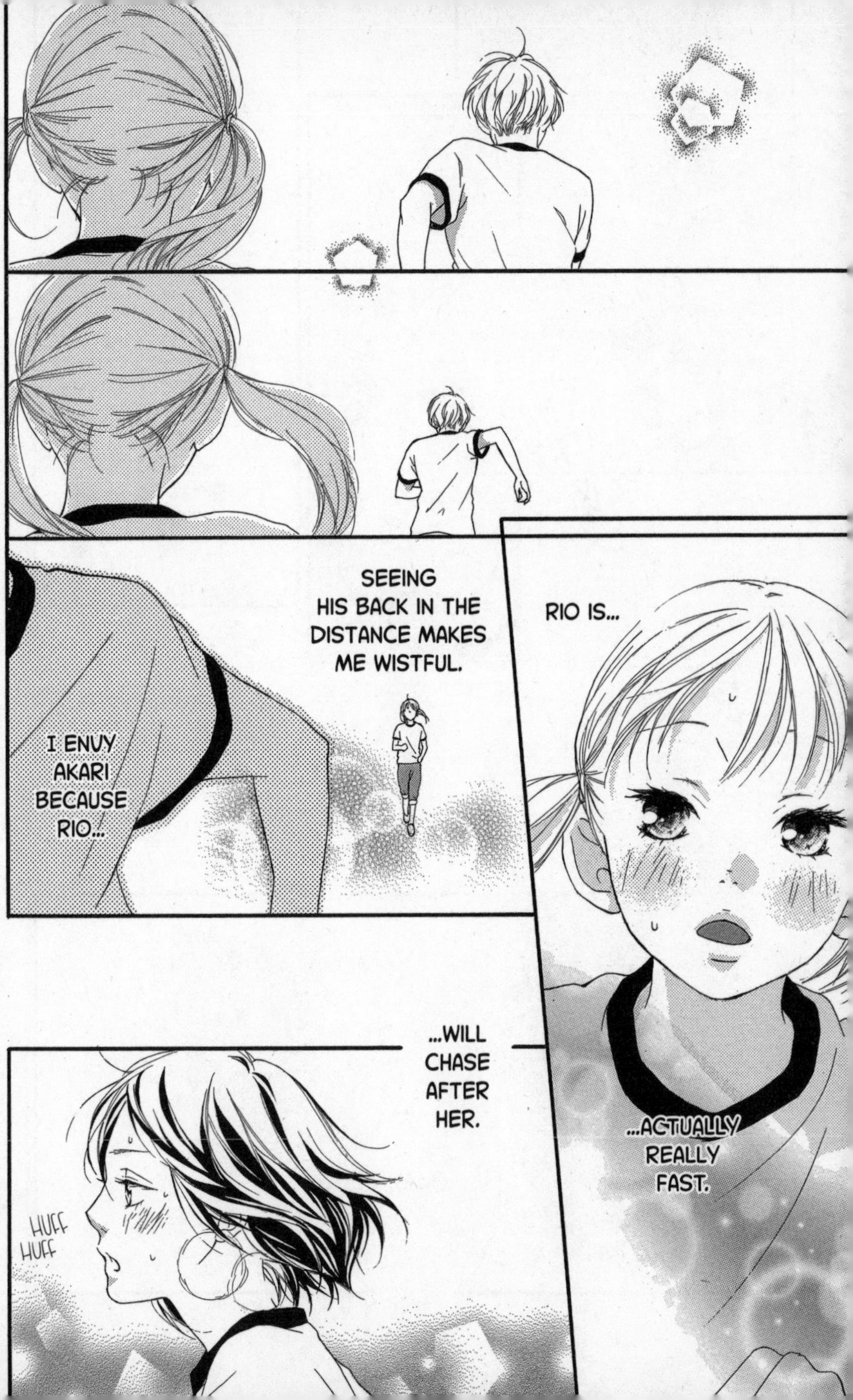
RIO IS...
...ACTUALLY REALLY FAST.
SEEING HIS BACK IN THE DISTANCE MAKES ME WISTFUL.
I ENVY AKARI BECAUSE RIO...
...WILL CHASE AFTER HER.
HUFF HUFF

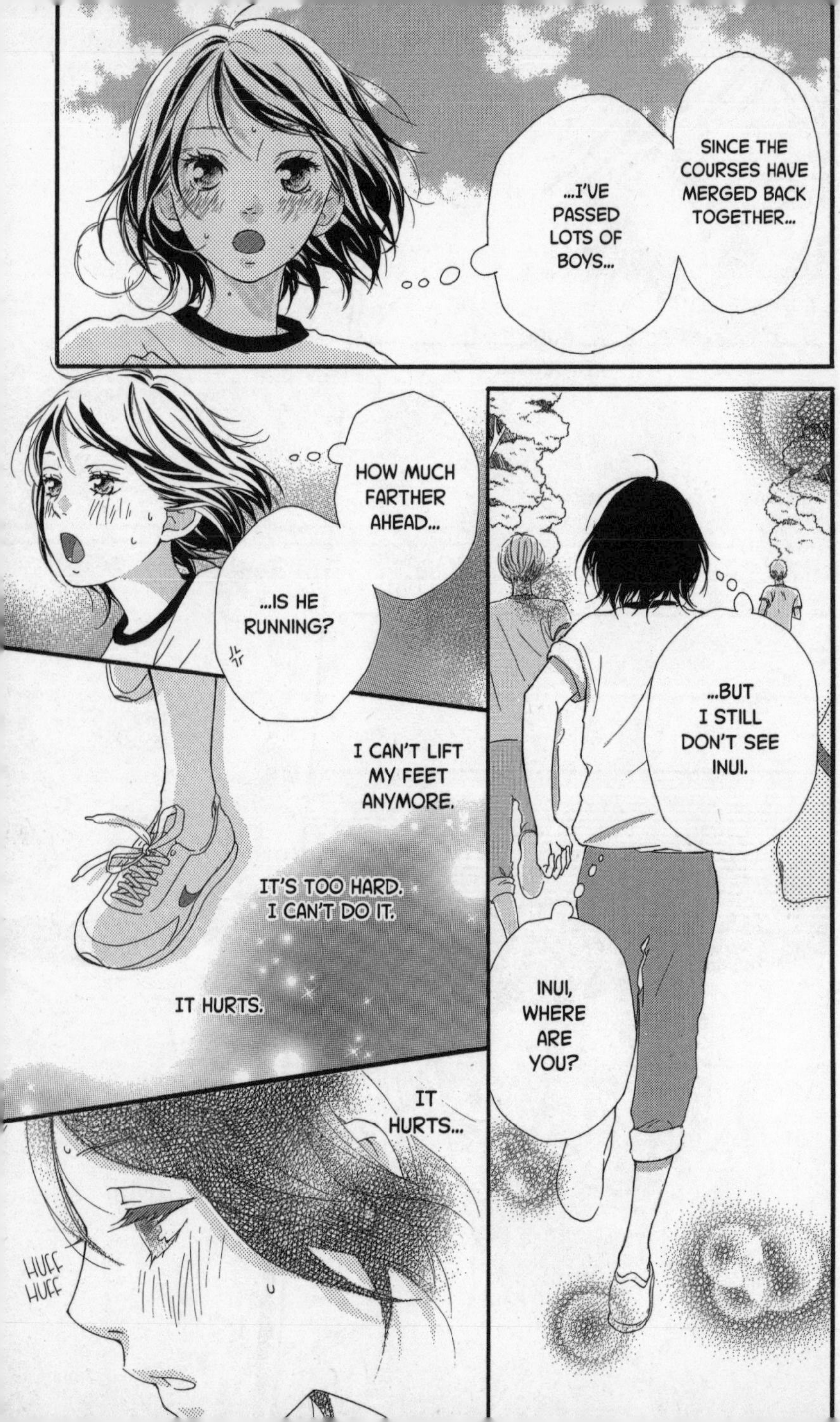
SINCE THE COURSES HAVE MERGED BACK TOGETHER...
...I'VE PASSED LOTS OF BOYS...
...BUT I STILL DON'T SEE INUI.
INUI, WHERE ARE YOU?
HOW MUCH FARTHER AHEAD...
...IS HE RUNNING?
I CAN'T LIFT MY FEET ANYMORE.
IT'S TOO HARD. I CAN'T DO IT.
IT HURTS.
IT HURTS...
HUFF HUFF

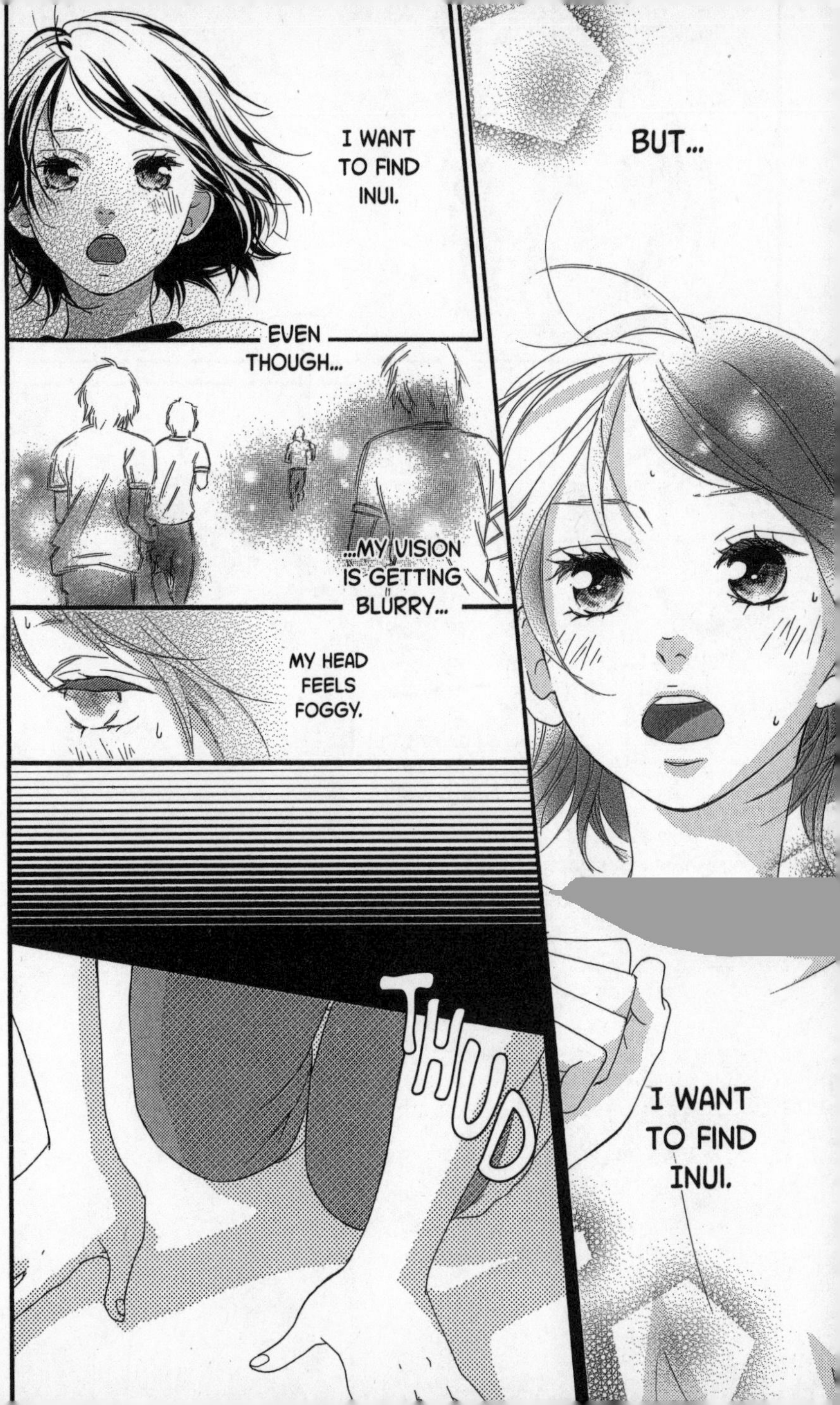
BUT...
I WANT TO FIND INUI.
I WANT TO FIND INUI.
EVEN THOUGH...
...MY VISION IS GETTING BLURRY...
MY HEAD FEELS FOGGY.
THUD

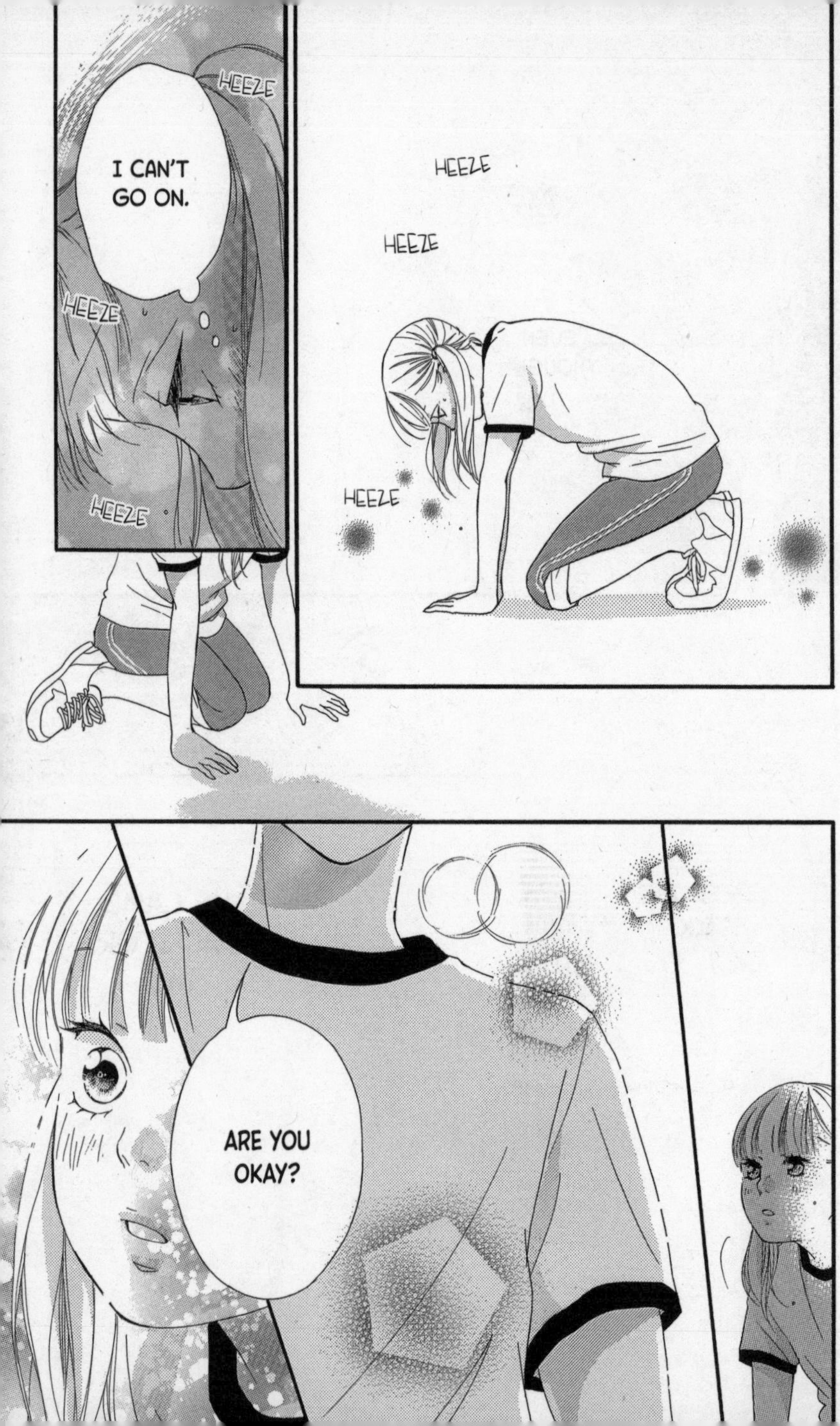
HEEZE
HEEZE
HEEZE
HEEZE
I CAN'T GO ON.
HEEZE
HEEZE
ARE YOU OKAY?

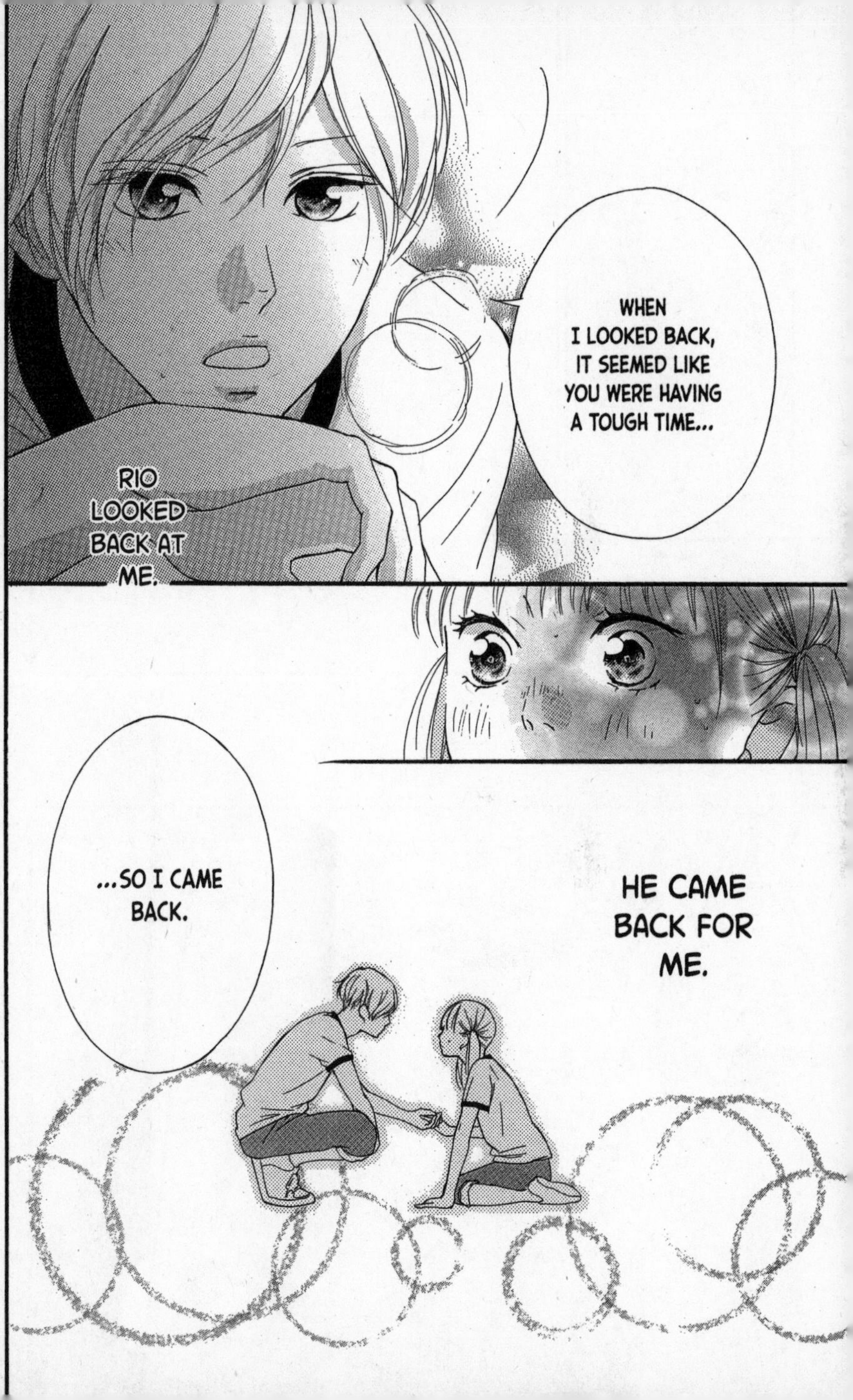
WHEN I LOOKED BACK, IT SEEMED LIKE YOU WERE HAVING A TOUGH TIME...
RIO LOOKED BACK AT ME.
HE CAME BACK FOR ME.
...SO I CAME BACK.

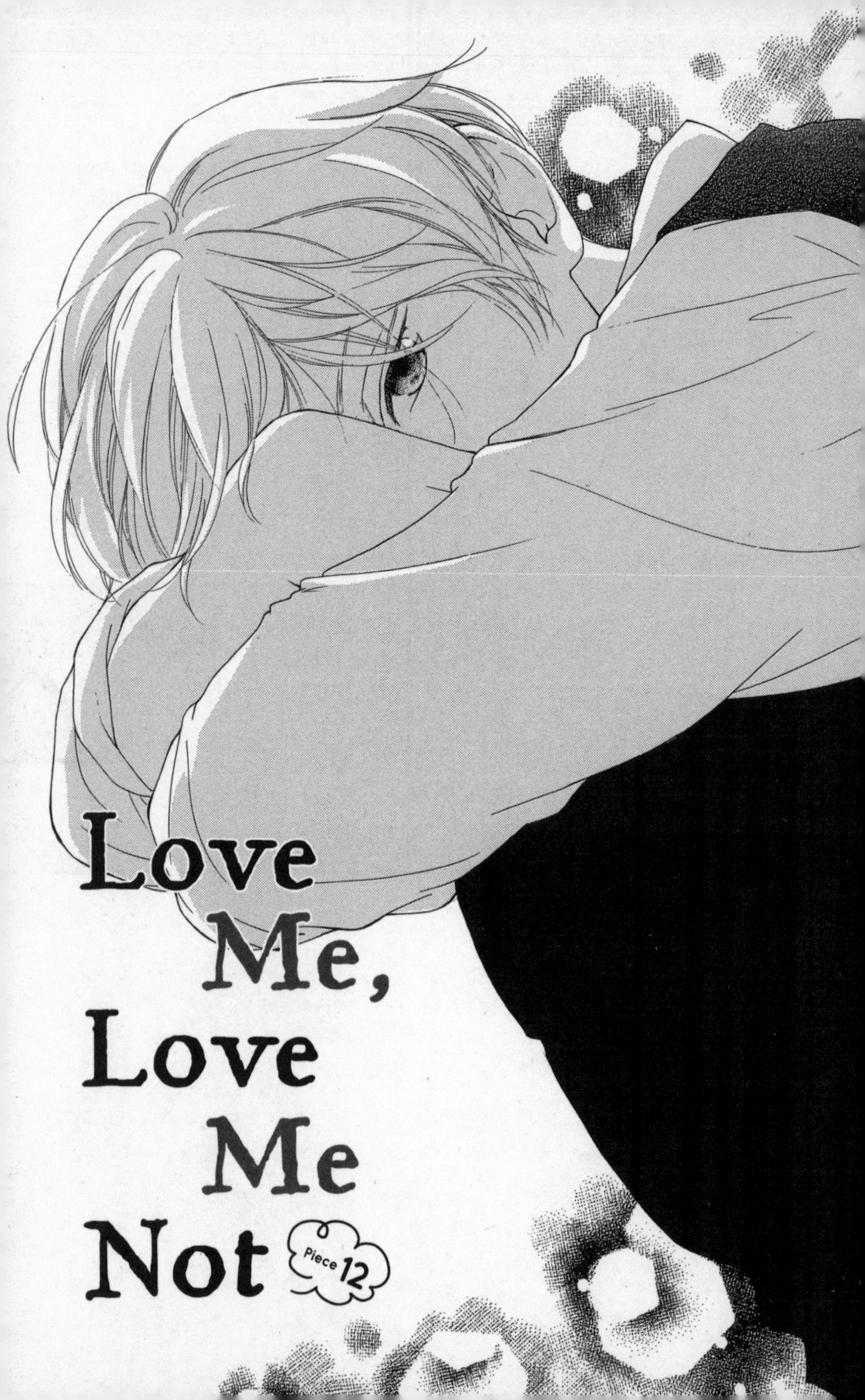
Love Me, Love Me Not
Piece 12

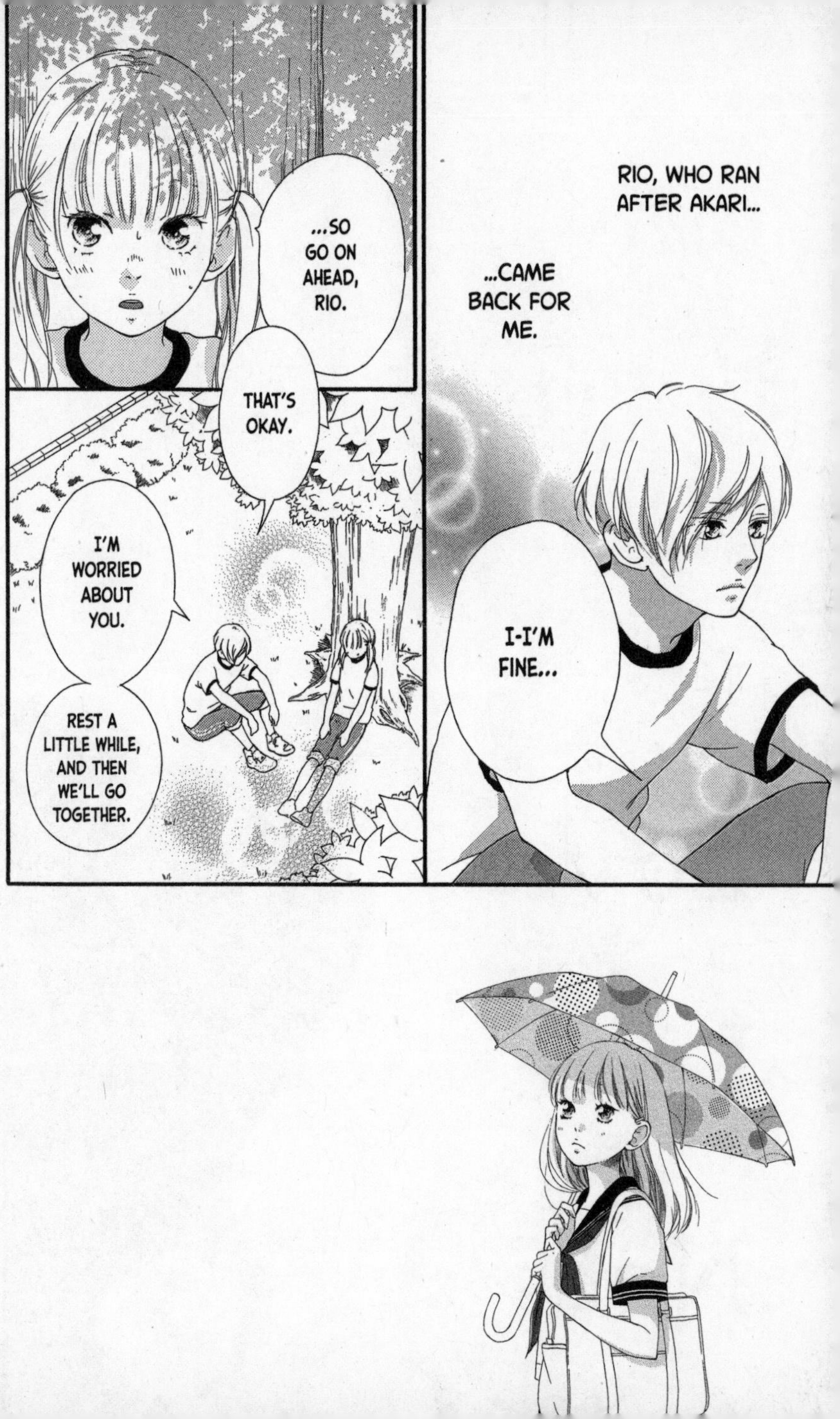
RIO, WHO RAN AFTER AKARI...
...CAME BACK FOR ME.
I-I'M FINE...
...SO GO ON AHEAD, RIO.
THAT'S OKAY.
I'M WORRIED ABOUT YOU.
REST A LITTLE WHILE, AND THEN WE'LL GO TOGETHER.

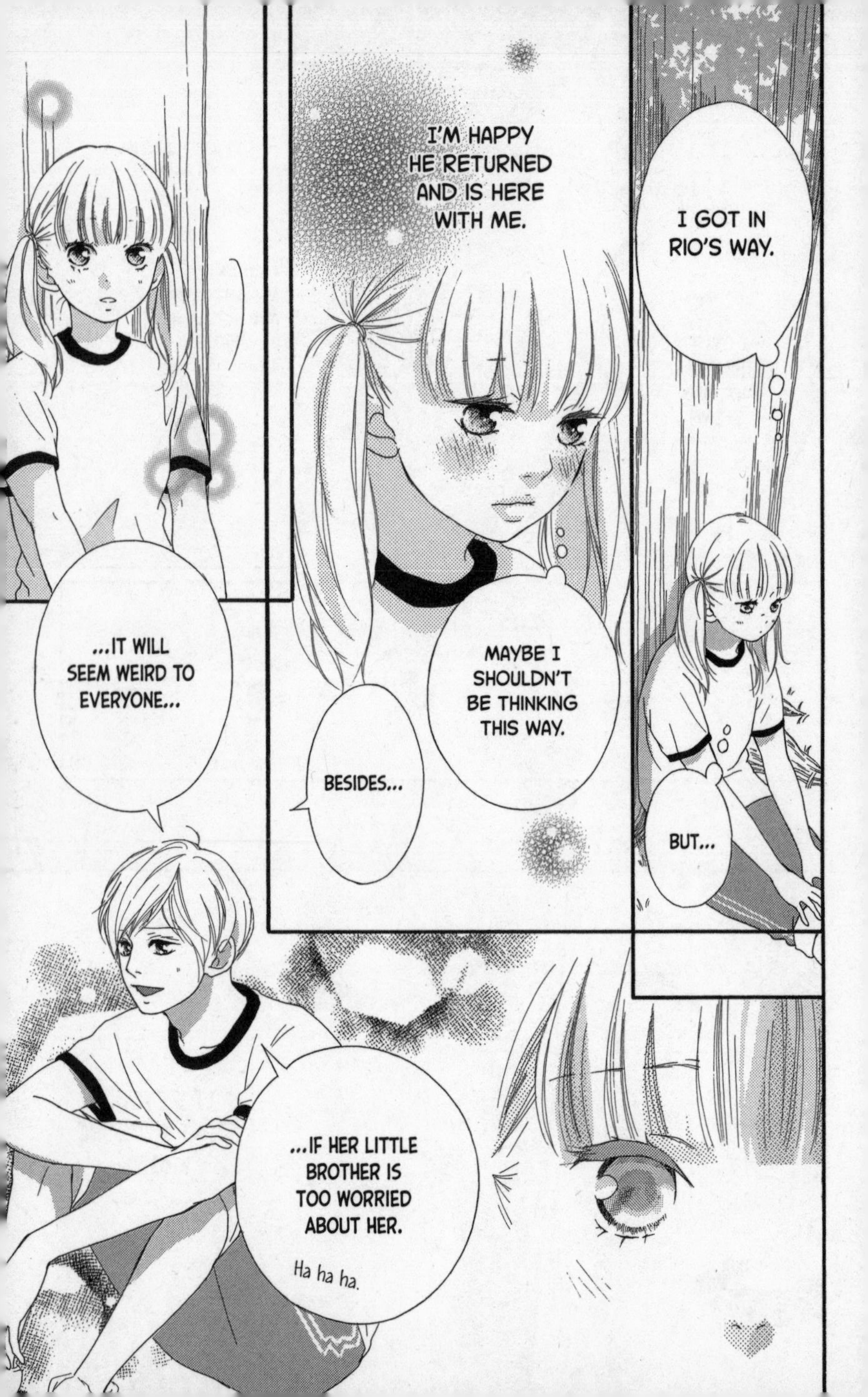
I GOT IN RIO'S WAY.
BUT...
I'M HAPPY HE RETURNED AND IS HERE WITH ME.
MAYBE I SHOULDN'T BE THINKING THIS WAY.
BESIDES...
...IT WILL SEEM WEIRD TO EVERYONE...
...IF HER LITTLE BROTHER IS TOO WORRIED ABOUT HER.
Ha ha ha.

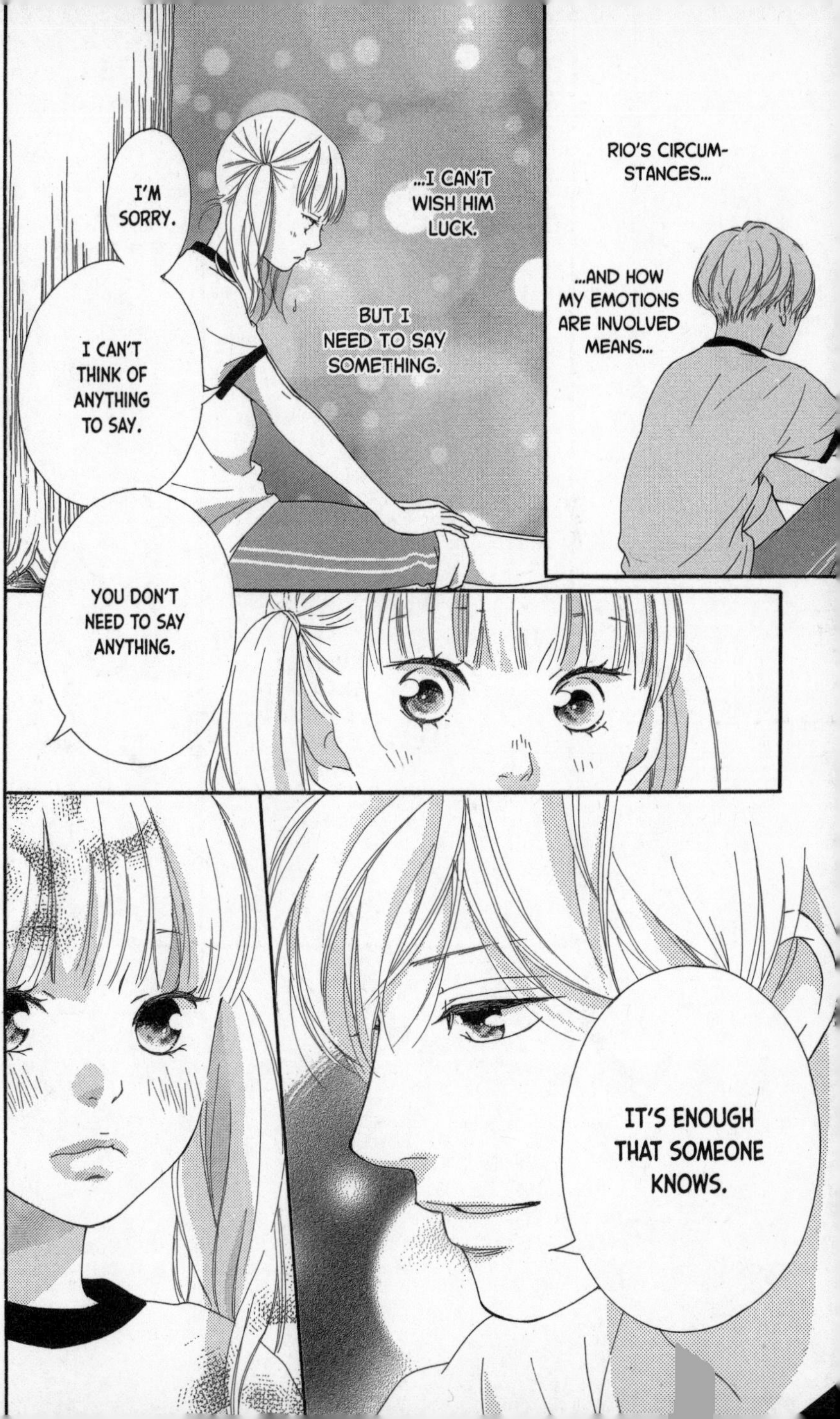
RIO'S CIRCUM-STANCES...
...AND HOW MY EMOTIONS ARE INVOLVED MEANS...
...I CAN'T WISH HIM LUCK.
BUT I NEED TO SAY SOMETHING.
I'M SORRY.
I CAN'T THINK OF ANYTHING TO SAY.
YOU DON'T NEED TO SAY ANYTHING.
IT'S ENOUGH THAT SOMEONE KNOWS.

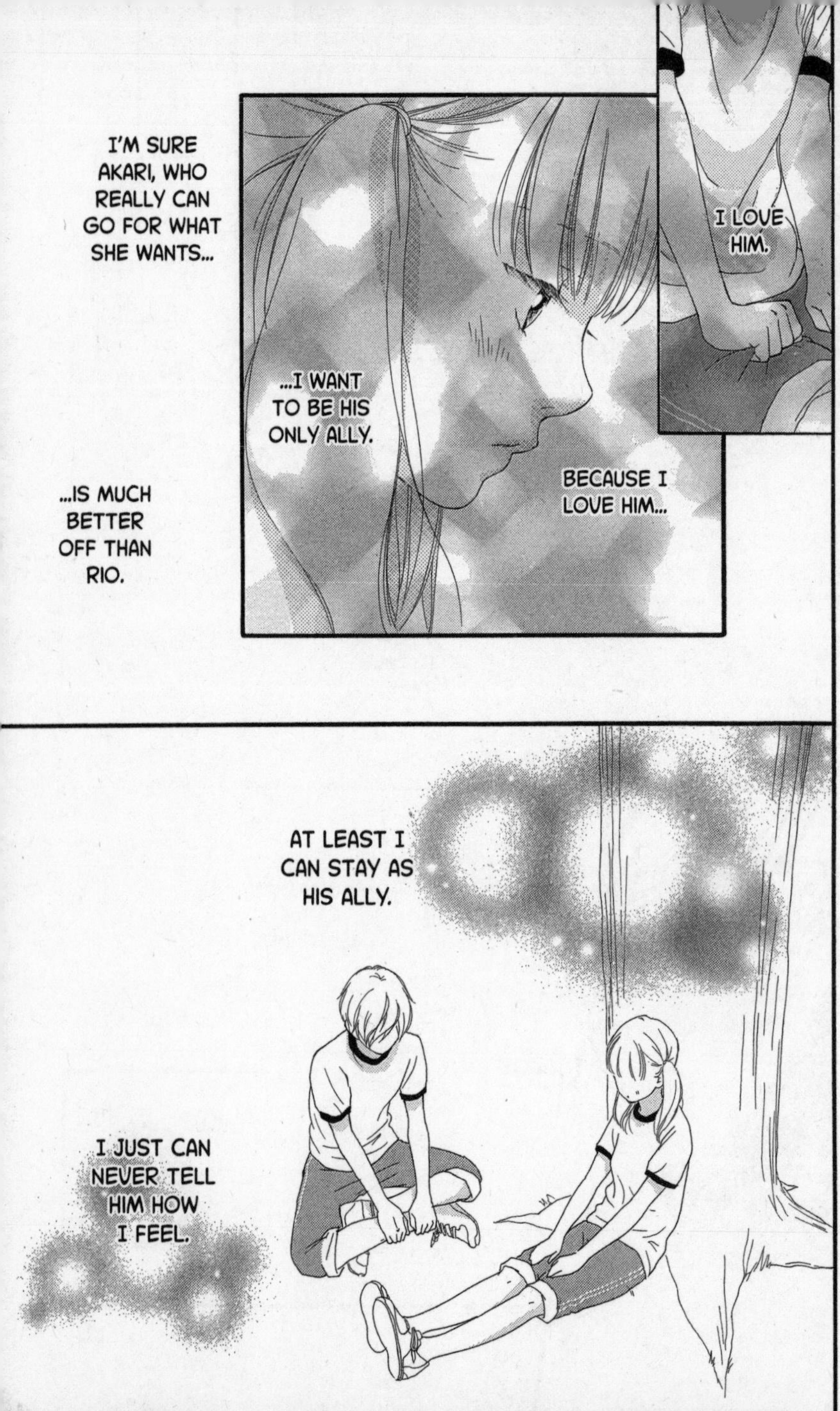
I LOVE HIM.
BECAUSE I LOVE HIM...
...I WANT TO BE HIS ONLY ALLY.
I'M SURE AKARI, WHO REALLY CAN GO FOR WHAT SHE WANTS...
...IS MUCH BETTER OFF THAN RIO.
AT LEAST I CAN STAY AS HIS ALLY.
I JUST CAN NEVER TELL HIM HOW I FEEL.

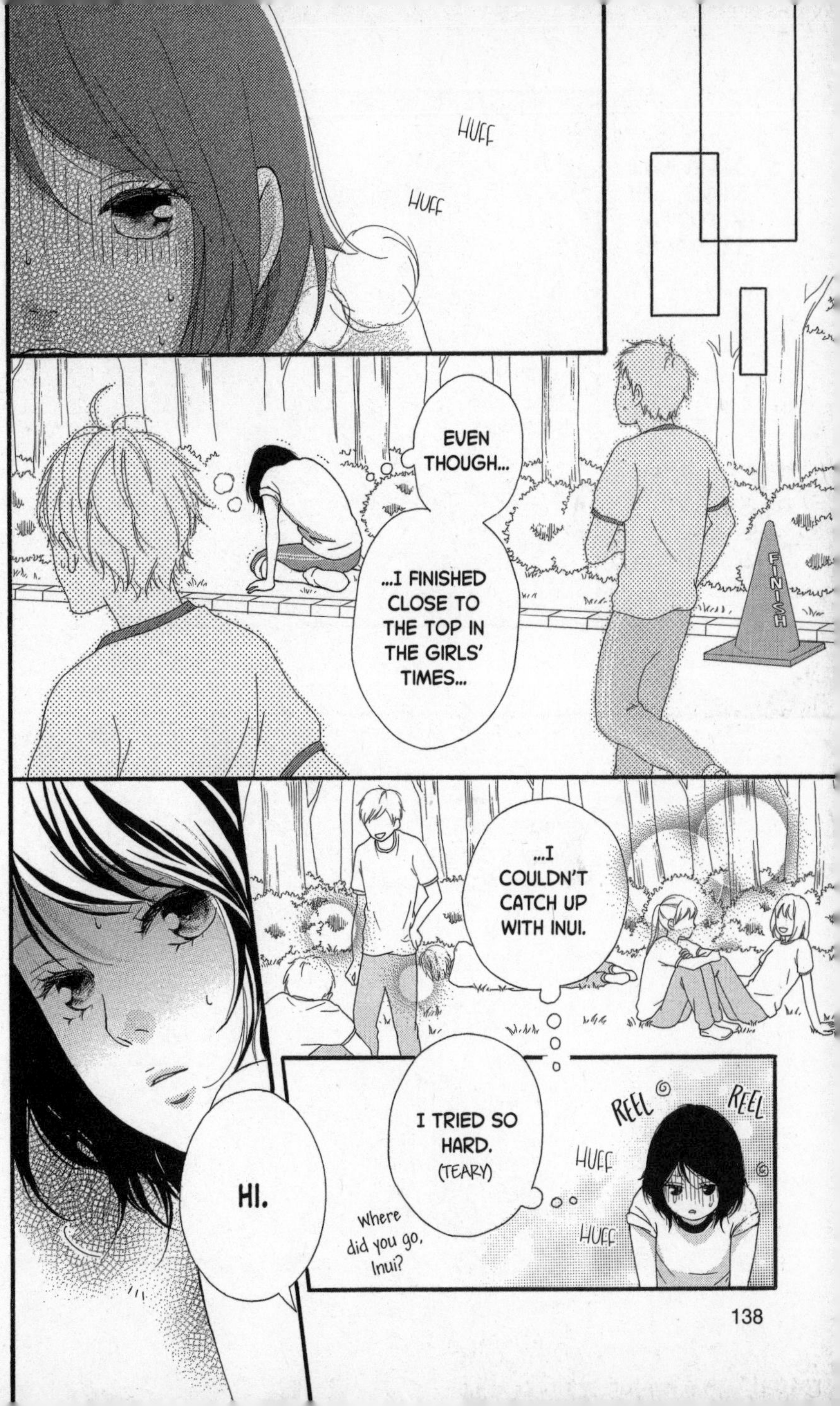
HUFF
HUFF
EVEN THOUGH...
...I FINISHED CLOSE TO THE TOP IN THE GIRLS' TIMES...
FINISH
...I COULDN'T CATCH UP WITH INUI.
REEL
REEL
HUFF
HUFF
I TRIED SO HARD. (TEARY)
Where did you go, Inui?
HI.

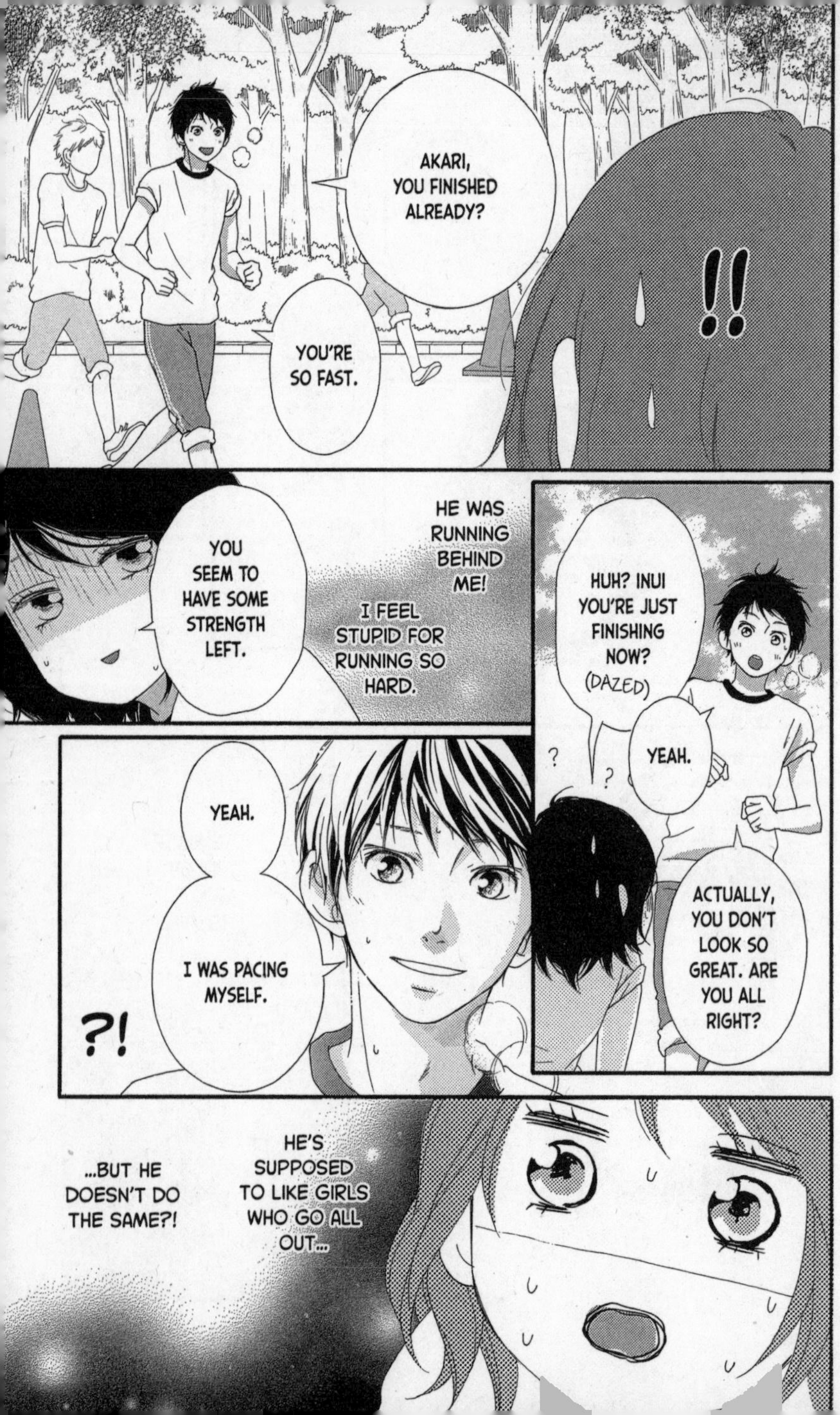
AKARI, YOU FINISHED ALREADY?
YOU'RE SO FAST.
!!
HUH? INUI YOU'RE JUST FINISHING NOW?
(DAZED)
YEAH.
? ?
ACTUALLY, YOU DON'T LOOK SO GREAT. ARE YOU ALL RIGHT?
HE WAS RUNNING BEHIND ME!
I FEEL STUPID FOR RUNNING SO HARD.
YOU SEEM TO HAVE SOME STRENGTH LEFT.
YEAH.
I WAS PACING MYSELF.
?!
HE'S SUPPOSED TO LIKE GIRLS WHO GO ALL OUT...
...BUT HE DOESN'T DO THE SAME?!

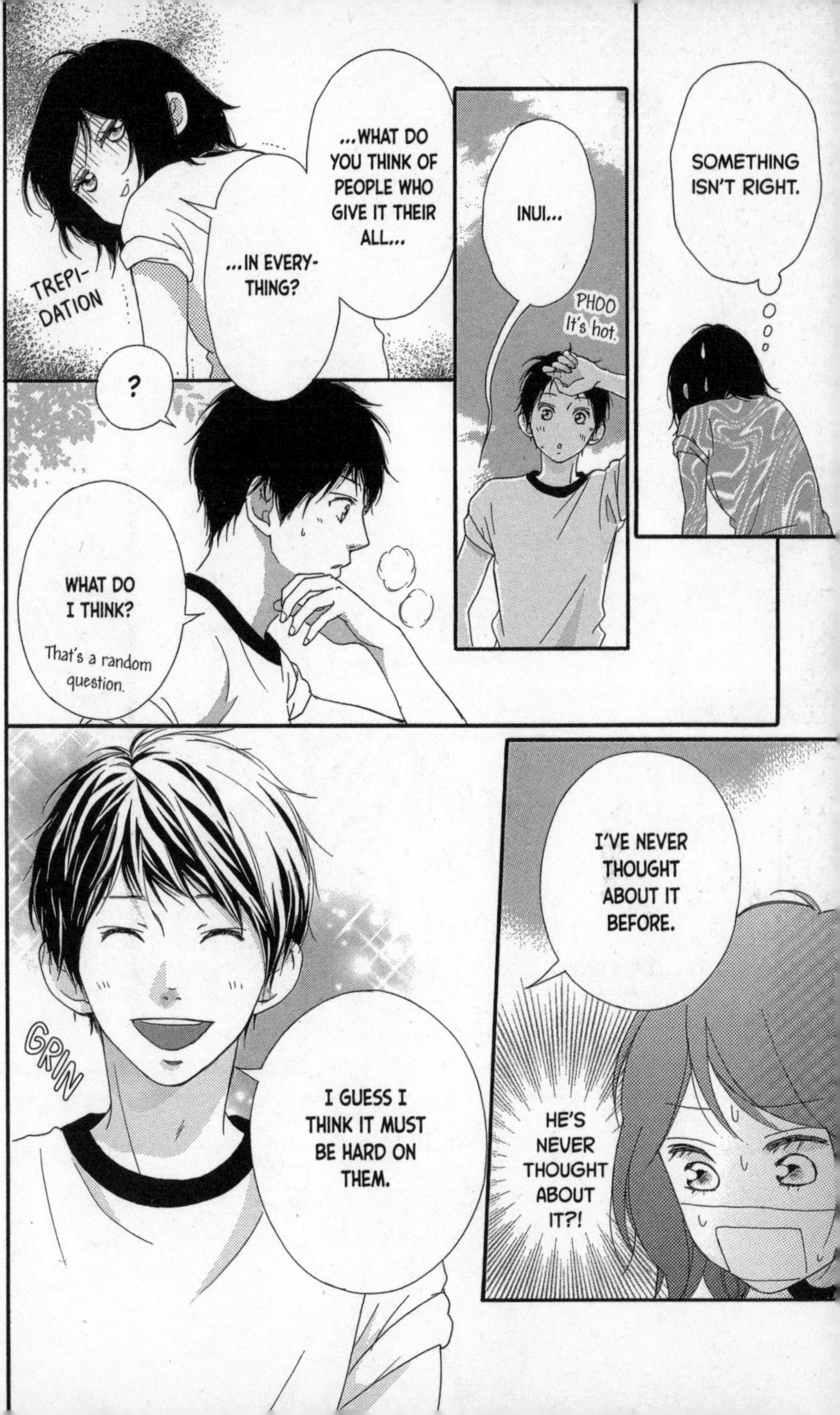
SOMETHING ISN'T RIGHT.
INUI...
PHOO It's hot.
...WHAT DO YOU THINK OF PEOPLE WHO GIVE IT THEIR ALL...
...IN EVERYTHING?
TREPIDATION
?
WHAT DO I THINK?
That's a random question.
I'VE NEVER THOUGHT ABOUT IT BEFORE.
HE'S NEVER THOUGHT ABOUT IT?!
GRIN
I GUESS I THINK IT MUST BE HARD ON THEM.

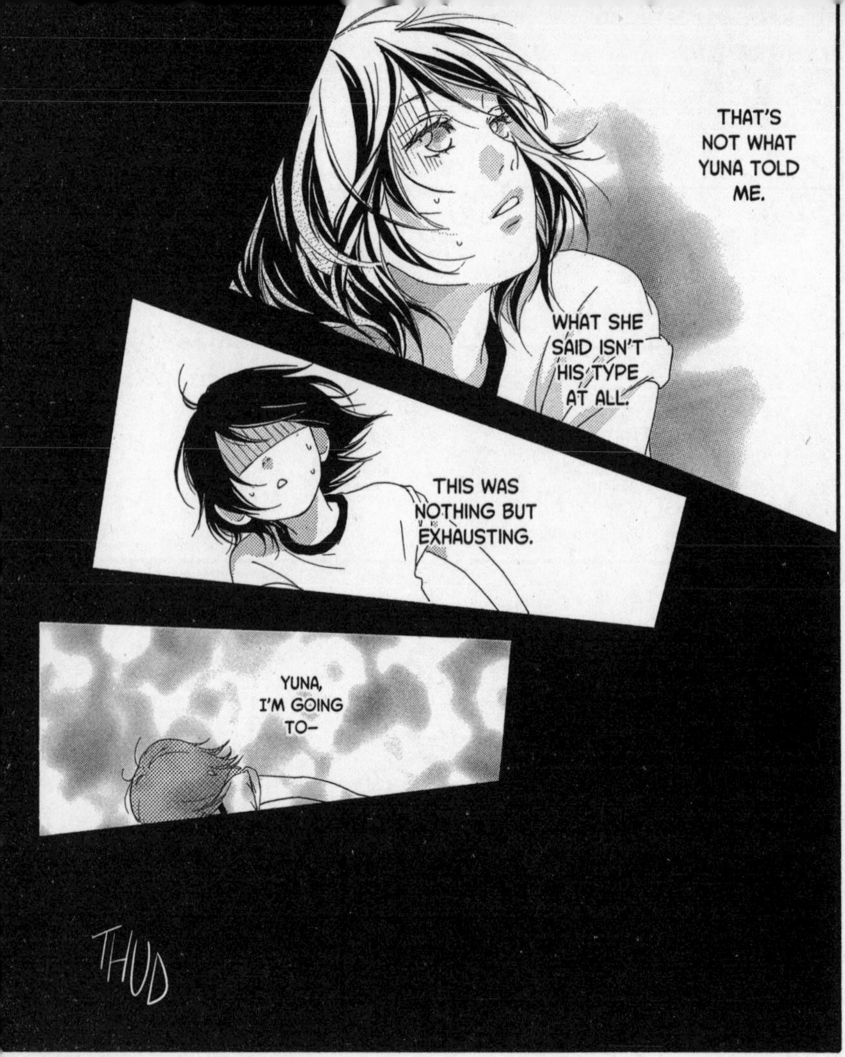
THAT'S NOT WHAT YUNA TOLD ME.
WHAT SHE SAID ISN'T HIS TYPE AT ALL.
THIS WAS NOTHING BUT EXHAUSTING.
YUNA, I'M GOING TO–
THUD

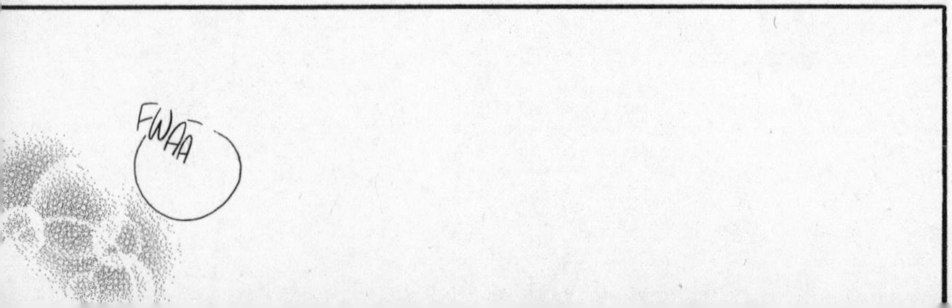
FWAA

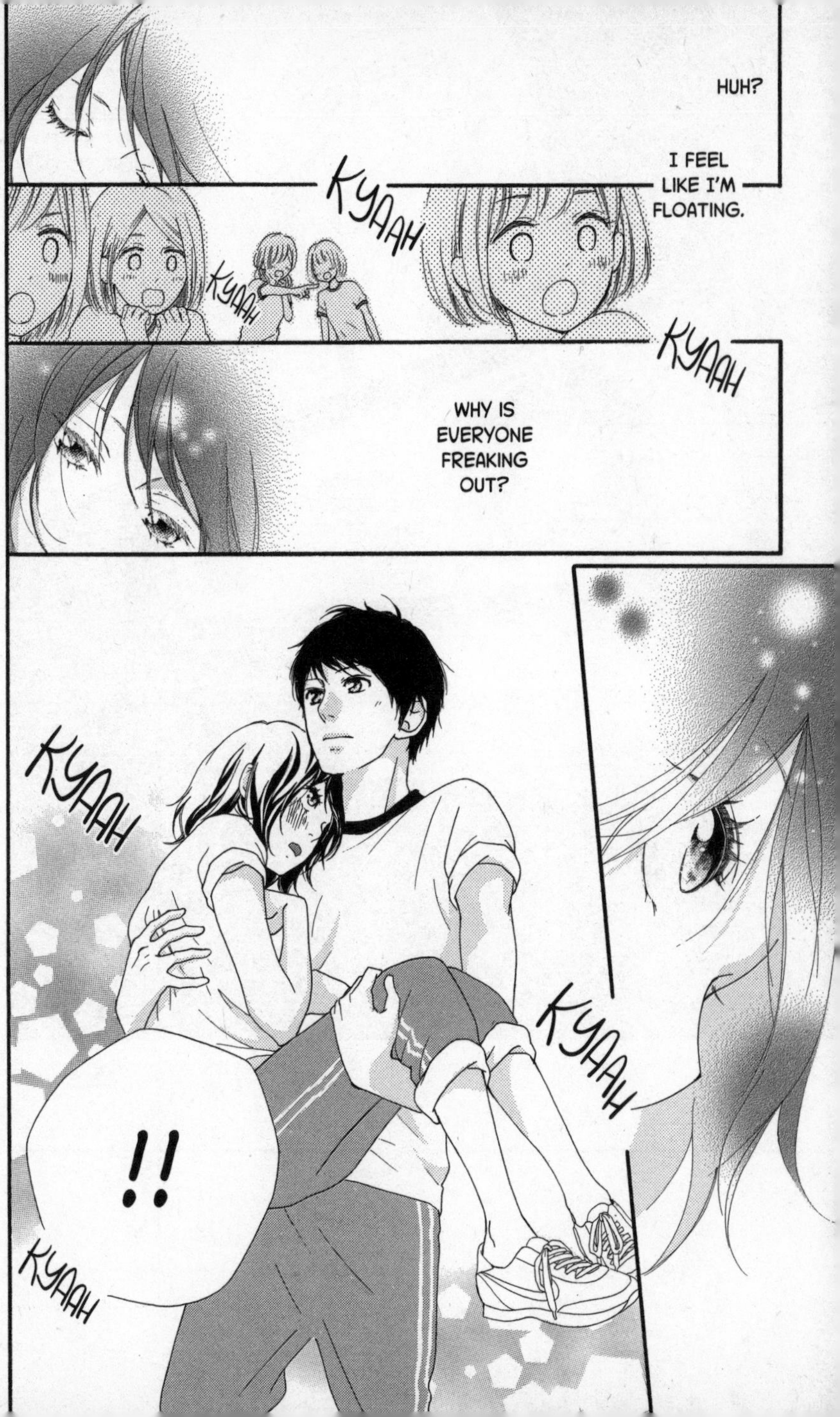
HUH?
I FEEL LIKE I'M FLOATING.
KYAAH
KYAAH
KYAAH
WHY IS EVERYONE FREAKING OUT?
KYAAH
KYAAH
!!
KYAAH

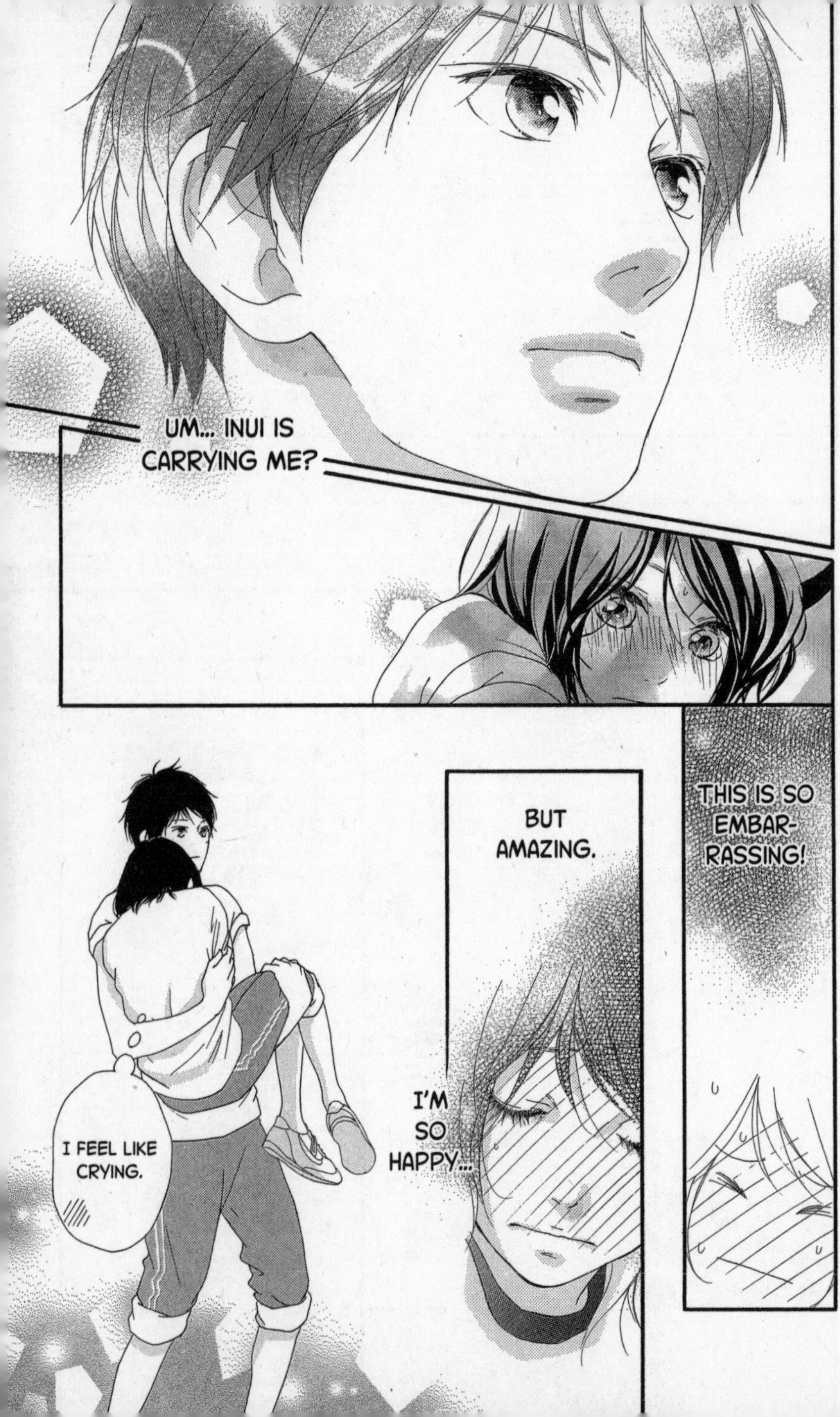
UM... INUI IS CARRYING ME?
THIS IS SO EMBAR-RASSING!
BUT AMAZING.
I'M SO HAPPY...
I FEEL LIKE CRYING.

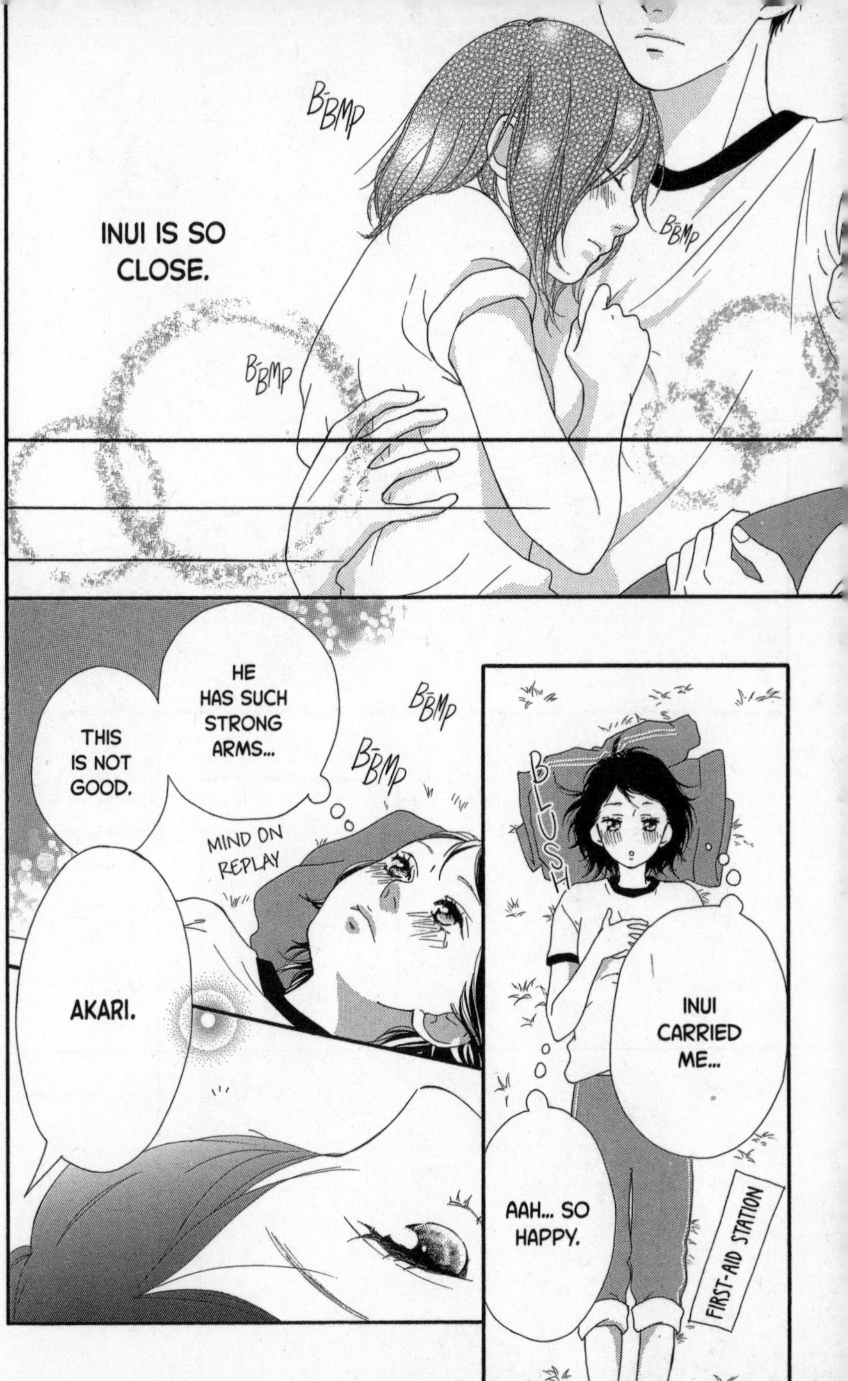
B-BMP
B-BMP
INUI IS SO CLOSE.
B-BMP
BLUSH
INUI CARRIED ME...
AAH... SO HAPPY.
FIRST-AID STATION
B-BMP
B-BMP
HE HAS SUCH STRONG ARMS...
THIS IS NOT GOOD.
MIND ON REPLAY
AKARI.

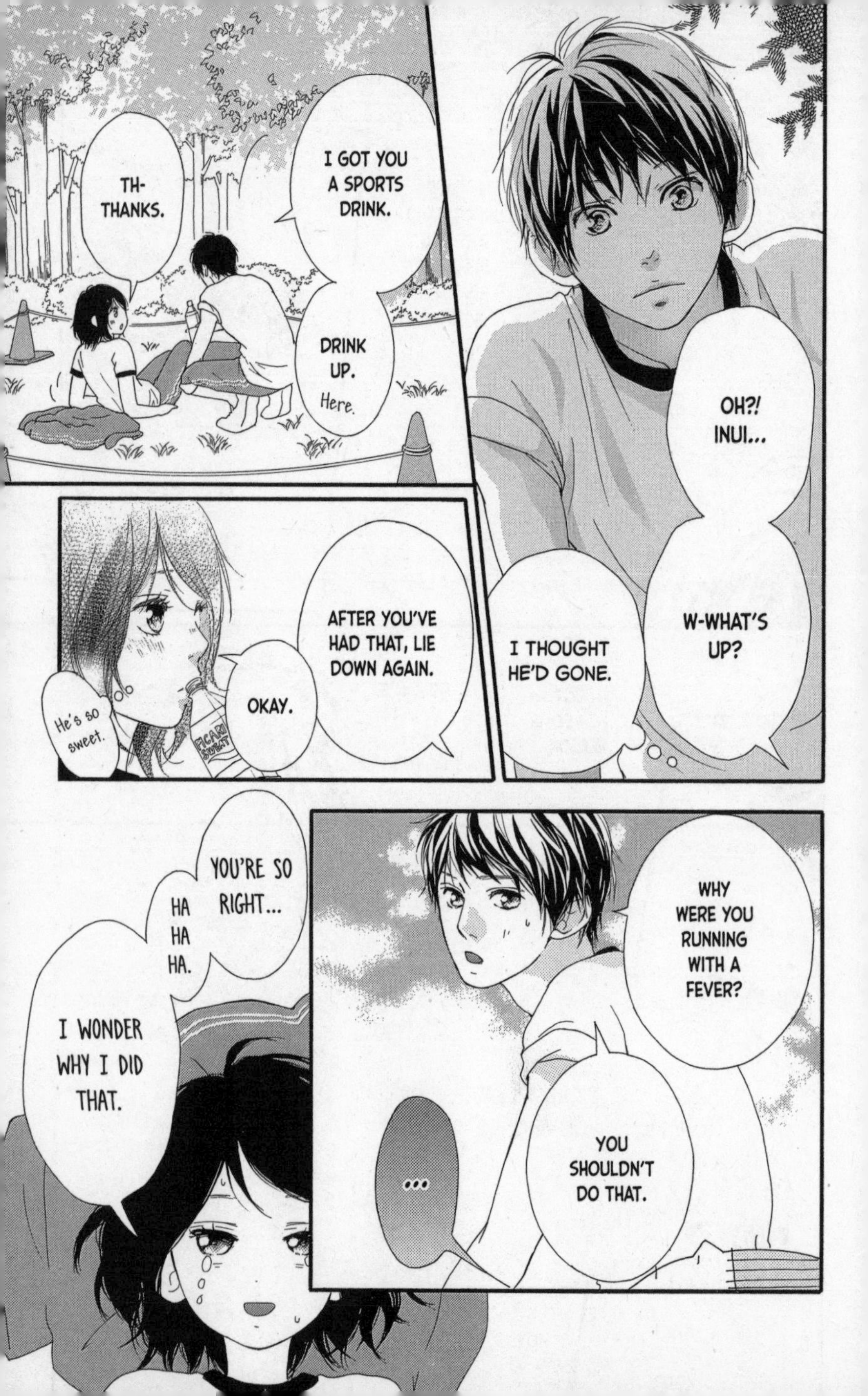
OH?! INUI...
W-WHAT'S UP?
I THOUGHT HE'D GONE.
I GOT YOU A SPORTS DRINK.
TH-THANKS.
DRINK UP.
Here.
AFTER YOU'VE HAD THAT, LIE DOWN AGAIN.
OKAY.
He's so sweet.
WHY WERE YOU RUNNING WITH A FEVER?
YOU SHOULDN'T DO THAT.
...
YOU'RE SO RIGHT...
HA HA HA.
I WONDER WHY I DID THAT.

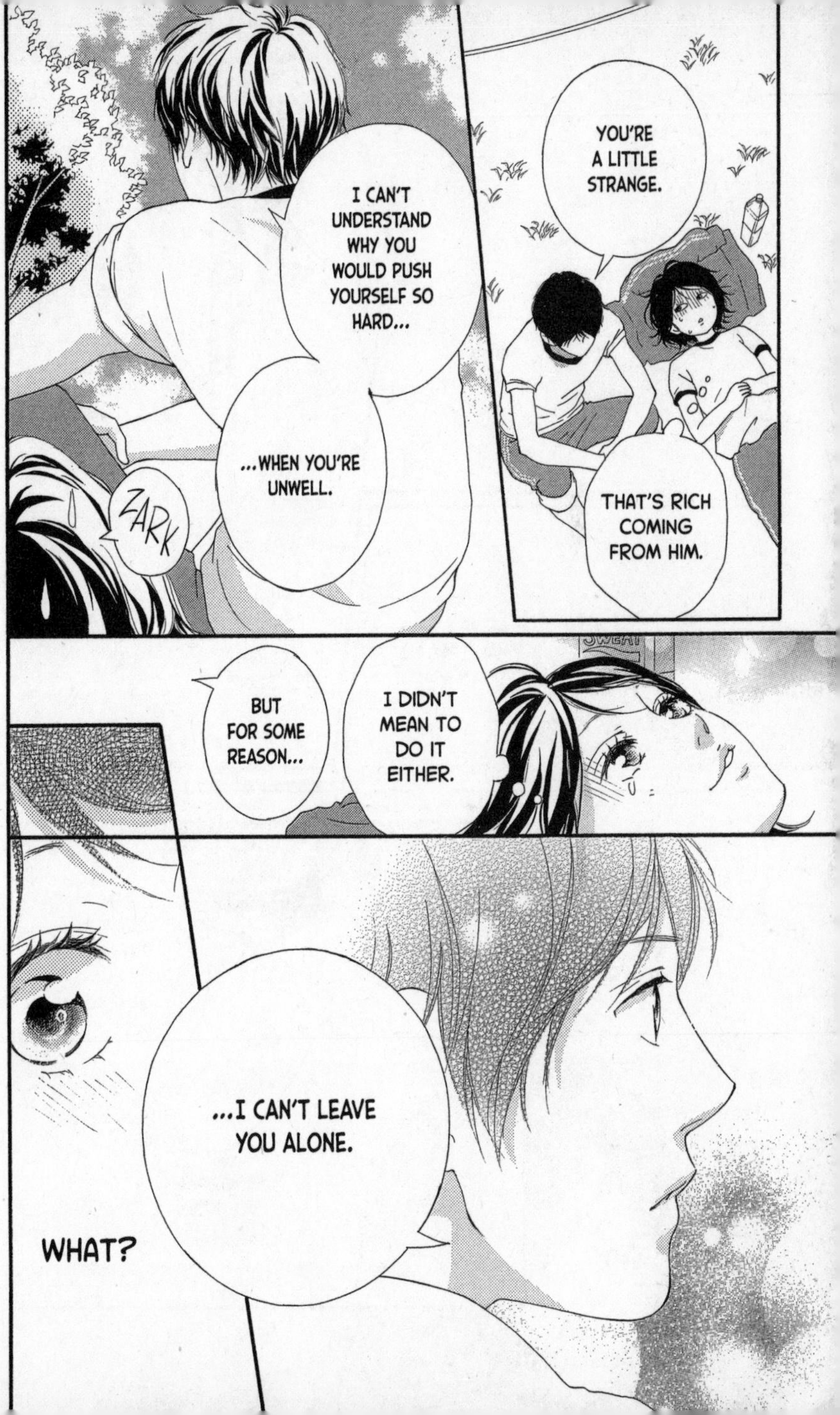
YOU'RE A LITTLE STRANGE.
THAT'S RICH COMING FROM HIM.
I CAN'T UNDERSTAND WHY YOU WOULD PUSH YOURSELF SO HARD...
...WHEN YOU'RE UNWELL.
ZARK
I DIDN'T MEAN TO DO IT EITHER.
BUT FOR SOME REASON...
...I CAN'T LEAVE YOU ALONE.
WHAT?

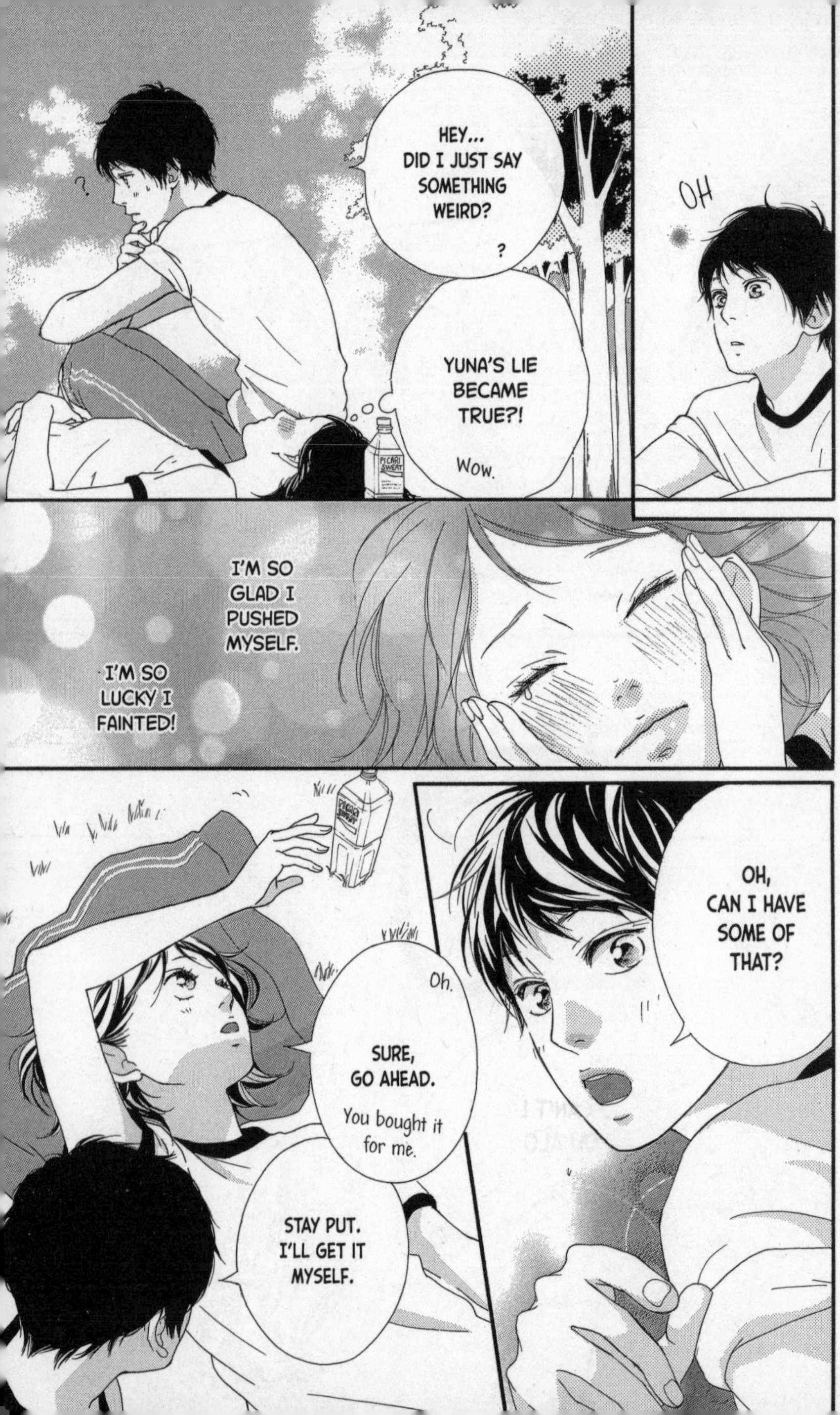
OH
HEY... DID I JUST SAY SOMETHING WEIRD?
?
YUNA'S LIE BECAME TRUE?!
Wow.
PICARI SWEAT
I'M SO GLAD I PUSHED MYSELF.
I'M SO LUCKY I FAINTED!
OH, CAN I HAVE SOME OF THAT?
Oh.
SURE, GO AHEAD.
You bought it for me.
STAY PUT. I'LL GET IT MYSELF.

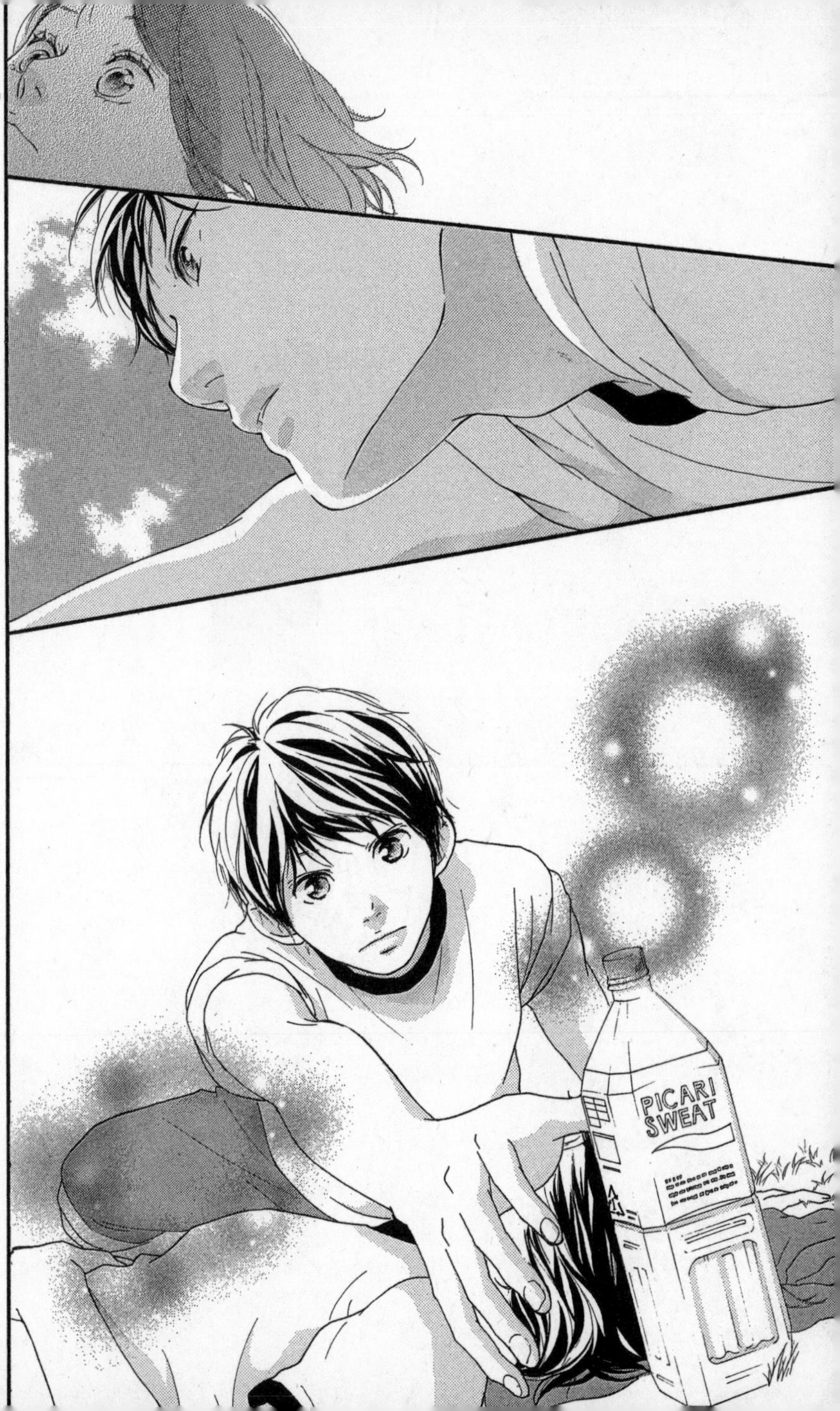
PICARI SWEAT

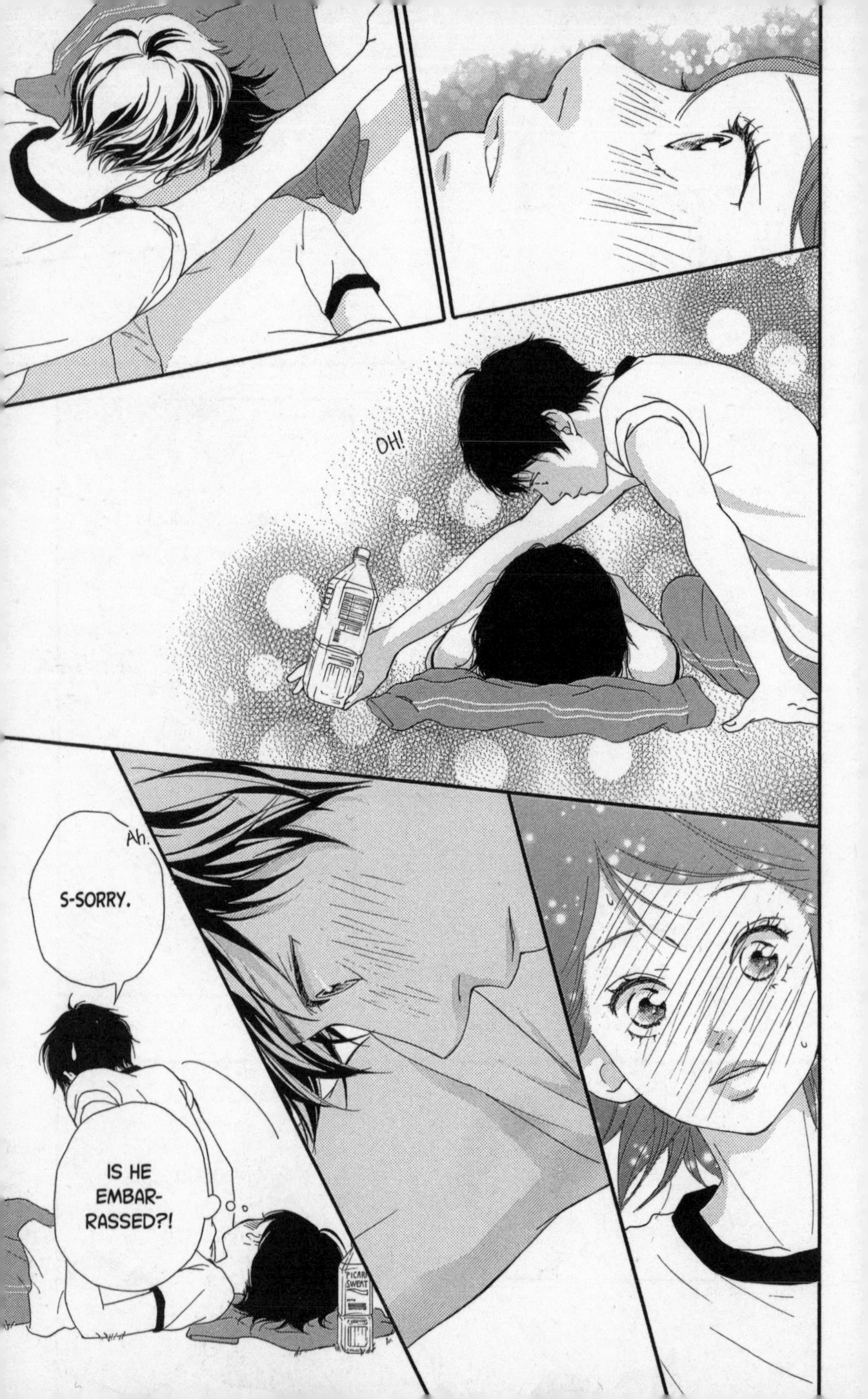
OH!
Ah.
S-SORRY.
IS HE EMBAR-RASSED?!
PICARI SWEAT

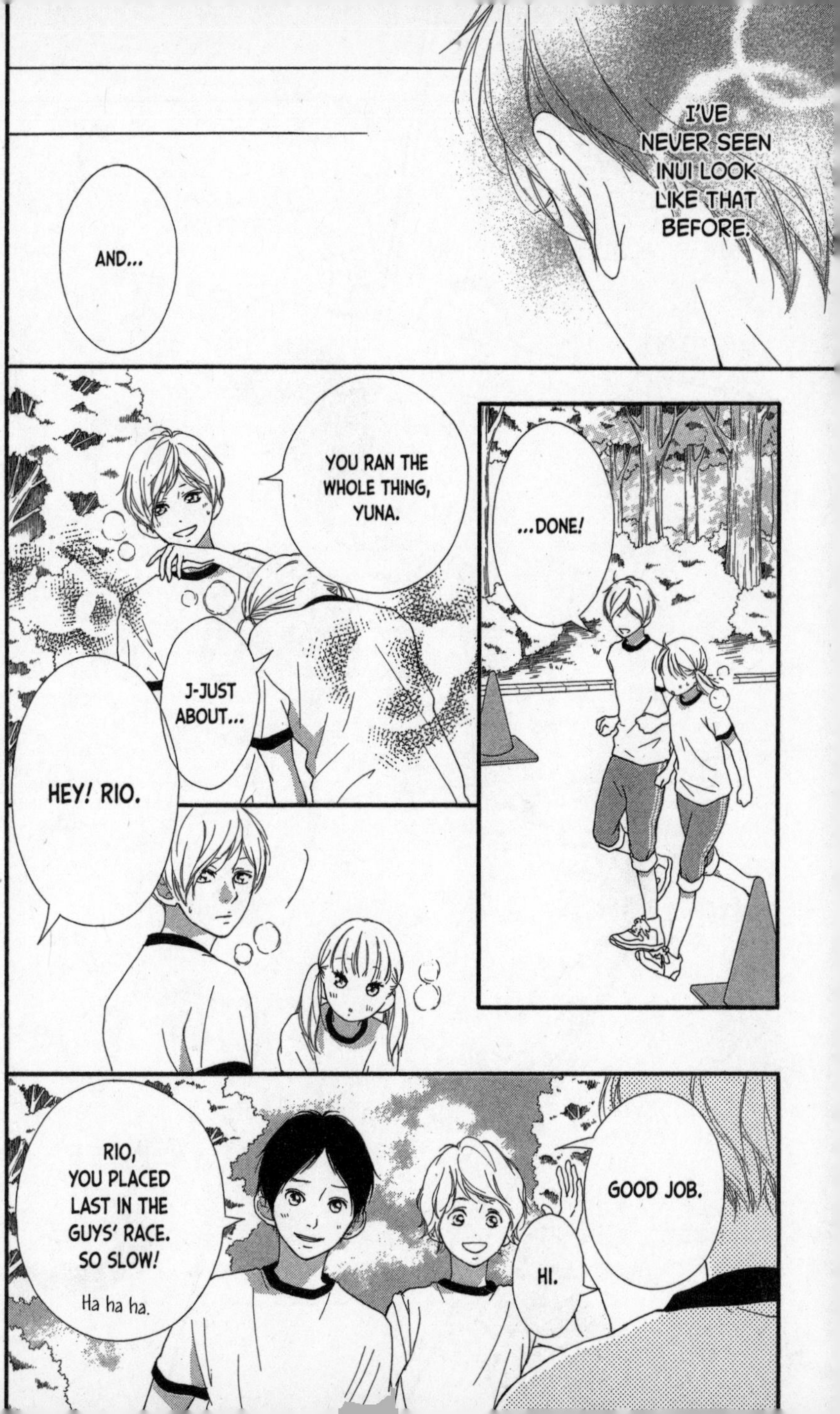
I'VE NEVER SEEN INUI LOOK LIKE THAT BEFORE.
AND...
...DONE!
YOU RAN THE WHOLE THING, YUNA.
J-JUST ABOUT...
HEY! RIO.
GOOD JOB.
HI.
RIO, YOU PLACED LAST IN THE GUYS' RACE. SO SLOW!
Ha ha ha.

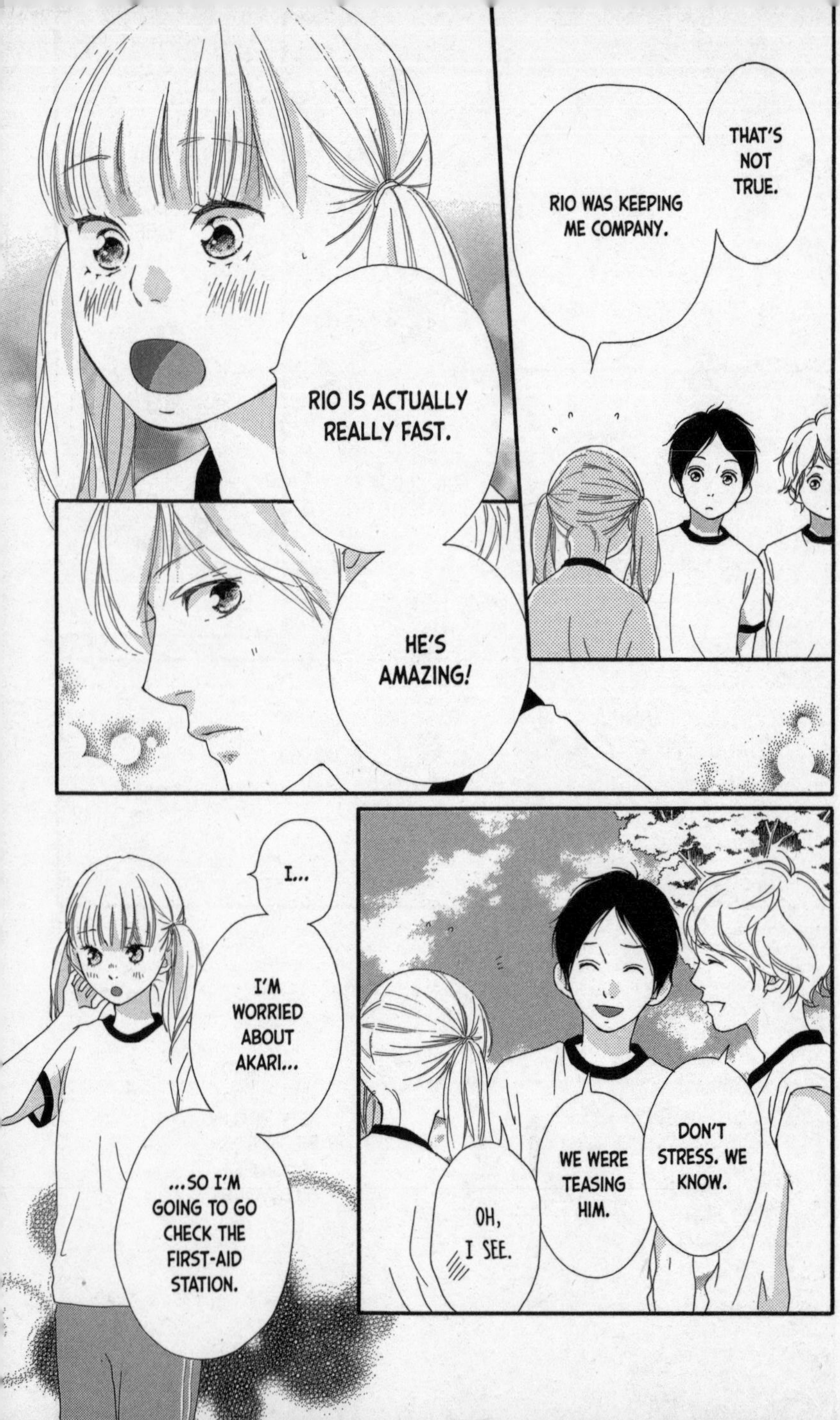
THAT'S NOT TRUE.
RIO WAS KEEPING ME COMPANY.
RIO IS ACTUALLY REALLY FAST.
HE'S AMAZING!
DON'T STRESS. WE KNOW.
WE WERE TEASING HIM.
OH, I SEE.
I...
I'M WORRIED ABOUT AKARI...
...SO I'M GOING TO GO CHECK THE FIRST-AID STATION.

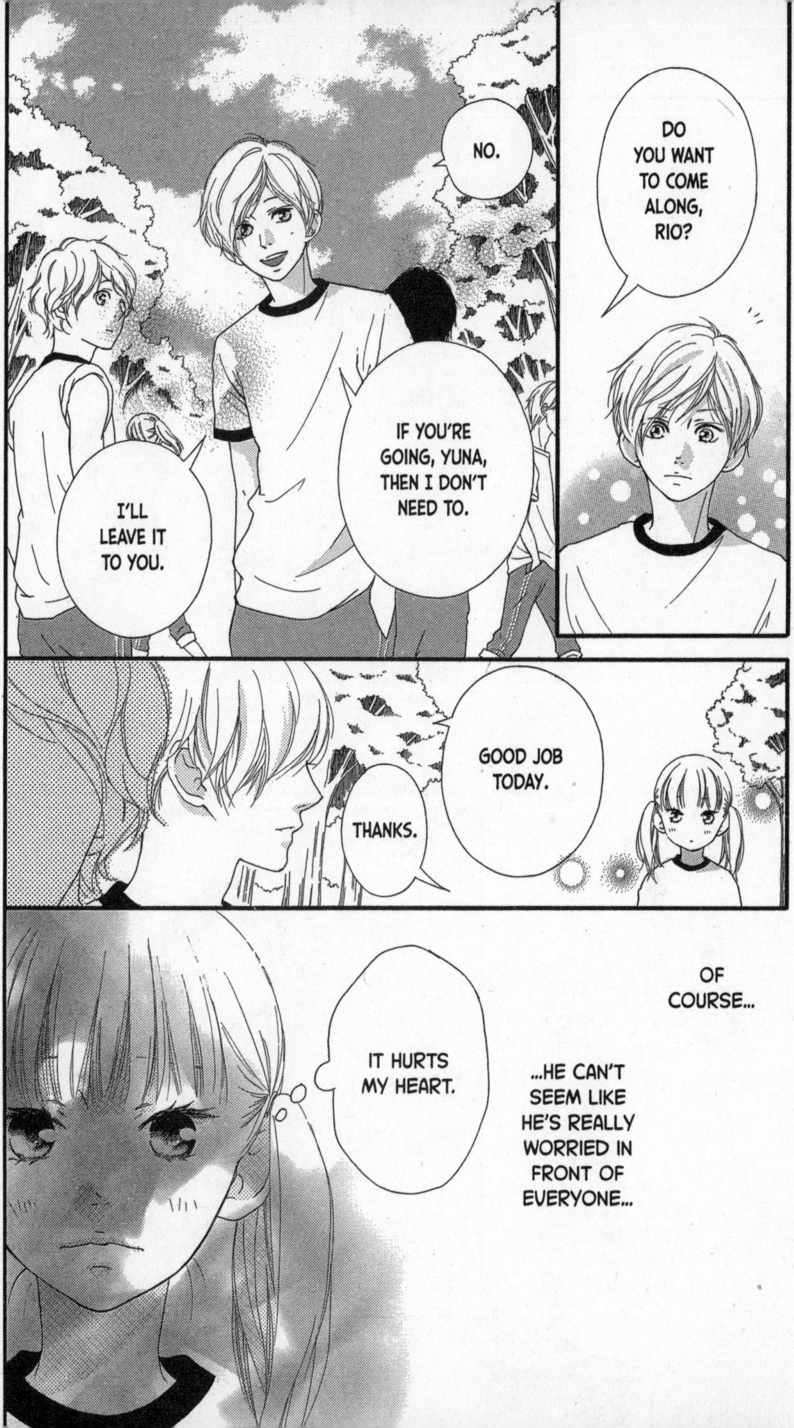
DO YOU WANT TO COME ALONG, RIO?
NO.
IF YOU'RE GOING, YUNA, THEN I DON'T NEED TO.
I'LL LEAVE IT TO YOU.
GOOD JOB TODAY.
THANKS.
OF COURSE...
...HE CAN'T SEEM LIKE HE'S REALLY WORRIED IN FRONT OF EVERYONE...
IT HURTS MY HEART.

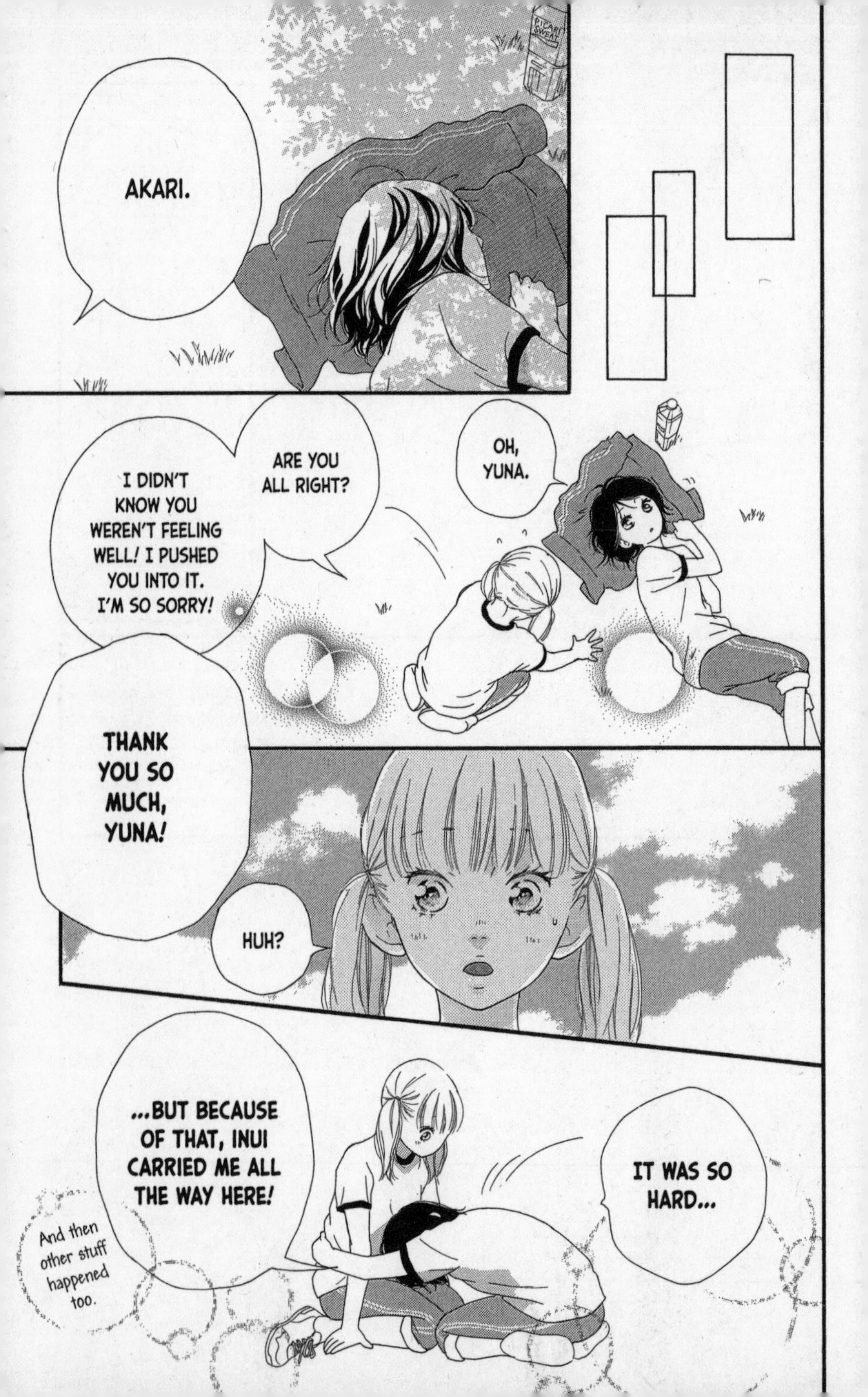
AKARI.
OH, YUNA.
ARE YOU ALL RIGHT?
I DIDN'T KNOW YOU WEREN'T FEELING WELL! I PUSHED YOU INTO IT. I'M SO SORRY!
THANK YOU SO MUCH, YUNA!
HUH?
IT WAS SO HARD...
...BUT BECAUSE OF THAT, INUI CARRIED ME ALL THE WAY HERE!
And then other stuff happened too.

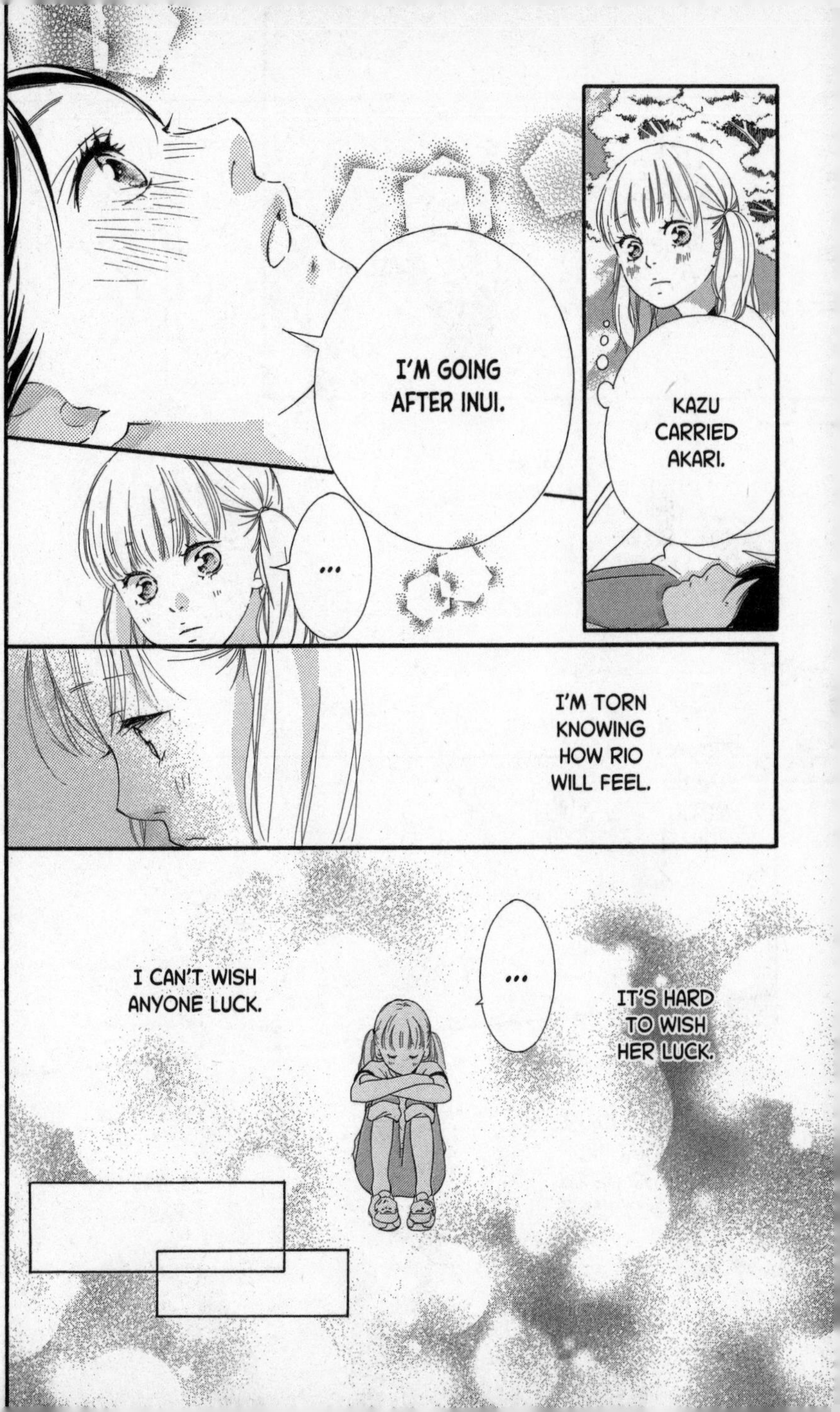
KAZU CARRIED AKARI.
I'M GOING AFTER INUI.
...
I'M TORN KNOWING HOW RIO WILL FEEL.
...
IT'S HARD TO WISH HER LUCK.
I CAN'T WISH ANYONE LUCK.

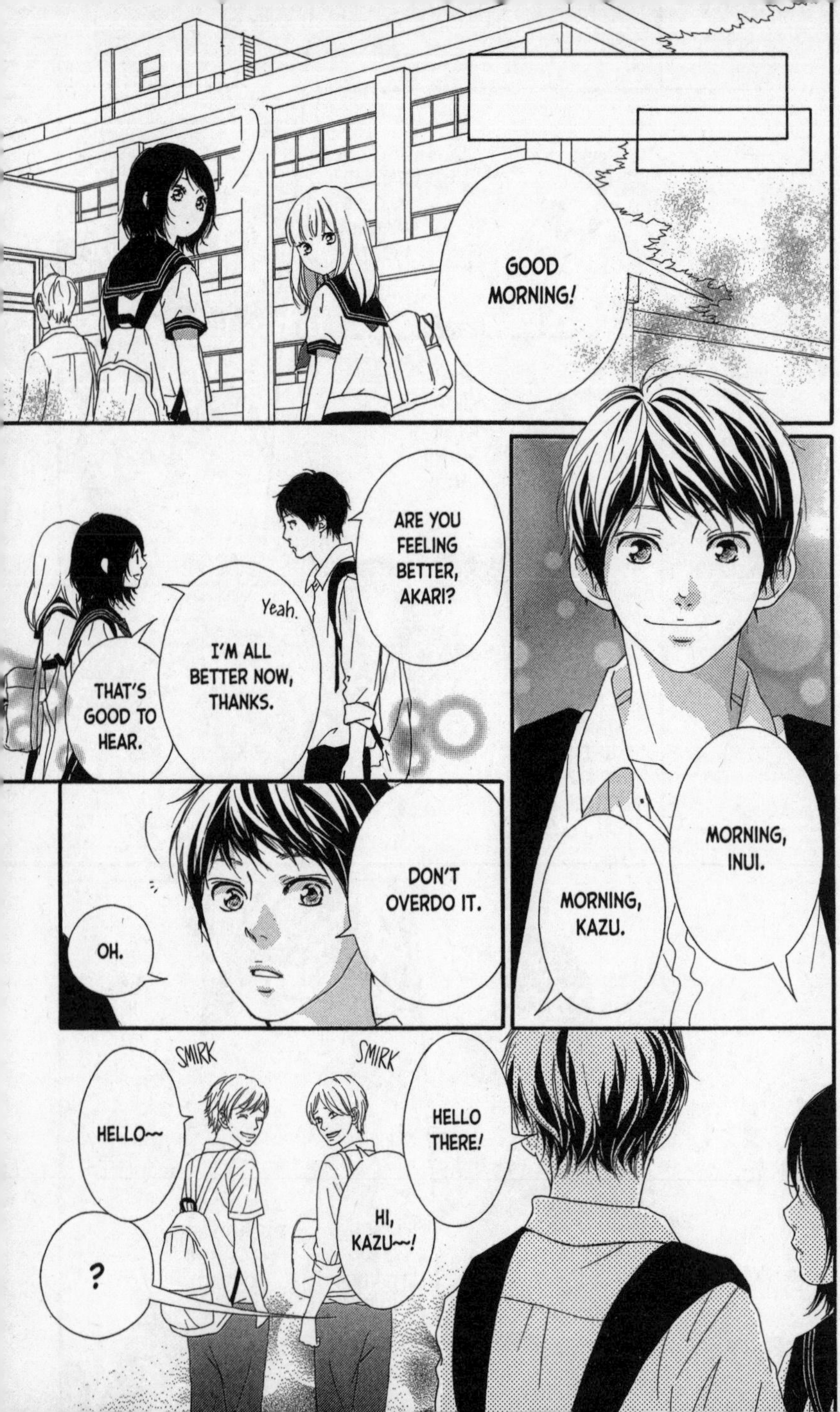
GOOD MORNING!
MORNING, INUI.
MORNING, KAZU.
ARE YOU FEELING BETTER, AKARI?
Yeah.
I'M ALL BETTER NOW, THANKS.
THAT'S GOOD TO HEAR.
DON'T OVERDO IT.
OH.
SMIRK
HELLO THERE!
HI, KAZU~~!
SMIRK
HELLO~~
?

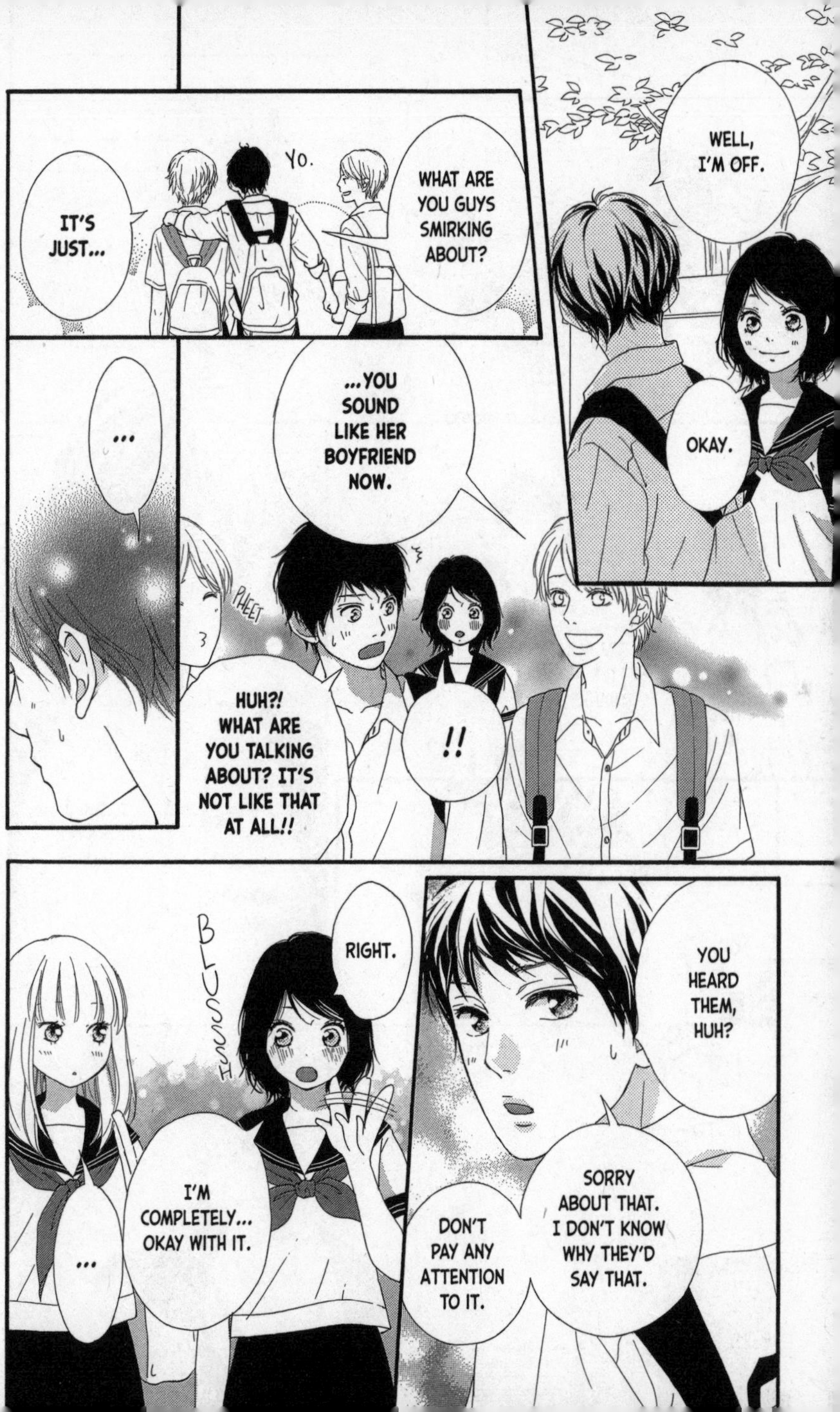
WELL, I'M OFF.
OKAY.
WHAT ARE YOU GUYS SMIRKING ABOUT?
YO.
IT'S JUST...
...YOU SOUND LIKE HER BOYFRIEND NOW.
PHEET
!!
HUH?! WHAT ARE YOU TALKING ABOUT? IT'S NOT LIKE THAT AT ALL!!
...
YOU HEARD THEM, HUH?
SORRY ABOUT THAT. I DON'T KNOW WHY THEY'D SAY THAT.
DON'T PAY ANY ATTENTION TO IT.
RIGHT.
BLUSSSH
I'M COMPLETELY... OKAY WITH IT.
...

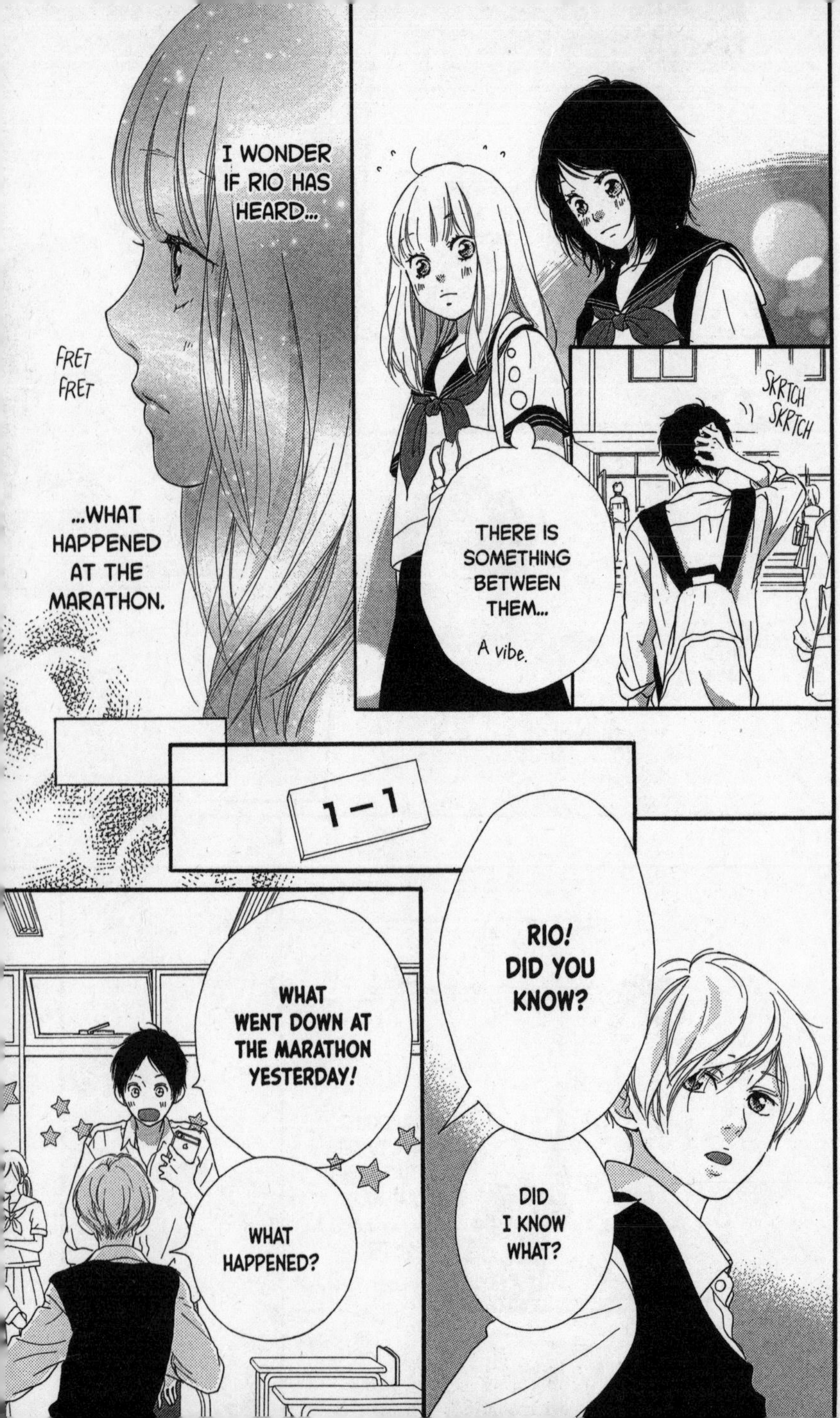
THERE IS SOMETHING BETWEEN THEM...
A vibe.
SKRTCH SKRTCH
I WONDER IF RIO HAS HEARD...
...WHAT HAPPENED AT THE MARATHON.
FRET FRET
1-1
RIO! DID YOU KNOW?
DID I KNOW WHAT?
WHAT WENT DOWN AT THE MARATHON YESTERDAY!
WHAT HAPPENED?

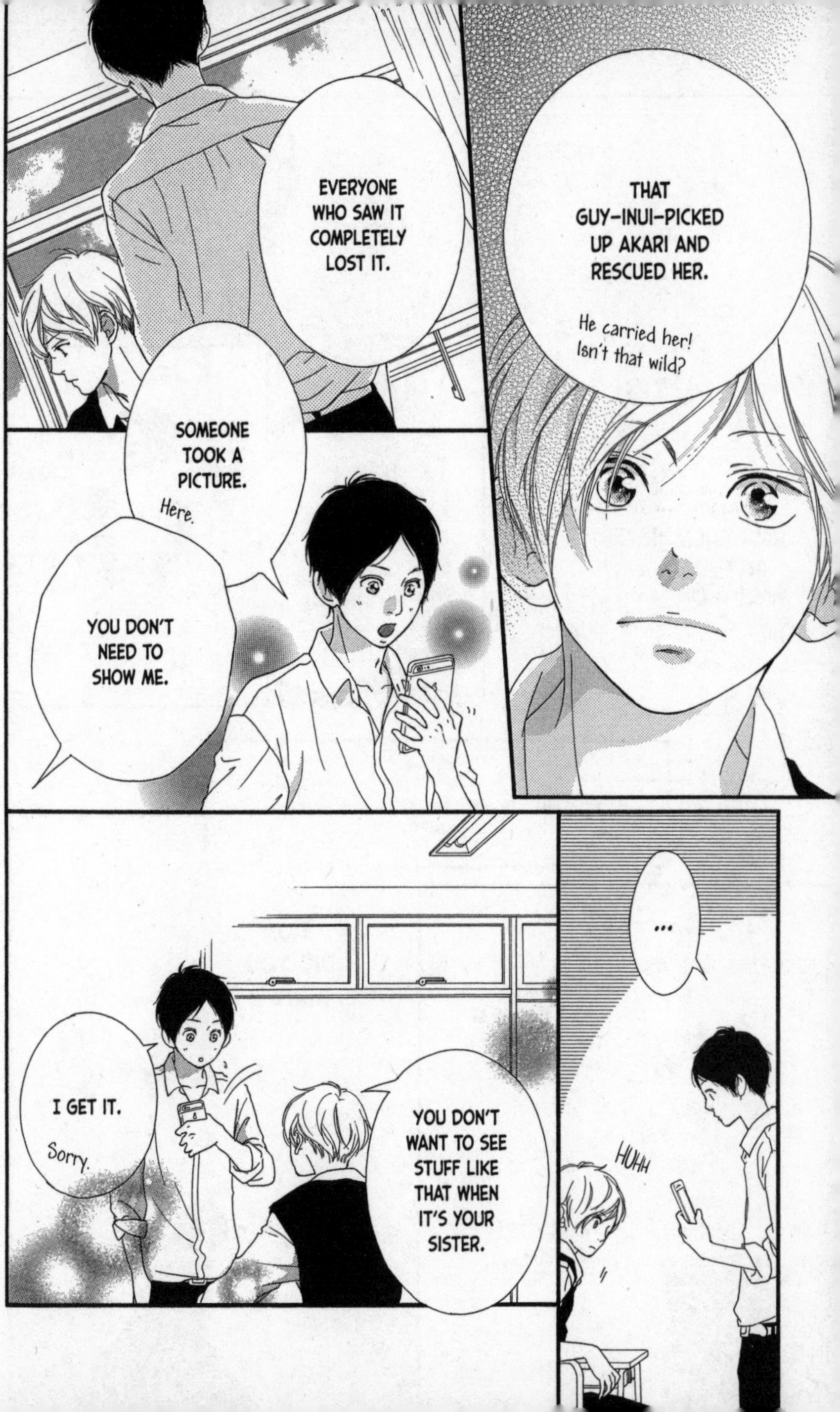

THAT GUY—INUI—PICKED UP AKARI AND RESCUED HER.
He carried her! Isn't that wild?
EVERYONE WHO SAW IT COMPLETELY LOST IT.
SOMEONE TOOK A PICTURE.
Here.
YOU DON'T NEED TO SHOW ME.
...
HUHH
YOU DON'T WANT TO SEE STUFF LIKE THAT WHEN IT'S YOUR SISTER.
I GET IT.
Sorry.

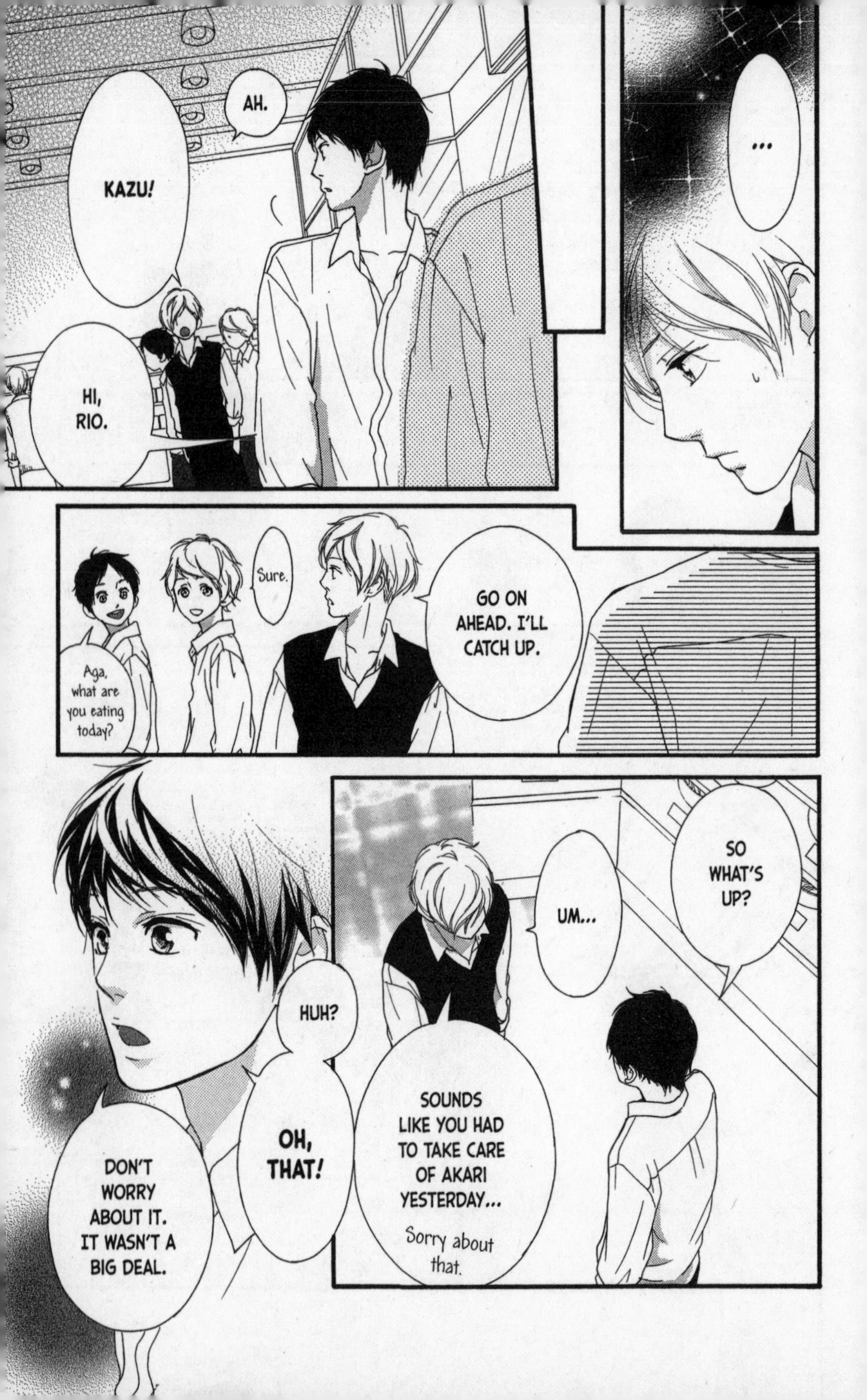
...
AH.
KAZU!
HI, RIO.
GO ON AHEAD. I'LL CATCH UP.
Sure.
Aga, what are you eating today?
SO WHAT'S UP?
UM...
SOUNDS LIKE YOU HAD TO TAKE CARE OF AKARI YESTERDAY... Sorry about that.
HUH?
OH, THAT!
DON'T WORRY ABOUT IT. IT WASN'T A BIG DEAL.

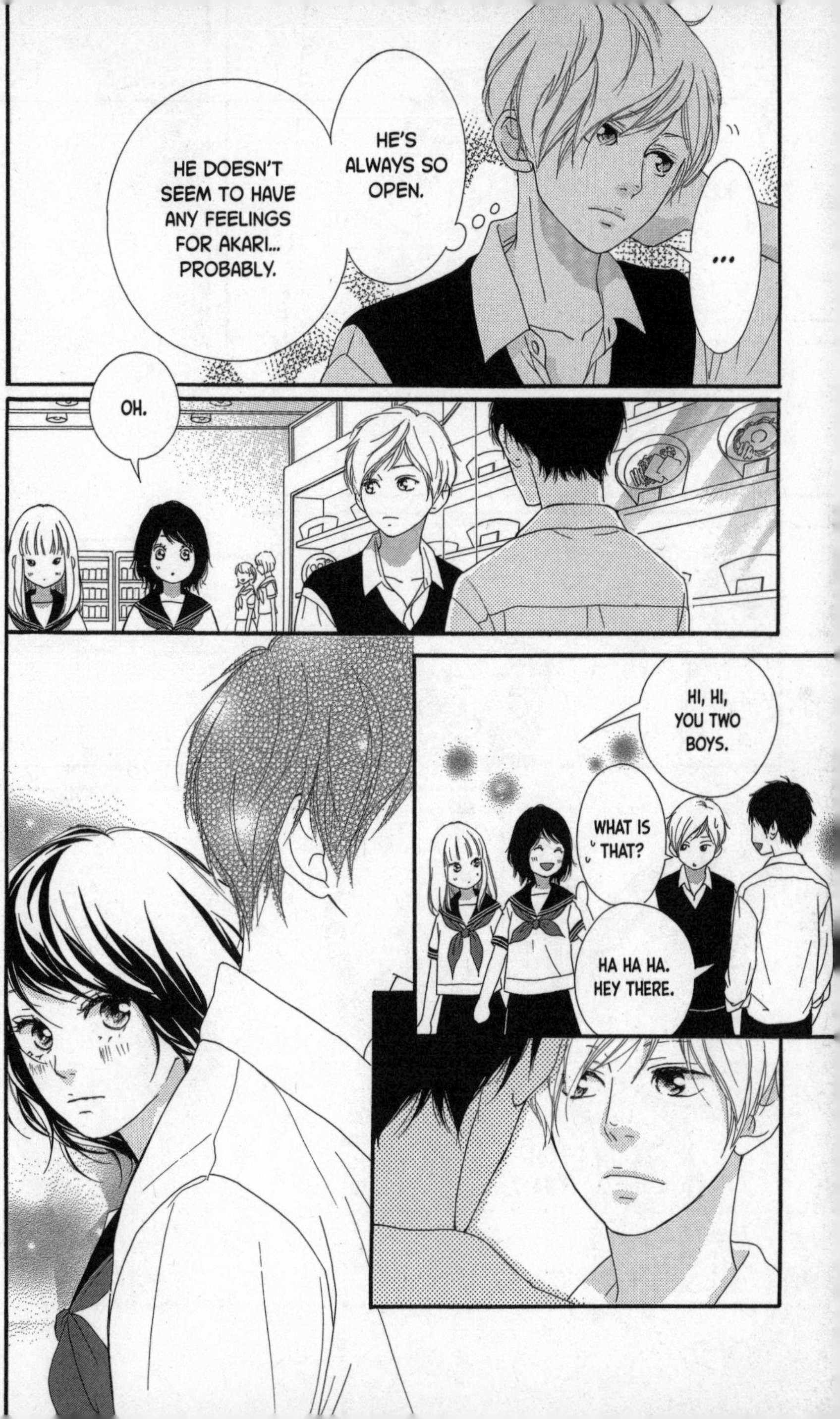
...
HE'S ALWAYS SO OPEN.
HE DOESN'T SEEM TO HAVE ANY FEELINGS FOR AKARI... PROBABLY.
OH.
HI, HI, YOU TWO BOYS.
WHAT IS THAT?
HA HA HA. HEY THERE.

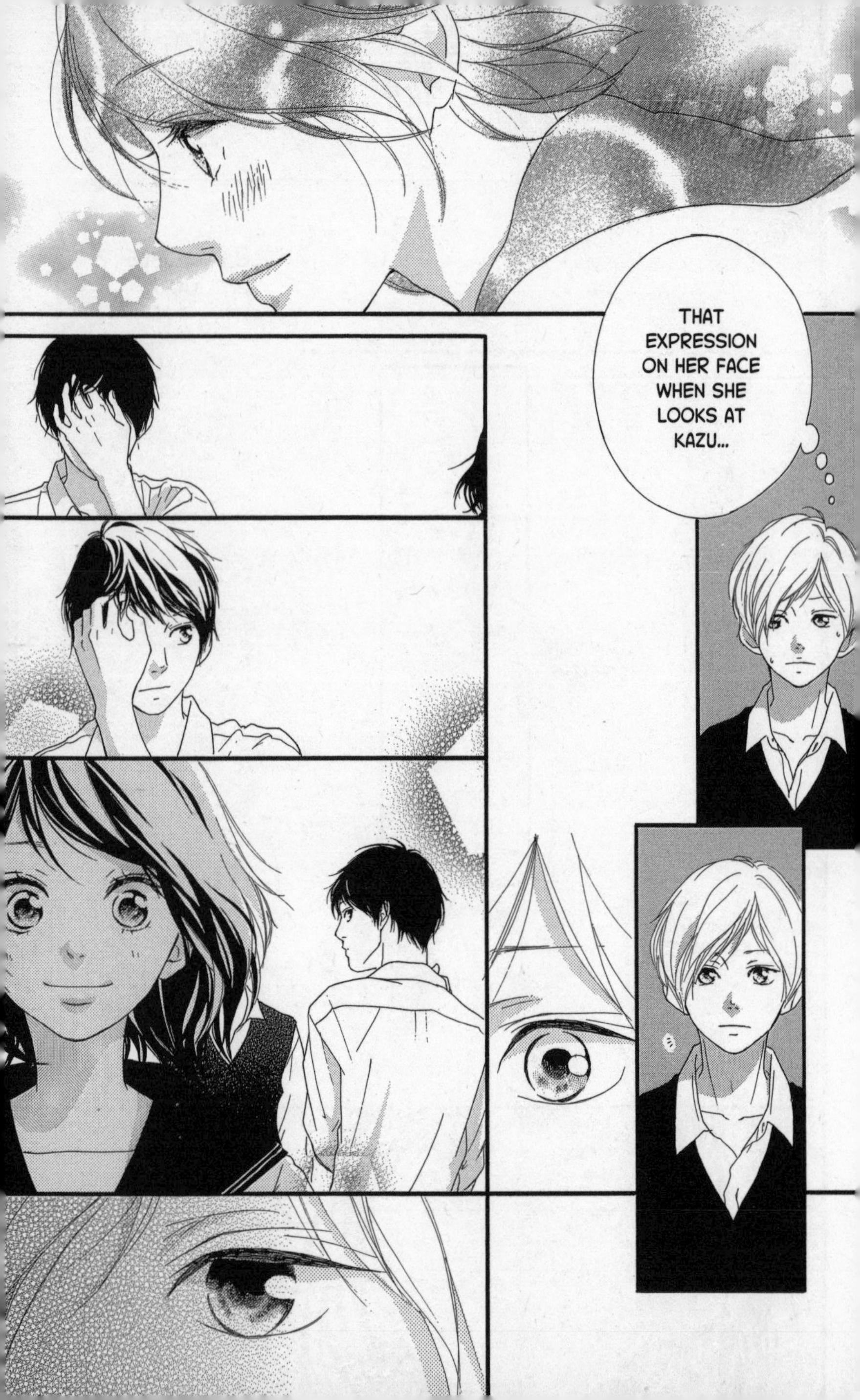
THAT EXPRESSION ON HER FACE WHEN SHE LOOKS AT KAZU...

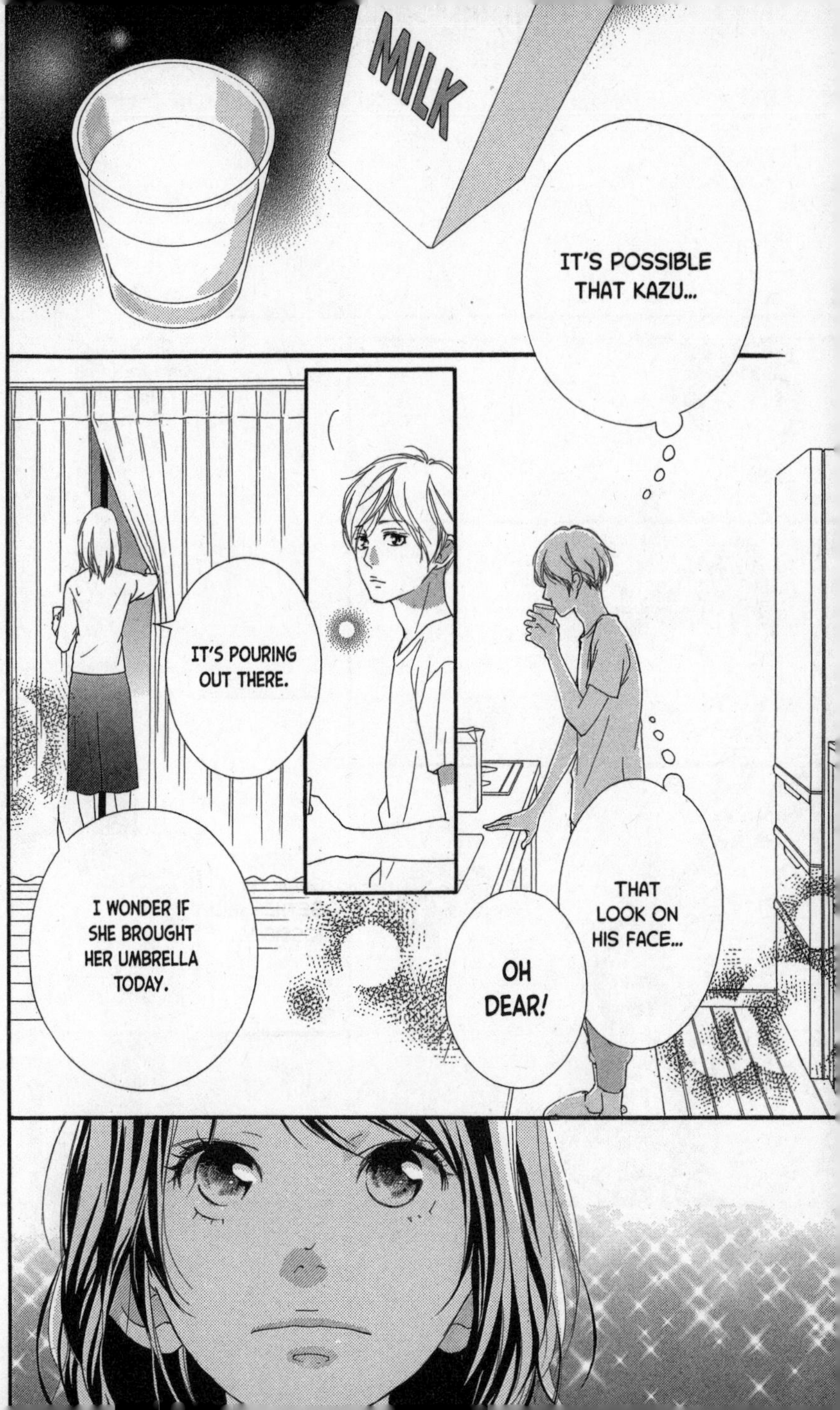
IT'S POSSIBLE THAT KAZU...
THAT LOOK ON HIS FACE...
OH DEAR!
IT'S POURING OUT THERE.
I WONDER IF SHE BROUGHT HER UMBRELLA TODAY.
MILK

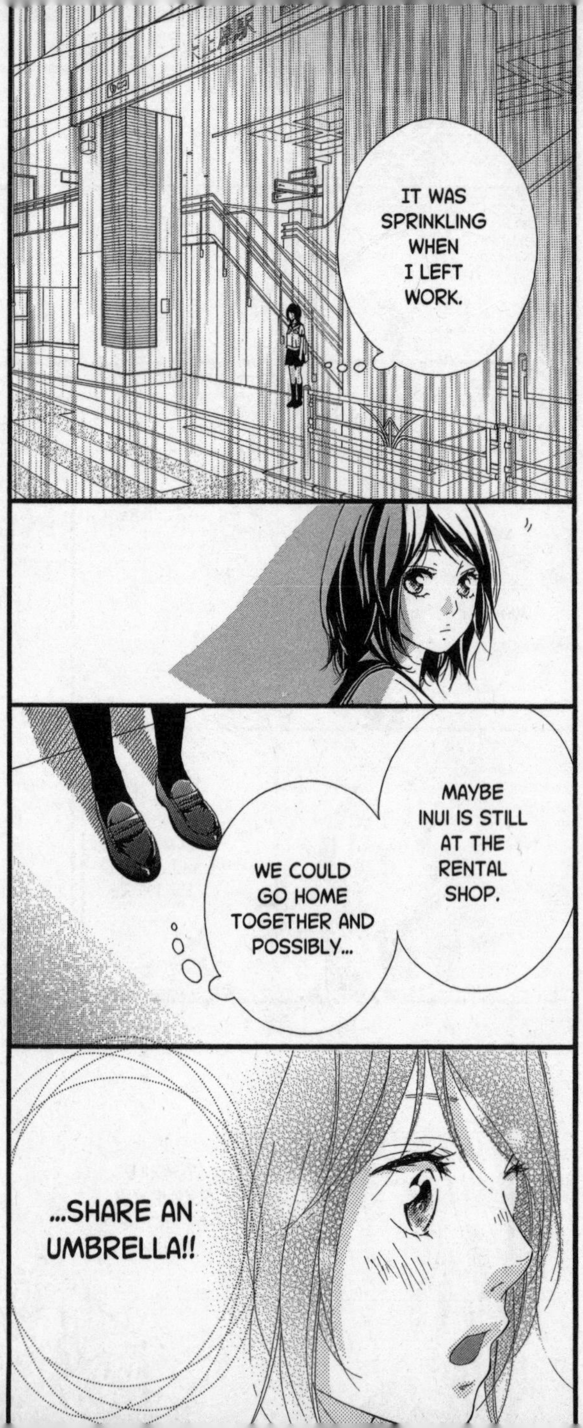
IT WAS SPRINKLING WHEN I LEFT WORK.
MAYBE INUI IS STILL AT THE RENTAL SHOP.
WE COULD GO HOME TOGETHER AND POSSIBLY...
...SHARE AN UMBRELLA!!

We went to see SHINee at Tokyo Dome. Six of us artists who are SHINee fans went together. We decided if we were going to go, we should go all the way. So for the first time in my life, I made paper fans to cheer them on. We went together to buy materials, and even doing that was super fun. I found time in between work to put my fan together bit by bit, but it was a lot harder than I thought. I panicked thinking I might not finish in time...but I got it done. It was fun seeing everyone's fans—each one was unique. Even though we made them, our seats were so far away that there was no way SHINee would ever see them! *(laugh)*
I learned for the first time that it's an effective item to get you in the spirit of things.
Speaking of getting in the spirit—the chanting! I had half given up on learning the chants because I didn't have enough time. But I learned as much as I could up until the very last moment, and those chants are the best! It increases your feeling of participation and gets you all excited. So much fun!!

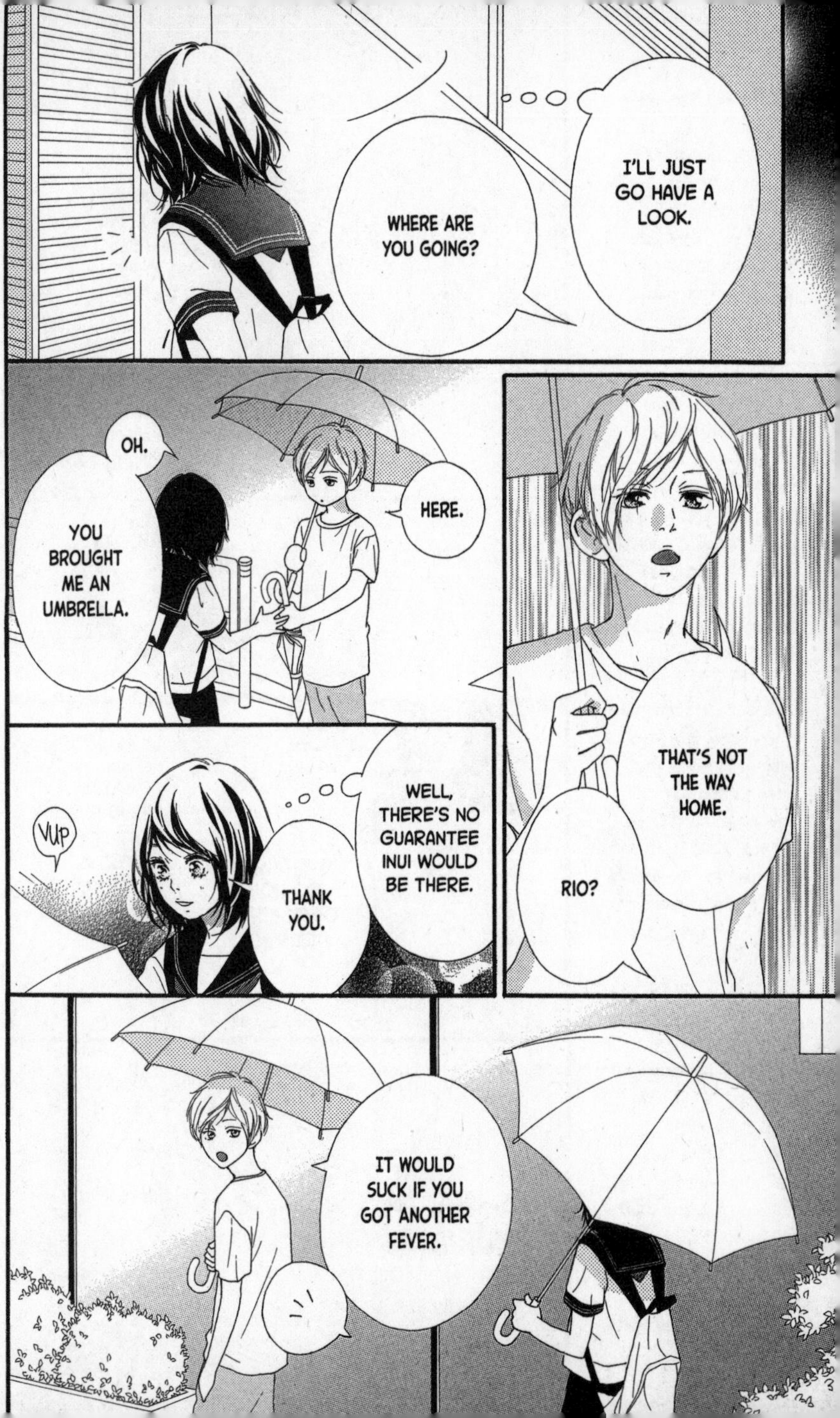
I'LL JUST GO HAVE A LOOK.
WHERE ARE YOU GOING?
THAT'S NOT THE WAY HOME.
RIO?
HERE.
OH.
YOU BROUGHT ME AN UMBRELLA.
WELL, THERE'S NO GUARANTEE INUI WOULD BE THERE.
THANK YOU.
VUP
IT WOULD SUCK IF YOU GOT ANOTHER FEVER.

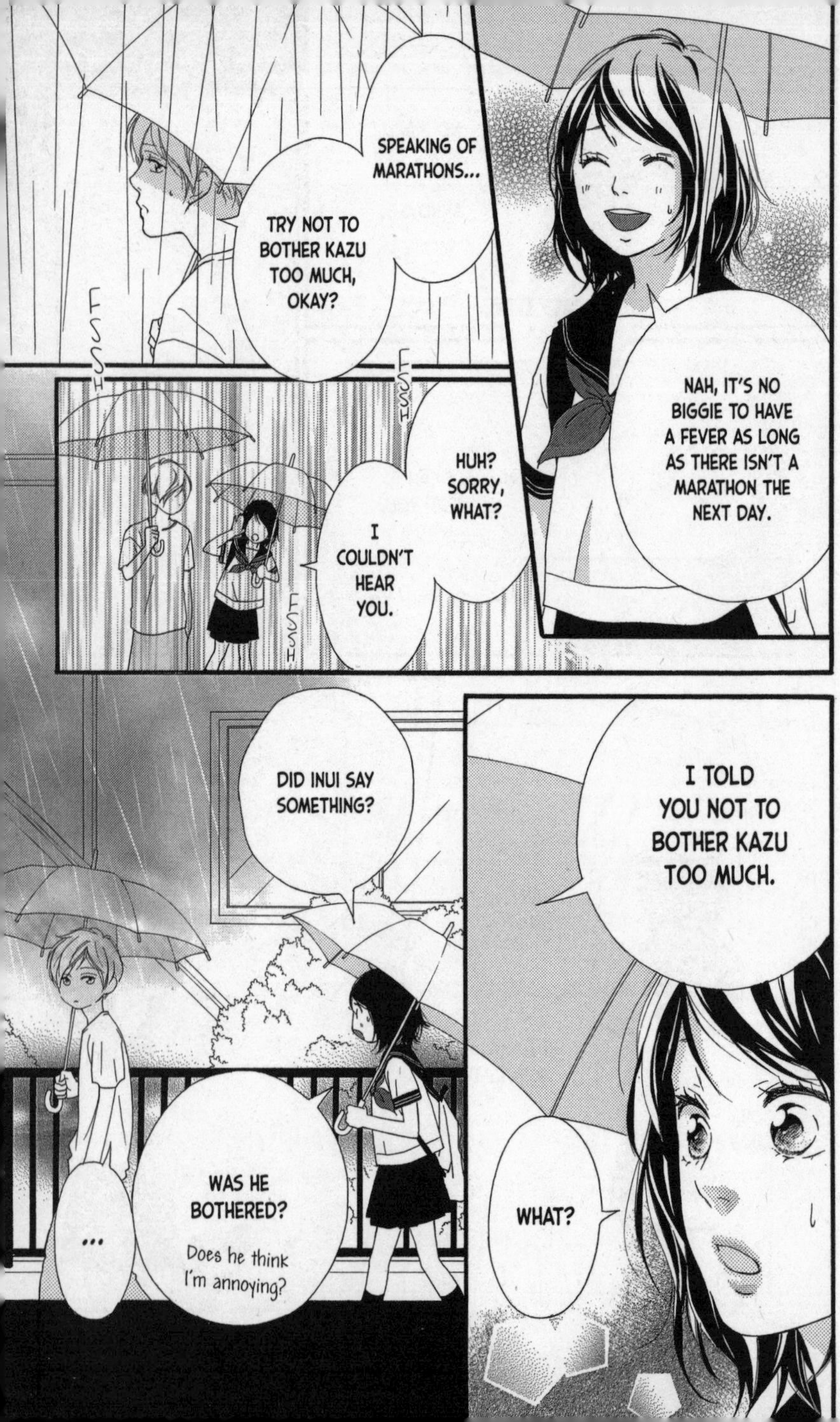
NAH, IT'S NO BIGGIE TO HAVE A FEVER AS LONG AS THERE ISN'T A MARATHON THE NEXT DAY.
SPEAKING OF MARATHONS...
TRY NOT TO BOTHER KAZU TOO MUCH, OKAY?
FSSH
FSSH
HUH? SORRY, WHAT?
I COULDN'T HEAR YOU.
FSSH
I TOLD YOU NOT TO BOTHER KAZU TOO MUCH.
WHAT?
DID INUI SAY SOMETHING?
WAS HE BOTHERED?
Does he think I'm annoying?
...

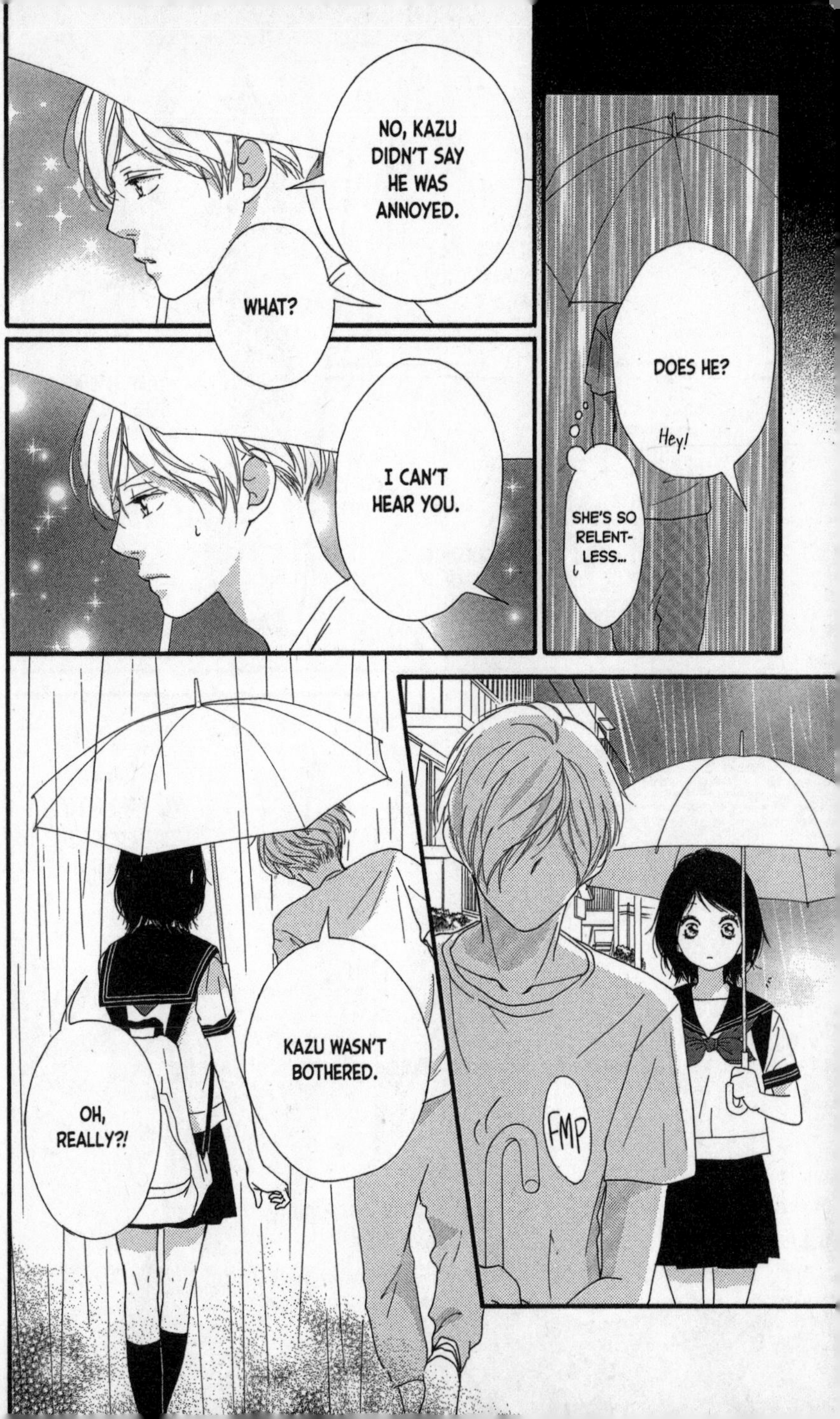
DOES HE?
Hey!
SHE'S SO RELENT-LESS...
NO, KAZU DIDN'T SAY HE WAS ANNOYED.
WHAT?
I CAN'T HEAR YOU.
FMP
KAZU WASN'T BOTHERED.
OH, REALLY?!

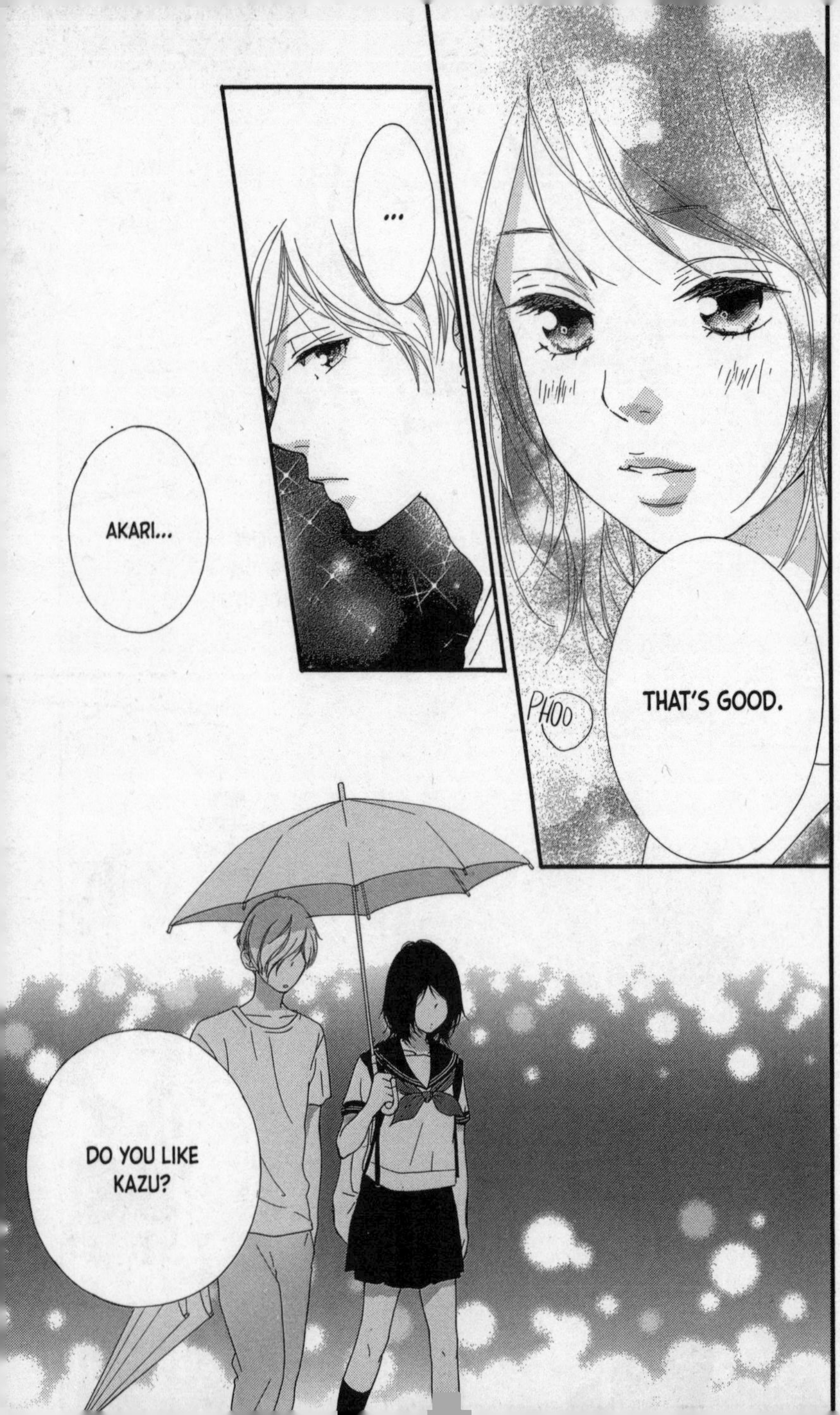
THAT'S GOOD.
PHOO
...
AKARI...
DO YOU LIKE KAZU?

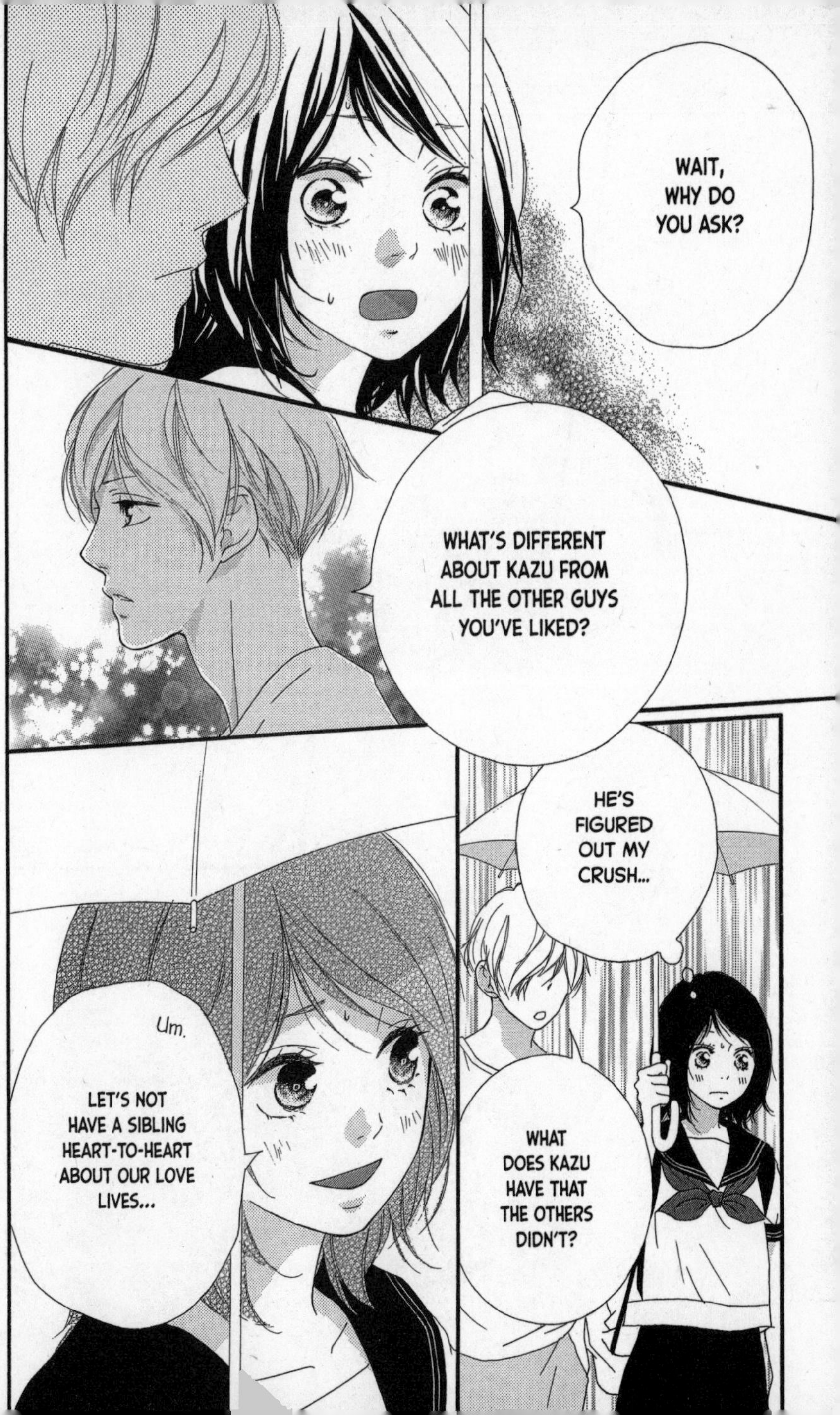
WAIT, WHY DO YOU ASK?
WHAT'S DIFFERENT ABOUT KAZU FROM ALL THE OTHER GUYS YOU'VE LIKED?
HE'S FIGURED OUT MY CRUSH...
WHAT DOES KAZU HAVE THAT THE OTHERS DIDN'T?
Um.
LET'S NOT HAVE A SIBLING HEART-TO-HEART ABOUT OUR LOVE LIVES...

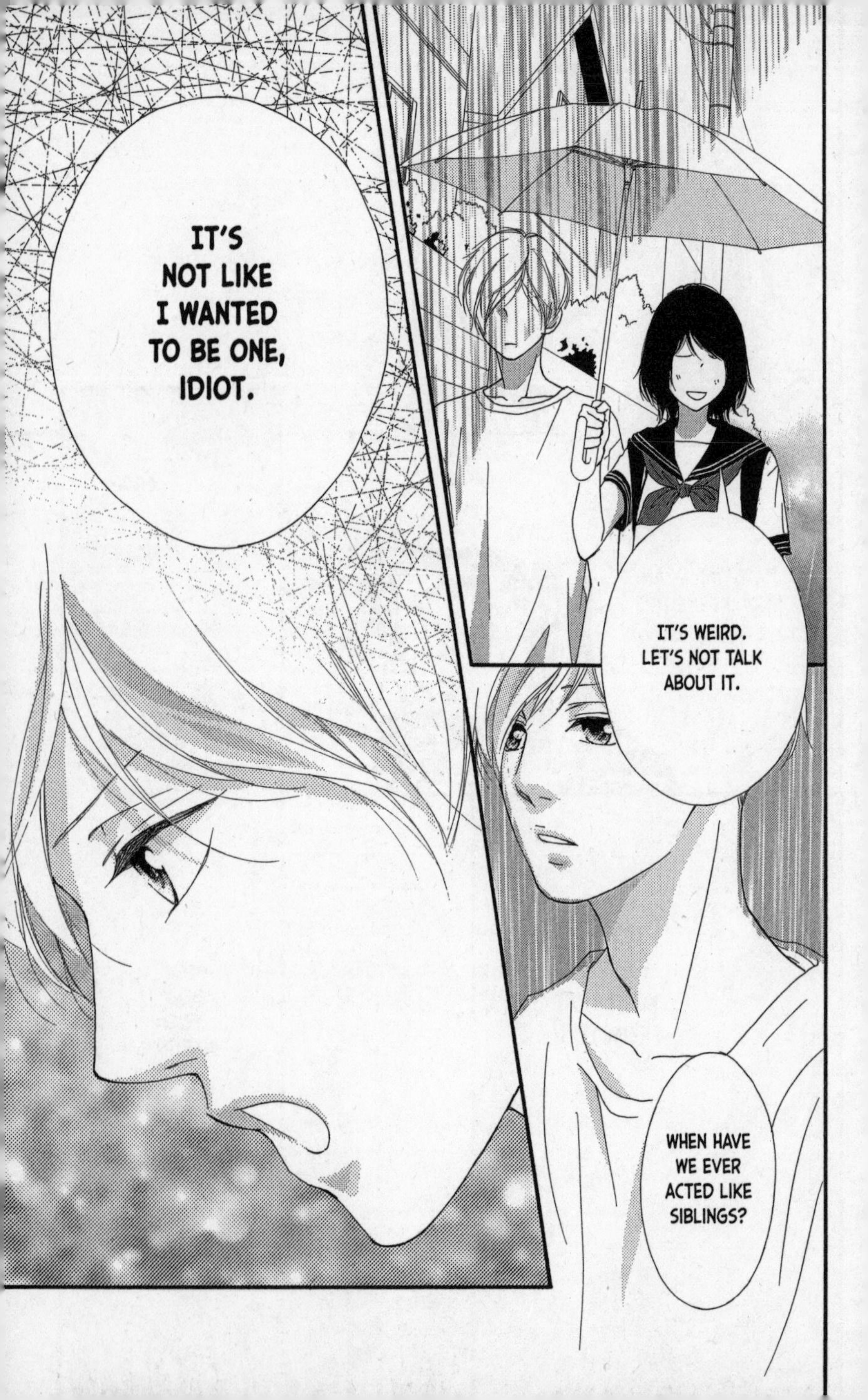
IT'S WEIRD. LET'S NOT TALK ABOUT IT.
WHEN HAVE WE EVER ACTED LIKE SIBLINGS?
IT'S NOT LIKE I WANTED TO BE ONE, IDIOT.

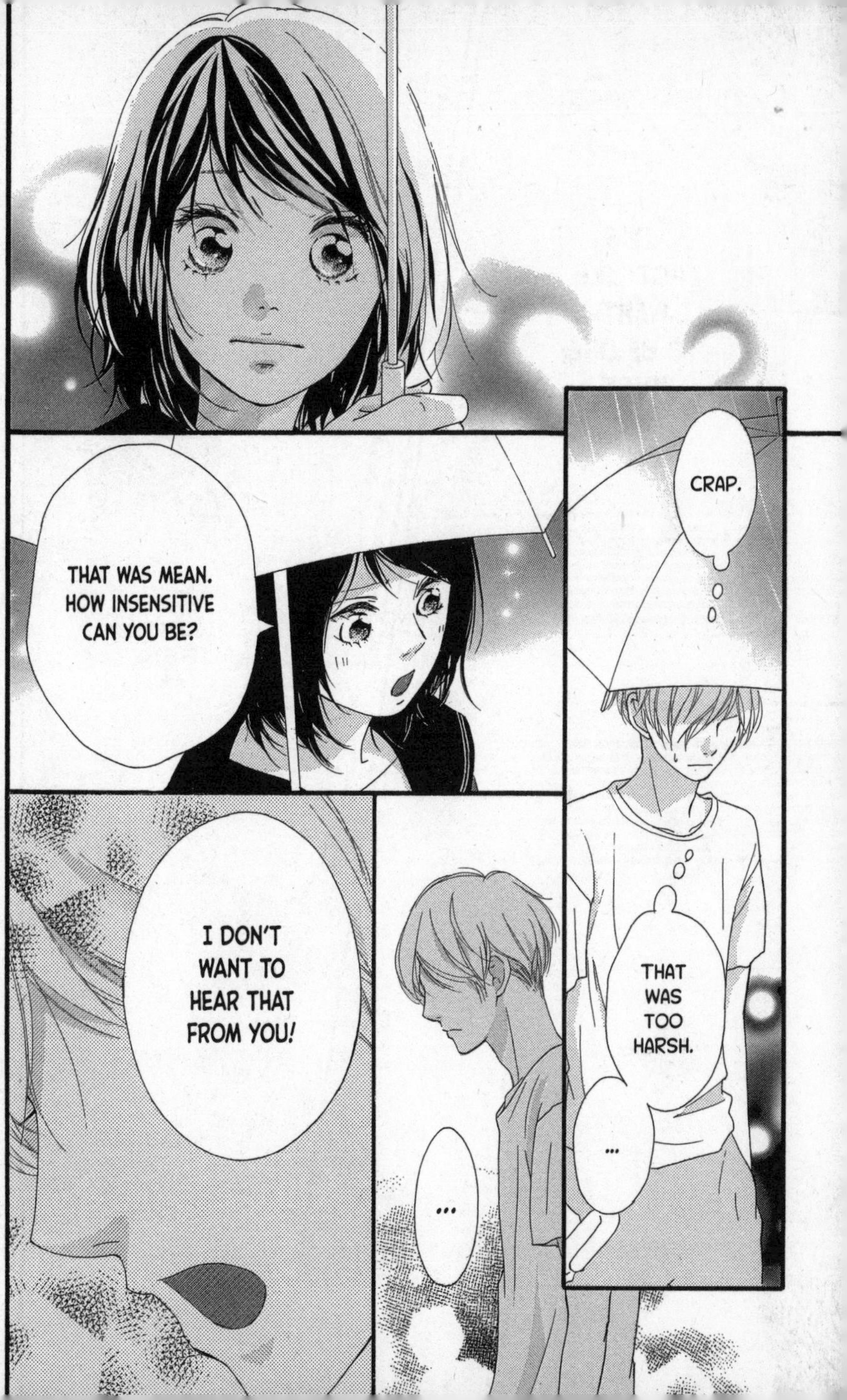
CRAP.
THAT WAS TOO HARSH.
...
THAT WAS MEAN. HOW INSENSITIVE CAN YOU BE?
...
I DON'T WANT TO HEAR THAT FROM YOU!

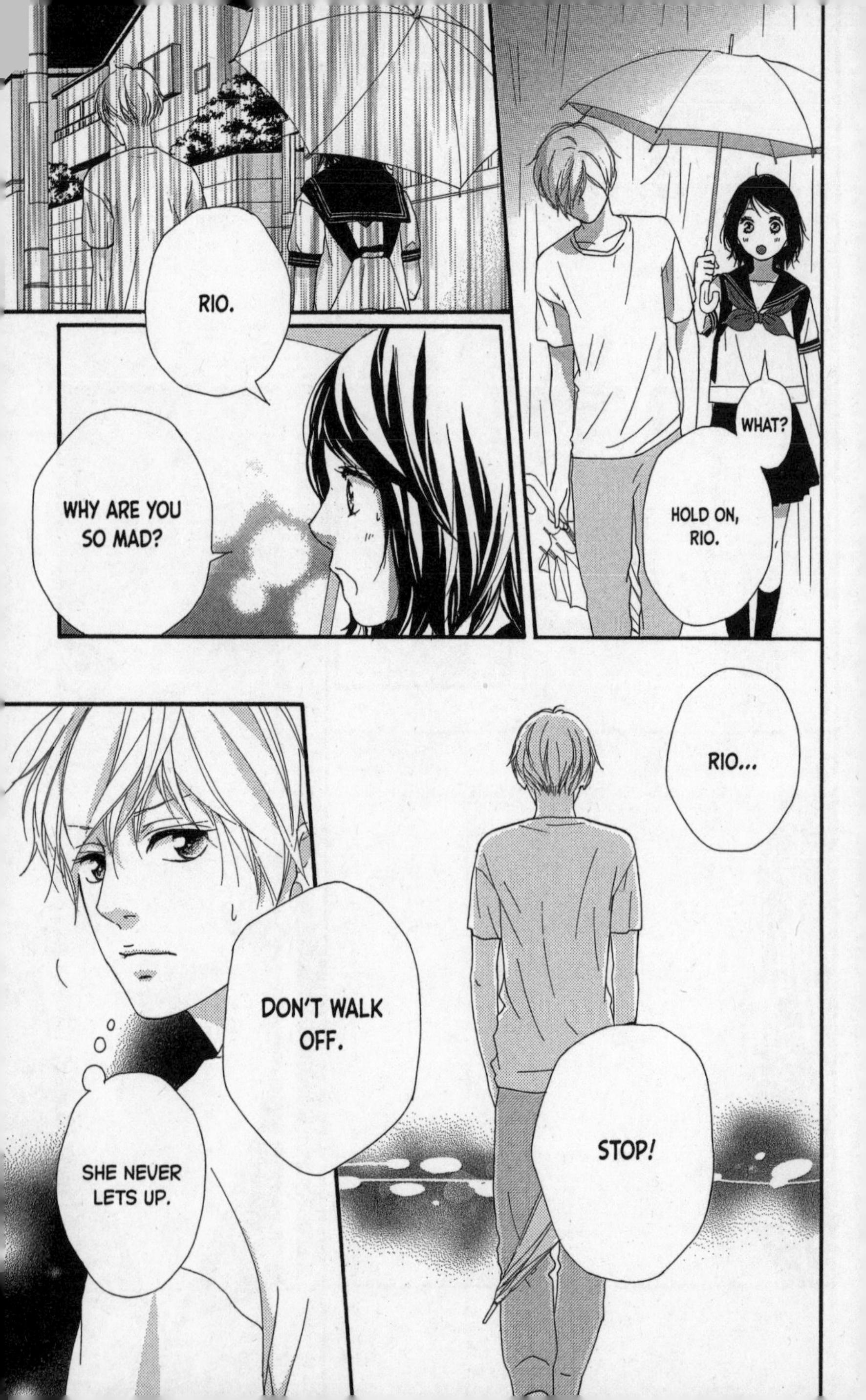
WHAT?
HOLD ON, RIO.
RIO.
WHY ARE YOU SO MAD?
RIO...
STOP!
DON'T WALK OFF.
SHE NEVER LETS UP.

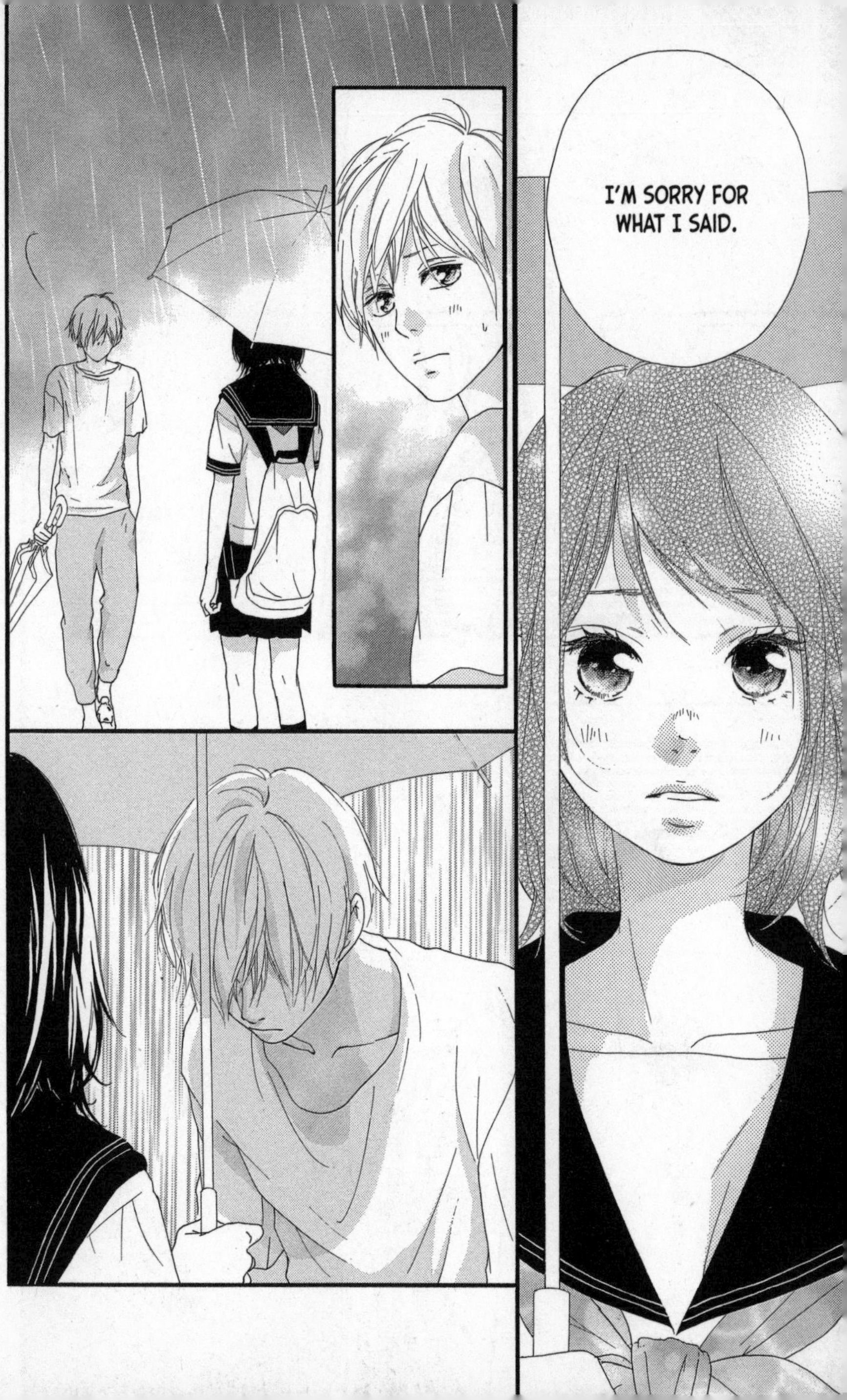
I'M SORRY FOR WHAT I SAID.

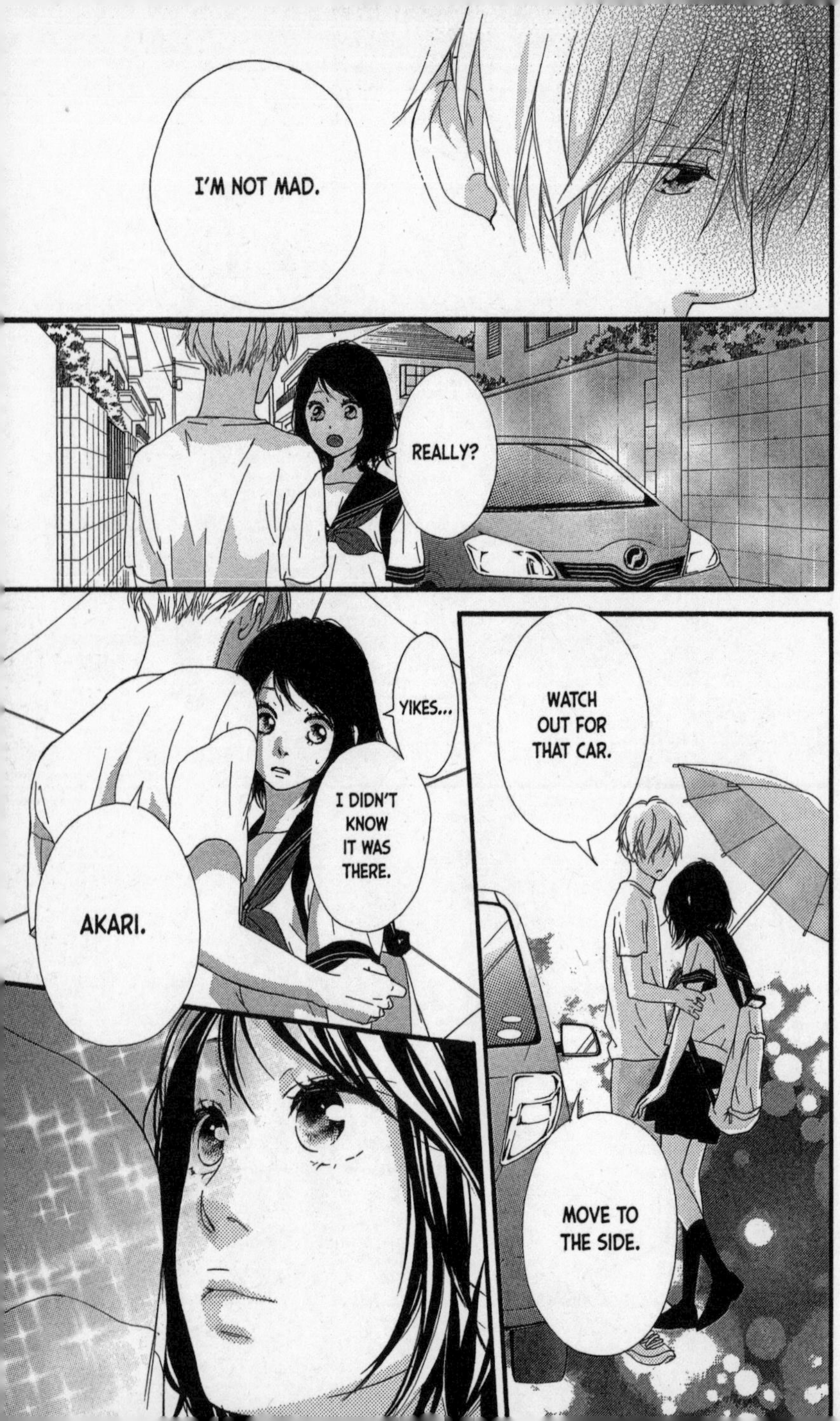
I'M NOT MAD.
REALLY?
WATCH OUT FOR THAT CAR.
MOVE TO THE SIDE.
YIKES...
I DIDN'T KNOW IT WAS THERE.
AKARI.

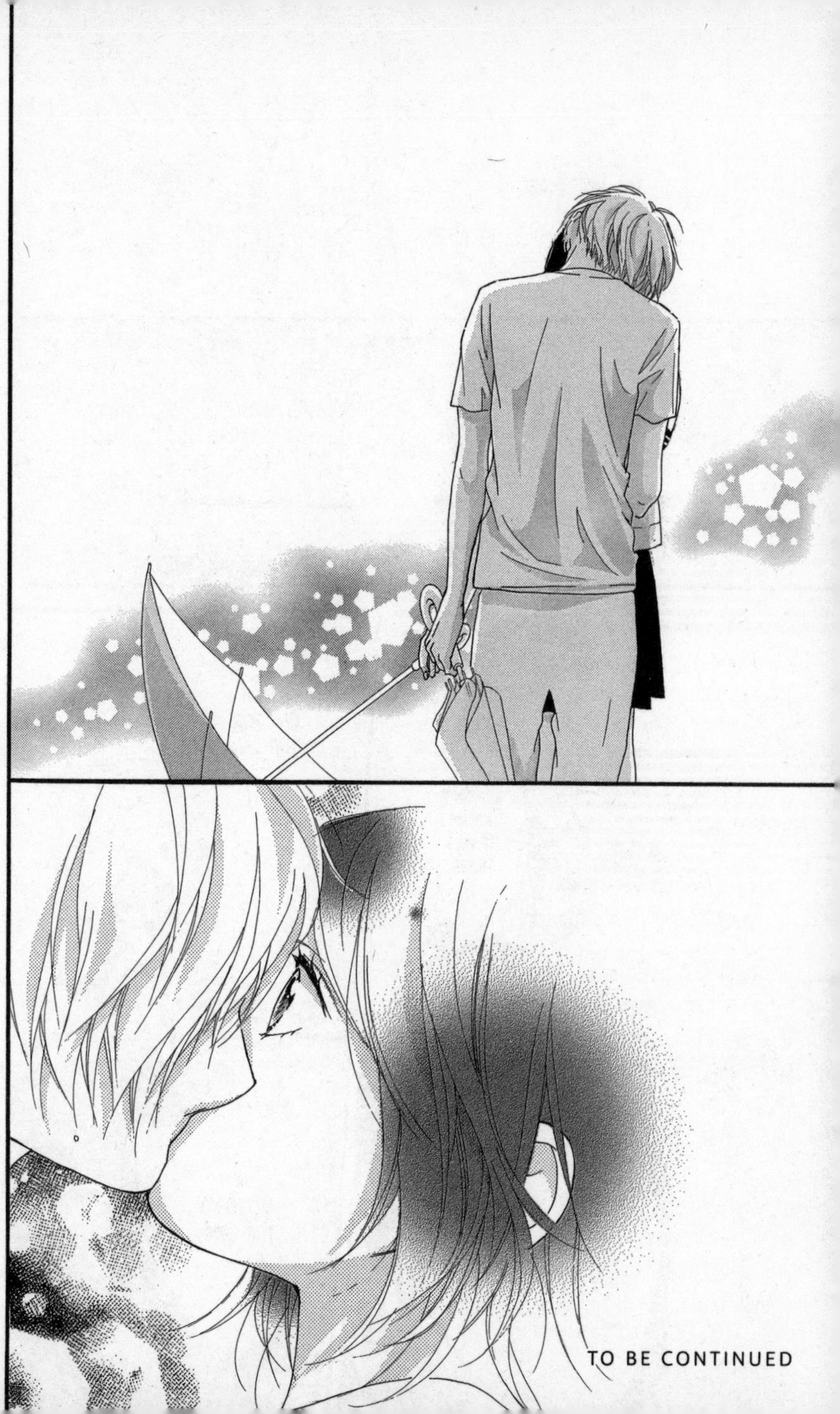
TO BE CONTINUED

GREETINGS

Thank you for reading this to the end.

I read in a book I bought about five years ago that "the youth of today have no ambition" or something like that. For those who are young now, some of you may have read that quote and felt irritated. I bought that book five years ago, but it was originally written about 30 years ago. I laughed when I realized young people past and present have always had the same thing said about them. I wondered what the adults a hundred years ago were thinking about the youth of their day. I speculate that they probably said the same thing. Maybe it's something people want to say when they become adults—it makes them think they're proper grown-ups. Will those of you who are young now grow up to say "the youth of today..."?

To those of you who are young now, please just ignore it and never think you have no ambition. Just live freely. These were my thoughts on reading this volume again recently. See you in the next volume!

Io Sakisaka

I decided walking is the answer to my lack of exercise. I got all excited and bought clothes and shoes and set off, but it lasted only a day. I haven't been since, but I'm trying to figure out how I can make it fun so that I continue.

Io Sakisaka

Born on June 8, Io Sakisaka made her debut as a manga creator with *Sakura, Chiru*. Her series *Strobe Edge* and *Ao Haru Ride* are published by VIZ Media's Shojo Beat imprint. *Ao Haru Ride* was adapted into an anime series in 2014, and *Love Me, Love Me Not* will be an animated feature film. In her spare time, Sakisaka likes to paint things and sleep.

Love Me, Love Me Not

Vol. 3
Shojo Beat Edition

STORY AND ART BY
Io Sakisaka

Adaptation/Nancy Thistlethwaite
Translation/JN Productions
Touch-Up Art & Lettering/Sara Linsley
Design/Yukiko Whitley
Editor/Nancy Thistlethwaite

OMOI, OMOWARE, FURI, FURARE © 2015 by Io Sakisaka
All rights reserved.
First published in Japan in 2015 by SHUEISHA Inc., Tokyo.
English translation rights arranged by SHUEISHA Inc.

Printed in the U.S.A.

Published by VIZ Media, LLC
P.O. Box 77010
San Francisco, CA 94107

10 9 8 7 6 5 4 3 2 1
First printing, July 2020

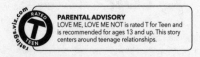

viz.com   shojobeat.com

STORY AND ART BY
IO SAKISAKA

Ao Haru Ride

Futaba Yoshioka thought all boys were loud and obnoxious until she met Kou Tanaka in junior high. But as soon as she realized she really liked him, he had already moved away because of family issues. Now, in high school, Kou has reappeared, but is he still the same boy she fell in love with?

Honey So Sweet

Story and Art by Amu Meguro

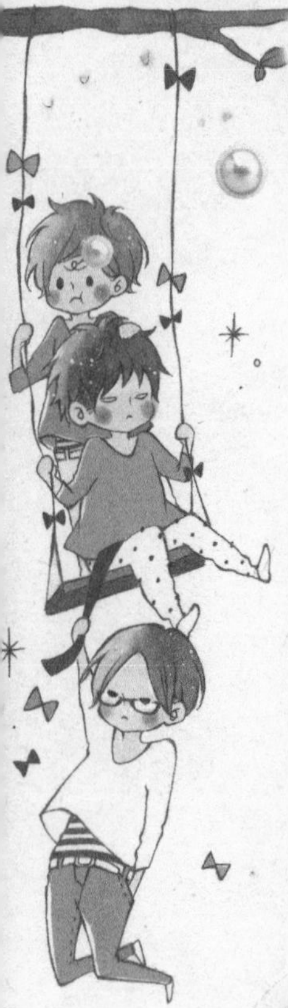

Little did Nao Kogure realize back in middle school that when she left an umbrella and a box of bandages in the rain for injured delinquent Taiga Onise that she would meet him again in high school. Nao wants nothing to do with the gruff and frightening Taiga, but he suddenly presents her with a huge bouquet of flowers and asks her to date him—with marriage in mind! Is Taiga really so scary, or is he a sweetheart in disguise?

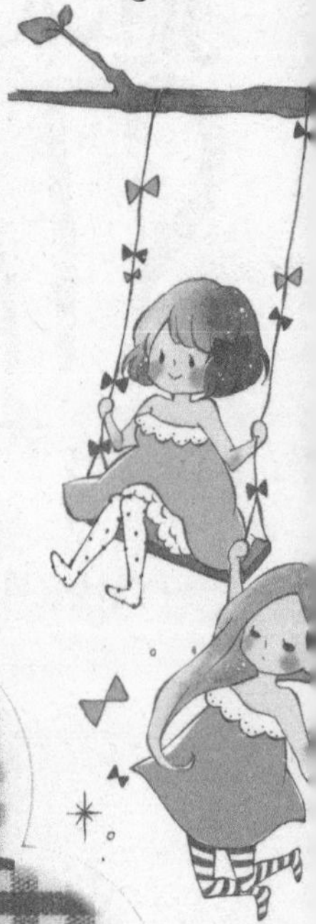

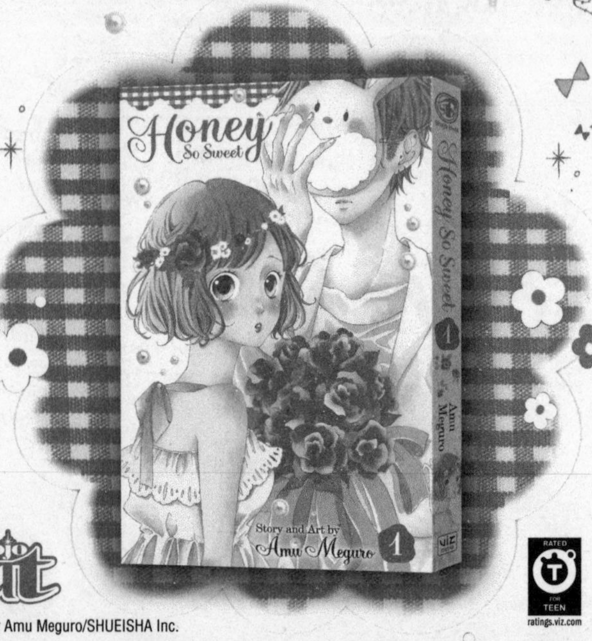
Honey So Sweet
Honey So Sweet 1
Amu Meguro
Story and Art by Amu Meguro 1
viz

Shojo Beat

RATED T FOR TEEN ratings.viz.com

viz media viz.com

DAYTIME SHOOTING STAR

Story & Art by
Mika Yamamori

Small town girl Suzume moves to Tokyo and finds her heart caught between two men!

After arriving in Tokyo to live with her uncle, Suzume collapses in a nearby park when she remembers once seeing a shooting star during the day. A handsome stranger brings her to her new home and tells her they'll meet again. Suzume starts her first day at her new high school sitting next to a boy who blushes furiously at her touch. And her homeroom teacher is none other than the handsome stranger!

HIRUNAKA NO RYUSEI © 2011 by Mika Yamamori/SHUEISHA Inc.

VIZ

SHORTCAKE CAKE

STORY AND ART BY
suu Morishita

An unflappable girl and a cast of
lovable roommates at a boardinghouse
create bonds of friendship and romance!

When Ten moves out of her parents' home
in the mountains to live in a boardinghouse,
she finds herself becoming fast friends with
her male roommates. But can love and
romance be far behind?

VIZ

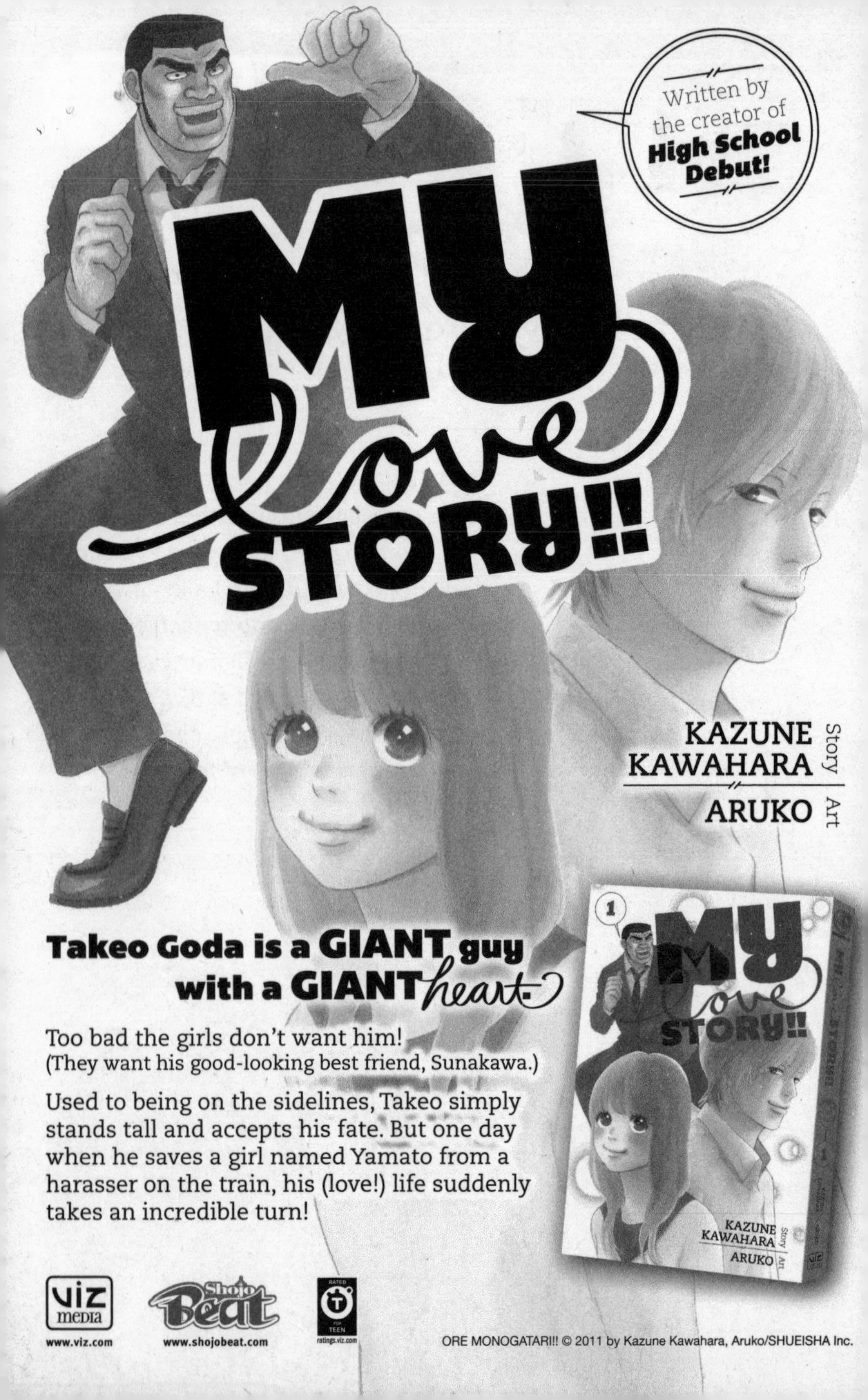
Written by the creator of High School Debut!
MY love STORY!!
KAZUNE KAWAHARA Story
ARUKO Art
Takeo Goda is a GIANT guy with a GIANT heart
Too bad the girls don't want him!
(They want his good-looking best friend, Sunakawa.)
Used to being on the sidelines, Takeo simply stands tall and accepts his fate. But one day when he saves a girl named Yamato from a harasser on the train, his (love!) life suddenly takes an incredible turn!
1 MY love STORY!!
KAZUNE KAWAHARA Story
ARUKO Art
viz media
www.viz.com
Shojo Beat
www.shojobeat.com
RATED T FOR TEEN
ratings.viz.com
ORE MONOGATARI!! © 2011 by Kazune Kawahara, Aruko/SHUEISHA Inc.

Stop!

You may be reading the wrong way.

In keeping with the original Japanese comic format, this book reads from right to left—so action, sound effects and word balloons are completely reversed to preserve the orientation of the original artwork. Check out the diagram shown here to get the hang of things, and then turn to the other side of the book to get started!

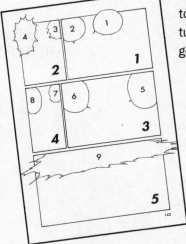